The Mind Changer

Patricia Sabella

DORRANCE
PUBLISHING CO
EST. 1920
PITTSBURGH, PENNSYLVANIA 15238

The contents of this work, including, but not limited to, the accuracy of events, people, and places depicted; opinions expressed; permission to use previously published materials included; and any advice given or actions advocated are solely the responsibility of the author, who assumes all liability for said work and indemnifies the publisher against any claims stemming from publication of the work.

Dorrance Publishing Co
585 Alpha Drive
Pittsburgh, PA 15238
Visit our website at *www.dorrancebookstore.com*

ISBN: 978-1-4809-9504-8
eISBN: 978-1-4809-9577-2

"We don't meet people by accident. They are meant to cross our path for a reason."

Unknown

"All saints have a past and all sinners have a future."

Oscar Wilde

For Bill

Prologue
December 1918

The young girl remained frozen in a fetal position on the bed.

"Make her listen to me," demanded the photographer to the other man in the room. "We don't have all day to get this done."

The man quickly moved from the wooden chair in the corner of the dreary tenement to his young wife lying on the bed. "You will not have to be told again to do what must be done, do you hear me?"

He turned to the photographer. "Remember you said you will hide her face in these pictures."

"Stop worrying. I know what I'm doing. Believe me, it won't be her face buyers will be looking at."

For the rest of the afternoon, the young girl gave in to the prodding and positioning for poses being demanded of her. She had no choice.

When the photographer finished taking the photographs, he closed his camera. The girl covered herself, quickly climbing under a blanket.

"This went well considering…," the photographer said to the young man without finishing his sentence. "Help me pack up." He then paid the man from a wad of bills he took from his jacket pocket.

They carried the photography equipment through the dark hallway and down the three flights of stairs. A cab was hailed and the photographer was gone.

Still naked but completely covered by the blanket, the girl remained unmoving. As if to remind herself of all the tears she had already shed, a single tear slipped down from one of her hazel eyes. It softly passed her cheek and found a resting place in the crevice of her bosom.

Her husband called her name, but she refused to answer him.

The pictures had aroused him, so he walked into the bedroom and closed the door behind him.

Sciacca, on the southeastern end of the island of Sicily, was set between the sea and dramatic cliffs. Before the war, wealthy visitors traveled there for the thermal springs and its rugged coastline beauty. Ancient architectural remains could be found throughout the land giving evidence of the many invaders from far-away lands who inhabited the region through the centuries. Times were hard now as the European war waged. Most of the young men of the village had been conscripted into the Italian army or had emigrated to America.

"No one's going out today with the storm coming. I would have to be a fool to take my boat out this morning." Roberto had been a fool once and it had cost him a son.

"Good. So why don't you go back to bed and rest. It's barely day break." Rosa knew he would not but she said it anyway.

"I'm awake so I'm going to take a walk," he told his wife.

Their small weathered stone cottage had been handed down from previous generations of the Amato family. It stood on a hill overlooking the sea and he could see the fishing boats, including his, safely sheltered in the harbor.

Roberto had a special place at the top of the hill where he could think quietly and where he had made most of the important decisions in his adult life. With the sunrise, the birds began to sing and the bees began buzzing among the hundreds of yellow wild flowers. The dark storm clouds coming in from the west would cover the sun very soon. He waited to hear when the birds

1

would go silent and the bees disappear in anticipation of the storm. He watched the branches of the olive trees dance gracefully as the wind grew in strength. The black storm clouds continued to gather and a distant rumble of thunder could be heard.

Although Roberto and Rosa Amato had created a life that met their humble needs, they desired more advantages for their children than could ever be had from a life dependent upon fishing.

In a good season and with favorable weather, Rosa's garden and small orchard supplemented Roberto's fishing. If the harvest was especially good, then she would the use the excess vegetables and fruits to barter with neighbors for goods she needed.

Basilio, their remaining son, left for America in 1914 just before war broke out in Europe. He and his wife, Carmela, like so many who had left their village for America, owed their passage expense to a patronne. The agreement for repayment of the lender's loan was harsh with high interest rates and a mandatory employment contract as a laborer in a factory of the patronne's choice.

Roberto wanted very much to send their daughter Mina to live with her brother in Boston. But he could not agree to have her burdened with the same untenable terms of repayment for her passage that his son had incurred.

Unexpectedly, an answer came when the Vitale family approached him about a marriage arrangement to their son who was already in America and living in the Italian North End of Boston. The offer included Mina's passage being fully paid by them.

As he stood looking out at the fleet of anchored fishing boats, he knew he would rely on first vetting the arrangement with Father Nunzio, his trusted parish priest, before he would visit the Villa Vitale himself to speak with the boy's father, Don Vitale.

Returning from a visit to a sick parishioner, the priest met Roberto on a road outside the village. "Let's talk as we walk," said the old priest, who had pastored the church for decades.

"So, Father, what news do you have for me?"

"I did as you asked and spoke with a number of contacts in Palermo and Corleone who know the family and I visited the Vitale parents, myself. As it is well known, the Vitale family has connections as far back as La Mano Nera, the Black Hand. But I was given assurances that their son, Carlo, does not and

"Don't worry, it is just a precaution. You can have it back when you come out," said the older of the two guards seeing the concern on Roberto's face.

"*If* you come out," sneered the younger man, taking advantage of Roberto's apparent nervousness.

"Silencio, Paulo!" ordered the guard in charge as he gave the younger one a shove.

"Disregard this fool. Again, what is your business with the Don?" repeated the older guard.

"It is a personal matter concerning an offer he has made me."

"Will you tell me what this business is?"

"No," responded Roberto firmly, surprising himself as well as the guards.

The older guard stared at him for a minute and then, without a word, walked back through the gate to the main house, leaving Roberto at the entrance gate to the villa.

Roberto did his best to look calm, knowing the remaining guard was hoping for some excitement in his otherwise boring job. *Well, he's not going to get any excitement from me,* he pledged to himself.

Within a few minutes, Roberto was granted entry through the gate. He was escorted to the main house where a servant was already waiting at the huge front door for him.

"Buongiorno," he greeted the maid.

She returned a smile but remained silent. She led him into a large receiving room after taking his cap and wool jacket from him. He would have preferred to have kept them but did not want to appear impolite.

The room's immense casement windows filled the room with eastern morning sunlight. Although no fire was burning in the huge fireplace, the smell of a recent wood-burning fire still filled the room. The largest oak desk Roberto had ever seen caught his attention first, followed by the many expensive-looking upholstered chairs and side tables. He knew he could never fit even one of these pieces of furniture in his small cottage.

The stone walls were covered with large portraits of generations of the Vitales. Bookcases, filled with hundreds of books, surrounded the huge stone fireplace. It was apparent that this room was where the Don conducted business and Roberto realized that, to Don Vitale, this marriage arrangement was business. In any case, Roberto would not allow the awesome décor of the room to deter him from his mission there.

Bruno Vitale entered, crossing the room to greet him. Close up, Roberto noticed that the Don's skin color was darker than his own. Close up, Roberto realized that the Don was shorter and heavier than he was.

"Signor Amato, welcome. We hoped to see you and now here you are". They shook hands as the Don gestured for them to sit.

Seating themselves in cushioned armchairs, the Don offered Roberto a drink which he accepted to be polite even though, by his clock, it was still morning. Roberto realized that his acceptance was a mistake when they both saw his tremor in holding the heavy crystal glass.

"Salude," they toasted as the Don pretended not to notice his shaking hand. Taking a sip, Roberto placed his glass down on the side table, unlike Signor Vitale who emptied his glass in one quick gulp.

"Amelia, come join us," the Don called out. His voice echoed through the large cavernous stone house. Dressed in a white silk dress with a lace scalloped hem that draped past her ankles, the lady of the villa entered the room so quickly after being summoned that one could safely guess that she deliberately hovered nearby waiting to be called.

The Don's appearance was quite a contrast to his wife's. While he had an olive complexion and the thick body of a Sicilian laborer, she was willowy and fair and appeared to be a few inches taller than her husband. Although the Don could never be described as handsome, no one would ever question either his intelligence or his ruthlessness, although many doubted that he could read the books in his library.

Roberto stood when she had entered the room and found himself bowing at the waist as a sign of respect. Around her it was too easy to feel like a serf.

"This is my wife, Signora Vitale. Our eldest son, Carlo, is named for her father. He is her favorite son so you can guess this marriage proposal for Carlo is very important to her."

"Bruno, why do you say such things? You know perfectly well that I love all our sons equally. And remember you were the one who did not want the name Bruno for our first born or we would have named him after you instead of my father," she responded to her husband defensively. Her husband only shrugged and moved across the room to refill his glass.

She turned to face Roberto directly. "Please forgive my husband's poor memory." She smiled and sat in a chair close to where Roberto sat, giving him her full attention.

"Signor Amato, we are so pleased to meet you finally, especially since we will be family once our children are wed," she said with a twinkle in her gray eyes. "We see your lovely daughter at mass every Sunday so we know she is as lovely inside as she is outside."

With all three seated and the Don speaking, Roberto tried to concentrate on what was being said, but couldn't get the thought out of his head about what the signora had said. The thought that such a marriage would connect Rosa and him to the Vitales *as family* had never crossed his mind. He could never imagine his Rosa and the signora having a meaningful conversation together. The thought frightened him more than pleased him, but he kept smiling since it seemed to be the wisest choice at present.

"Not so quick, Amelia. I believe Roberto is here because he is still considering our offer. Am I correct, Roberto, since I have yet to receive your answer?"

"Don Vitale, I have heard all good things from Father Nunzio about Carlo, but I need to have them confirmed by you, father to father. I believe you have all sons and no daughters. Daughters need a father's special protection, as you can understand."

"Sadly, my prayers were never answered for a daughter," lamented the Don's wife, interrupting her husband who was about to speak. "Once our children are wed, your Mina will become our daughter, as well."

"But I have given you three healthy sons, so be grateful, Amelia," her husband reminded her in a tone that ended her participation in the conversation. "I wanted you to meet Signor Amato but now we must discuss business."

With a beat of silence and the eye contact between them, a signal was clearly given for her dismissal. Amelia slowly, but elegantly, rose from her chair and with a noticeable flicker of disappointment, bade Roberto farewell.

"Of course, I will leave you gentlemen to come to a happy conclusion for us" and she left the room.

Roberto's impression was that she was lonely and eager for any outside company. However, the life she chose or was chosen for her, excluded that. He stood again as she left the room remembering the manners taught him by the nuns in his early school days. Bruno Vitale had remained seated as his wife made her exit.

"I do understand your position, Roberto, so what do you need to hear from me so your decision can be made?" The Don lost no time getting to the point of the meeting.

"Do you think your son will enlist in the Boston Cosa Nostra?" as Roberto also got to the point. He amazed himself with his own question's directness. "As her father, I want a normal and safe life for my daughter if she goes to America. I would wish for her a good life filled with happiness and free of fear. Respectfully, I ask if you can understand my position as a father?"

"I am grateful that you have spoken your mind, Roberto, and I do understand what you want for your daughter because Amelia and I want the same for Carlo. We will not allow his entry into any syndicate but let me explain."

The Don offered another drink which Roberto declined. He had barely touched the glass that still remained on the table.

The Don crossed the room to an antique marble table and refilled his glass from a crystal decanter there. He began to speak in a restrained but well thought out manner.

"I am going to share private information with you because of your hesitancy regarding the marriage. My son will not be part of the life our family has chosen. To be initiated there are requirements for an inductee. A recruit must be of full Italian descent. He must have no connection to the police, either himself or members of his family. An Omertha code of silence is also required and, if broken, could mean a serious penalty."

When he stressed the word 'serious', he glanced at Roberto to see if there was a reaction. With Roberto's stone face, the Don went on. "Carlo would easily meet these first three qualifications. However, he would have to be sponsored by a soldato, a soldier who has already been made a permanent member. This will be impossible for him because, unknown to my son, word has gone out of my opposition to any such sponsorship. Anyone going against me understands they will risk my retribution, even as far as America."

He stopped briefly to judge Roberto's reaction. Seeing none, he went on. "Finally, some familia have another requirement that you will find troubling. Before earning initiation, a test is required to prove loyalty, sometimes one that is best not mentioned. I know that hurting others is not in my son's nature. Do not misunderstand me. I do not want to paint my son as innocent, as he is not. He has his flaws. And his decisions are not always mature enough to my satisfaction. But that may be my fault because I allowed his mother to spoil him as our first born. He has always had more of his mother's soft side than mine."

The Don took a deep breath and continued. "That's why we sent him to America. We wanted to remove him from the dangers inherit in our family business. We decided to allow him a fresh start for the sake of the grandchildren we expect from him after he is wed."

Roberto reached for the glass of liqueur and drank hoping it would steady his nerves after hearing what had been unexpectedly shared with him. He remained silent and maintained a poker face, unsure if Don Vitale was finished speaking. He wasn't.

"So, my answer is that because I will not allow this life for Carlo, he will never be Cosa Nostra. I will prevent it from happening, regardless if it is something he may want because it is familiar to him. His mother and I are in agreement with this."

"Our younger sons must be part of our business and they will carry on our work here at home, but not Carlo. Believe me, we have enemies in this line of work and men seeking vendettas against my family. So, as you can see, we must protect ourselves with walls and guards. Even though my wife grew up this same way in Palermo, she made me promise that our children would be spared. I can only keep that promise for our oldest son, Carlo, not the other two, and she still holds that against me."

The degree of openness by the Don was unexpected and left Roberto fazed. He was rattled thinking of how to respond when the Don added, "Roberto, regardless of your decision I expect that everything that I have told you will be kept with your fullest discretion. Capisci?"

Roberto understood only too well the importance of keeping their conversation confidential. "Don Vitale, nothing you have told me will ever leave this house, other than reassuring my wife with your word that Carlo will not be part of Cosa Nostra in America. You have my word that I will have my answer to you shortly." Roberto felt proud that he said this with no sign of temerity.

The two men stood and shook hands without another word being said. The servant appeared out of nowhere and silently led him to the entranceway, opening the massive oak door. Roberto glanced back and could see the Don's wife looking at him from the balcony above the stairs. There was a tentative smile on her face but Roberto was handed his cap and coat and escorted out so quickly that he had no time to give her a reciprocal smile. For that he felt badly. He actually felt sorry for her. She lived in a gilded cage.

As he walked toward the gates of the villa, he nodded at the guards and put out his hand for the return of his knife.

The older guard handed it to him saying, "Looks like your business is completed."

"Almost," he replied.

Filled with an emotion he could not explain, Roberto sniggered to himself as he began his walk on the dirt road that would lead him home. The long trek gave him the time needed to ponder his options. Simply there were two choices, either refuse the Don's son in marriage or permit it. Allowing the marriage would gain Mina's entrance into a new life in America.

Although he was convinced of the Don's resolve that his son would be free of any mob connections, before a decision could be made, he needed his wife's input.

The arrangement will provide passage to America for Mina to join her brother. Once there, only God knows what will happen, he thought with trepidation. *Our daughter can change her mind about anything and everything, large and small.*

He decided to wait for the upcoming feast of San Andreas before broaching the marriage offer with his wife. He believed that discussing the marriage offer would be best presented during the celebration in the village.

At least, being out in public, Rosa will not yell at me for considering a marriage for Mina into a criminal family. She will avoid a scene until we reach home. He knew that from past experiences with the passionate woman to whom he was married. *By then I should be able to convince her that the offer may be Mina's only chance for a better life.*

The procession through the village and to the harbor for the blessing of the fishing boats to celebrate the feast of St. Andreas, the patron saint of fisherman, was an annual event in Sciacca.

"With the war waging in the north, we all need this festival right now. The music and dancing will be good for us, but especially for you and the other young people," she told her daughter who did not seem to share her mother's enthusiasm.

"I think the old people like it better than the young ones," Mina remarked rubbing her feet since her Sunday shoes, that she insisted on wearing, hurt her feet. Rosa had warned her how the shoes were not meant to be worn for long processions but, like all young girls, she was more vain than wise.

"Nothing seems to please you sixteen-year olds," Rosa said as she watched Mina roll her eyes. "Anyway, we are here so let's make it a happy event, please."

The statue of the patron saint had been carried through the village with the procession ending with Father Nunzio's blessings at the steps of the Duomo. Everyone wore their best clothes and the musicians would play local music that would get young and old dancing. In the past, before the war drained the young men of the village, the celebration was an opportunity for match making between families.

Rosa sat chatting with her daughter while they awaited Roberto. Then they could set out their meal. If one looked quickly, they would have thought the two women were sisters. It was never questioned that Mina inherited her mother's loveliness and sweet temperament. Although, neither parent took the blame for her inherited tendency towards vacillation which was a fault they were still trying to cure.

"Look at your father, Mina, busy in discussion when he should be sitting here with us eating. Men! Do you see the typical Sicilian discussion? Hands flying in the air, voices being raised and no one agreeing on anything."

"They mostly speak about the war, Momma. That's all everyone talks about anymore."

"Mina, I am grateful that your brother is safe in America. Now we have no sons for the government to draft to fight and die in a war over some foreign duke's assassination that is no concern of our people."

"Then make sure you tell Papa that you only want to listen to the music and not hear talk of politics. Otherwise, that's what you will be hearing from him."

As Mina was unwrapping the lunch Rosa had prepared for her small family, Brigida, her best friend, tried to pull Mina out to the open plaza to dance the *Fasola* with her.

"Mina, come dance with me," she pleaded.

"I have no intention of dancing and what for?" Mina replied pointing to the villagers. "Look around, Brigida. All that's left to watch us dance are withered old men and little boys."

"Suit yourself, Mina," replied the disappointed Brigida who turned to join the other dancers.

But within seconds, Mina rushed to her feet and took her friend's hand. "Let's dance," she said, as if it was her idea.

Brigida turned and placed both hands on her hips. "Mina, why is it that you always say one thing but do the opposite?"

Hearing this, Rosa sighed as she knew exactly what Brigida meant. As a little girl, Mina's quirk was endearing but as a young adult was growing tiresome.

As she watched them dance, it never ceased to amaze Rosa how the two girls were such pictures of contrast to each other. Mina's Roman ancestry blessed her with luminously dark hair and hazel eyes in contrast to Brigida's redheaded Norman ancestry. They, like so many Sicilians, were living proof that Sciacca's population carried the genes of many ancient and diffuse conquering invaders.

The two teenagers were slim, but then with the war, everyone was slimmer than in previous years. Dressed in their dark blue striped skirts and aprons, they were lovely to look at. They knew it and they flaunted it. Brigida's long red hair was tethered in a silver clasp that caught the sunlight each time she twirled and Mina wore her hair in a loose bun displaying the gold filigree dropped earrings inherited from her grandmother.

"Oh, to be young and carefree of the realities of life," Rosa mumbled to herself as she watched them happily prancing about to the music. Even Father Nunzio joined in making everyone laugh as he tried to keep up with the girls.

Rosa knew that each of the girls believed, without a doubt, that their families would eventually approve good marriages for them once the war was over and the young men returned.

"Oh Dio! please let all return who left," she prayed, sadly knowing that will not happen with so many names of casualties already being posted on the church's door weekly.

The young are untethered from what is real. For now, let them live comfortably in their own imaginations because this war will break hearts soon enough when less young men return than had left, Rosa could not help thinking.

Mina was torn between her desire to join her brother in America and staying with her aging parents. Unlike Brigida, who never wanted to leave Sciacca, Mina wasn't sure. That's why Rosa insisted that she continue her English lessons with Father Nunzio who was educated in Rome but chose the life of a humble pastor in Sicily. Unlike most other Sicilian priests, his education included being fluent in English so he was only too pleased to give Mina English lessons weekly.

Rosa and Roberto encouraged their children to emigrate in order to remove the children's guilt for such a move. As their only remaining son, Basilio had to be thoroughly convinced that it was their wish for him. He promised them that one day he would find a way for them to be all together again. No one had any solution as to how that would ever happen nor how to find a way to pay Mina's passage to America, but it continued to be discussed at home and in letters.

As Rosa patiently awaited her husband and daughter to join her, an elderly neighbor waved to her, slowly making her way over. Rosa made an inaudible groan.

"Scusa, Rosa, please make room for me on the bench". The request came from Eugenia, the village gossiper and firm believer in all things evil eye. Eugenia never seemed to lose weight even as everyone else in the village became thinner as the war waged and food supplies decreased. Eugenia lived alone and, behind her back, the children called her the Sciacca Witch.

"Last night while I was praying, I heard the baying of your dog. Surely, you heard it, too?" she questioned Rosa as she slowly and carefully sat her large body down on the narrow wooden bench.

"Our dog is always baying so we pay him no mind," responded Rosa as politely as she could without antagonizing the woman.

"*Mal notaria*, Rosa, bad luck is coming to you."

"Eugenia, your concern is noted. Tomorrow, I will remember to put my first stocking on my left leg to ensure good luck."

"It is too late for that, Rosa, too late," warned Eugenia. "Be on your guard is all I can warn you."

Although Rosa reluctantly offered her something to eat, Eugenia surprisingly refused. With effort, she raised her hefty body to a standing position and looked around to see who she would visit next. *I wonder why she never appears to lose weight like the rest of us*, Rosa thought unkindly. *Maybe she does have some kind of magic.*

After repeating her warning for a second time, she bid Rosa a good afternoon.

"Bonasera to you, too, Eugenia." Rosa answered halfheartedly wondering how she was supposed to have a good afternoon after being told of an imminent evil omen? *Is it any wonder that I try to avoid her?*

Rosa had prepared pasta con le sarde for her family. Sardines, raisins and capers were still readily available but it took bartering on her part for the pine nuts. Bartering had become a war time necessity for the village and Rosa was quite adept at it because of the yield from her productive garden.

Roberto finally joined his wife and, as she placed a dish in front of him, he piously recited the traditional Sicilian prayer, 'whatever I eat today, may I eat it next year.'

"With the large fish avoiding my nets this week, it is a good thing I like sardines," he said teasingly to his wife. Rosa silently prayed to St. Andreas to not forget the fishermen when next the men go out.

Rosa called Mina to join them but her daughter replied back that she was not hungry.

"Remember when we preferred dancing to eating?" smiled Roberto as he carefully moved his hand under Rosa's buttocks. Pushing his had away, shyly hoping no one saw, Rosa replied coyly, "I remember we preferred *something else* more than we preferred dancing or eating." With that said, Roberto again moved his hand under her backside as they sat together laughing softly.

Then within a heartbeat, Mina joined her parents and ate hungrily before again joining in the dancing. Her parents had grown accustomed to Mina's in-decisiveness. Her flighty ways were known to all and, although frustrating at times, everyone made allowances for it because of her sweet temperament.

Roberto knew he could no longer delay. Now that he and Rosa were alone he was about to bring up the marriage offer. But before he had a chance, Rosa's worried look made him hesitate.

"What is it, Rosa? Why do you look worried?"

"The old hag Eugenia told me to expect bad news. She's so often right, I'm concerned. Look at her. Now she is sitting with the Aguglia family probably depressing them, too."

Roberto knew he had to turn this around quickly if he was to accomplish what he had to.

"Well, I have good news not bad news. A husband has been matched for Mina. His name is Carlo Vitale. He is a bit older at 26 but he lives in Boston and works with Basilio at the same plant. Most importantly, should we accept, the Vitale family will pay Mina's voyage in full." He said all this in one breath to prevent Rosa interrupting him which he knew would result as soon as she heard the name Vitale.

"God Almighty, the Vitales are Cosa Nostra, Roberto! What are you thinking?" Alarmed, she would never agree for Mina to become part of that world, regardless of the luxuries such a life would afford her. "Everyone knows of their connections in Palermo and Corleone. They live in that large villa pretending that it was not bought with blood money."

16

"Not their son, Rosa. Father Nunzio learned that Carlo Vitale earns an honest salary at his job. In fact, he works in the same plant as Basilio. He has no criminal connections."

Roberto wanted to believe everything he told her but his Sicilian cynicism was always there deep down. It helped cushion the inevitable disappointments life brought with it. But he continued to speak optimistically anyway in order to convince his wife. If necessary, he would try to repeat Father Nunzio's sermon on taking risks and having trust and something about human angels, although he knew it would never sound the same coming from him.

"Sure, it is hopeful news that the Americans have finally joined the war and will bring it to an end sooner, but we all know that Sicily's hardship will not end any time soon after that. No one is counting on the post- war period being much better than it is now. We will have to face the same problems we have now with food shortages, no jobs for our returning soldiers and political unrest. Our country's problems may even get worse before they get better so we should be in agreement in taking advantage of the Vitale offer for Mina's sake."

"But I am worried for our daughter."

"Look, Rosa, we have to face facts. The Vitale offer will provide Mina's passage to America. As you know, that is a very generous offer. Who knows? Maybe if their son backs out, no repayment will be required and Mina will remain living with Basilio and Carmela."

"No young man would ever reject Mina!"

"I am only saying that getting Mina to America is the priority."

"Not if she is locked in an unhappy marriage for her lifetime with a man she does not love and who is related to criminals."

"Be reasonable, if a Sicilian searches hard and long enough, I suppose most of us can find a relative with a mob connection of some kind."

"How can you say such a shameful thing, Roberto? I do not believe that and you should not either."

"Let's not argue the past when the present is our main concern, Rosa. You hardly knew me when our parents arranged our marriage. Has it been so bad?"

He knew her answer before it was given. She leaned over and took his hand in hers.

"Not so bad."

"That's why once we can agree then we can inform Mina. We will let her make the final decision."

Roberto held back telling Rosa that he still felt that the Don didn't describe his son the way a proud father would be expected to, but it was all the information they would be getting on Carlo.

"Rosa, consider that Mina will have Basilio and Carmela living near her after she is wed. This will work out to everyone's satisfaction. Another thought…maybe before you and I are too old, our son and daughter may find a way for us to join them in America. Miracles can happen. Picture holding little American grandchildren in your arms." He made a swinging motion with his joined arms as if he was rocking an infant to sleep.

Rosa hugged her husband. He always knew how to appeal to her heart. Not because she always fully agreed with him but because she knew his decisions were never made lightly or without much thought. She would acquiesce to his judgment in this as she had always done in the past in matters of importance.

"I know we had hoped for this and we still do not know what Mina will decide. But I cannot help thinking that this could be the bad news predicted by that witch, Eugenia?"

"No, this is good news, Rosa!" he insisted firmly. "It is for Mina's future. We both know there is nothing worthwhile for her here anymore. But we will wait for Mina's opinion tonight after we speak with her about the offer."

"We will miss her terribly if she agrees. I still miss both our sons every day. The loss never leaves me. The fact remains that we may never see our children again in our lifetime," she lamented and which he shared but would not speak of it.

"When will this happen if she agrees to it?" she asked with a tremor in her voice and tears beginning to form in the corner of each eye.

"Soon," he answered consolingly.

That evening at home, Roberto poured the wine made at harvest from their healthy vines into three glasses. It was suspicious the way her father was treating her like an adult but Mina decided to enjoy it while it lasted.

"Mina, we have talked about America for quite a while. Would you wish to go if there is a chance?" questioned her father slyly.

"No, I don't think so, Papa. I want to stay here with you and Momma."

"What is here for you, Mina? Do you have a young man we don't know about?"

"I truly wish I could answer yes, but of course not, Papa."

"Do you trust me to find a husband for you?"

"Probably," Mina answered with a bit of hesitation. "What are you saying?"

She kept glancing at her mother who was silent. Her mother was never silent so that was perplexing.

"What If I found passage for you to America and a husband at the same time?"

"Then I would think you can work miracles, Papa."

"Then call me Saint Roberto because I have accomplished both recently."

Mina didn't know how to respond but she knew her father well enough for belief.

"Momma, what is this all about? What is Papa talking about? Where could he find a husband when the only young men left in any of the villages have something wrong with them?"

"What if I found him already in America?" her father asked as he began to explain the proposal to her, especially assuring her that there was no criminal association involved even though the young man's father was the Don.

All that was known was shared with Mina. He addressed each of her questions with an answer as honestly as he could. He tried to make her understand the special opportunity the offer presented.

"At the end of my visit with him, the Don gave me his son's picture for you. The Don had said, 'Roberto, my wife insisted that you give Carlo's picture to your daughter so that she can see that Carlo has his mother's looks, not mine, which should please her.' So, what do you think?" her father asked.

Taking her time, Mina studied the picture. Roberto had no idea the color of his eyes when Mina asked but told her that Signora Vitale's were a light color. He could not answer her question as to Carlo's height.

"What if he's very short? His father is short."

"I am sure that regardless of his height he will be taller than you," retorted her father trying to be patient.

Listening to her, her parents began to feel that she was having a positive reaction to all that was being discussed. She brought up that she would find it exciting to live with Basilio and Carmela. She added she would learn all she could about Boston from Father Nunzio. She talked about the adventure of the sea voyage across the Atlantic. It was no wonder that her parents expected that she was excited and eager to accept the offer.

Then she shook her head and said, "No, please turn down the offer. I hope you are not disappointed with my decision but it is for the best," Mina answered as gently as she could.

Stunned, Roberto thought he would make it clear that she had no choice but, in his heart, he could never demand that she go against her will. He looked at his wife for support but all he saw was relief on her face in that she wouldn't be losing her daughter, after all.

"Very well, Mina. I will inform the Don tomorrow." He would keep his word that it was her decision to make, not his, regardless of his deep disappointment.

He swallowed the remaining wine in his glass in one gulp, dreading another visit where he would have to inform the Don that the offer was rejected, not to mention, his concern about potential repercussions. Living in a small village like Sciacca, such news would not go unknown for long, he knew only too well. The Vitale family's honor could be at stake.

But before his disappointment had time to fully sink in, Mina changed her mind.

"Maybe I will agree, Papa, out of respect for your recommendation." Actually, it took just a few minutes to picture herself with having a handsome husband, living in a modern American apartment while seeing the sights of Boston with her brother and sister in law. She saw herself purchasing a beautiful wedding dress and enjoying a lovely wedding reception.

What was I thinking to turn this down? she rebuked herself. *I cannot wait to tell Brigida,* she thought excitedly. *She will be so jealous!*

Mina 's parents exchanged surprised looks. Now Roberto's was a look of relief while Rosa's face returned to her original look of anticipatory loss.

were, turned and smiled at them, although Mina could see his smile was directed at Fiona more so than herself. When Fiona almost lost her balance on the stair, he was the one who caught her arm preventing her fall.

"Good grief, how embarrassing if I fell. Thank you so much," Fiona said, relieved that she was spared an injury at the start of her voyage.

"Well, the way they have us packed in like sardines, I doubt you would have been able to fall very far. The truth be known, you more or less just landed on me rather than my rescuing you."

"You are very kind to say that but thank you anyway."

As they continued descending the stairwell, he introduced himself. "I'm Brian Kelly."

He had turned to face them and was descending the stairs backwards as he spoke to them.

"Do be careful or you will be the next to fall, Mr. Kelly."

"Don't worry about that. I have great balance. And what are your names, may I ask?"

"I'm Fiona Burke and my friend is Mina…". Fiona realized she did not know Mina's last name.

"Well then, hello Miss Burke and Miss…?" Brian answered looking at Mina to provide her surname.

"Amato," Mina responded and in broken English asked Brian to call her Mina, seeing there was no reason for formality when they were all around the same age.

"Please call me Brian, Ladies," he called over his shoulder to them as he followed his family to their assigned area.

"Then first name basis it will be," declared Fiona loudly enough for him to hear, pleased that she had made two friends already and was no longer as alone as she had been just minutes before and months before that.

Once the steerage deck was reached, the passengers were divided into three sections, one for families, one for single women and the last for single men.

February, 1918

Boston

Upon learning that his sister would be joining him, Basilio was excited to have the responsibility for her care and for the planning of her marriage.

"I know it means stretching our income, Carmela, but it will mean so much to me to have Mina here." Carmela was delighted, as well, and told him that she had always thought of Mina as one of her own sisters.

Being a stickler for details, Carmela reviewed all the steps Basilio would need to take once Mina passed processing at Ellis Island in New York.

Jokingly, Basilio reminded his wife that he doubted much had changed of the processing procedures since they went through Ellis Island in New York harbor upon their entry to America not so long ago.

"Carmela, if anything has changed, I certainly hope it is for the better because neither of us would ever wish to go through that journey again."

"I will pray to St. Christopher, patron saint of travelers, that you have a safe trip to New York and back to me." Carmela seemed to know every patron saint, their feast days and the grisly ways each was martyred.

"I am taking an ordinary train, Carmela, not joining a wagon train heading out west," he laughed but knew her worry meant her love for him.

As much as loved his young wife, he did wish that she would try to assimilate more into American society. Carmela always spoke in the dialect in which she was raised and avoided learning any English. She felt she had no need to learn since almost everyone in the tenements came from somewhere in Sicily. Carmela, although not a beauty, had a wholesome look with her curly brown hair and deep brown eyes. Although their families had recommended the match, the couple fell in love with each other very quickly. As a provider, Basilio was an excellent and caring husband and Carmela a wonderful wife. They represented a successful marriage match made by their fathers.

Each week together they would sort his paycheck to pay the household expenses and to pay down their passage debt.

"Carmela, you should have been a banker," Basilio teased her because Carmela's frugal ways were resulting in some savings, small but still savings even after their debts were covered.

Carmela was renowned for her cooking and sewing and for her charity work within the building, especially baby- sitting whenever asked. Although both desperately wanted children there had been no pregnancies in their three years of marriage. When the public health nurse would visit the tenements, making her rounds explaining forms of birth control to the women who had more babies than they could feed, Carmela would hide her tears and pray she was not permanently barren. Her talks with the nurse were about conception, not prevention. Although sometimes the nurse was accompanied by a Negro girl training to be a doctor, the women in her tenement preferred to listen only to the white nurse.

"I know your little sister will be as lovely as ever and will make me look like an old matron next to her." She held a mirror to herself. Carmela was barely five feet tall in stature and, at twenty, already had a thickening waist line. With dark hair and eyes, she looked like most of the other Sicilian women in the building. Although her looks would be described as 'plain', she had an inner beauty recognized by all who knew her.

"I love your extra pounds because there is more of you to fondle," her husband replied, hugging her closely and placing his hands all over her body to prove his point.

He picked her up in his strong arms and carried her to the bed while telling her, "I love trying to make babies with you, Carm, and even if no babies come, I sure do enjoy trying every night!" Carmela felt secure in adding love-making to the list of her other skills.

Basilio was learning English quickly out of necessity because not all his coworkers were Sicilian. The plant had many American, Irish and Scandina-vian workers. Sadly, he learned not long after his arrival in the country of the prejudice against Sicilians. He and Carmela were aware that even the mainland

Italians unfairly considered Sicilians as lowly peasants. Compared with the mostly uneducated Sicilians who took the laborer jobs, many Italians came to America with trade skills that provided elevated status in the workforce. However, whether the Italians or the Sicilians had skilled occupations, the unions kept them both out.

"Carmela, I try to listen to everyone around me so I can learn how to be American. What I have seen is that the Norwegian workers seem to assimilate easiest here because they look more like the Americans than we do. We cannot change our looks but we can learn English and the ways of the Americans. I am sure that all we need is time to prove ourselves."

"Even after all this time, I'm still more comfortable being in our tenement enclave with our people, speaking our language and doing things our way," said Carmela. "Maybe I'm a coward and afraid to venture out too far, but I doubt I will ever change. Basilio, you are the one for whom I pray every day so that you are strong enough to put up with the discrimination everywhere."

"Carmela, believe it or not, slowly things are getting better. The Irish are the most difficult even though many are new immigrants themselves and, like us Sicilians, mostly unskilled laborers, too. Everyone says that their intolerance of us is for the same reason we have been made unwelcome in their parish churches. They see us as border line pagans because our celebration of Catholicism differs from theirs. They see our celebration processions of the saints as a form of idolatry, even though they raucously celebrate their St. Patrick's Day getting drunk! Although some of our elderly may believe in the 'evil eye', incredibly, the Irish believe in leprechauns and fairies and have their own superstitions, too. They even kiss a rock called the 'Blarney Stone' for good luck. Wish I could understand why they think we are so different from them when I think we all are a bit crazy."

Basilio was not religious but lived by the golden rule of treating others as one would want to be treated and was flummoxed when others did not. As the years passed, Basilio learned to ignore the insulting derogatory names used behind his back. He prayed that Carmela would never hear the news of the three Sicilian men recently lynched in New Orleans for minor infractions, with little evidence and no one defending them. *That would be all she would have to hear and she would have us swimming home to Sciacca.*

Basilio had a thirst for learning and embraced the future that America offered. He hoped to be able to practice English with Mina since Carmela had no interest. Being taller than most Sicilians, he radiated a handsomeness and intelligence that set him apart from many others. His dark hair and hazel eyes were the same as his sister's. Had he not been five years her senior, they could have passed as fraternal twins. The difference was that he was born with a club foot with his right foot a few inches shorter that the left which resulted in a limp which he took great strides to hide. He padded his shoe each day to compensate for his disability. It had kept him from being conscripted into the army but never hindered him otherwise. He was determined to assimilate and earn respect from his peers and his bosses as an honorable man and a good worker. He planned to have his future children educated so that the next generation would be as American as anyone else. In time, he hoped to earn passage for his parents but that was a long-term goal since he had yet to pay off his and Carmela's substantial debt for their own passage.

When his father wrote of Mina's match to his co-worker Carlo Vitale, he had mixed emotions. He was excited to have his sister join him in Boston but there were rumors that Carlo had a gambling problem. Although he did not know him well, Basilio decided to make a point of spending time with him. Carlo was older than Basilio and had a separate group of friends. Nevertheless, he hoped the impending marriage between their families would give them common ground for friendship.

After receiving his parent's letter, he made a point of seeking Carlo out since he worked in a different area than Basilio's. He found Carlo speaking with two men so he waited until Carlo noticed him.

"Ciao, Carlo. I am Basilio Amato, Mina's brother," as he reached to shake Carlo's hand. "I wish to offer my congratulations."

As Carlo introduced his coworkers, Basilio followed the Italian custom of saying 'ciao' to each individual while shaking each man's hand. At that point, the two men politely excused themselves assuming the conversation would involve family matters and, to Sicilians, nothing is more confidential than family matters.

Once alone and with only a few minutes left for the break, Basilio said, "Carlo, I look forward to being brothers with your marriage to my sister. I just wonder why you never mentioned this to me knowing of the match?"

"That's because I'm old fashioned, Basilio. I believe it was your place to come to me. We may live in America but let's not forget our traditions," he lectured the younger man. Basilio still found it odd but left it at that with both men agreeing to plan more time together.

While he worked, Basilio thought back how often Mina had written that she never wanted to leave home for America. He reminded himself how he would have to get accustomed again to his sister's odd way of making decisions, especially from their years growing up together. After months of letters with Mina's protesting that she could never leave Sciacca, he learned from his parents that she was thrilled when told of the match and the journey. *Always expect the unexpected from my sister*, he reminded himself.

Although Basilio had planned to meet Mina alone, Carlo insisted that the two men travel together to New York City to bring Mina to Boston.

Basilio finally agreed after much deliberation and Carlo's insistence. Although he was glad to have company on the train ride, he hoped that it would not be too awkward for Mina to meet her future husband on a dock in New York City instead of a family dinner arranged at home which had been the original plan.

Carlo Vitale threw away the letter but kept looking at the small picture that had been enclosed. It was a relief when he received the news that his family had found him a pretty Sicilian girl to wed. Philomena, called Mina for short, was described in his mother's letter as pretty, pious and obedient. Her picture was a bit grainy but, from what he could see, she looked pleasing and had a nice smile with straight teeth.

"I like the description of 'pretty' and 'obedient' but could do without the 'pious' part," he jokingly told his friend forcing a smile. "She's only sixteen but my mother wrote that she is already an excellent cook and is learning English. She had better not be some educated type with a snooty air." This time he was serious.

"You can always send her back if she is," said Mario, his friend and frequent gambling companion at the social club owned by the Boston mob.

At twenty-six and with no responsibilities, Carlo was a 'man about town'. All he had to do was work his job and have fun every evening. He was a frequent visitor to the social club where he was known for his gambling habit. He was also well known among the puttanas who hung around the Italian social club looking for business. He liked the whores because there were no rules as to what could be done with them and he didn't like rules. That was one of the reasons he left Sicily when given the chance. His father ran his home and his gang ruthlessly. He pitied his mother but was grateful that he had inherited her good looks, although he blamed his father for his short peasant stature.

He saw the arranged marriage as something that would not necessarily require any preliminary romantic work on his part. It would give him a wife to care for his needs and yet not interfere with his private life. When children arrived, she would see to their proper upbringing like all good Sicilian mothers. It pleased him every time he thought about having a woman in his bed every night. His family finally did him a favor.

"American girls have too many crazy new ideas," he told Mario, when he shared the news of his forthcoming arranged marriage.

"There's nothing like a Sicilian wife who knows when to be seen and when to be heard but are you sure you trust your mother's description of 'pretty'? She could be a dog face, you know," responded Mario.

With no marriage prospects in his near future, Mario hoped that she would be ugly because he resented Carlo's privileged life. He also worried he would lose his gambling buddy when Carlo married. Carlo's good looks were a magnet that drew the women over to them which never happened when Mario was alone at the club. With an undercurrent of jealousy, Mario Russo resented Carlo's family ties to the Sicilian syndicate and how a laborer's job was in place for him as soon as he had arrived in America. Mario had the lowliest job in the city.

"I'm still waiting for you to keep your word about getting me a better job," he reminded Carlo, not for the first time. "I'm tired of working with the coons. Nobody white wants my job," he complained.

While Carlo was a laborer in the distillery plant, Mario's job was to cart out the 'night soil' from the tenement outhouses. Every night, he would shovel the excrement from the tenement outhouses into barrels that would be carted to barges and dumped out to sea. Very often, illegally, short cuts were taken and dumping was made in the river.

Too often, Mario brought the smell of his job with him making him the butt of constant jokes because of it. He had a vile temper and a foul mouth which only added to his ostracism from the people with whom he came in contact. Why Carlo befriended him was a mystery to both of them at times. Perhaps it was because of Carlo's need to feel superior. With Mario it was easy to do.

"You keep promising to use your family's influence to get me a job at the molasses distillery so why hasn't that happened yet?"

"I keep asking but my father has more important matters than you."

Mario could only think that Carlo was either unable to do so or did not want to do so. An underlying resentment continued because of that.

To prevent the conversation from going downhill, Mario brought up something he considered great fun the previous Sunday. "We did have a good time throwing horse manure on those suffragette marchers, didn't we? 'Specially with the cops not stopping us. I hope those lesbians plan more marches real soon 'cause I'll be right there for the free fun."

"Before I think about marches I need to start winning my money back," replied Carlo with a trace of concern in his voice. They were heading to the neighborhood gambling club together as they did most early evenings before Mario had to go to his job at midnight.

"We both need to, Chum, but I have to say, your losses have been real bad lately. You better hope your family back home will help you out again 'cause the guys don't have a lot of patience when you owe them big money." Mario enjoyed bringing up Carlo's bad luck at the tables every chance he had.

"Maybe tonight's my night and I won't need my family. But if I do, I know that they always come through for me. Look, didn't they just buy me a Sicilian wife?" he laughed patting his friend's shoulder. "I am their golden boy."

Although strings had been pulled to place Carlo in a job at the Purity Distilling Company, the steady weekly paycheck rarely covered his expenses. The loan sharks found him to be a frequent customer. But Carlo rationalized that his future involved more than a laborer's salary so his losses would be covered shortly. He continually invoked his family to make mafia contacts for him in Boston or New York, but their answer was always 'be patient, Son.' He had already become known to the local mob on his own but only by his gambling loans and losses. Sometimes, the loans made to him were late in repayment. Too often, it required the influence of his family to prevent repercussions. He could not understand his father's delay in obtaining his entry into the local syndicate and was becoming very frustrated.

Carlo promised himself, *that no matter what happens, I will never become a Sicilian ritornati who returns home to Sicily because they couldn't make a success of themselves. Let those losers go back to the homeland where there is always one crisis or another, with centuries of la miseria with grain failures, phlloxera disease destroying the grape vines and fishing boats lost in storms. I will remain here and become someone who everyone looks up to as soon as I gain entrance into the Cosa Nostra family here in Boston. If my father doesn't help then I will do it on my own.*

He continued to hope that his Sicilian family's mob connections would enable him to rise quickly to a better life in Boston once he became a member of the local mob. He spent most of his non- working time gambling and hanging out trying to get the notice from them that he craved. He used his father's and grandfather's names freely and could not understand that it did not get him the results he expected. *Don't these idiots know they are important Dons in Palermo and Sciacca?* he questioned.

February, 1918

Steerage

The steamship rules were such that women traveling without male escorts had separate quarters from families traveling together and from men traveling alone. Basilio and Carmela had each other during their voyage, so Mina felt vindicated in going against her brother's advice and partnering with a companion. Basilio's admonition to be wary of strangers on board was well intentioned but Mina preferred to have a female friend and confident for the voyage. The voyage was far too long to be alone. Depending on weather and storms, the voyage could last for a full month.

As they walked to their assigned compartment, Fiona told Mina that she was from Dublin, Ireland. "I am heading to New York where I have relatives who reside in a place called Brooklyn. Where is your destination, Mina?"

Mina could only interpret part of what she said because her Irish accent made words sound quite differently from Father Nunzio's Sicilian pronunciation during their English lessons in Sciacca.

"I am to go to Boston, to my brother," Mina shared slowly using her limited English. She was pleased that Fiona seemed to understand her even though her sentences often contained a mixture of English and Sicilian words.

"So, we have established that you are Sicilian. Well, that's fine. We can still make this work. Since I will never be clever enough to learn your language, we will have to practice English together," the Irish girl said in a cheerfully positive tone.

Fiona stood out wherever she went, not only because of her ethereal beauty but also because of her exceptional eyes. Mina could not help staring at them as she had never seen anyone with two different eye colors. Fiona laughed when she noticed Mina's perplexed look.

"I'm used to people staring at my eyes. For some inexplicable reason, I was born with one blue eye and one brown eye, making me a freak of nature, I suppose. Quite unusual, Si, yes?" as she made a face while enlarging her eyes in exaggeration, wondering how much of what she was saying was being understood by this Italian girl.

"Well," she continued speaking more to herself than her new companion, "I will have you know, even though I doubt you are understanding me, once upon a time, these eyes helped me earn money. But that's another story for another time… probably, never," she finished with a smile so warm it that could melt a glacier.

Although a skein of laws had been recently passed to improve conditions in steerage, many steamship lines ignored them. The young girls learned this quickly. The berths were 2 tiered, six feet long and two feet wide with only two feet of space above each. No space was allocated for baggage so steerage passengers had to keep their belongings in and around their berths.

"Jesus, Mary and Joseph," exclaimed Fiona at seeing where they would be spending the weeks ahead. She began to look closely at the straw- filled mattresses hoping not to find vermin. Each berth had only one thin blanket per person and Fiona wondered how they would cope with the cold. There was minimal lighting and ventilation but she decided not to say anything about that since she could already see her new companion was not coping well. She guessed that this Italian girl, though poor in money since she was traveling in steerage, most probably had lived a life with sunny skies and open fields and never really knew hunger as did the Irish.

As the girls were choosing berths next to each other, they became aware of men standing in the doorways observing the women and making crude remarks. There should have been stewards to move them away and back to their own area, but none were present. A few older widowed women threatened that they would report their behavior but it seemed to make little difference as the men continued to lean against the doorway.

Alarmed, Mina gave Fiona a worried look and said, "Oddio, niete privacy!" voicing her words for "no privacy," which was easily translated by Fiona just by the look on her companion's face.

An older German spinster yelled 'lustmolchs' at the idling men in the doorway. Derogatory terms were aimed at the lingerers in a number of other languages, as well, by the other women trying to settle into the quarters.

But it was Fiona who took charge of the situation with "Don't you gentlemen have better things to do than to spy on us?" as she approached them with a shooing away gesture.

"Miss, this is the best entertainment we could hope for on this god forsaken boat," quipped the wise guy of the group, making no attempt to move on as he slouched against the wall.

"Then I can assure you that we will find a way to put an end to your entertainment". She turned away and back to Mina with a 'stop worrying' look.

Later on, Fiona organized the single women into an agreement that when it was time to dress and undress, they would take turns holding up blankets for each other's privacy. It solved the peeping Tom problem.

Undressing one night, Mina noticed Fiona's unusual necklace. Pointing to the amulet, Mina admired it with "So pretty."

Fiona bent her head to kiss it and offered it to Mina with "You may kiss it, too. It may bring you luck although it doesn't seem to work all the time for me."

Mina politely refused, thinking that seemed unholy. She knew she would kiss it if it held a relic of a saint but not some pagan Druid amulet.

The few lavatories were separated by sex and only held a minimal number of basins that could not accommodate the 800 steerage passengers effectively. Passengers were required to bring their own towels and soap. There were a few faucets offering cold salt water and only one faucet that provided warm water which most used to wash their soiled dinner utensils.

Many men continued to linger around the women's baths, as well as the doorways. As much as the women passengers complained to the staff, no noticeable action was ever taken. It reassured Mina of her decision to partner with Fiona for safety. As demure as Fiona appeared, she had a noticeable toughness when needed. Mina found comfort in Fiona's strength because she frequently questioned her own. It also became apparent that Brian Kelly appeared frequently to escort them, and the women in his family, through the hallways to the disappointment of many of the male harassers.

Each passenger was given one dinner pail for the duration of the trip. The girls learned quickly to guard these since theft was rampant and replacements next to impossible to obtain. Sometimes, they even carried them whenever they could find space to stand on the small steerage deck and away from the odors that were accumulating quickly below in the compartments.

Meal time was poorly coordinated with people shoving and pushing as soon as the bell rang announcing the meal. A single line would eventually form and the crew would ration out food from large pots into each passenger's dinner pail. Only very young children were eligible to receive milk which often ran out before the end of the voyage. The food was not of good quality and the servings were small. Apparently, this was done deliberately so that many passengers, who could afford it, would purchase food from the ship's private canteens.

Unlike the first and second levels, there were no dining areas in steerage. People ate sitting in their berths or balancing their pails on shelves that had been built along the wall of the passageway corridor. Arguments were constant with space being at a premium.

Mina had secured a space on one of the shelves than ran along the wall and was used as a table by those quick enough to grab a few inches on which to place the dinner pails. A German woman moved Mina's pail where it would have spilled on the floor had it not been for a large gentleman who was seated alongside of them with his family. He not only caught the pail in his large hands but proceeded to stand over the German calling her rudeness out in front of everyone.

"Look, Lady, let me remind you that your country is losing the war and none of us are going to tolerate aggressive German behavior ever again anywhere and certainly not here on shipboard."

Speaking no English, she answered in German until another passenger, seeing the commotion, translated for her. "She is saying that she was only trying to make seating for her small son, that's all. She says there is no need to be nasty and no reason to argue." By then, the German woman's husband arrived and took their three children back to their berths to eat, with his wife following closely but looking back angrily at the tall man who had berated her.

"Why do they hate us, Kurt? I did not intentionally try to spill the girl's food. It was an accident," she explained to her spouse.

"Germany started a war that is ruining lives and killing hundreds of thousands of people, Elke, that's why. We must be low key and accept that we will be facing prejudice for being German. But once I am working and we all learn to speak English and our girls make school friends, it will get better for us. Until then, we must be patient, my Love," as he led his family back to their berths to finish their meals.

Mina was lost for words, still stunned by the unexpected scene that had just taken place. Fiona immediately filled in the awkward moment by attempting to introduce herself and Mina to the tall gentleman, but he paid her no attention since he was still engrossed watching the Germans walk away. Most of the other passengers in the area cheered his warning to the Germans while a group of German passengers could be seen comforting the woman and her three children, who had been thoroughly shaken by the argument. The German children could not understand why the Irish man was so angry with their mother since they had been unable to understand anything that had been said to her by him.

The man looked at his wife and remarked sarcastically "Well, no friendship formed there, I guess," still exchanging angry looks with the German woman as she was being led away by her husband.

"Well, I just hope you haven't started another war down here, too, Jack," his wife replied leading him back to where their two children were seated.

Smiling and grateful, Mina and Fiona introduced themselves again now that they had the man's attention. He politely introduced himself as Jack Turner from Cork, his wife Winnifred, and their young daughters, Kate and Sara.

Jack Turner was a red head with a handlebar moustache the same color. He stood over six and half feet tall, so he towered over all the other immigrant men on the ship. When asked about his height, he attributed his physical attributes to the Vikings.

"Some tell that the Viking raiders ended up liking the Cork Irish women so much that they settled there. Hundreds of years of fathering tall red heads resulted in the likes of me," he joked.

"Look at Brian, here's another one if you don't believe me!" Brian Kelly had joined their group after hearing the commotion.

"Brian isn't a carrot- top like you, Jack. With his dark auburn hair and blue eyes, he is quite a catch for some lass," attested Winnifred, winking at Fiona.

Brian blushed at Winnifred's compliment but turned the conversation back to the encounter with the German woman by telling Jack Turner how he agreed with everything Jack had said.

"You did the right thing to speak up, Jack. It's always the same with the Krauts, thinking they are superior to everyone else."

"I know that my Black Irish wife agrees. She lost a brother in the war they started."

Winnifred was what some called 'Black Irish' because of her jet-black hair and olive skin. Some believed that when the Spanish Armada sunk near the Irish coast, the sailors who survived remained in Ireland mixing their genes with native women, but there are more who disagree with that explanation than accept it. Because she was small boned, she looked fragile next to her strong husband but she still had a stubbornness that matched or exceeded his.

"Many seem to be leaving their country now that the tide of the war has turned, thanks be to America," said Winnifred.

"Everyone is a victim of war in one way or another," Fiona added pensively with her eyes lowered and looking away from her companions.

Following the meal, they sat together sharing stories of their pasts and plans for the future. Being Irish, Fiona hit it off right away with the Turners and the Kelly family. The Turners and the Kellies were neighbor tenant farmers in southern Cork. Many a night the fathers would talk of emigration, tired of working for landlords with little to show for their labors. Both families benefited from having relatives already settled in America.

Jack's bachelor brother, Timothy, invited them to change their lives, as he had himself a few years earlier when he landed in New Jersey. Surprising them, he had done well in the construction business where his earnings enabled him to cover the passage expense for Jack's family. He told both Jack and Sean Kelly, Brian's father, that there was construction work for them, even work for Brian. **But I encourage sending the younger children to school instead of working right away. The way ahead for them in America is with an education. Come to America, I'm lonely for family and old friends,** Tim wrote. **Leave Ireland's political troubles behind and start anew in New Jersey in peace.**

The Turners sold their few animals and their meager furniture, consoled their daughters that their pet goat would be fine with their neighbor and said their farewells, never looking back. Similarly, the Kellies did the same.

In his letters, Tim promised a place for Jack's family in his rented home. Knowing that there was a home waiting for them upon arrival gave Winnifred the security she needed before she would agree to the life-changing decision. They were filled with excitement in contrast with many others on the ship who could not hide their anxiety about what was ahead for them in the new land.

"It is a grand thing that your brother has an actual house with so many rooms and a *basement* and an *attic* and a *yard and a front porch with a swing. C*an you imagine how grand the house must be?" Winnie was thrilled that such luxury awaited them as she accentuated each individual section of the house as Tim described in his letter.

"Whenever I feel blue, I picture myself sitting on the porch with a cup of tea and my troubles leave me." Winnie reveled in the thought of all the space the house offered after spending her life in a two-room cottage with a leaky thatched roof.

Tim wrote that he deliberately rented a house large enough for everyone and one that would accommodate the large family he hopes to have some day himself.

"Tim is making it easy for us until we find our own place, and we will have our own place once I begin working, I promise you, my girls," Jack swore to his three females as they hung on to his every word.

"Jack, it is so exciting to think about. Tim is an angel, is he not?" beamed Winnie.

"If Tim is an angel then he is a hardworking, hard drinking, foul mouthed one. I should know having grown up with my older brother."

"Say what you want, he is guiding us and paving our way into a new and better life. For that I am so grateful."

"True enough. But I will find us our own home with a yard for your garden and a front porch with your own swing. Just trust me."

Jack knew that Tim's offer of a home awaiting them allayed much of Winnie's nervousness and without it she may have never agreed to leave the homeland. The fear of the unknown had always been a constant in her life which Jack recognized. Her insecurity was caused by being raised in abject poverty with a drunkard father. Married to Jack lessened her fears of the unknown to some degree but not to the level that Jack had hoped after all their years of marriage. Uprooting the family took a great deal of courage for her to make such a leap. But he was proud knowing it was because of her trust in him.

Unabashedly and in front of everyone, Jack went on to say to Winnie, "We are both in our twenties, so we have many years ahead of us to make a new life and to see to a proper education for the girls ……and for their brothers and sisters who come along in the coming years." He winked at Winnifred

43

who immediately started to blush while Mina and Fiona began to tease Winnie about how Jack knew how to turn her face red so easily.

"After all, we are obligated to procreate as good Catholics, aren't we, Winnie?" he continued to ask to his wife's embarrassment. She gave him a playful shove but no one could doubt the affection they had for each other.

The first few days into the voyage were extremely stressful. The winter storms over the Atlantic were relentless. Everything in steerage moved from side-to-side with unsecured luggage dangerously falling and skidding across the floor. Fiona fell to her knees when the swaying of the ship was too much for her. She broke out in a sweat and became nauseous. Mina immediately diagnosed her with sea sickness and told her that there were numerous passengers already sick.

Steerage became even more unbearable than it had been from the start. The constant vomiting left the air unbreathable and the floors wet and sticky. Pots were overrun and required emptying all the time. Bed coverings and clothes had to be hand-washed with salt water, exhausting those who were caretakers of the sick.

Mina was tiring of being Fiona's nurse. *I am sorry that she did not have my benefit of coming from a fishing family but she is going to have to start cleaning up after herself from now on.* Mina resolved that being Fiona's nursemaid had to end after discovering Fiona's vomit under her fingernails and in her hair. But within minutes when her friend had another vomiting episode, Mina changed her mind. *How can I abandon my new friend when she is in such a state?* and held the pail while Fiona bent over it.

As Fiona retched, she kept apologizing "Mina, I am so sorry to be such a burden. I had no idea about seasickness! Without you, I could never get through this ordeal. You are more like a sister than a friend." Then Fiona leaned over the pail again and again.

Mina held the pail with her left hand while the right one gathered Fiona's loose hair to keep it away from the emesis. *How can she be so pretty even when she's so sick,* Mina questioned, maybe even with a bit of jealousy.

Brian stood in the doorway and offered to help.

"Don't let him see me like this," Fiona ordered.

Ignoring Fiona, Mina said "Si, thank you, Brian. Could I ask you to empty the pot so I can stay with Fiona?"

44

"Sure, I've been emptying my family's pots so I'm getting very efficient at it."

"You look well, Brian, thank goodness."

"You do, too, Mina. We are the lucky ones, aren't we now? I bet you have been on boats before just as I have, right?"

"Si, I am a fisherman's daughter. But not so Fiona, poor girl." Mina walked over and handed him the pail.

"Fiona, I hope you feel better soon," he called out to her from the distance of the doorway.

"Oh God, why does he have to be so nice all the time?" Fiona groaned.

"I think he likes you, Fiona. I see many of the girls trying to get his attention."

"If you had any idea of my life, you would know that involving myself romantically at this time is out of the question. But you are right. Brian is thoughtful and kind and will make someone a wonderful husband someday, no doubt. I wish it could be me, but it cannot."

As the retching seemed to decrease, Fiona laid down with her head in Mina's lap. *Perhaps, when she is feeling better we can learn more about each other. Then she will be less a mystery to me.*

The Turner family fared better than most of the other families with only Jack being the one with any sea sickness symptoms. Winnifred and the children were surprised themselves that they had weathered the illness that was so prevalent among the passengers. What upset Winnie the most, besides the deplorable conditions, was that the ship's staff ignored them. Everyone complained but steerage passengers were told that staff was far too busy with the ill passengers in first and second classes.

Jack recovered relatively quickly because his 'nurses', as he called Winnie and his daughters, waited on him hand and foot. However, his appetite was diminished for days following his recovery.

"No loss considering the food served here," he joked. "But you girls collect my share and eat it. Don't let a morsel go to waste no matter how bad the taste. We don't want Uncle Tim to be picking up four skeletons, do we now?"

Survival in steerage was dependent on the support and kindness of family and fellow passengers. For those most vulnerable, the infants and the elderly, there were cases of fatal dehydration that resulted in death. The saddest burials were always of the children who died during the voyage. The wailing of the parents broke even the hardest of hearts.

One day, the young German Werner girls and Mina found themselves emptying their pails of vomit at the same time. The sisters wisely went everywhere together for safety, which Mina thought was very sensible. Although they only spoke German and Mina did not, Mina made a funny face to reflect how disgusting their work was in emptying the vomit pots.

The older girl smiled in return saying," Ich habe die Nase voll davon," which Mina later learned meant "I'm sick of it, too". The girls were pretty but pale. They looked much younger than the ages they shared with Mina when they used their fingers to answer Mina's question on how old they were.

Malnourished in Germany, of course, poor darlings, as Mina gratefully thought of her father's fish and her mother's garden back home growing up, war or no war. *Probably, this German family had been city people*, Mina surmised.

Regardless whether the passenger belonged to first class or steerage, burial at sea was finally the equalizer. Corpses of the deceased had to be dropped overboard. Each body was wrapped in a canvas cover and lifted overboard following a brief prayer service by a chaplain. It was the Lutheran minister who could be seen most often consoling families who had lost loved ones, long after the other clergymen had left steerage. Mina observed him to be a comfort to anyone in need and not limited to just those who shared his religion.

Even after the sea sickness diminished, some passengers continued to appear ill. Many had chronic coughs and, from the conditions in the lavatories, there were signs of dysentery. Washing the floors, more often than less, became the voluntary burden of the passengers since the staff neglected their cleaning duties and appeared not to be held accountable for their neglect. Steerage did not provide a healthy environment which added to the passengers' anxiety about the health examination awaiting each passenger at Ellis Island. Those who did not pass would be separated from their loved ones and either placed indefinitely in the island's infirmary or sent back home with no entrance into America permitted.

"God, Mina, do you hear the German woman saying 'geh rein 'and 'steht noch' to her ailing son all day? I think she is ordering him to practice being quiet and to stand still as if that will fool the health inspectors if his cough continues when we dock. I'm amazed that the frail little boy made it through the sea sickness."

"I truly feel sorry for these families and grateful we have only ourselves to worry about," said Mina in broken English but enough for Fiona to understand.

"So true. I can't imagine the stress involved with having sick children and worse, burying one at sea."

All the Italians and Sicilians were Catholic but the Irish had a deep divide between Catholic and Protestant, Mina observed. Every Sunday morning, a Roman Catholic priest and an Anglican Protestant priest would come to the steerage level to provide Sunday services in different corners. The few Russian Orthodox Catholics attended the Roman Catholic service and later in the morning, the Lutheran minister would arrive for the few Scandinavian and German Protestants.

This odd experience was not lost on Mina who attended the Roman Catholic mass on one side of the room while noting that Fiona attended none of the religious services.

Kate Turner, being an observant child, asked her mother why some of the Russian passengers made the sign of the cross 'backwards', as she described it.

"What I know is that the Russian Church differs from our Roman Church. They have a different pope from ours and their priests dress differently and they cross themselves from right to left instead of our way of left to right. But both our churches have the same beliefs. So, you see they are not doing anything backwards, just doing the ritual the way they have been taught."

"Do you understand the differences better now?" asked Winnie, proud of her youngster's observation skill and the type of thoughtful questions she asked.

When the services were completed, the clerics made their way up the stairs out of steerage looking relieved to be doing so. It was understandable since the steerage stench was intolerable most days. However, it was very noticeable that the Lutheran minister did not rush away after his service was completed as the other clergymen did. He remained below in steerage and spent time with his small congregation, learning their names and backgrounds.

Mina was pleased to have noticed that he befriended the Werner family who always seemed so isolated, especially after the episode with Jack Turner. She later learned that Reverend Mayerhoffer was said to divide his time between being a shipboard chaplain and being the founder of an orphanage for immigrant children whose parents die during the ocean crossings. His reputation was that of a kind and caring man.

Using her English words and pointing at the clergymen as they were leaving, Mina questioned Fiona, "Which religion are you?"

"None. Gone, flew away years ago." Fiona used her hand imitating a bird flying off into the sky.

"Mi dispiace, I mean, I am so sorry, Fiona," as Mina switched to English. Although she knew she was not the most religious person herself, unlike Fiona, she still held on to her faith and wondered what happened to make Fiona lose hers so she asked her.

"When you pray but terrible things still happen to you, it's easy to lose your faith. Simply put, that's my story, Mina."

"I am so sorry that terrible things happened to you but you cannot blame God."

"Mina, that is easier said than done but let's talk about something else, please," so the conversation ended and was never brought up again.

Later in the afternoon, after the Turners spoke of their past and future, it was Mina's turn. She described Sciacca and her carefree life growing up in her bucolic village. She suddenly became quite homesick again for Sicily.

Her voice quivered as she described, "I am blessed with the most loving parents who have always doted on me being their only daughter and their youngest. Although times have been hard, we live in a beautiful village with the sea on one side and the mountains on the other. And unlike this freezing weather, there is almost constant sunshine in Sciacca." When she spoke of her arranged marriage she could not help notice concern on all their faces.

Winnie could not help but question such an arrangement. "So, you have never met your future husband, Mina? Forgive my nosiness but aren't you afraid you may be disappointed?"

"Jack and I grew up together and have known each other our whole lives. You can understand how unusual your upcoming wedding is to someone like us."

"It is a Sicilian custom and one found in other countries, too, to trust your parents in such matters. Our families have spoken and we have pictures of each other and our parish priest's recommendation. I will surely have time to learn more about Carlo during the pre-wedding weeks while I live with my brother and his wife, so I am quite sure that everything will be fine."

"Tell us more about Sicily, Mina. Did you know that we all come from islands? Ireland and Sicily are both islands." Eight-year-old Kate Turner was proud of her knowledge of geography.

Deciding to capture the children's immediate attention, Mina told them about Eugenia, their village witch. Everyone giggled except the children who listened with wide eyes.

Six-year-old Sara questioned Mina, "Is she an evil witch or a good witch?"

To prevent nightmares, Mina responded, "A good witch, who tries to help people," although she knew Eugenia enjoyed scaring people with her visions more than anything else.

Not letting the subject change, Sara continued with "How does she help people?"

"Well, she sees a little into the future and warns people about what to do or not do."

"Did she see into your future, Mina?"

Pondering it for the first time, Mina replied more seriously than before. "I don't think she did because no one ever told me." But the thought lingered for a while with Mina even as the others went on telling their stories.

When Fiona's turn came she related that she was orphaned young and had lived with a spinster aunt in Dublin who saved up to generously pay Fiona's passage. She denied having any siblings.

"Having no brothers or sisters would be lonely. Were you lonely, Fiona?" Both Turner girls moved closer to Fiona with genuine sympathy, even putting their arms around her.

"Yes, I was, but now I am grown-up and have you two as my little sisters." She said that as she began to tickle the girls who squirmed all around enjoying themselves. Fiona quickly turned the subject away from herself by asking Winnifred a number of questions about their village in Cork. It was apparent to Mina that Fiona did not want to add any details about her life beyond what she had already said. It was not the first time that her stories were noticeably vague and seemed incomplete.

Respectfully, neither the Turners nor Mina questioned Fiona further, but one could see that Brian wanted to learn more about her. Perhaps, being Irish, they all had a better understanding of her reasons for discretion and her need for privacy.

Mina, attributed her secrecy to the possibility that she had something to hide. *Whatever it may be, I'm going to ask her to tell me about the many missing parts in her story when we are alone tonight.* But then Mina changed her mind. *It's really none of my business.*

As the Turners realized Mina's English was limited, they turned the otherwise tedious hours into English lessons for her. They made her use English words when they played card games and when they would look at the American maps Jack had bought.

"The maps are very important or we won't know where the hell we are going when the ship docks." Jack insisted everyone look and learn as he laid the American North East maps out for all to view.

"Jack, watch your language in front of the children," Winifred admonished with a smile, but eagerly she was the first to ask, "please show us New Jersey first."

"It makes better sense to start from our landing if everyone agrees?" They all nodded letting Jack take the lead, as usual.

Jack began with Manhattan Island and Ellis Island where they would view the Statue of Liberty as the ship would enter the harbor. Then pointing with his finger, he moved it in the directions they would be taking after passing through the admission process and, afterwards, to the ferries and then the trains to New Jersey and Boston.

Mina questioned the distance between New York and Boston which appeared so small on the map until Jack explained how to accurately measure distances in mileage using inches. "Oh, that will mean a very long train ride, yes?" as Mina realized after performing her calculation.

"But a lovely one, I'm sure," encouraged Winifred. "Think of all the American scenery you will see from the train window, Mina."

Fiona seemed to direct everyone's attention to a passenger who started playing a fiddle with a few children beginning to dance a jig to the music. She didn't express any interest in viewing the map which left Mina perplexed.

"Fiona, you need to let Jack show you Brooklyn while he still has the map laid out," Mina insisted. "Aren't you interested in seeing where you will be going?"

"Of course, I am. Please show me Brooklyn, Jack." Moving Fiona's pointer finger around New York and its boroughs of Manhattan, Queens, Bronx and Westchester, Jack ended the trail with her finger finally landing on Brooklyn.

"Do you know which section of Brooklyn you will be living? If you do, then maybe we can narrow it down some more," said Jack, enjoying his role as navigator.

"I don't remember exactly, Jack, but my family can tell us when we all meet at the end of the trip."

"As we can see, Manhattan, Brooklyn and New Jersey are very close to each other. In fact, amazingly, New Jersey is just a very short distance across the river from Ellis Island," Jack said still mesmerized by the map's information. "Look at that, just a small amount of water between the two land masses."

"So, we have no excuses for not visiting once we are all settled in our new homes," said Winnifred.

"Sadly, not so easily from Boston," lamented Mina.

Winifred truly cared for Fiona and Mina. The thought of their friendships potentially ending saddened her. "We will all write and plan visits, even from Boston, Mina. We must pledge to never lose our special relationships."

"Of course, we will find a way to visit," Fiona responded as she continued looking at the map with Jack. But to Mina, it appeared that Fiona was feigning interest in the map rather than expressing a true interest in her destination. It remained a mystery to Mina, one she hoped would be solved before the ship docked.

Then Brian came over and asked Jack, "May I intrude? I'd love a look at that map if you wouldn't mind?" But Fiona guessed that it may have been an excuse to be near her. She hoped so yet knew it would be best not to encourage him.

"Sure, Brian. Here's Chatham, right here," as Jack's large finger pointed to the city in New Jersey where the Kellies and Turners were heading.

Brian looked at Fiona and Mina proudly explaining, "My father and I will be working construction with Tim and Jack but I am going to try real hard to become a fireman. In fact, Tim wrote us that construction just started on the new municipal building that will house the mayor's office, the library, the jail and the new fire department. Right now, the Hook and Ladder and

Hose Company is working from a barn so the city is modernizing every day and we will be part of it."

"You will make a wonderful fireman, Brian," Mina replied. Fiona just smiled. She could truly picture Brian dressed in a fireman's uniform rescuing children and kittens from fires.

The five members of the Werner family kept to themselves as best as they could in the crowded compartments, especially after the confrontation with Jack Turner. Because of the war they were only too aware of the backlash against anyone who was German.

"I miss my friends in Munich," voiced the oldest daughter, Gerda.

"Gerda, you know very well that Munich is no longer the same with the war. Even your friends have probably relocated to safer locations by now."

"What will happen to our grandparents?" asked Elke, the second daughter. Both parents looked at each other to see who would answer.

"We have already told you that the grandparents refused to leave. We asked them to come with us but they are old and want to stay German, not become American like us," Kurt repeated the explanation once again to his worried children. He and his wife, Elke, had the same worry but kept it to themselves.

Before the war they enjoyed a comfortable middle- class life in picturesque Munich, the beautiful city known for Octoberfest and Mendelssohn's music. But the war ruined German lives that had been built up through years of education and hard work, leaving the people impacted physically and psychologically devastated.

Unemployment was rampant. Homes went unheated as the coal supplies were used for transporting troops. People were starving. Farmers had been drafted and their fields destroyed in the fighting. When the Werner's watched their church bell lowered to be melted down for munitions, they knew it was time to leave. Fortunately, because of Kurt's civil service position, he was able to obtain the necessary papers for emigration with the choice between Canada or America but chose America for his family. Regardless of their urgings to their parents to leave with them, they were refused. Leaving them was the most difficult decision they had to make. The other serious worry concerned the health of their youngest child.

"Kurt, I am so worried for Ernst. It was a miracle that he passed the pre-boarding exam, but if his coughing worsens, will he pass the entry physical on Ellis Island?" Elke Werner whispered to her husband so the children would not hear. Their youngest son, at four years old, had suffered more than his sisters during the 'turnip winter' when the German populace had only turnips to eat because food supplies had been redirected to the troops on the front lines.

"Our poor baby Ernst has paid the price of having no potatoes or meat," his mother lamented, as she looked at her sleeping malnourished boy whose head was on his sister Gerda's shoulder. The three children slept together for warmth.

"And Gerda and Erika are too thin and too short for their ages, too. I pray we will see their health improve with nourishing American food, God willing."

"Elke, 'langsam, langsam', little by little, we will manage each step placed before us and get us all through the immigration process. We just have to keep Ernst as warm as possible and see if the ship's doctor has something for his congestion. As young as he is, we have to make him understand the importance of not showing the officials that he is weak. We must give him extra food from our share of the ship rations to build him up. The girls are stronger and will understand."

"You don't speak of it but we are entering an America that is very anti-German. Everyone says that there is discrimination to the point that some German Americans are changing their surnames. Even some businesses are changing the company names to sound less Germanic. The German language is no longer being taught in the schools and the German language newspapers have been forced to close. If all of these rumors are true, then how will we be treated upon arrival when we speak so little English? Would Canada have been a better choice for us? Look how we are already being treated here on the ship." Elke looked to her husband to calm her fears.

"Elke, there is discrimination in Canada, too. I believe if all that I have heard is true, then America will have more opportunities for our family. We will live in the city at first and learn more about the other states where Germans have been moving, states with names like Wisconsin and Minnesota. We will have choices, I promise you."

Elke continued, "You saw what happened and how I was treated when I accidentally knocked over the Italian girl's food! I was only trying to make room for our children to sit. If only I could speak English, then I could have explained that it was not intentional but an accident. We are at a great loss not being able to speak to Americans."

"Be strong, Elke. I believe the worst is over for us and you should believe that, too," as he took her hand in his and squeezed.

She wished with all her heart that she could have the same confidence as Kurt.

During the final week of the journey, there was a strong awareness of hunger among the passengers. Rumor was that the ship was running low on food because the of the unexpected storms that had added five extra days to the usual three-week Atlantic crossing. In order not to deprive upper class passengers, food had to be rationed in steerage.

"Can you believe that they stopped milk for the children?" an irate woman shouted to her fellow passengers when a steward denied her request.

"Why?" many asked in unison.

"Because they have only enough left for first class passengers! That's what I was told."

The stewards were mobbed for an explanation as to how this could happen, but it was useless. For the remainder of the voyage, there would be no milk.

Up to that point, Mina had been hiding the dried food packed deep in her bags. Basilio had warned that it would be needed, especially in the last days of the voyage. Although she was determined to follow her family's instruction to never share, she had a change of mind when she saw Fiona dramatically losing weight. *There will be nothing left of her, especially after losing weight from her sea sickness.*

The final straw was the sight of the two Turner children. Guilt and shame made her change her mind about hoarding the food for herself. She decided to share what food she had left with her friends.

"Fiona, I am ashamed. I have kept food for myself that my family had hidden in my valise and not shared with you. Seeing how weak you have become, please share with me what I still have left."

She then took Fiona aside and privately showed her the dried fruit, nuts and crackers still remaining edible. She sorted some for Fiona and told her that the rest would be given to the Turners. Fiona graciously told Mina that she understood and that she would have probably done the same if their circumstances had been reversed.

Fiona repeatedly told Mina that she was in her debt, not only for getting her through her week of sea sickness but for sharing the much-needed nourishment. "I don't know how or when but someday I will pay you back, I promise," said Fiona gratefully as they ate sitting on Mina's bunk.

When Mina slipped Jack and Winifred Turner some dried fruit and crackers for their children, Winifred, a quiet and reserved young woman, unexpectedly kissed Mina's hand in gratitude.

"Stop, Winifred. This is the least I can do for good friends."

"Thank you, Mina. My family is my life so I am very grateful for your charity". She reached again to kiss Mina's hand but instead Mina pulled her into a hug. As they ended their embrace and faced each other, Mina could not help notice that Winifred appeared to have an infection in both eyes.

"Winnifred, your eyes?" questioned Mina alarmed at how sore they appeared.

"Not to worry. Jack and I have been using salt water on them. Salt water can cure anything so we are sure they will clear up before departing the ship. They have to," Winnifred stated determinedly.

Mina truly hoped she was right. There were many depressing stories of passengers denied entry, separated from families and not allowed entry because of medical issues. She could not even imagine such a tragedy as that to happen to the Turner family. Her hope was that whatever Winnie suffered with, it could be treated quickly in the infirmary.

"Dear God, please spare this wonderful family," she prayed under her breath.

While she prayed for the Turners, she saw Frau Werner hugging her small son who was having difficulty breathing. His continuous coughing reminded Mina of the childhood diseases in Sciacca called 'le grippe' and whooping cough. *Uffa*, she thought, *what will happen to them when they arrive at Ellis Island?*

Jack Turner was making them all laugh about something his brother Tim had promised when they disembarked.

"Tim said that he would fill all our empty stomachs with those Coney Island hot dogs everyone talks about, and that goes for you two, as well," as he included Mina and Fiona. "And, Uncle Tim wrote that he will be buying us tickets to the new thrill ride called a 'roller coaster' in a place called Coney Island that will scare the hell out of us when it goes up and down hills at speed that will knock your socks off!"

"Jack, again your language!" Winifred reminded him. "Stop saying hell," which only made the children laugh more upon hearing their mother repeat the word. The thought of a hot dog cheered the hungry children, as well as the adults. Obtaining vendor food on the wharf at the end of the journey was everyone's hope.

Like Fiona, Jack promised to someday repay Mina for her kindness in sharing her food. Although she insisted no repayment was necessary, Jack said, "I have your brother's address, Mina, so you can expect repayment one of these days."

"Just use our addresses to stay in touch, that's all," said Mina. But then she remembered that she needed to remind Fiona again to write down her address in Brooklyn.

To get through the tedious hours of boredom on the ship, the future was a favorite topic of Mina's. She, more so than Fiona, reveled in detailing her future and upcoming marriage. She had provided Fiona with her brother's address in Boston and spoke of Basilio and Carmela and less about Carlo since she had yet to meet him. Fiona spoke once of family living in Brooklyn who would be taking her in but never added any specifics.

"I still cannot believe you will be marrying someone you don't know," said Fiona while they sat on their bunks.

"But it is our way, Fiona. Our families do the planning and rarely is there an unsuccessful marriage."

"But what about love?" Fiona asked. "I've had little love in my own life so far but, I know if I ever do marry, I will have to be head over heels in love with the man."

"Love comes in time although it must be earned. I am sure Carlo will earn it by being a caring and gentle husband," Mina explained in her much-improved English.

As close to the same age as we are, Fiona could not help think, *what a trusting child Mina still is. She has led a blessed life so far, surrounded by a loving family and she probably has never experienced hunger or danger a day in her life. She will now move from her father to her brother for care and protection. I only wonder if that has weakened her instead of prepared her for what may lie ahead?*

The girls originally communicated with hand signals and pointing, as well as individual vocabulary words, at the beginning of the voyage. Mina would frequently repeat the words she was learning. Noticeably as the voyage was coming close to an end, Mina's English greatly improved which she attributed to her friend, Fiona, but also to the Turner family who made a game of teaching Mina. The children would point to things for Fiona to identify and laugh their heads off when she would make a mistake.

Sara, the eight- year old, pointed to a valise. "What is that called, Mina?"

Mina could see the Italian word in her mind but would just blurt out anything when she couldn't recall the English noun. She knew the girls would be amused at her expense and it was fun for her, too.

"A box?"

"No, Silly! A valise!"

"My turn," as the younger daughter, Kate, pointed to her eyelashes. "What are these called, Mina?"

As the children corrected Mina again, Winnifred broke in saying, "Mina's doing brilliantly but it takes time to learn a new language. Can you imagine if we had to learn Italian?"

Mina was truly grateful for all the tutoring she was receiving which led to her question. "With all of you as my teachers, will my Boston brother be surprised when he hears me speak English with an Irish brogue?"

"Don't worry. From what we hear, everyone in Boston already speaks funny," Fiona replied with a shrug and a wink.

Fiona was furious one afternoon. As she was walking in the corridor, one of the group of harassers placed his hand on her buttocks as she passed. This group of men were becoming more brazen as the journey was coming closer to an end. When Fiona confronted him, he apologized with an insincere smile while his friends laughed. They all radiated an unwelcomed boozy cheer.

"Miss, it could not be helped with the corridors being as narrow as they are."

"You are full of shit and whiskey so keep your dirty hands to yourself or you will be sorry. We will not tolerate having to walk though gauntlets each time we go anywhere because of you bog Irish." She kept her voice down because she didn't want the other passengers to hear her using foul language.

"Miss, with a mouth like that, I cannot help but think we have met somewhere. If I keep straining my memory, it will come to me."

Another Dubliner in his group joked, "Kevin, the only women you know are tarts." At that, the others joined in the laughter at Kevin's expense, poking him good naturedly as drunks do with each other.

"No, it will come to me. I know her from somewhere," he repeated to his friends. Then looking at Fiona again, he asked, "Help me out, do I look familiar to you as you do to me?" Fiona was stunned by his possible recognition of her but could not afford to show any emotion.

"Absolutely not. And I'm not surprised by what your friend just said about you knowing only tarts," she responded in an airy way as if she was levels above these men.

"She's a feisty one, she is," was said loudly behind Fiona's back as she walked away quickly returning to the women's quarters.

"Fiona, what surprises me is that you did not slap his face," said Mina, who had witnessed the harassment. Placing her hand on Fiona's wrist she added, "Come, we will report his behavior."

Reporting this was the last thing Fiona wanted to do. Instead, she needed time to think the threat through. If the man does finally recognize her, he would ruin her new identity. Even worse, she would be sent back to Ireland since prostitutes were ineligible for entrance into America. Her forged papers would be uncovered.

"It would be useless to report, Mina, because we are nothing to the people in charge. But don't worry, I will get even when the time is right," she responded in a cold controlled voice. After saying this, she turned away from Mina. She could feel the internal rage that sometimes erupted within her when she perceived an injustice and she did not wish for Mina to notice this. *We are defined by our family*, Fiona knew and accepted the realization.

A few nights later, there were screams from the pretty Polish girl a few berths away from theirs. A man had tried to attack her in her sleep but her screams scared him off. "He pushed the blanket into my mouth and lifted up my night gown," she explained via another woman who translated for her.

"If I had not been able to pull the blanket from my mouth, I would not have been able to scream and he would have succeeded in raping me." She was still shivering even with a number of blankets taken from their beds with which to cover her.

"You will be alright, Bertha, you are just in shock right now. Be strong." Fiona said trying to comfort the girl in her own pragmatic way.

"What would have happened to me if he had made me pregnant?" she cried, more with relief than fear at that point.

Just the verbalization of the possibility horrified everyone because they all knew that such a result would have ruined the innocent girl's life. And no one knew that better than Fiona.

Because she could not describe her attacker, nothing could be done by the ship's staff after she reported it. That did not stop the women. Since the girl was very young, only spoke Polish and was travelling without family, the women agreed to ensure her safety together as a group. Turns were taken to escort Bertha back and forth from the toilet since she had the unwanted attention of too many of the single men who lingered outside the women's areas.

No one thought that any man would actually enter into the women's sleeping quarters. With an awareness of this new danger and for the rest of the voyage, Mina and Fiona, like many of the younger women, wore their clothes to bed each night.

Not long after both episodes, Mina was stunned to see Fiona conversing with the man who was the leader of the harassers, even smiling at the man. When she noticed Mina glancing at them, she ended what seemed to be a friendly conversation with him and walked back to where Mina was standing.

"How could you speak with such a pig, Fiona?"

"Oh, it was just about the weather, Mina. No sense in having enemies while we are down here locked in together."

"He's the one who tries to get your attention by saying that you have met somewhere, right?"

Measuring her words, Fiona answered carefully, "Believe me, we have never met."

Mina looked at Fiona, who deliberately, it seemed, did not return her glance but kept her gaze fixed on the floor. Fiona's silence was new to her. "I don't understand you, Fiona. You will never see me speaking with that detestable man about anything."

Mina never understood Fiona's quick reversal from revenge to forgiveness. But then Fiona continued to be a mystery in many ways. In the days that followed, no mention of it was ever made again. *The way I tend to change my mind, I suppose I am the last person to criticize others for doing so,* Mina admitted to herself.

In the middle of the night, Fiona waited until she could hear Mina's light snores. She put on her shoes and headed to the deck which was empty being well after midnight. She was alone so she leaned over the railing taking in deep breaths of the salty sea air. Suddenly, a man came up from behind her, clamped his hands over her breasts and roughly began kissing her neck. Fiona smiled at him. Then abruptly, she leveraged her weight and using a maneuver she had learned in her previous life, she pushed the surprised man overboard. It happened so suddenly there was no time for him to issue a scream loud enough to be heard.

She hurried back to her bed as silently as she had left it. Unknown to her, Mina had seen her leave earlier but had rolled over back to sleep, confident that Fiona was probably just having a sleepless night…. all too common in steerage.

The next day, the man known as Kevin was reported missing and all the crew and passengers were questioned. With no information and with his history of repeated drunkenness, he was listed as lost at sea. Mina never asked Fiona about it but she had a suspicion that seemed to linger since she had seen Fiona speaking with the same man the day before. *I should ask Fiona when we are alone,* she decided. But in the next minute, she changed her mind once again. *How can I think that Fiona could have been involved in his disappearance? Shame on me,* Mina reprimanded herself, wiping away any suspicion she may have had.

October, 1916

Dublin

Kieran Burke and his wife, Anna, hid the smuggled guns under the parlor floor. As staunch patriots dedicated to the riots to free Ireland from the British rule of tyranny, they risked everything for their beliefs. As soldiers of the IRA, their role was to hide the guns delivered to them and then to transport the same guns to the locations secretly passed on to them through messages written on notes placed in milk cans. The identities of the Irish republican soldiers were kept as secret from each other as possible to prevent identification under torture if captured.

Only the oldest child, Fiona, their teenage daughter, knew of her parents' dangerous politics. She was proud of them although always frightened of the horrendous reprisals the British would inflict if they were ever found out. She worried not only for them but for herself and her two younger brothers.

"What will happen to us if you and Mum are found out," was his daughter's serious question to her father. Kieran took her in his arms and assured her that if anything bad happened, she and her brothers would have a safe home with their mother's sister.

"Your Aunt Irene wants nothing to do with the political troubles so she is not worth anything to the Brits. You would always be safe there. Sometimes, I think we should send you to her now but, selfishly, I would miss you children around me. I hope you can understand," he told her and she could hear the angst in his voice.

Every day, the cost to free Ireland resulted in stories of ghastly deaths on both sides. From what she learned, a quick death was preferable to an imprisonment in an English prison where the patriots were starved and tortured. Disregarding their demands to be considered political prisoners, Britain labeled them criminals and subjected them to the harshest treatment. Reports indicated that even under torture, there were no traitors among the brave men and women who died miserably without ever forfeiting the names of fellow IRA members. Poems and songs were already being written about them.

"Come to supper," called their mother as the evening Angelus rang from the corner church bell. "But, first wash those dirty hands before coming to table," were the last words spoken to her sons by Anna Burke.

The front door crashed in and the small front room filled quickly with British soldiers.

"Arms up," screamed one while another shot Anna in the head even before she had time to comply. The boys went to the floor cradling their mother but were pulled away and led out into the street. Neighbors gathered outside and could be heard cursing the British soldiers while the soldiers pushed them back trying to control the hostile crowd jeering curses at them.

Hearing the shots from the yard while gathering coal for the stove, Kieran Burke ran to the chaos in the house from the back door only to be brought down by two soldiers while a third held a rifle at him. He slowly raised his arms once they allowed him to stand.

His heart seemed to stop in his chest when he saw his wife's body lying near the table with a visible bullet hole in her forehead. *No time to grieve for Anna now, find the children*, his immediate thought.

"My children, what have you done to the children," he yelled enraged with worry.

The commanding officer looked him up and down with distain. "Your traitor children will be dealt with, you can be sure of that. In fact, I believe my men have started with your daughter."

Kieran knew that all hope was gone for any escape. His immediate concern was for the boys and his daughter. What misery will they be subjected to since the British held no constraints on torture regardless of age for the Irish.

Although he promised himself to be stoic in front of the enemy, the sight of Anna lying on the floor with an apron still in her hand brought on the tears he had hoped to hold back. But at the same time, he felt relief that the British could no longer hurt Anna. They both knew the odds involved in being Irish freedom fighters. The concern now was for the children.

"Where are my children?" he asked over and over before the officer hit him with the butt of his pistol and then had him ordered back to the yard to be beaten for information. Meanwhile, as the crowd objected, the soldiers tied the boys' hands and feet before placing them in the army truck.

Kieran had not seen the three soldiers who had forced his daughter onto a bed in the back room and began to take turns gang raping the fifteen-year-old but he did hear her screams and it tore him apart with anguish and guilt.

"Your men are animals, she's just a child. Stop them if you have any compassion left in you," he begged the commanding officer standing before him and who knew exactly what was taking place in the house.

"You should have thought of what would happen to your family when you decided to become a traitor to the Crown. The real guilt is on you," the officer replied with the same condescendingly superior tone used for centuries by the British with their subjects around the globe.

"You decide what to do next. I leave him in your hands," was his next order to his soldiers surrounding the prisoner as he casually walked out of the yard and to the front of the house.

Burke yelled to his daughter, "Be strong, Fiona" and "Up the IRA" as he was forced to kneel in the dirt with soldiers holding him down.

Her father's screams took her mind away from the cruel rape she was undergoing. She called out to him with no answer other than hearing his continued screams. She was spared the sight of the soldiers who were pitch capping him by applying pitch and gunpowder to his head and setting it on fire.

Fiona never knew if her father died in their backyard that evening or if they allowed him to survive only long enough to be imprisoned and later hanged. For the rest of her life she would never know his fate.

When the soldiers finished with her, they crudely teased each other about their sexual prowess as they left her face down on the bed crying. An officer came to the doorway and harshly ordered her to dress. As she achingly moved to a standing position, she wiped the blood and semen from between her legs. Defiantly, she gathered her ripped clothes from the floor where they had been tossed.

She inspected the damage as she dressed. The buttons on her blouse had been torn off but her skirt was still in one piece. Her underpants were too torn to wear, so she threw those back to the floor. She found her torn stockings with her shoes kicked under the bed.

Fiona wanted to make her hero parents proud so she held her head high, wiped away any trace of tears and walked into the front room still crowded with soldiers and constabulary. Her mother's body had been removed but the blood stain where she fell was still visible.

She limped as she was escorted outside to the front of the house with all eyes on her.

Because of her abuse, she had trouble stepping up into the wagon, requiring someone from behind to lift her into the prison wagon to join her brothers. Most neighbors silently stood in groups watching her respectfully. Others shouted obscenities at the soldiers who were given an order to ignore them. Fiona knew that among the crowd there were IRA members and that there would be reprisals made to avenge her family.

She found her brothers crying huddled like the orphans they now were. "Fiona, the soldiers shot Mum," Thomas, the younger one, cried out reaching for his sister and innocently thinking she did not know.

The older one, James, looked at her ripped clothing, the blood on her legs and asked "What did they do to you, Fiona?"

"Never mind, I'm here with you now. Be brave and things will work out. After all, we are only children so what can they do to us, other than take us to Aunt Irene's?" With all her heart she hoped she was right.

The saying that bad things can happen to good people certainly could apply to this young girl sitting before me, thought the old priest as he recorded his notes on the case.

As he wrote, he would periodically glance up at the silent girl who seemed resigned to her fate.

Fiona Burke, fifteen, unmarried and three months pregnant, sat quietly with her hands folded in her lap, awaiting transport to the Dublin Magdalene Asylum for Fallen Women, also known as the Magdalene Laundry.

The priest wrote in his record, **according to the limited history provided by the authorities, Fiona's parents were Sinn Fein republican activists for Ireland's independence and traitors to the Crown. Both paid severely for their politics when they were killed resisting arrest for treason in the October 1916 raid in their home by British military.**

The young girl states that her pregnancy is a result of that same raid, although there is no evidence in the official record to substantiate her claim of rape. The two younger children have been domiciled in an aunt's home and will continue to be cared for by her. As per this aunt, the stigma of Fiona's pregnancy precludes the family caring for her any longer. Today, she is being admitted to the Magdalene Home.

Sadly, the child is being penalized for her rape and the guilty soldiers go unpunished, thought the priest, although he does not add that opinion to his written notes.

As she entered the grounds of the Magdalene Home, better known as the Magdalene Laundry, the first thing Fiona noticed was the ten-foot high cement wall surrounding the property with broken glass scattered over the tops. At the iron gate, she was handed over to a nun by the transporting constable. The nun signed a paper without a word while the constable tipped his hat. As he began to leave, he gave Fiona a sympathetic nod and informed her about the nuns' vow of silence. "They are mostly a quiet bunch here but they will take good care of you and your baby."

"Constable, is this a laundry or a prison?"

Bending his down to her level, he whispered, "A bit of both, Lass."

The nun gestured for silence by putting her finger to her lips and led the way to a huge empty dormitory. A cot was pointed out to Fiona as was a small closet with two uniforms and one pair of used ankle high boots. The room was sunless, only lighted by a few high windows that ran close to the ceiling. There was a familiar odor of bleach reminding her of her aunt's home where she lived after her parents were killed. It sadly brought back the memory of her aunt's rejection once Fiona's pregnancy began to show.

Following the raid, she and her two younger brothers had been taken in by her mother's sister, Irene. Fiona never spoke of the rape, not even to her aunt. She tried to remove it from her memory. Because her aunt never asked any questions, it was never spoken of. Although times were hard with the extra mouths to feed, life went on the first month until Fiona 's monthly period was missed. Once she started experiencing morning sickness, she feared what it meant. She had seen her mother vomiting in each of the early stages of her pregnancies with Fiona's younger brothers. She tried at first to hide it but, in such close living quarters as theirs, such secrets were impossible to keep.

It was in her third month when her aunt told her that she must leave because she was bringing shame on the house. Fiona tortured herself replaying their final conversation in her mind.

"Aunt Irene, please don't send me away. I'll care for my brothers and do whatever you need. I won't ever leave the house so neighbors won't see my pregnancy. Please, I'm so afraid to be sent out," she had begged clinging onto her aunt. "You know I'm a good girl and the soldiers did this to me against my will. Mum would turn over in her grave if she knew that you were abandoning me when I am in such a sorry state." Without any sign of compassion, her aunt remained adamant in her decision.

That is the harsh memory I will have to live with that has led me to this place, thought Fiona.

The nun interrupted Fiona's train of thought by gesturing to her to undress and put on one of the uniforms hanging in the locker. Fiona felt shy about having to undress while the nun stood by but the nun did turn her head to allow Fiona some privacy.

"Sister, this dress is too large," as she pulled the ties around her tiny waist as tightly as she could. Is there a smaller size?"

The nun ignored her question and pointed to the boots. Like the dress, they did not fit properly either but Fiona could tell that was no concern of the nun who appeared to have a set plan for her once she was dressed in the assigned clothing.

When the nun noticed Fiona's Celtic spiral amulet around her neck, she gestured for her to remove it. Fiona refused. It had been a birthday gift from her parents who laughingly told her of the pagan Celts belief that it would always bring an infinite flow of optimism and good energy to the wearer.

"That is our wish for you always," her parents had said to her with hugs and kisses on her fifteenth birthday. The happy days.

"No jewelry permitted," the nun said, this time reverting to spoken words in a barely audible whisper so no one could hear her breaking the rule of silence.

Fiona became tearful and refused to remove the necklace. "Sister, this is all I have left of my family, all I have left of my parents. They were brutally murdered by the British just three months ago fighting for Irish independence. Your independence, too!" Tears and snot began running down her face even though she tried to hold back the flood of emotions that had built up in her since the tragedy.

In an unexpected moment of empathy, whether personal or political on her part, the young nun allowed it but warned, "you must keep it covered always or there will be trouble for both of us." So, Fiona obediently concealed it under her dress where it could not be seen by anyone.

The large interior room's floor was littered with hair. The two very pregnant girls in the room reminded Fiona of shorn sheep with their new short haircuts. A third younger girl was seated while an older nun with scissors was busy at work cutting her hair. Fiona wondered if the girl was pregnant because her belly was still quite flat. The girl kept fidgeting and complaining which only irritated the nun.

"Stop your nonsense, Joan, or I'll shave your head rather than cut your hair. Do you hear me? See how well behaved the other girls were for their haircuts? You will learn that insolence will not be tolerated here." Apparently, this nun wasn't bound to silence. She turned to the young nun who had delivered Fiona and informed her "Sister, you may take them away now as I am finished with them." To Fiona, she said "see that broom over there, start sweeping up the floor until your turn."

Guessing that she was among other new arrivals, Fiona knew it was best to follow orders. Quietly obeying, she began to sweep the different colored hair from the floor, regretfully knowing that her own platinum blonde tresses would soon join the pile of brunette and red hair already there.

Following her hair cut, the kind young nun with whom she now shared the secret of the retained necklace, silently escorted her to a large work area. It was a huge laundry where over fifty young women were working …sorting, washing, ironing and folding. Because of the heat in the laundry, sweat dripped down the reddened faces of the young women and large circles of sweat stains formed on the backs and under the armpit areas of the uniforms. With a nod of her head, the nun left after assigning Fiona to a pregnant older girl, who appeared to be the person responsible to orient her.

The girl said in a monotone voice, "My name is Margaret," and she said nothing else and kept folding linens.

To fill in the silent void, Fiona answered, "That's a pretty name." *Why did I say such a stupid thing?* she rebuked herself.

"So, what's your name?"

"Fiona."

"You pregnant or just caught whoring?"

"Raped and pregnant, because ……..."

"Never mind that. We all have our stories. Just watch me and learn," the insouciant girl interrupted before Fiona could finish her sentence.

"All I can tell you is to keep quiet and work hard and maybe someday you can get out of here, if what you say is true about being raped. That may work in your favor."

None of the workers spoke and the noise level was high from all the machines. Three nuns walked the premises as watchful supervisors. Even above the noise of the machines, the rattling noise of their long rosary beads that hung down their habits could be heard whenever they walked close by.

After a nun passed, Margaret gave Fiona an iron and in a low voice instructed how the linens were to be pressed and folded. "What you have to watch out for is burning yourself. I've done that and you don't want that to happen."

"Is there any medical help here when that happens?"

"There is an infirmary but their main concern is delivering babies." Margaret then put her finger to her lips signaling that conversation was over and she went back to her own work. Fiona looked at her assigned pile. She began to iron her first sheet using the heavy iron and trying to be careful not to burn herself.

In a very short time, Fiona began to wipe the sweat dripping from her forehead. She whispered to Margaret, "how can the sisters stand this heat wearing their full habits and veils? It's a wonder they don't faint."

Margaret first glanced around and then answered under her breath, "Because they're too mean to faint." Then she finally smiled at Fiona.

As the weeks passed, Fiona performed her work dutifully and tried to mind her own business. She particularly tried to stay out of the way of one clique of girls who were bullies. Her goal was to do what she was told to do until she delivered when she imagined she would be released after placing her newborn up for adoption. Each time she inquired about her future release plan, the one social worker in the home would tell her, "We'll see, Fiona, no promises."

One night as the girls were undressing readying themselves for bed before all the dormitory lights went off, one of the girls from the clique noticed Fiona's Celtic amulet. Carelessly, it accidentally dangled from her neck when she was removing her socks.

"Well, what do you have there, Missy Rule -Breaker?" asked an older girl who was taller and heavier than Fiona.

Another from the clique, who seemed to be the leader, reached for Fiona's prized talisman saying, "I'll do you a favor and just take it away so you don't get in trouble."

"Over my dead body," said Fiona with both hands on her necklace.

"Idiot, can you count.... there are five of us and one of you so hand it over or I'll rip it from your neck."

"Just try," came a voice from behind. As the group turned, they saw it was Margaret and, without a word, each went to their cots. The lights went off before Fiona could thank Margaret. As she lied in bed, still shaken, she watched the full moon appear through the window near the ceiling, providing light that the Magdalene Home would not.

Over the months, she and Margaret became close or as close as any girl could under the long periods of mandatory silence and the ever-watchful eyes of the nuns. As friends, they were able to share the forced silences together more comfortably. In response to the constant religious diatribes, they rebelliously communicated by rolling their eyes or with a mocking smile.

The bullies were wary of Margaret and Margaret became Fiona's protector. Fiona's mother would have described Margaret as being 'big boned' which was a politer description than 'manly'. Sometimes Fiona worried that Margaret wanted more from Fiona than friendship but that worry never became realized.

"If anyone bothers you, tell me. I'll beat the shite out of them". Fiona believed Margaret meant every word. And she and the bullies knew she could do it.

Only during the quiet of night could Fiona grow contemplative and dream of her release and her future. She promised herself that she would change the current landscape of her life. However, in the ink black of the night, sometimes her fear that she couldn't overcame her.

Some days Fiona felt she must have ironed and folded all of the linens in Dublin. She listened to the gossip and learned about her surroundings. She learned that the Church and County received payments for the free laundry work provided by the inmates. What was disconcerting was learning that the infants were taken away from the mothers who wanted to keep them and sent overseas for adoption, mostly in America and Canada. The mothers had no say in the matter. Although Fiona felt sympathy for those girls who would never know their babies, she still had trouble accepting the child in her womb as hers and knew adoption would be the best course for both her and the infant.

Margaret's newborn infant was taken from her at birth. "I wasn't even permitted to hold my son, not even once. They told me that was to prevent me from becoming attached to him. There are evil people here pretending to do God's work and someday they will be found out," Margaret tearfully confided.

"I don't know what to say that will help you, Margaret, I truly wish I could ease your heartache." Fiona decided that it was best to just allow Margaret to vent her feelings.

"Mina, my stupid dream was that I would be released, find work and return for my child. I kept telling myself that it would be possible when all the time I should have known I was only deluding myself."

Margaret never saw her son again. Her only consolation was that he was healthy and was adopted quickly by a well- off Canadian couple. Mother Superior had told her this and she wanted desperately to believe it.

One night with abandon, because she figured her imprisonment might be coming to an end now that she had delivered her child, Margaret shared with Fiona everything she had learned at the Home. Angrily, she described that, because there were more infants than adoptive parents, many infants were left in cribs, failing to thrive and dying in the first few weeks through lack of love and neglect.

"Imagine a wee babe left in a crib, never being held or loved, Fiona. At least my son escaped from here. Have you any idea how many infants they bury in the yard? And these little baptized souls buried in unmarked mass graves as if they never existed."

She went on. "Worse for the infants who become young children here. They go to the public school but are treated as pariahs and segregated from the local children. Some are called the devil's spawn and told that they will eventually grow horns. They live with an undeserved shame, never knowing a mother's love."

Fiona thought back to her own school days and remembered the children from the home being isolated from the other classes and in the play yard, but she had never paid it much attention then.

The following month, when Fiona went into labor, she gave her amulet to Margaret knowing she couldn't hide the forbidden necklace from the staff in attendance in the delivery room.

After hours of painful labor, a midwife said "she's ready" and she found herself on the delivery room table. She heard them say the word 'breech' which troubled her but finally she felt the small body pass through her. There was a flurry of activity but Fiona could only hear whispering between the midwife and the delivery room nun. She kept waiting to hear the infant cry but the silence in the room was deafening.

"We are sorry, Fiona, but your baby girl is a still-born."

"But the baby was kicking me the whole time. How can that be?"

"Sometimes close to delivery, the cord wraps around an infant's neck preventing enough air to breath. It's sad but happens." The midwife seemed truly upset. She then placed the silent, unmoving infant in Fiona's arms for a final goodbye.

As she held her dead infant daughter, Fiona begged God to forgive her guilty relief. At first, when she learned that her rape resulted in a pregnancy, she wanted the British bastard in her womb to die. But as time passed she realized that the baby was as much a victim of the crime as she was.

When she returned to the dormitory, she crawled into her bed and felt her flat belly. Then Margaret sneaked over to Fiona's cot in the dark and returned the amulet she had kept hidden. She placed it around Fiona's neck. "I hope having this around your neck again gives you some comfort, Fiona," was all she said before crawling back to her own bed. And it did.

September, 1917

Dublin

Beds at the Magdalene Laundry were needed due to the war and the increase in unmarried girls impregnated by soldiers. The Home provided a place where these young women could be hidden away from the eyes of society, the society that was failing them. The fact that they provided a lucrative free labor pool with proceeds going to the church and county was given little mention.

"Margaret, do you think we can expect to be released soon?" Fiona whispered while pushing the laundry cart.

Margaret nodded in agreement. Her concern was why she had not heard about her release since she had delivered her child weeks before Fiona.

Days later Fiona again questioned Margaret as to how they can learn about their release dates. They had both left messages to speak with the social worker with no success. They had planned to leave and find work together for a fresh start once they both regained their freedom. Together they knew their chances were far better than alone.

"I am going to have to request a formal hearing. This delay is unfair," Margaret responded. Surprisingly, her request was granted by the administrative nun the same morning of her request.

Fiona went on with her work hoping she could learn Margaret's release date before bedtime since dinner, like all meals, had a mandatory requirement for silence. When Margaret was escorted back to the washers, Fiona could see by her friend's face that there was something wrong. Even when Fiona would find a reason to be near Margaret for a possible whisper, her friend would turn away from her.

That night, sitting on Margaret's bed in the dark, Margaret broke the news given to her that morning. "Because I had to whore to feed myself, the sisters decided that additional rehabilitation and penance are required before allowing my release."

Fiona thought to herself, *or could it be economic because Margaret's work productivity is greater than everyone else's here.*

Cold faced she told Fiona, "You will have to accept that they have shattered our plan to leave this place and start over together. I have accepted it and now you will have to, too, and make a new plan for yourself."

Fiona couldn't bear to witness her friend's crushed rebellious nature. It had been Margaret who had been her savior all along, like an unexpected guardian angel, albeit a fallen one, sent to her to get her through the misery of her incarceration.

Softening her words somewhat, Margaret continued to add, "Fiona, you are a different case from those of us who had prostituted ourselves. You were an innocent victim and they are aware of that fact, even if they never admit it. And with no record of crimes or mental illness in your file, you will be released far earlier than I. So, get out of here and don't wait for me. Go to your aunt's home and beg to be back with your brothers. Find work and start your life where you left off. Find a good boy and marry and never look back, that is my advice."

Margaret hesitated a bit but then wrote something down on an edge of paper torn from one of the assignment sheets hanging on the wall.

"Take this address, Fiona," said Margaret, as she slipped the sliver of paper into Fiona's hand. "With life being as unkind as it seems to be for the two of us, we must prepare ourselves for the very worst. I pray to God you will be able to return to your aunt and never have to use this address. Remember that you are to use it only as a last resort as I had to once. Do you understand me?"

With that said, Margaret pulled the blanket over her head not waiting for a reply. She turned her back to Fiona who climbed back into her own cot heartbroken for her friend, as well as for their dashed plans. As she lay awake, she realized how much she relied on Margaret who treated her as she imagined an older sister would, always with love, practical advice and protection.

Unceremoniously, early the next morning, Fiona was returned her suitcase, given a few quid and her old coat and escorted out the Home's back door without even any breakfast or a chance to bid Margaret farewell. Fiona never saw Margaret again. Months later she wrote her but never received a response.

Upon her release, Fiona nervously went to her mother's sister, unsure of her aunt's reaction to her return. The walk from the Home to her aunt's row house took almost three hours to cover on foot so she was exhausted as she neared her destination. Although her aunt physically resembled her mother, she was nothing like her otherwise. Irene had always been a fearful and nervous person frightened by the politics of the time and only wished for the status quo. She never married and worked as a cleaning woman in the local brewery at night. When she began knocking on the front door, Fiona realized that she would probably be waking her aunt who slept during the day.

As Fiona expected, her aunt finally answered the door dressed in a robe. She appeared shocked to find Fiona standing there and hurried her into the small parlor. Before she shut the front door, she glanced around as if to see if anyone had seen Fiona's arrival.

No greeting, not even a hug, but Fiona never remembered her aunt to be an affectionate person. *How different it must be for my brothers living with her after having our loving mother's hugs and kisses*, Fiona thought sadly.

But she knew she had to be grateful for her aunt's care of her brothers even though she had sent her away for being pregnant.

"I am so happy to see you again, Aunt Irene, and cannot wait to see my brothers. I know they are in school right now but it will be so wonderful to surprise them when they come home."

As Fiona removed her coat and hat, she began describing the loss of her baby and how happy she was to be returning home to family. But she was quickly interrupted by her aunt.

"Do you realize what grief we are still suffering because of your parents? We are constantly under surveillance by the British because of their rebellious politics and my relationship to them. I worry that my job could be threatened with your return. We can barely put enough food on the table for three as it is, so what would happen if I lose my income. There is no way you can live here, Fiona, you must accept that. I am truly sorry."

Fiona never imagined for a moment that her aunt would turn her out now that she was no longer pregnant. "But I'll find work and help, Aunt Irene, please have pity. I have nothing and nowhere to go," Fiona said, still believing she would convince her aunt and not be sent away again.

But she was turned away. Her aunt handed her the valise and the coat she had just removed and guided her to the door. Repeating over and over "so sorry, Fiona, so sorry," as she closed the door with a click of the lock.

Fiona stood on the sidewalk, put down her valise and put on her coat. It took every inner strength she had not to cry in public with passersby walking on the street. For a few minutes, she could not even think straight. *Parents and grandparents all dead and an aunt who disowned me. I am sixteen years old and have no one in the world*, she thought despairingly. Then she realized that her parish church was just a short distance. With nowhere else to go, she thought that her parish priest would surely help her find shelter and work.

The same priest who had sat with her awaiting the constable's arrival earlier in the year answered the door after she rang the bell.

"Father, I doubt you remember me but my name is Fiona Burke and I was just released from the Magdalene Home."

"I do remember you and am pleased to see you again, Miss Burke." He invited her into the rectory and told her to take a seat. He hesitated asking about the pregnancy and decided to let her speak first. Fiona explained the loss of the baby and how her aunt refused to take her back into her home.

Instead of hearing positive suggestions as to how she could receive help, the priest began to drone on with spiritual advice when she really needed food and a roof over her head.

She listened patiently for a time and then interrupted him. "Father, I haven't eaten all day and am still weak from delivering the baby. May I have a cup of tea and anything else you can spare?" she asked, embarrassed by sounding so needy.

"We priests have a cook who prepares our meals here in the rectory, but she is not here right now I am sorry to say. I can get some tea and scones. That is the best I can manage for you."

"Thank you, Father, anything is appreciated."

Fiona tried her best to politely and slowly eat the small amount of food presented to her but it was difficult since she was famished. Her tea was gone within a few swallows and she was too ashamed to ask for more. She had hoped more would have been offered, but that did not happen.

Dark distant storm clouds were rushing the day towards dusk as the late afternoon was progressing quickly into evening. Fiona waited for him to have a suggestion for where she could spend the night but no suggestion ever came. When the extended silences became very uncomfortable, Fiona put on her coat. With the little pride she still had, she left without a backward glance.

There must have been a light rain while she was in the rectory because the wind shook raindrops from the leaves of the trees from under which she walked. She hoped the rain would not resume while she was wandering aimlessly adding to her desperate state.

With no emotional or financial support Fiona realized how hopeless her situation was. Real fear set in. She began to miss the security the asylum provided compared with her current condition but mostly she missed Margaret's friendship.

With her small valise, she wandered the streets trying to appear as if she was heading to a specific address. She had never before been homeless and she felt shame when she passed pedestrians, knowing they had homes and families. After all she had experienced, she still had some pride left.

To add to her dilemma, she needed a toilet badly. She was too shy to ask while at the rectory. When she saw his discomfort at the mere mention of her delivery, she knew she could not bear to see it worsen with the mention of a need for a toilet. This late in the day, holding it in was no longer an option. It was getting dark and she headed to the nearby park.

Fiona walked around the park looking for an area where she could find some modicum of privacy. She kept changing direction so that she wouldn't appear loss to people walking in the park. Finally, as night fell and people left the park, she found a corner behind an area with bushes along a concrete wall. Once she relieved herself, she huddled in a corner close to the wall that helped to block the night wind. She prayed it would not rain. She prayed she would be safe.

She struggled to keep her clothes clean but she knew that even sitting on grass left stains. *How can I go on like this?* she asked herself. *I have become a vagabond.* Despairingly, she stared at the small pond and for one brief moment contemplated suicide which, as a Catholic, she quickly ruled out. *Eternal hell as punishment for taking my life would be far worse than this, no matter how bad this is.*

As exhaustion overwhelmed her, she dozed off. Just before dawn a policeman, making his rounds, came up to her, gently tapping her awake with his Billy-club. For a fleeting moment, she imagined help had arrived. Instead, he leered at her and then told her what he wanted from her if she did not want to be arrested for vagrancy and prostitution.

After he left, a shaken Fiona stumbled to a water fountain in the park, washed out her mouth, cleaned her hands and face and took out the address that had been given to her by Margaret.

It took her most of the day to locate the address on the other end of the city. She was weary and hungry and her feet were blistered. Her valise seemed to get heavier as she got thirstier. The fact that it was a brothel did not surprise her for two reasons. First, because Margaret told her that she became pregnant working in a brothel and, secondly, because Margaret had hoped that she would never have to use it. It was to be a last resort.

Well, I am at my last resort right now so I only hope there is room for me here, she thought with more acceptance than despair. Heartsick with this downward turn in her life, she rationalized she would still have better living conditions in the brothel than she would have fending for herself on the street. She had no other options left to her so she braced herself for what was to come.

A Negro woman answered Fiona's knock, looked her over and allowed her to enter. "You wait here for Madame," she said and left Fiona standing in the vestibule. Within a few minutes, a tall woman with too much make-up and a fancy dress appeared. Without a word, she turned Fiona around to look her over and lifted her skirt to look at her legs.

"I assume you want me to take you in, correct?"

"Yes."

"How did you hear of my house?"

"A friend."

"I see. Are you a virgin and don't lie to me?"

"No." Fiona waited for the woman to ask more but she did not.

Instead, she asked as routinely as if she were asking for the time of day, "Do you have any sores around your private parts?"

"I do not."

"I may have to check you to be sure. I cannot be having our clients catch syphilis."

Fiona stood silently not knowing what to say. Instead the woman in charge studied her face saying, "it is uncanny how much you resemble my daughter who passed away last year from tuberculosis."

"I am sorry for your loss. I lost my family, too, but not to disease."

"How then?"

"British military."

Madame offered no condolences but silently stared at Fiona for a few moments. "You are to call me 'Madame'. This is my house and everything and everyone in it belongs to me. You can settle in and observe the other girls starting now. Learn from them how things are done here. You will be excused from having customers tonight but you will be expected to take your share starting tomorrow evening."

She then ordered the Negro worker, "Give her Victoria's room, get her cleaned up and take away her clothes."

"But, these are the only clothes I own," Fiona responded fretfully when she heard the woman's order.

"You don't require clothing here," she informed Fiona with her crooked smile.

Perhaps, if nothing else positive could be said about her situation, it could be said that the brothel did improve her otherwise hopeless position. She had a roof over her head, a comfortable bed and meals served in the morning and early evening before the customers arrived.

It helped that she reminded Madame of her daughter, Victoria. The resemblance played in Fiona's favor because she was given the best room in the house, other than Madame's. The unfairness did not escape some of the prostitutes with seniority, either. Fiona appeared to have become Madame's favorite. Being a young blonde beauty with her unique eyes of different colors, Madame groomed Fiona as a courtesan and marketed her as such to the wealthiest clients.

Fiona learned what men wanted and gave it to them. She learned things from Madame that, although shocking to her at first, became her trademark, often setting her apart from the other girls. She hated what she did with every fiber of her being but she knew that the answer was to excel at it. In time, she would find her way out from this shameful life.

"Ma Chere, you are young enough for us to be together for many years," she told Fiona, so pleased with the money Fiona was bringing into the house with her long list of clients who placed appointments with Fiona exclusively. Some paid exorbitant rates for extra hours or an all-nighter with her.

"You are an oddity with those eyes. Even on the outside, there is talk about the girl with both a blue and a brown eye. In fact, I have a photographer friend and business partner who will be told about you. Let us just say that he is looking for a special model for his provocative photo business." Madame was always finding new avenues for illicit business opportunities.

Within the month, the photographer visited the brothel and met with Fiona with Madame closely overseeing. He looked her over, then looked her over again, this time from under the black hood of his new Kodak camera lens and agreed she would do very nicely for the photographs he planned to take.

"She will be a good model. She has a combination of angelic wholesomeness and worldly wisdom for her young age behind those magnificent eyes," he told Madame.

"Another thing, Madame. The latest fashion is for women to shave the hair away from the underarms. Since 1915, many fashionable women have been using this tool called the 'Milady Decollete'," as he removed the razor from his bag and handed it to Madame.

"Fiona, take this and shave," she instructed Fiona as she and her new partner discussed business.

That was Fiona's introduction into the underground erotic French postcard business for which the photographer and Madame agreed to partner and split the income.

After months of prostitution, Fiona did not believe that there could be anything that could shame her again until the realization that now there would be permanent pictures of her in shameful poses.

"Fiona, you could become famous. The underground pornography world, with its international appetite for these special pictures is a very profitable business," the photographer explained to her. "My photographs are purchased by royals, bankers and wealthy businessmen who have an insatiable appetite for them."

When Fiona returned from her room, after shaving her underarms, the session began with the photographer. Madame acted as his assistant in arranging the background scenery and posing Fiona as the photographer instructed.

Would anyone recognize me in these pictures? But then Fiona consoled herself with *who is left to recognize me? and what would it even matter anymore if someone did?* She accepted that she had no choice but to agree to this new arrangement. Refusal could result in being turned out to the streets which was still her greatest fear.

Hours later, after the photographer left, Madame was ecstatic about the new business venture. She boasted to Fiona that someday they would go to

America where the photographer had an office in New York City where there would be lots of money for them. Madame paid Fiona a small amount of money following the session which took Fiona by surprise. Slyly, Madame was aware that this session was mainly an introduction and that, going forward, Sam would be expecting bolder pictures.

"Ma Chere, I remind you that I saved you when you were desperate. You would be dead had it not been for my kindness in taking you in. I know that you will always understand your debt to me and fully cooperate with anything asked of you."

"Oui, Madame," Fiona responded affirmatively, using the same tired French expressions used so unsuccessfully by Madame in her attempt to have people believe she was French. She always did her best to placate Madame, but Fiona had other plans. She just needed time and money.

November, 1917

Dublin

Madame was a former whore herself who, as she aged and lost her looks in her thirties, used her business experience and savings to open her own brothel. The police whom she paid and who were frequent free customers, looked the proverbial 'other way' so her house prospered. With Dublin's poverty generated by the war and the Church's powerful overreach in society, there was no shortage of hungry girls needing work and shelter.

No one knew Madame's real name. She insisted on being addressed as Madame. Her pretension of having a French background fooled no one, not even the least sophisticated girls in the home. However, she instilled fear among the whores who feared life on the street should one be penalized with immediate eviction.

One evening, an older police official shared with Honey, one of the whores, that he knew Madame twenty years ago when she was Peggy Walsh and he had arrested her father for burglary. She had been the oldest child of five motherless siblings who all died within a short time of cholera.

"Poverty brings out the best and the worst in folks. Some become saints and others sinners. I believe it brought out the worst in Peggy morally, but she sure turned into one hell of a businesswoman," he laughed as he fondled the topless girl sitting on his lap and swore that he would arrest her if she ever told Madame what he had just told her.

Fiona had no experience as to knowing what constituted a high-end brothel from a lower one. She could only guess that Madame's had to be better than most based on the affluence of the client base. Wealthy business men, judges and local politicians frequented the house. All were well dressed and educated.

Madame had a few silk dresses and paraded around the premises like the lady of the manor. All the girls had laundered pinafores and clean underwear every day thanks to the two Negro women workers. The kitchen also had a Black woman who cooked, named Beth, and, in the evenings, an old Dubliner came to play music on his tin whistle. If his song navigated into a sad one, which was frequently the case with Irish music, Madame would shake her fist at him demanding happy music.

"No sad music in my house!" she would rant at the musician.

The house itself had rooms on the second floor and the attic. Newer girls were assigned the attic rooms which were always colder in the winter and hotter in the summer. Even though she was the newest girl, Fiona was rewarded with Victoria's second-floor room which angered the others. Everyone thought it was because Fiona looked like Madame's deceased daughter. The late Victoria had left a room that was furnished with the most comfortable bed Fiona ever slept in. Sadly, she had to share it nightly with men lining up in the downstairs parlor but she had it to herself during the daytime when the house closed and everyone slept.

Madame planned to keep Fiona, her rising star, very busy with the wealthier customers. Since many of them were older, Madame made it easier for them to climb only one flight of stairs to reach Fiona. And because many of them were older, Fiona knew exactly how to make them happy with less exertion demanded on their part. For this, they were always grateful and would always request Fiona. Madame allowed her to keep a bottle of whiskey in her room which pleased Fiona. She knew that, after a few drinks, some of the older clients couldn't do much more than just 'look and touch', which suited Fiona just fine. Their secrets were safe with her and that contributed to her success.

Madame had all the rooms decorated with scarlet red drapes and fancy linens and artificial flowers, the likes of which impressed Fiona having come from a poor row house. The housekeeper even sprayed cologne periodically in each room after a customer was finished.

Madame would ask Fiona," Ma Chere, tu es content?" as if she really cared whether or not Fiona was content with the business arrangement. Fiona was not fooled. She understood that Madame was completely compassionless and cruel after witnessing her vile temper numerous times. Her leverage with the girls was the fear of trying to survive on the outside. Conditions were hopeless for women alone. Starvation, prison and worse laid outside the brothel. Fiona's past experience being alone and penniless still haunted her. The brothel provided security but the loss of morality, dignity and freedom was the price.

Just that day at dawn with the last customers gone, the girls watched Madame count the night's income. Outraged that her expectations were unmet, she angrily called a girl to her. The very young girl, who Madame named Pepper because of her racial mixture of Irish and African, was only thirteen years old.

Madame spoke loudly enough for everyone in the house to hear, "Pepper, au contraire to what I thought of you, you are not bringing in enough business so there is no room for you here any longer."

"Can you believe that Madame had auctioned off Pepper's virginity just a few months ago and is now tossing her out to the street," whispered the whore named Honey. "Keep in mind that could happen to you or to any one of us by that bitch."

Honey was a few years older than the other girls and was the one who disparaged Madame the most behind her back when the girls were alone. Fiona predicted that someday, if Honey wasn't careful, Madame will over hear her or one of the other girls will tell on her, and she will end up on the street like poor Pepper.

Madame's diatribe continued as the racially-mixed child stood trembling, "The men don't ask for you, they prefer the white girls. I told you from the beginning to do something extra special for your customers but apparently you are not exciting enough for them. One customer told me that you made him feel guilty. I cannot have that." With that, she walked out of the room, signaling the Negro workers to escort the young exile out.

Those were Madame's last words to the child she named Pepper. It was Madame's custom to choose a name for each new whore. For some inexplicable reason known only to Madame, Fiona kept her name unchanged.

Before retiring to her room to sleep for the day, Fiona did see the Negro women consoling the youngster in the back alley and taking a great risk in handing her a package of food and an old blanket. The memory of sleeping in the park came back vividly to Fiona but she pushed it away as it made her heart ache with self -pity, as well as pity for what she knew awaited the girl. *I can never let that happen to me again. When I leave this place, it will be on my terms,* she swore to herself.

December, 1917

Dublin

Fiona was patient. She learned her trade. She was very aware of how disingenuous Madame was. Never for a moment did Fiona believe Madame truly cared for her or any of the other girls. It was always only about the money they brought in. But Fiona had learned how to bide her time until she had a better option. There were tricks to this trade and she promised herself that she would learn them all.

She realized that the competition for repeat customers was fierce. Most were jealous of Fiona's unique prettiness but two girls nearer Fiona's age befriended her.

Sugar and Spice were their Madame-given names. "Our real names are Rose and May, but real names are never to be used here, remember that or Madame will have a fit."

"What is your real name?" Spice asked.

"It's Fiona and it's my real name."

"We wondered about that. It is truly unusual how Madame allowed you to keep your name. She seems to name us all after condiments." Both girls giggled at that.

"Maybe it would have been better to have had it changed. Did you ever consider that?" asked Sugar seriously.

"Not really. What would that serve?"

"We like to think these are our temporary 'stage names' and maybe someday we can return to our own identities again. Then no one will ever know what happened to Sugar and Spice and we can become ourselves again."

Fiona wondered if their idea was idiotic or brilliant but she was impressed with their goal that someday they would be done whoring. She hoped they were right.

They explained that their customer specialty was ménage a trois, three-somes. They were rarely moody like the other girls and were even playful. In fact, one late afternoon before the brothel opened for business, they made a game out of 'schooling' Fiona. They laughed and acted like the teenagers they really were in contrast to the painted tarts they appeared to be each evening. Even the worker women had to hush them, at times, concerned about Madame's temper if she heard them playing games instead of resting for the work ahead.

"OK, Fiona, just two more lessons and you will know everything we know. Very important, you must learn how to handle an unruly customer," said Sugar. "It is a self -defense move, with a funny name called 'ju-jitsu'. My brother learned it in the army and taught it to me before the malaria got him. He caught that disease when the army sent him to India. The little I remembered, I taught to Spice and we practice it on each other. It's fun and exercise. We only had to use it once on a crazy customer so it came in quite handy." Practicing with both girls, Fiona became adept, but not until receiving more than a few aches and pains following the lessons.

"Remember, in this business, ju-jitsu can save your life someday."

Lessons with the two girls continued with Spice play acting the whore and Sugar the customer. "This is what you do to look as if you are drinking whiskey but you really are not. When the client isn't looking, you dump the drink in the chamber pot or the flower vase but not before wetting your lips. That way, you will taste like whiskey to your customer which will please him into thinking how much more compliant you will be. You must always stay sober and keep your wits about you or the wrong type of man can hurt you." Fiona was grateful to Sugar and Spice for the important lessons they taught her. Lessons that she would remember and use when needed.

One Sunday morning, Sugar and Spice woke Fiona asking if she would attend Mass with them.

"Sorry, Girls, but my Sunday Mass days ended a long time ago. Frankly, how can you think to go to church when you whore every night?"

Taken aback, Spice answered somewhat truculently, "We may be whores, Fiona, but we are still Catholics. We know we commit sin but missing Mass is a mortal sin so we never miss."

"And we sit in the back of the church and we don't take communion," Sugar clarified.

"You'll just have to pray for me, then," said Fiona as she turned over to go back to sleep.

Fiona learned quickly to implement everything she learned which resulted in gratuities from her generous clients. Unknown to Madame or anyone else in the house, she hid her money. She would ask in her winsome way for a tip and the men would happily oblige to please her.

"But please do not tell Madame," she would purr to her clients and they apparently obliged since Madame never learned about her secret cache.

Her main concern was hiding her savings, not only from Madame who would punish her severely, but also from thievery by the others in the house.

She loosened a floor board under her bed as she had learned from her rebel parents who hid documents and guns from the British. It took a toll on her hands using a bread knife pilfered from a customer's plate but she succeeded. Since Madame supplied the girls with creams for their faces, Fiona laughed to herself each time the cream was used to heal her scraped hands instead.

"Why does she get the best clients?" complained the other whores when time proved Fiona was bringing in the most income to the house.

"Because they request her, that's why, so try harder to please," retorted Madame, as she deliberately created dissent and jealousy among the girls in order to create competition and more income for her house.

Then one winter evening when as her girls were gathering in the parlor, Fiona was found to be missing.

"Now what is keeping Fiona?" Impatiently, Madame ordered one of the Negro women to go upstairs and see why Fiona was delayed. Madame demanded that all the girls be positioned in the parlor before she opened the door for business. It made a client's selection easier.

When the worker returned, she fearfully reported, "Madame, Fiona is not in her room, or the toilet. I checked both."

"When did you last see?" Madame's irritation beginning to turn into alarm.

"Early this morning when we closed and her last customer left, that was the last time I see Miss Fiona," she said with her Caribbean accent getting thicker as her fear increased. She had witnessed Madame's temper too many times.

"Sugar, Spice, where is Fiona?" she screamed at the two girls closest to Fiona. Both concerned as to what Madame's reaction would be if Fiona was truly gone.

"We don't know, Madame. We really don't know," they repeated frightened by Madame's anger. "She never told us anything about leaving the house."

"Fiona?" Madame screamed over and over, as everyone in the house kept their heads down and their eyes on the floor, although the jealous ones truly hoped that she was gone for good. With her face a rictus of fury, she was incredulous of Fiona's disloyalty. As the realization of Fiona's escape sunk in, she became manic. Only because customers were knocking on the door for the brothel to open that she composed herself.

"Now you wash the floors!" Similar sarcastic remarks were widespread among the steerage passengers as they watched the crew finally cleaning the floors and lavatories that had been neglected throughout the voyage and left to the passengers to clean. No one was fooled that the only reason was because of the imminent inspection of the ship at the port of entry. But the passengers were too excited to have reached port so nothing could damper the euphoria of entering America felt among one and all.

Standing on the deck with Fiona awaiting disembarkation, they both held their hats as the wind ripped around them. Without the ability to wash clothes, the dresses they wore were not as clean as they would have liked. There was a surrounding sour odor from the many unwashed bodies circling them. They hoped that their periodic sponge bathes sufficed for them. Fortunately, the excitement emanating from the passengers was contagious. There was a universal feeling of gratitude, relief and happiness. But then, looking around at all the other steerage passengers, the girls counted their blessings in comparison.

Some children had shoes tied with cord to hold them together and many adults wore patched clothes and carried raggedy bundles of their worldly belongings. Women wore peasant scarves on their heads and some appeared without coats, insufficient coverage for arriving in New York City in the middle of winter.

Mina could see that the Statue of Liberty was even grander than Basilio had described. Some of the women passengers were crying with happiness while the men were removing their hats in respect. Numerous languages could be heard but all were speaking of the sight of the majestic monument that promised freedom to all. While most were in awe, the few French passengers cheered and reminded all on deck that the statue was France's gift in 1886 to America. "Liberte and equalite"! one Frenchman loudly boasted.

But then, someone standing behind Mina was heard to say that Ellis Island can be called by another name, 'the Isle of Tears.'

"What do you mean?" she inquired turning behind her to ask the man who had spoken. Fiona turned, as well, but she already knew the answer.

"Because some passengers will be sent back home if they don't pass the medical or reading tests, that's why. Wouldn't you be crying if that happened to you?"

"Don't worry, Mina, that is not going to happen to either of us. There's always a kill-joy in every crowd," Fiona said consolingly while giving the outspoken man a dirty look. "Stop scaring people. For all you know, it could be the Isle of Tears for you," she warned.

Up until this time, Mina felt nothing but confidence but overhearing that comment diminished it a bit. She was told by her brother in his last letter that he would meet her at the area called 'the Kissing Post' which was the happy name she thought of when she thought of Ellis Island.

It got its name because of the kisses everyone receives from all the relatives awaiting to greet the new arrivals, Basilio had written. Needless to say, she was determined to think of the 'Kissing Post' and not the 'Isle of Tears'.

Because the waters around the island were too shallow for the transatlantic ships to dock, steerage passengers were transported by ferries for processing on Ellis Island. First and second-class passengers were exempted from traveling to Ellis Island and, instead, were processed aboard ship before departure. Providing that no illness was identified, these passengers were free to enter the US through customs at the piers.

As they made their way onto the island, Mina grabbed Fiona's arm. "Just in case we are separated, remember to wait at the Kissing Post."

"Of course, Mina. In fact, Brian also insisted that we meet there. I had to explain to him that the Kissing Post is the place where families waited to greet their arriving relatives. I truly think he had a different idea of the purpose." Both girls could not stop giggling at that.

Mina visualized hugs and kisses all around as family members introduced each other. She also saw it as an opportunity to get the Brooklyn address still needed to write Fiona. She and the Turner and Kelly families had already shared theirs.

"And don't forget that I still need your address, Fiona."

Fiona smiled and shook her head in agreement. "I must get it from my relatives, Mina, then I'll share with you, I promise."

Mina was surprised that Fiona seemed unusually quiet among the excited voices surrounding them. Parents were embracing children and the older passengers filled with relief that they had finally reached the final steps of the journey. Mina took her hand, surprised that this time she was comforting Fiona instead of the other way around.

The immigration process started with the passengers following the assigned interpreters, who were known to speak multiple languages, through the main doorway and up steps to the Registry Room.

"This is where it looks like we will be separated, Mina. You will have to go on the Italian line and I with the English speaking. I can see Brian and his family up ahead with the Turners. Your line is longer since the majority of the passengers are Italian. Now remember, you will need to pass the reading test in Italian. Even though your verbal English has come so far, do not ask to take the test in English because you are not ready for that," she warned.

"I know that, Fiona, no worries. Just wait for me at the Kissing Post. No matter what or how long it takes me, promise?"

"I promise." But Fiona had an entirely different plan.

Unknown to most of the passengers, as they walked in line through the immigration station, was that they were already undergoing a preliminary health observation by a doctor who was looking for any outward signs of any physical or mental illness. If the physician perceived a potential condition, he would mark the person's right shoulder with a chalk mark, such as PG for pregnancy, TB for tuberculosis, M for a mental disability and so on, which would result in the passenger being directed for a closer physical examination. If a condition was one that could be treated in the Island's infirmary, then the passenger was admitted to the facility before admission into the country was approved. For passengers where a condition required long term care or was one that was deemed to be an unacceptable disability, the patient was denied admission and would have to return to Europe.

As they passengers entered the Great Hall, everyone became anxious. All dreaded the health inspection point as it was common knowledge that a passenger was not allowed to proceed if marked with chalk. Passengers were already in a weakened state from the voyage and some were being chalked and removed from the lines as everyone watched and worried.

Because of the war, German passengers were met with more of an underlying current of suspicion that those from other countries. Mina had seen the small German boy's coat marked with a 'P' and his family removed from the German speaking line. She wondered if 'P' meant 'pneumonia' or 'pleurisy'. Although the family tried, it was impossible to conceal the small child's condition from the medical professionals.

Mina realized that Frau Werner must have had a suspicion when those last days ship board were filled with instructions to the children, especially her youngest, to hold back coughs and sneezes and to be silent and stoic when passing through the entry process. As Mina continued through the process where her next step was the literacy test, she turned her head to see the German family distraught and all three youngsters crying inconsolably.

"Oh, that poor family. How heartbreaking for them if they are turned away and returned to war-ravaged Germany." Mina had grown fond of the two young daughters and prayed for them.

As they passed through the Registry Room, Mina's heart went out to every one of the passengers who appeared to have various chalk marks on their clothing. What could possibly be worse for some of these peasant families than having to return to places where there is no one and nothing to which to return.

Then Mina's attention was drawn ahead to Fiona's English line where she saw Winifred being separated from her family. Winifred's coat had been chalked with a large letter that Mina could not read. Standing between an inspector and a physician, Winnifred could be seen pleading to be allowed to go forward with Jack and the children. Mina guessed it was the reddened and crusty infected eyes that Winifred had tried to hide unsuccessfully by lowering the brim of her hat. She could hear the children crying and Jack being pushed forward down the line escorted by security guards because he refused to leave his wife. It seemed that he and Sean Kelly had pooled their money to try to buy Winnie's authorization but their effort failed. The amount they raised apparently was not enough to entice the inspectors who were well known for accepting bribes.

Oh, dear God, thought Mina. *After this long voyage to have it end this way.* She prayed it would be a hospital stay and not deportation for Winifred. It would be the Isle of Tears for them, after all, which sickened her because she already thought of them as dear friends.

On the English -speaking line, Fiona saw Jack Turner in a huddle with the security agents. The agents had pushed the Kelly family forward. She knew there was nothing that she could do to help. All she could do was to promise herself that she would write Jack as soon as she could. She was sure that Winnie's eye condition would be treated in the infirmary and the family reunited again.

Sean Kelly had tried to interject on behalf of Winnifred, calling the agents cruel to separate a mother from her children, but the irritated agent ordered him to move on.

"You are no relation to this family. Keep moving if you know what's good for you." Then the agent looked at the other agent. "Another loud mouth Mick, just what the country needs."

"Go, Sean, see to your family," Jack advised. "You don't need any trouble, go on. We will be alright once we work this out." He tried to sound confident for his loved ones who were all but clinging to him with worried expressions.

"Jack and Winnie, we are so sorry. God be with you," said Sean Kelly as he led his son and family forward. "We will be praying for you and waiting outside." They moved forward to where the irritated agent was pointing.

Once a passenger passed the medical examination process, then the man or woman had to go before an inspector who sat at a desk accompanied by an interpreter. Each passenger was questioned on the original thirty-one answers that had been given at the beginning of the voyage and recorded in the ship's manifest. These pertained to name, nationality, occupation, health, finances, destination and any other questions for consistency with the information contained in the ship's manifest log. Then those passengers over sixteen years of age took a literacy test which was a printed passage in the passenger's native language. Once all these steps were completed satisfactorily, a landing card was pinned to the clothing of each immigrant.

As Mina awaited her turn, she could see Fiona on the English-speaking line moving through the process very quickly. In no time, Mina could see that she had finished all the requirements while Mina still had not yet taken the literacy test.

From the distance, Mina could see that with her charm working as usual, Fiona had her gruff-looking agent laughing as he pinned her landing card to her coat. *Fiona could escape hell by charming the devil himself,* she thought admiringly.

Mina passed her literacy test with no problem. She moved forward with great relief knowing she was just finishing the final steps in the processing procedure leading to her approval for entry.

Thank you, God! she prayed as her landing card was pinned to her coat. She also thanked the agent who wished her "good luck," which he probably said hundreds of times each day as immigrants reached this final point in the arduous process.

Fiona's worry had been the Manifest questioning and was overjoyed that it went smoothly. She had Sam to thank for having her papers listing her occupation as a catalogue model employed by him. *How ironic to be listed as a model who poses with clothes on rather than off!* She wondered about the Turners and if Mina witnessed what happened to them. Regardless, Fiona knew that her priority was to leave the area immediately and hope to get the ferry to Manhattan before Mina and Brian realize she's gone.

Mina knew that the Turners were being held back but she could not understand why Fiona wasn't waiting for her. She found herself not only disappointed but also annoyed with her.

"Have you seen Fiona?" asked Brian. His family could be seen embracing his aunts and uncles. "Where could she have gone?"

Mina answered, "I have no idea but let's give her a few minutes before we begin to worry."

They both searched the crowd which was slowly breaking up. Many were heading to the Kissing Post to find their waiting relatives, as the Kelly family had done. Brian was called away to join his family.

"I cannot wait, Mina. My uncle is taking us someplace to eat and then to the barge that will take us to New Jersey. Please write and remind Fiona to write, too. Tell her how sorry I am to have missed her." He looked heartbroken so Mina assured him that she would do both.

Many of the passengers sought out the ferries and money exchangers. Many headed directly to the food vendors lining the area. But then her attention quickly turned to a man waving as he ran to her. She was thrilled and relieved to see her brother Basilio, even more handsome than she remembered having put on some bulk and muscle. As per his letter, he had been reliably waiting at the Kissing Post area. Just as he promised and just as she knew he would be. *But who else is that with him? Could that be Carlo Vitale? But, still, where is Fiona?*

"Little Sister, welcome to America," were the first words from her brother as he put her in a tight bear-hug. Ending his long hug, Basilio turned to introduce Carlo. The landing was noisy so they could barely hear each other but she did hear her brother say, "... Carlo insisted on being here to greet you, too."

Smiling and politely taking her hand, Carlo welcomed her. Mina could not help noticing that he seemed to be evaluating her and was disheartened to be judged when she felt so disheveled. *How could he expect me to look my best after such a long journey?* She would have chosen a better time for their first meeting if she had been given a choice. But after a few minutes, he did seem pleased if his furtive glances counted. She hoped it wasn't just wishful thinking on her part.

Although his parents had sent a picture of her, Carlo knew that seeing the girl in person right away was very important. *In case they had pawned an ugly old maid on me, I would have enough time to get out of this arrangement. But, so far, I have no complaints since the girl in front of me is pretty*, he thought.

Mina tried to concentrate conversation with her brother but would slip glances at her future husband whenever she could without it being too obvious and often caught him doing the same. *He is good-looking like his picture, but I do wish he were taller, like Basilio. When I write Brigida, I will not mention his height, though.*

"Who are you looking for?" Basilio asked as he watched his sister searching the crowd.

"My good friend who was supposed to meet us here. I don't understand why we cannot find each other? The crowd is thinning out so we are easy for her to see us standing here."

When Mina sighted a blonde head in the dwindling crowd, she felt relieved but it was only momentary. It was Bertha, the Polish girl who had travelled alone and was now happily surrounded by her welcoming family. *I'm so glad for Bertha, but where in God's name is Fiona?*

"There is an hour wait between ferries, just a reminder." Carlo seemed to not give much concern for Mina's missing friend, which was not lost on Mina. He seemed to have tired from standing and shifted from one foot to the other. She thought of her brother with his disabled foot politely handling his discomfort uncomplainingly.

"Let's wait just a few more minutes, please," she pleaded. It was not supposed to end this way. Her brother recognized her disappointment and agreed to wait a while longer.

It was a nightmare for the Werner family upon being informed that their son was being denied entry into America. Ernst had been chalked with a large letter 'P'. The physician's opinion was that Ernst's condition was a chronic respiratory one, as the medical professionals bounced around names of conditions such as asthma and pleurisy, pneumonia and tuberculosis.

"The child must return to his country of origin," was the ultimatum given by the medical official in charge and whose word was the last word. There was no appeal available to the immigrant family.

"Das ist bescheuert, ridiculous! How can a four-year-old child return to Germany? What are you saying?" Kurt demanded. He was confused with what was being stated about his four-year old being returned to war-torn Germany.

"We are sorry but the regulations must be strictly enforced when a serious health issue is identified. Your son is a sick child. He suffers with a chronic condition which requires prolonged medical care which disqualifies his entry. I'm very sorry," said the physician through the German interpreter. Even the interpreter was upset having to relay the physician's message knowing he was playing a part in the tragedy that had befallen on the family.

"Bitte,Ich verstehen nicht?" Not understanding, Kurt asked the interpreter, a fellow-countryman, why Ernst could not be treated in the infirmary rather than being deported?

Compassionately, the interpreter explained "Sir, as I am hearing it, your son is too sick for admission into the island's infirmary. Only short-term cases are treated there and these doctors have diagnosed your boy as requiring longer care, convalescent care that could take months. I am so sorry."

"Nein, they are being cruel because we are German," cried an anguished Frau Werner who had listened intently to the interpreter. She began cursing the agents. Her husband told her to hush. He looked at the interpreter hoping he would not pass on her derogatory comments to the doctor. The interpreter did not.

"What happens to us next?" asked Kurt Werner trying to remain as calm as possible and hoping there was some option for them other then returning to Germany. There had to be. His family had come too far to turn back.

"Sir, if your boy was twelve years or older, he could be sent back alone. But he is only four. So, you will have to decide which parent will return with him or if you choose to return as a family."

Kurt and Elke could not have heard anything more devastating. Shocked, they were moved to a quieter area where they were informed that they would have to make the decision quickly. Once the realization set in, they were devastated.

Anguished and confused, both parents looked to each other for solace as to making the right decision. Do they choose to return as a family, or one parent return with Ernst and the other start the new life in America with the daughters?

Even at his young age, Ernst sat shivering with shame knowing that he was the cause of the problem that was causing trouble for his family. His sisters kept kissing him and telling him everything would be better, although they were confused and miserable and had no idea what their parents' final decision would be.

"Schatzi, all will be solved, please do not fret. Momma and Poppa will make a good decision for all of us," said their mother as she tried her best to console her distraught son.

Kurt decided he would return with his son. Trying to sound braver than he really felt, he looked at his tearful son. "Ja, Ernst and I will make the voyage back and it will be easier with just the two of us and no females to worry about, right, Ernst?"

"Nein, Liebling, it cannot be that way. You can earn a living here in America. I cannot. How could I support the girls and myself alone in this country, unable to speak English? You are the one who must stay and carry out our original plan." Elke's rational Germanic nature took over even with a broken heart. She became very stoic and resigned with each word.

Before her husband could argue, Elke continued, "There is no way that I will agree that the whole family return, so do not suggest it, Kurt. We have come too far and sacrificed too much. The practical answer is for Ernst and my return. That is the realistic way to solve this tragedy. You and our daughters must complete the entrance process and establish a home in this country, as unwelcoming as it seems to be for Germans."

Kurt kept disagreeing but he lost every argument he could make. Elke remained adamant and nothing he could say could change her decision. Their daughters began to cry hysterically filled with the anticipatory loss of their mother and brother and even begged to remain together even if it meant everyone returning to Germany.

"Ernst and I will go to my parents' home, we will be fine." But to soften her children's anguish, she added, "and as soon as Ernst is well, we will join you again, I make you that promise. That is why you must help your father to make a nice home that will be ready for our return."

Elke knew it was a promise that could never be kept. It was one desperately needed to be given to her children at that point as they huddled forlornly, shivering in the cold hall with their dream as a family shattered.

Kurt pulled his wife out of the hearing distance of the children. "And what if you cannot find your parents or find mine? Bombing and hunger were already forcing people out of their homes in search of safety even before we left. Then what will you do? I cannot live with your decision, Elke."

"Nein, Kurt, it is the only choice for us," she said stubbornly. Our parents are old and I'm sure that they have not left their homes. We will go home to them. It is the best plan we can make under this horrible outcome. We took the risk knowing our boy was sickly and we lost. At least our daughters will have a safe future that you will create for them."

As they walked back to the children, both parents explained their decision and the logic behind it. Comforting her children, Elke reminded them that someday soon they would be together again. She stated this firmly to give them the hope they needed as she wiped away their tears, as well as her own. She reached for her daughters to smother them in kisses as she knew, even as they did not, it would be the last time she would ever see them or her husband again. Distraught, Kurt knew that, too.

As Elke held Ernst' hand and carried a suitcase in the other, she walked over to the agent in charge of returnees and joined the line of rejected passengers. Her daughters watched their mother and brother leave as they held each other weeping at the sight. Although Elke did not turn around, little Ernst turned to give his sisters one last pitiful wave good-bye.

"Stop, Frau Werner, stop immediately. Do not go through that gate!" Two men were calling out the order to her as they were running up to her and Ernst.

Out of breath from running, Reverend Mayerhoffer, the Lutheran chaplain, accompanied by a supervising federal agent shouted, "We have a solution if you will agree to it."

Stunned but hopeful, everyone was led into a conference room. The minister asked the Werners for their complete trust in order for his proposed solution to work. It had already received approval from the federal staff because of the reverend's respected reputation for his charity work among the immigrants. He explained slowly and in detail that if the Werners signed papers giving Ernst to the orphanage, the child could remain in America where he would be treated medically until his respiratory condition resolves.

"You can visit him every day and as soon as he is well, you sign another paper to 'adopt' your son. Then no one has to return to Germany."

Elke kept thanking God, over and over, still in shock at how the circumstances had changed at the very last minute. Little Ernst was relieved that he and his mother would not have to undergo the dreaded return to Germany even though it still meant he had to separate from them. The reverend carefully explained the plan to him so that he fully understood and would have no fear when he would leave with the minister. The reverend kept reassuring Ernst that the orphanage's hospital section would get him well again so that he could join his family.

The weeping and embracing that followed, after everyone in the family eagerly and gratefully accepted the reverend's plan, was due to relief and love for the man who was a stranger they met in steerage on Sundays and who changed their lives forever.

The preliminary health inspection on Ellis Island was frequently discussed onboard the ship during the voyage. With Winnifred's conjunctivitis, the family coached her to evade detection by having her wear her hat lowered and her eyes looking at the ground as she passed the medical observers.

Jack and the girls became alarmed as soon as Winnie was pulled aside for a closer examination and her coat immediately marked with an E in chalk. They stayed close to her as the family was allowed to continue until the final exam would take place.

"Dear God in heaven, Jack, what do you think will happen next?"

"Winnie, you must stay calm. This will work out, trust me."

When Winnie was led to a line with others who had been chalked, her nervousness could be seen across the room where Jack and the girls waited. Once the doctor completed his exam of Winnie, which he completed within just a minute or two, she was told she would be temporarily detained in the infirmary until her eye infection cleared.

Her husband was called over and given the same news while Winnie burst into tears. Seeing their mother crying, the girls became hysterical thinking the worst.

Jack was already in trouble for unsuccessfully trying to bribe the agents to allow Winnie through, so he knew better than to try to bribe the physician. All considered, he actually felt relief that the decision did not involve deportation as he saw was happening to the German family.

"Darling, please stop crying. This is actually good news. While it does involve a slight delay for you in their infirmary, your eye condition is curable. Think how wonderful that will be after all these weeks of suffering with the infection to have your eyes back to normal? No worries, as I will visit you and take you home as soon as you are discharged. The girls and I will have everything ready for your homecoming. You won't have to lift a finger unpacking or getting the rooms ready. Won't that be grand?" Jack was always convincing if he truly believed in something. And he truly believed in what he was telling Winnie.

But Winnie only half heard her husband. All she knew was that she would be separated from her family and placed in a hospital for the first time in her life, with no one committing to a timeframe for her discharge. She tried to recall some of Jack's last words about coming for her and good news about her eyes but none rang true to her. She could find no good news in the new ordeal she was facing.

Jack tried to allay her fears. "The voyage was the worst and we got through that, didn't we? We will get through this stay in the infirmary, too. Think about the poor souls who are being returned and count our blessings, Winnie. Can you imagine such a horror? We are so fortunate, thank God, that you just need some time in the infirmary that is a thousand times better than steerage, for sure. I would even bet you that the first infirmary meal you eat will be a thousand times better than the one the girls and I will have today with Tim's cooking!" Even now, Jack was able to elicit a smile from Winnie, albeit a slight one that disappeared as quickly as it had come. "So, rest and recover quickly so we can bring you home to New Jersey. Do all my women agree?"

Their daughters stopped crying and hugged their mother while Winnie continued to be anxious and worried. Jack quietly worried, too, not about the infirmary but about Winnie's inability to be alone. She had never been alone having come from a large family and marrying Jack at seventeen. He prayed she would cope. He wrote down Tim's address for her to keep safely in her purse. Then he gave her the money still left in his pocket and told her to use it should she be required to pay for infirmary food. With kisses and wet eyes, the family had to continue through the entry process without her.

As Winnie entered the infirmary, the admitting clerk told her, "This facility is run by the US Public Health Service with highly professional staff, so no worries, Mrs. Turner. You will receive excellent care."

She was taken to the female contagious disease ward where her treatment and recuperation would take place. The ward held twenty beds side-by-side, ten along each wall. She was given a gown to wear and a screen was moved over for her privacy as she undressed. Once in her assigned bed, the screen was removed and she found herself between two non-English speaking patients with only a few feet between their beds. They spoke to each other in Italian which made Winnifred even more lonely with having no one nearby speaking English. She looked around the ward and saw that there were a few patients who appeared to have similar conditions involving eyes. Some wore patches or were bandaged, while some patients were having their eyes irrigated with a medical solution by the nurses.

Loneliness set in and she could not stop her fear and depression which grew instead of diminished, no matter how hard she tried to be brave and accepting of her situation.

She dreaded not having Jack to make decisions and to lead the way. She feared that since she had this eye condition for so long, she worried how long it would require treatment before any improvement would result. She knew she had to do something.

I cannot endure weeks of detention and what if it takes months to cure, not weeks? What if they cannot even cure my eye infection? Do I even have enough money to pay for food and expenses here? What if I run out of money?

God forbid, what if they returned me to Ireland? Would they tell Jack after they sent me back to Ireland and not before? If that were to happen, I would never see my loved ones ever again. I would be lost without my loved ones who are my life!

Winnifred stressed herself to emotional exhaustion. A tenant farmer's wife, she relied on Jack for everything so this became too much for her to bear. She never felt so alone. All her life she was surrounded by her parents and brothers until they died. By then she was married to Jack and then came along the children. She never knew what loneliness was until now.

Then and there, she decided she would have to determine her own fate and not leave it to others. *If I want to be sitting on the front porch of Tim's house sipping black tea, then being here is not going to get me there.* She thought back to how often during the voyage her family studied the maps to learn where their new home was located. With Mina and Fiona, they all became familiar with the locations on the map for Manhattan, New Jersey, and Boston.

In a desperate emotional state and not thinking clearly, she again recalled the map they had studied on the ship. *It is only a short distance to the New Jersey shore from Ellis Island. I can swim it.*

Fiona cleared processing before Mina did. All she knew was that Mina had not caught up to her. Whatever it was that was delaying Mina, Fiona was grateful, as it was making her escape easier. She braced herself knowing that although she was physically a part of the crowd, she was all alone among them. She had lied about a family from Brooklyn. No one was going to be meeting her at the Kissing Post. There was no home in Brooklyn awaiting her.

She glanced over to the waiting area and saw two men whom she guessed were waiting for Mina. The tall one, who looked so much like Mina, had to be her brother. He was just as Mina had described him with his dark good looks and wide smile and openly friendly manner. She could see that, as he awaited his sister, he was politely answering passenger requests for directions to the money exchange booths and the ferries.

Fiona prided herself in being a good judge of men. She observed the second man, who she assumed could be Mina's future husband. Although nice looking and well dressed, he had an air about him as if he found being in the throng of new arrivals was beneath him. She could see it in his facial expression and body language. Even with just a few moments of observation, Fiona knew the type.

But in what position am I to judge, she reminded herself as she set off with her bag, the same expensive carpet bag she had stolen from Madame's closet. She spotted Brian Kelly with his extended family happily talking and walking towards the restaurant area. She was relieved that they were not immediately heading to the ferry as she planned to do. She knew it would not be easy to forget him…with his strong young body and gentle personality.

She knew she would truly miss Mina and she sincerely hoped Mina would have a happy life. *Although she could be a bit spoiled and she did have that most annoying habit of changing her mind*, Fiona knew she would truly miss her friend. The crossing would never have been bearable without Mina's friendship and even her vacillation had been amusing at times. It saddened her to think that both her friends, Margaret and Mina, were lost to her and she was once again alone in the world. For one fleeting moment she again allowed herself to recall how Brian looked at her with longing and affection every time they were together. But she forced herself to erase the visual from her mind's eye because he deserved a girl as innocent as he.

Now I have to make a clean start, she promised herself. She remembered Margaret's favorite quote from Oscar Wilde that 'all saints have a past and all sinners a future.' She clung to that belief as a sinner. *No more prostitution ever again and, eventually, I'll find a way out of the dirty picture business, too. I just need some time and some luck.*

After quickly exchanging her Irish money for American dollars at the Money Exchange, the cashiers pointed to where she would take the ferry to Manhattan. She quickly began to walk away and surrounded herself with other passengers who were hurrying to board the ferry that was already at the dock and already more than half full. She hoped Mina would be further delayed looking for her and would have to catch the next ferry. She agonized over how hard pressed she would be trying to explain the situation should Mina make it to the same ferry.

Her plan worked. The ferry filled up quickly, closed the gang plank and made its way across the water to New York City. Mina would have to wait for the next ferry. As she sailed across the bay, she wondered how Mina was handling both her disappearance and meeting her future husband. How she would have loved to share her thoughts with her as they had done on shipboard on everything.

She felt around herself to ensure that the money hidden in various parts of her clothing and shoes was secure. From her bag, she pulled out the address of the photographer.

During his last visits when Madame had left them alone, the photographer had secretly promised her continuation of the erotic modeling job if she came to New York and, as if to prove the truth of his offer, he had bought her passage ticket and had ensured that there would be a legitimate occupation listed on her traveling papers.

Fiona found his generosity a bit disconcerting. Did he want more from her than posing for his dirty pictures? Fiona knew that she would never allow that to be part of the arrangement.

He told her that his name is Samuel Goldman, that he was born and raised in New York. He said he was unmarried. Being middle aged and in a distasteful occupation, Fiona thought he was probably being truthful. He and Madame had gone into business quite accidentally when he visited her house as a customer. But, as there is no honor among thieves, he apparently had no compunction about cutting Madame out of his business once he lured Fiona out of Ireland. Fiona had accepted his offer. She wanted nothing more than an opportunity out of prostitution even if it meant undressing for provocative pictures. It seemed the lesser of two evils.

Madame still haunted her thoughts. Uninvited, reminders of her sinewy watchfulness and malevolent behavior would come to mind. She wondered how badly Madame took her escape and hoped she did not take her anger out on the others in the house, especially Sugar and Spice. There was a deep sense of relief having three thousand miles of ocean between them but Madame uninvitedly frequented her thoughts

As soon as I am financially able, I will end the shameful picture posing work with Sam, too, and become the woman I was meant to be before the troubles hit.

It was late when they arrived at Basilio's tenement. They had to convert the little amount of Sicilian money Mina had left into dollars at the Money Exchange and then had to buy tickets to Boston at the rail road office. They missed the ferry just as it pulled up the gangplank so there was a wait for the next one.

The train ride was long but Mina was too excited to notice. The two-hundred-dred-mile trip from New York to Boston may be considered uncomfortable by most people but she was relieved to be above ground with fresh air after so many days at sea. As exhausted as she felt, she did not want to lose one minute from viewing out the window at her new country for as long as daylight allowed.

She and Carlo did not speak much. Mina felt shy and was grateful that Basilio carried most of the conversation although she was taken aback by the number of times Carlo seemed to correct Basilio on one matter or another.

Looking continuously out the window helped avoid conversation. To be truthful, Mina was trying to hide her disappointment. She would steal looks at her future husband when he was speaking with her brother. Although he had handsome features, her girlish dream was that the man she would marry would be taller instead of being the same height as she.

When dreams meet reality, dreams usually suffer, Mina thought with a degree of disappointment. If Brigida were here, and she was glad that she was not, she knew that her friend would point out Carlo's height and would also cattily whisper to her, "look how Carlo's hair is already thinning?"

Her disappointment carried over to her new home, as well. The tenement buildings were all row houses made of faded brick and all were five story walk-ups. Basilio's building was located in a dreary area in the North End of Boston.

As she stood outside the building, Mina decided, *I will not complain and I will present a grateful attitude. I will act maturely and not display my disappointment with my new home.* Then, as was her way, Mina changed her mind and complained to her brother and Carlo, instead of following her first inclination to be polite and grateful.

"How long will it take me to adjust to this crowded tenement life? Everything looks old and dirty. I think I will be homesick very quickly."

"Sister, you will adjust but it does take time. Carmela and I count our blessings. We are in America, I am employed, we are healthy and our lives will only get better in time with hard work and determination. You will see, so will yours."

Mina fell silent but had her doubts. She also could not help notice a look of impatience that Carlo gave her but he said nothing.

After climbing the three flights of stairs, Carmela heard them and opened the door. She rushed to greet Mina. They folded each other in a tight embrace. Then Carmela moved to wrap her arms around her husband, smothering him in kisses.

"I'm so relieved that you are home safe and sound." Mina stared at them thinking *I want a marriage like theirs.*

"Carmela, you are finally getting to meet Carlo. And Carlo, my wife, Carmela.," Basilio said introducing them as Mina watched for reactions.

"Welcome, Carlo, please sit down. You all must be tired and hungry." As she brought the pasta, wine and bread to the table, Carmela kept surreptitiously sneaking glances at Carlo. She could not wait to hear Mina's reaction of this stranger to whom she is promised in marriage. *At least I knew Basilio when our parents arranged our marriage, thank goodness,* she could not help think.

Trying not to be impolite, Mina glanced around her new home as inconspicuously as possible. She couldn't count more than two rooms. Both rooms were dingy looking and the furniture sparse. She glanced at the smallest kitchen area Mina had ever seen and a closed door which she imagined led to the couple's bedroom. The main room in which they were all seated had a table and 4 chairs and a small dresser in a corner. She could see that part of the living room had been separated by a blanket hanging on a clothesline across the width of the room which she assumed was prepared for her since it was obvious that there was no second bedroom. She was horrified about her loss of any privacy and Carmela picked up on her distress.

"Let the men drink their grappa, Mina, and we will talk together in my bedroom where we can have some privacy." A bottle of the liquor was set on the table as the dishes were cleared by the women. The men could be heard discussing their jobs and politics as the women adjourned to the bedroom. Mina quickly realized that she would only be able to speak English with her brother but even then, not all the time because Carmela only spoke Italian, as did Carlo and the building's inhabitants. This was concerning to her after all the effort she had made to learn English and it seemed like a step backwards.

With the door closed, Carmela explained that the sleeping area they arranged for her would only be for a short time. Soon she will be married and have her own apartment. Behind the hanging curtain, there was a mattress on the floor and a few hooks in the wall on which to hang her clothes. Her suitcase would have to serve as a dresser for her smaller items of clothing.

"The weeks before the wedding will go by quickly, you will see. I bet Carlo's apartment is larger than ours and since everyone knows about his family connections, he probably receives some extra income from his family, too."

"Carlo has no mafia connections, Carmela, surely Basilio told you that. His family has demanded that he lead an honest life as his father gave his word to mine or there would have been no marriage."

Carmela wanted to believe her sister-in-law but had her doubts. Instead, girlishly, Carmela was eager to know what Mina thought of Carlo and asked her.

"I wish he were taller, like Basilio, but so far he seems polite and smart. The next few weeks will allow us to learn more about each other, I'm sure."

Carmela was surprised at how Mina had grown in maturity since last seeing her three years ago. It was a relief to hear her positive reaction to a man who will be so important to her in her future.

As Carlo prepared to leave he gave Mina a chaste kiss on her cheek, and said "Mina, I promise you a wonderful future."

"Thank you, Carlo. And I promise you that I will be a wonderful wife. Will I see you soon?"

"Of course," he promised but it was almost a week before they met again. Mina hoped that he was not disappointed in her. *Could that be possible? Could he have found her disappointing as she had found him for being shorter than she hoped?*

Her brother's concern centered around the talk at work of Carlo's gambling every night but he kept silent about it. *I cannot judge until I have more information. Besides, if he is always winning money, then that would be a good thing, not a bad one.*

That first night, after Carlo left, Carmela took Mina downstairs to the toilets. The tenement's outhouses were located in an alleyway and consisted of a rectangular wooden building with four doors next to each other. Men and women were using any door that became available. The seats in each compartment were divided by only a thin wood wall so privacy was next to impossible which had Mina troubled. She never experienced anything like this in Sciacca. Lines had already formed so Carmela spent the waiting time introducing Mina to neighbors already in line around them. Everyone she met was Sicilian. She heard no one speaking English.

"We have a chamber pot under our bed and I put one out for you, too, Mina, but it is preferable not to use it unless necessary, such as in the middle of the night. Frankly, it is dangerous to come out here after dark and certainly you are never to come out alone. Besides, you will see the trouble involved in emptying these pots each morning, carrying the full pots down the stairs to be emptied in the privies in the alley. Some lazy people actually empty them by tossing the contents out the windows instead of using the privy for disposal, which is just awful! That's why you are to remember to always walk closer to the street and not close to the buildings when you are outside."

The lesson continued. "Each night the city's cleaners come to take the 'night soil' away in trucks so you may hear the noise since our apartment is on the side of the alley. But the good news is that everyone has running water up to our third floor. Those on the fourth and fifth floors do not and so we are very fortunate for that…and because of that we have a higher rent."

As Carmela was speaking, an elderly woman finished her turn at the privy and noticed Carmela waiting in line.

"Carmela, how are you?" she asked in between a bout of coughing.

"I'm well, Mrs. Jacobs. Are you not well?"

"Oh, this cough? It comes and goes. Don't grow old, Carmela."

"Please, I want you to meet my sister-in-law, Philomena. She just arrived a few hours ago all the way from Sicily."

"Nice to meet you but you may call me Mina, Mrs. Jacobs."

"How are you getting along, Mrs. Jacobs, with winter almost here?" Carmela asked with some concern.

"Winter and all the seasons bring me 'tsuris'. Girls, that's the Yiddish word for 'trouble'. In this building we are either freezing or melting."

"No time for chit-chat," yelled an irritated voice further down in the waiting line.

"You are right, we apologize," the old woman responded to the unfriendly person while whispering to Carmela, "come visit me soon, please, I will make you delicious Kreplach soup."

Mrs. Jacobs lived on the third floor, too, not far from Carmela's apartment. As they watched the old humped woman carefully hold onto the wall for balance as she walked away, Carmela wondered how much longer she would be able to navigate all the steps to her apartment.

"Kreplach soup?" Mina asked.

"She's a Jew but a nice one. I'm sure that's a Jewish soup and I'm sure it will taste fine. Did you notice how perfectly she speaks our language?"

"Si. Are there many Jews in this building?" Mina inquired. She couldn't remember even one living in Sciacca.

"No, I think she is the only one. She puts up with a great deal of discrimination in our building so I'm sorry for her. She should have left years ago when the Jews left the North End for better places. Sad to say, but I think it will take us Sicilians a longer time than the Jews to move out of the tenements."

Mina could not breathe because of the stench in the toilet area once her turn came. She held her breath as long as she could and rushed to quickly escape back upstairs once she was finished. She rushed so quickly that she forgot to hold the door open for the person next on line, as was the custom. She pretended not to hear the disparaging remark aimed at her.

A small mongrel dog loitered near the entranceway of the building. Mina bent to pet it. It distanced itself away from her but it was wagging its tail as if it was considering whether Mina was safe. *Poor animal probably has good reasons not to trust people*, Mina reasoned.

But before Mina could call the dog to her, Carmela stopped her.

"Don't, Mina! It is not a pet. Its job is to catch the rats. It always begs for food but there are enough rats to keep its stomach full. Promise me you will not become attached to this animal. No one can afford pets."

"I promise, Carmela," Mina replied in her little girl voice but already knew she didn't mean it having grown up with pet dogs and cats.

"St. Francis will protect it," Carmela added, hoping that would satisfy the younger girl as they began the accent to the third floor.

"Carmela, you are a font of knowledge when it comes to the saints, aren't you?"

As she pictured the stray dog in her mind, Mina couldn't help thinking that St. Francis wasn't doing a very good job for the starving little animal. It looked like it needed much more than prayer to survive the coming winter.

True to her reputation, Carmela half-jokingly stated that they should pray to Santa Bibiana, patron saint for hang- overs and headaches considering all the grappa the men had been drinking lately as wedding plans were being finalized.

After seeing Mina roll her eyes, Carmela reminded her, "You need to appreciate the saints, Mina. You were named after Saint Philomena, known for her modesty, remember that."

"How could I ever forget. Between you and my mother, it's a miracle I'm not a nun."

The two spent some time discussing Carlo. Carmela felt relief that Mina expressed complete joy with everything about her future husband, but she didn't believe her. Even in the short time he spent at dinner last night, Carmela found some behavior with which she was uncomfortable, such as his arrogance and his talking over Basilio every time her husband had something to say. *Maybe I'm being too defensive of Basilio,* she thought, promising to give herself more time to get to know Carlo.

"Time to get oriented to how we do things here, Mina," Carmela said cheerfully. She began by teaching Mina how housekeeping and laundering were done in the tenement building which was quite different from the homeland. Mina tried her best to be a good student as she knew she would soon have a wife's responsibility herself after the wedding. She learned tenement life which included the workings of the stove, the procuring of ice for the icebox and how to wash and hang wet clothes from the kitchen window as early as possible in the morning in order to have the laundry dry during the day.

118

The weight of carrying the wet laundry up the tenement stairs from the wash room was very exhausting but carrying full chamber pots down three flights of stairs to be emptied in the privies was her most dreaded task. She never realized how much easier tasks were in Sciacca when compared to the tenements.

"And you must be on your guard at all times in the hallways. They are dark and sometimes there are homeless people sleeping in them who would not hesitate to hurt you. Remember that."

"I can hear children in the hallways right now," voiced Mina.

"There are mothers who work nights who put their children out in the halls so that they can sleep for a few hours in the morning. It is unsafe as children have fallen down stairs but it is what it is when people are poor, Mina. There are other terrible things that I hate to speak of."

"Tell me, Carmela, I will need to know if I am going to live here."

After hesitating, Carmela explained, "Horribly, some children are sent out at night to sell themselves. I've even seen one little boy who wears a girl's dress to sell himself to perverts. But with his father's death, he is responsible to earn money for his family in this terrible way or they would starve. Anyway, there are many good things here and I promise you that they outweigh the bad ones."

Stunned by the mention of children prostituting themselves, Mina asked, "so what are the good things about this building?"

"Sicilians try to care for one another as much as possible. You will see women visiting the sick or caring for children when mothers must work. Our men provide some security, since the police never venture into the tenements unless forced to for a serious crime."

"Are there ever serious crimes?"

"Rarely anything that requires the police except last year when a husband murdered his wife on the fifth floor. He's in prison now and a new family moved in after that. Poverty and living on the highest floor with no running water and all those stairs to walk up and down all day only contributes to misery."

Mina was delighted when Carmela changed the subject and told her, "Let's go out today to the markets where you will learn shopping in our Little Sicily. It will get us out into the fresh air and into the sunlight, just like when we were home shopping in the village."

Carmela introduced her to the fruit and vegetable merchants and olive oil storekeepers, the butcher and the Italian bakery and the numerous pushcart peddlers. Together they walked through the Italian North End section of Boston where Carmela explained which stores were honest and which overcharged.

As Carmela was choosing peppers, a young Negro girl approached the vegetable cart. As she began to select tomatoes, in broken English, the Sicilian vendor said to her in a rude tone, "don't they sell tomatoes in your part of town?"

"This is America so the whole country is my 'part of town'." Her demeanor became defiant.

"Not here, it's not," as he took the tomato that she was holding from her hand. "I'm tired of you people stealing from my cart when my back is turned."

Taking Mina by surprise, Carmela joined in the conversation telling the vendor in Sicilian "how come it is alright for her Negro men to fight and die in the war overseas right now but you

can't sell her tomatoes? If you want to sell vegetables to me then you better sell her those tomatoes."

He returned the tomato to the black woman grudgingly and watched her deliberately choose a few more. He grudgingly bagged her order and took her money without another word said. He had no intention of losing a good customer like Carmela.

The young woman turned to Carmela." I don't know what you told that man but thank you for your good deed. I wish there were more white people like you." Once Mina translated to Carmela what the girl said, she was gone as quickly as she had arrived.

Carmela and the vendor continued to give each other the evil-eye looks, as only Sicilians can do, but she bought many vegetables from him anyway.

"He has the freshest vegetables even though he is a strunz," Carmela whispered to Mina, making them both laugh as they continued down the crowded street.

Mina loved the excitement of the streets crowded with shoppers and horses and delivery wagons but mostly the number of automobiles. Except for the Don's, rarely was an automobile ever seen in Sciacca. As they neared the harbor, Carmela warned that this area near the docks and warehouses was to be avoided.

"With sailors being sailors, there are houses of ill repute, gambling and much drunkenness around here, so decent women stay far away. It is too unsafe."

They continued walking to the garment business area where almost all the factories and shops were owned by Jews. There were tailor shops, stores with elegant bonnets and feathered hats and fashionable dresses in the windows.

There was even a large jewelry store. Mina window- shopped eagerly and wishfully. She had never seen the likes of such displays of fashions for both men and women. Fiona asked about a store selling wedding dresses.

"Mina, didn't Basilio speak with you about this? You will be wearing my wedding dress because we haven't any other choice financially. You understand, right?"

Mina gave not so much a smile as a lift of her dark eyebrows. "I understand, Carmela," although she immediately thought of another option. *I am definitely going to ask Carlo to buy my wedding dress. He will do it, even if he has to ask his father for money. I really want my own wedding dress.*

During the voyage, all she dreamed of was the wedding gown made with yards of luminous taffeta tight at the waist and stiff at the elbows and, in it, she would look like a fashion model in her dream dress.

But suddenly, she had an inexplicable premonition that Carlo would refuse and embarrass her for asking. It made her uncomfortable that she felt this way about him. So, she changed her mind.

"Of course, Carmela, I am very grateful to be able to wear your dress. I remember how lovely you looked in it."

"Mina, I am sure that you will look even prettier in it than I did!"

Unkindly, Mina thought, *I have no doubt about that.*

One morning after Basilio left for work and the morning chores had been completed, Carmela asked Mina if she would like to visit Mrs. Jacobs.

"Is she the old woman we met by the toilets on my first night here?"

"Yes, Mina. She is a very educated Polish Jew who repeats herself and tells the same stories over again so you must be patient. Sometimes, because of this, I limit my visits because she can keep you there all day if she can. She has been widowed for many years and is all alone in this world. Sadly, she and her husband never had children but I think that she was left enough savings from all their years of frugality that she doesn't seem as hard pressed as most of us in this building. She very often has groceries delivered to her which must be costly."

Upon hearing this, Mina thought of her own parents back in Sicily. "Carm, do you wonder about your parents as I do about ours. With Basilio and me here in America, I worry as they grow older and if one were to die, the other would be left alone."

"Thanks to God, there is less worry for me because my brothers and sisters are still in Sciacca. And, as I've assured your brother many times, your parents are our family, too, so mine will care for them as their own. You need not worry."

With that, Carmela had immediately lightened Mina's guilt so she was able to brush away the depressing thought of her parents being alone. Carmela had the gift of being able to make someone feel better. It was just one of her many endearing qualities. *That had to be Basilio's reason for choosing her over the many beauties in the village who did everything but throw themselves at his feet.*

"Mrs. Jacobs speaks our language but also a few others. Sometimes she mixes them up so be polite and pretend you don't notice."

Mrs. Jacob's apartment was neat but not clean. She was too disabled to bend and wash floors. Because of her age and the distance to the outside bathrooms, the odor from the unemptied chamber pots permeated the apartment. Although she owned nice pieces of furniture, the dust was thick on them. There were numerous books everywhere, some even in small piles on the floor.

To Mina's delight, she learned that the elderly woman was fluent in English in addition to her native Polish, Yiddish and Italian.

"My Irving taught me English and Italian," she boasted of her late husband.

"God rest his soul, he brought us to America from Poland for a new life away from the persecutions which killed our families. His father was a highly educated rabbi and head of a school for boys before the night of terror when our village was torched. He provided Irving with an incredible education. In time, and through his own perseverance, Irv found a translator position at the Boston Harbor Immigration building. With his knowledge of many languages, he worked translating for the agents and the immigrants. I was so proud of him."

Mina thought back to the amazing work of the translators she met on Ellis Island when she arrived. Overworked and, no doubt, underpaid, these men allowed the new arrivals to hear the questions and orders in their own language, eliminating any communication problems with the agents.

"He knew it was necessary for me to learn English, as well as Italian living in the North End. Our goal was to move when our Jewish neighbors were moving out but we waited too long, and then Irving died. So, here I remain with my memories. Anyway, I use my Italian all the time now but I have no one with whom to practice English," she lamented, "so sometimes I talk to myself in English. I'm sure that's why some people in this building think I'm a crazy old lady," she said with a forced smile.

"So that is why I have a proposition for Mina if Basilio will approve." Mina felt a bit peeved that the old woman continued addressing Carmela directly, as if Mina wasn't even in the room.

"That depends on your request, Mrs. Jacobs. Everyone knows that you can take the boy out of Sicily but you cannot always take Sicily out of the boy," smiled Carmela. "Like all Sicilian men, he is very protective of the women in his family. But I am curious, so tell me what you are thinking."

"If Mina would be willing to run some errands and some housework for me, I can pay wages for her work. For free, if she would like, I can have her reading and writing English in just a few months.... and we can work on getting rid of that Irish brogue she developed from her voyage!"

"I accept the job and would love English lessons, Mrs. Jacobs," was the excited answer from Mina, not waiting for a response from her sister-in-law.

"And it will be good for me, too, being able to practice the language again with another person. At my age, one must keep the mind engaged or lose it," she added, winking at the teenager.

"Carmela, you remember you refused my offer to teach you last year. I accepted your explanation then that you saw no reason being surrounded by everyone here speaking the native tongue. However, if you would change your mind, then my proposal is open to you, as well."

Unlike Mina, Carmela was not one to ever change her mind once she made a decision. She was comfortable with her 'small life', as she called it, in her Sicilian populated building and with the Sicilian-speaking vendors where she shopped.

"With whom would I speak English even if I learned?" Carmela reiterated once again with a finality in her tone. "However, I can agree that it would prove to be meaningful for Mina, especially since it would build on what she has learned from our pastor in Sciacca and during her voyage. It would be a shame for her to lose what she has already learned."

Mina was taken aback and delighted that she realized that she had Carmela's agreement to work part time for the Jewish lady. *That is all I needed,* knowing how Basilio rarely disagrees with anything Carmela recommends.

Maybe Carmela is smarter than I imagined, mused Mina. *Although she refuses to learn English herself, she recognizes the value for those who do want to learn.*

Mina persisted, "please let's not even tell Basilio. It will only be a few hours a day while Basilio is at work. Imagine when I can surprise him and Carlo with my new ability to speak, read and write English fluently and at the same time earn some money assisting Mrs. Jacobs. After that, I will able to help improve Basilio's and Carlo's English, too."

"Mina, I can see the value in this arrangement. Frankly, any money that you can earn will be a very helpful addition to your household. But remember, even if we keep this from Basilio, in a few weeks it will be Carlo who will have to give you permission to continue, you realize that, right? From just the few hours spent with him, my impression is that he tends to be very

traditional in his belief that a wife's place is in the home. I hope I am wrong since I can see how badly you want to do this."

"Thank you, Carmela, this means so much to me," Mina said hugging her and then hugging Mrs. Jacobs.

Mina was relieved that Carmela did not oppose the plan and agreed to keep it their secret for the time being. Carmela's warning regarding Carlo's questionable permission continued to bother her so she decided to postpone thinking about it. She would cross that bridge later. *Maybe I'll ask him a short time following the wedding. Then we will be happy newlyweds and, like Basilio with Carmela, he won't deny me anything I ask.* Growing up, she always won her way with her parents and her brothers, so she was convinced it would not be any different with a husband.

As they returned to the apartment, Carmela explained Boston's North End history. "You need to understand where you now live. This region had origi- nally been settled by Irish and Jewish immigrants. Eventually, assimilating into society and finding better jobs, these groups moved to the West and South Ends of the city, leaving most of the North End to Sicilian new comers like us." Carmela seemed to stop at that point.

"Go on, Carmela, this is interesting."

"Well, in Boston the Irish have been rising from poverty for years by en- tering politics where they often have the majority voting numbers and in public service jobs with many finding positions in police and fire departments and the military. It is harder for our men to compete with

those who arrived years before us and who only hire their own kind when good union jobs become available. So, for now, most of our men can only hope to find placement as laborers or barbers and vendors."

"What about the Jews? There were a few on our ship."

"The Jews are more fortunate, for the most part. They arrive in America with marketable skills, such as being tailors and butchers, so they are often more able to prosper in less time than other immigrants. Many have family and friends already in America who advocated for them and often the syna- gogues provide assistance to the new arrivals. Most admirable about them is that Jewish parents are known to make their children's education their priority, resulting in many entering professional fields. Then, as the children become doctors, lawyers and all types of other professionals, they move their parents out of the tenements to better neighborhoods."

"So why is Mrs. Jacobs still here?"

"As I told you, unfortunately, she never had children. When her husband died there was no family to help her move out of the North End when all the Jews were leaving for other parts in Boston. I don't believe there are any friends still alive, either, because no one ever visits her. Frankly, being a Jew in this building has left her quite isolated. Sicilians can be very anti -Semitic, as you know. However, she has lived frugally and everyone believes that her husband must have left savings because she doesn't seem to struggle financially. There were rumors that her apartment was robbed a few times when she was out shopping but that no money was ever found. However, I do pray to St. Paul for her conversion to our true faith and you should, too, Mina."

Carmela and her saints, again! Mina thought.

"Well, if you have taught me anything, Carmela, it is that Carlo and I had better make our children's education our priority. Isn't that what you and Basilio intend to do?"

Looking sad, Carmela answered with, "First we have to have children." Mina was angry with herself for her insensitivity knowing that for three years they had been trying.

Every Sunday, Mina attended Mass at St. Leonard's Church on Pine Street with Carmela and Basilio. It was the first church in Boston to serve Italian parishioners. Mina's church wedding was planned to be performed in June with a Sicilian priest officiating the ceremony. That gave everyone a comfortable feeling, reminiscent of weddings at home in Sciacca.

Carmela frequently stopped at the church on weekdays. One day after shopping with Mina, Carmela asked if she would like to stop in the church to say a prayer or to light a candle.

"You see, I try to visit our church whenever I can because I pray to Saint Felicity for a son."

"Then I will pray to her for you, too," said Mina.

Mounting the church's front steps, they entered the church's marble vestibule. Carmela was wearing a head scarf but realized that Mina was bareheaded. *Just like the young who hate to cover their pretty hair,* Carmela thought.

Carmela removed the scarf worn at her neck and offered it to Mina to use as a covering for her head.

"On second thought, Carmela, I would prefer to wait outside and enjoy the sunshine, if that is alright with you. Sunday mass is really enough church for me."

Although not pleased with this, Carmela was too tired from all the walking they had done to argue so she entered the church and crossed herself at the holy water font. Once she genuflected before moving into a pew, she bowed her head in silent prayer. The darkened interior of the church was lit with the flicker of the candles arranged in various areas in the church and by the streaks of sunlight that found their way through the large stained -glass windows, each commemorating a bible story. Carmela was delighted when some of the sunlight beamed down on her just in the spot where she knelt, almost surrounding her with a halo as seen in pictures of the saints. She bathed herself in this unexpected gift of warm sunlight and was enjoying the lingering fragrance of incense from an earlier ceremony.

Then Mina startled her when she bumped her way into the pew, noisily kneeling and wearing a handkerchief balanced on her head as a cover. *This is exactly what Basilio described when he warned me to be patient and accept Mina's exasperatingly odd habit of frequently changing her mind*, sighed Carmela.

As Mina looked around, she noticed how exactly alike the church was with her Duomo at home, only not so old. The same life-sized statues, the beautiful altar and the stations of the cross around the church's walls were exactly like the church Mina's family attended every Sunday in Sicily.

Situated in various pews scattered around the church, elderly women could be seen reciting their rosaries. With the morning masses over, the women whispered the Hail Mary repeatedly, creating a comforting chorus of prayer.

Mina turned her head to watch Carmela who was praying with her eyes shut tightly and her lips slightly moving. As a yawn overtook her, Mina closed her eyes, too, but not in prayer.

June, 1918

Just hours away from the wedding ceremony, a heavy North- Easter stormed into the North End. As Mina dressed for the wedding she whined to Carmela about the weather.

"This is terrible. We will be drenched before we even make it to the church's vestibule. Our dresses will be soaked and our hair ruined!"

"Some say a rainy wedding day brings good luck to the couple," said Carmela, always the optimist. Carmela had just finished her blue matron-of-honor dress the day before and was adding a matching ribbon to her hair.

Suddenly, the sun appeared brilliantly through the window. As Mina ran to look out, she could see the steam rising from the wet cracked sidewalks and small areas of yellowed grass. It had been seasonally hot last few days in June.

"Carmela, now that the rain is gone, is my good luck gone, too?" asked Mina teasingly, yet very relieved that now their walk to the church wouldn't leave her a bedraggled mess.

"The sun came out because the good Lord couldn't take any more of your complaining, Mina. And this is still a lucky day for you, rain or shine." Carmela hoped that it was true. No matter how hard she tried, Carmela did not like Carlo Vitale, but never said anything to Mina or Basilio.

"I think back to your wedding to Basilio in Sciacca. Birds were chirping and bunnies running in the grass while everyone of the guests danced and ate so merrily. I remember the pretty lights your Papa hung around the garden as the sun set and the evening descended and the celebration went on into the night. Your wedding was magical, Carmela. I have only inner-city concrete for my celebration."

"Shame on you, Mina. Today you will have a husband who will love you. And your brother and I have a wonderful party awaiting you and Carlo here in our home after the ceremony. You should be grateful for all your blessings," Carmela reprimanded her as she lost patience with Mina.

There was no full-length mirror in the apartment. Frustrated, Mina maneuvered herself around different angles using a hand mirror. In her home in Sciacca, a person could view oneself from head to foot in her grandmother's antique full-length mirror, even with its faded glass.

Mina sighed. Even with the alterations that had to be made in order to have Carmela's wedding dress fit her, the fit wasn't perfect. Mina, being taller, could see the hemline was still too short. And Mina's bustline was half the size of Carmela's well - endowed bosom, so there was too much extra room in the bodice. But all was forgotten once Carmela fixed the simple lace mantilla on Mina's head.

"The lace mantilla makes me feel like a princess. It is so beautiful!"

"Good, now are you happier? Put on the new shoes we bought with the money your parents sent."

"Just as I predicted. You look even prettier in my wedding dress than I did," chirped Carmela with genuine love for her sister-in-law and trying to elevate Mina's mood again.

"Thank you, Carmela." But out of Carmela's sight, Mina made a face. Then realizing how much she owed Carmela, she summoned a happy expression that conveyed her appreciation.

"And remember that the dress comes back to me for my future daughter," said a hopeful Carmela who was old fashioned.

"Of course, Carmela." *But Mina imagined that the modern girls in years to come will not be wearing anything like this shapeless dress with its matronly sleeves and high neckline."*

Following the ceremony at Saint Leonard's church, the reception was held at her brother's apartment. A large custard and fruit wedding cake was being served. It was Mrs. Jacobs generous gift, ordered from the local Italian bakery. Carmela served Italian coffee with it. Basilio used some of their savings to purchase wine and beer and noticed that some of Carlo's friends brought grappa and rye whiskey. Attendees were a mixture of tenement neighbors, friends and co-workers and the parish priest, Father Martino, who married them.

As with most social gatherings, the women and men separated into their own groups. The women gossiped and the men talked baseball.

"Do you really think that women will get the vote?" questioned a young woman who lived on the floor above Carmela.

"I certainly think it will happen soon," replied Mrs. Jacobs, always eager to discuss politics."

Only a few of the younger women ever brought up political issues as they did laundry together. They followed the news closely while the majority of the other women relied on the common Sicilian survival strategy to stay detached and uninvolved. Just as had been done in Sicily, most left it to the men.

"Let's change the conversation, please. I prefer we talk about our building's problems," voiced a neighbor who lived on the top floor. "The rats are worse than ever and did I hear that the iceman is refusing to deliver ice to the fifth floor?"

In one of the men's groups, an older man who worked with Basilio was overheard saying, "What about those Red Sox, uh? At Fenway the other day, I heard talk about them selling Babe

Ruth to the Yankees, for Christ sake! They do that, then the only championships will be for the Yankees is all I can say."

As Mina observed the visitors she noticed that Basilio's friends attended with their wives but all of Carlo's friends came alone. He introduced her to Mario, who he called his "best friend."

Mina wanted to like him but he immediately made her uncomfortable in the way he seemed to leer at her. He blatantly looked her up and down until his eyes settled on her chest as if he were calculating her measurements in his head. She was relieved when Carlo put his hand on her elbow and led her across the room saying he wanted to greet a special guest.

A well-dressed man sat in a chair while those around him were taking in his every word as if Pope Benedict was making an address to an audience from the Vatican balcony.

"Signor Lazio, this is my wife, Philomena. We thank you so much for coming to our small celebration. It means very much to us". Mina noticed her husband making a slight but still noticeable bow to the gentleman as he spoke. The strange gesture made her uncomfortable.

"Congratulations to you both and I wish you many happy years. Carlo, please let your father know that I was here and paid my respects," he said with a thick Corleone accent.

He then got up to leave after handing his empty wine glass to one of the men around him.

Carlo led Mina back towards Carmela and the other women when she asked "Who is that man?"

"That man is a Capo and, if you don't know what that is, then let me educate you. He is a senior member of the local mafia family. I hope that his coming here is a good sign for me."

"He said that he was here out of respect for your father."

Annoyed, Carlo resisted the urge to scold Mina. It was their wedding day and there would be ample time to train his wife later to either agree with him or say nothing.

"Carlo, are all your friends still bachelors?" Mina inquired with a playfully crooked grin. "I see no wives, not even girlfriends."

"They aren't as lucky as I am," he responded squeezing his new wife as they both laughed together.

Mina was proud when she later learned that Carlo had shared half the expense of the wine and beer with Basilio, who could never have afforded it alone.

Why did I change my mind when I originally thought to ask Carlo to buy me a wedding dress? she thought regretfully as she looked down at Carmela's dress with the stain on the hem that they had labored unsuccessfully to remove.

After the reception ended and Carmela refused Mina's offer to clean up, the couple walked hand in hand to Carlo's apartment. Mina happily looked forward to her new married life. Before they made love that night, he presented her with a gold necklace that had been his mother's. She had sent it to him so that he could give it to Mina as his wedding gift. She lovingly wore it to bed that night and rarely ever removed it.

"Every time you touch it, let it remind you of our love," he had said, surprising Mina with a poetic side she would never have guessed he had.

She thought she would have been bashful that first night but she wasn't. Maybe it was her hot Sicilian blood but for so long she had looked forward to finally experiencing the act she believed would be romantic and fulfilling between lovers and not the 'unpleasant wife's duty', described by the old women.

She changed into a white night gown, deliberately purchasing one that was so sheer that the nipples of her breasts and her dark pubic hair could be seen through the thin fabric. Nothing was hidden. She appeared before Carlo giving him a full view of her young and willing body as she turned in a slow circle displaying herself to him in the gaslight.

For her that night the love making act was over too quickly. She knew there had to be more to it than what had just taken place. Mina attributed Carlo's lack of energy to all the alcohol he drank at the reception with his friend Mario. In retrospect, it seemed that Mario had been deliberately encouraging Carlo to overdrink.

Although he was gentle with her, knowing it was her first time, it lacked the passion that she and Brigida had read about in books secretly obtained from Brigida's older sisters. She remembered how they would sit in her father's field hidden among the wildflowers and would read aloud the exciting passages in the books that would make them swoon and giggle while bees around them went from one blossom to the next and the cries of the seagulls could be heard in the harbor below.

Our love making will be better next time, I know it will, she convinced herself.

A week later, following dinner at Basilio's apartment, the newlyweds encountered two teenage boys in the alley tormenting the dog that Mina befriended against Carmela's admonition. Each day after working for Mrs. Jacobs, Mina would feed the dog with scraps saved from their lunch.

"Carlo, please stop them," she pleaded. "How can they be so mean to a helpless dog?"

As she was about to run into the alley herself, Carlo held her back. "Stay here," he ordered.

He grabbed one boy with his powerful arm and cursed the other as he ran out of his reach. "My wife feeds that dog and if anything happens to it, I'll get you. I am Cosa Nostra and I will find you," he said threateningly, as he released the boy after a strong shaking. The boys ran in one direction while the dog ran in the opposite one.

Mina kissed her husband affectionately. Whether he demonstrated a genuine kindness for animals or just addressed her request, she was pleased with him. *He has his faults but at moments like this I cannot help but love him.*

"Your lie about being part of Cosa Nostra worked, Carlo," she said with a smile. "You really scared them".

Carlo did not answer but took her hand again as they continued walking home in a comfortable silence.

Sam asked why Fiona never asked to see the pictures he had taken of her. "You are so beautiful in these, Fiona. You make a man's heart race just looking at your lovely body."

"I never want to see any of them, Sam, so never bring it up again," she said adamantly "You know that, so why do you keep asking?"

"OK, but I'm proud of my work. Let's talk about something else then."

Then Fiona sneezed.

"Zol zein gezunt!" exclaimed Sam.

"What did you say? I never heard you speak anything but English."

"Oh, I still remember some of my childhood Yiddish for 'bless you'. Don't tell me you are coming down with a cold?"

"Since you keep me mostly naked all day, is it any surprise if I am?" Fiona answered truculently.

Sam hesitated for a moment as if he had to make a decision.

"I been thinkin', how about I take you out on the town? Al Jolson has a new show at the Winter Garden. I love his songs, especially when he wears blackface and gets down on his knees and belts out a song with his whole heart in it. One of my favorites is 'Mammy'. Have you ever heard it?"

"No, Sam, I have not. As I just told you, I'm too tired after removing my clothes for your dirty pictures every day to do anything else," she said sarcastically.

"All the more reason we should go see a show. What do you think?"

"Your invitation does sound nice. I guess if I intend to be an American, I better learn American songs." *As long as Sam doesn't try to make this more than it will ever be between us,* she thought.

"You know Al Jolson's a Jew like me and his real name is Asa Yoelson. All these stars try to hide being Jewish but I don't fault him for it," as Sam relayed the additional information about the celebrity. "It's a mean world out there for us Jew boys," spoken as if from personal experience.

Sam made a promise to Fiona that at the end of each week he would treat her to a night out. It was a treat for Fiona since every night after modeling for Sam, she would pick up some food from a corner deli and retreat to her rented room until the next working day when she would repeat the same.

"Fiona, you need to get out and see the sights of the city," encouraged her land lady, Mrs. Murphy. Fiona, lived in a boarding house for young women. Mrs. Murphy only rented to respectable and employed women with references required. Sam had made it possible for her by producing two references. The first was a letter of recommendation from a non-existent priest in Ireland and then working papers stating Fiona was a secretary in his photography shop.

If Mrs. Murphy ever learned what I really did in the photography shop, she would have a heart attack on the spot, Fiona speculated.

Each evening after work, Fiona would arrive at the house and freshen up in the immaculately kept water closet shared by the renters. She would wash away the grit and ash of the city's streets from her face and hands. Then she would undress and remove her constricting corset, not that she needed a corset but it was the fashion. She would don the silk robe that Sam had given her as a birthday gift.

"Since you are so secretive about your actual birthday, this gift should suffice on this made-up birthday date," he had told her jokingly one day.

"Why not since everything else about me is made-up," she responded with tongue in cheek. She appreciated Sam's thoughtfulness which made it easier to work with him. He never pried into her early past. From meeting her at Madame's, he knew enough about her as it was.

Once comfortable in her room, she would spread out the newspaper which connected her with the world around her. She looked forward to reading every page to learn everything she could about the local and world news. Whenever there was an article on Ireland, she would read it carefully as she still felt a connection, no matter how she tried to renounce it now that she was in America. Dublin had so many sad memories for her. Some scorched as deeply in her mind as the burning tar that had scorched her father's body.

When she read that Britain, being dangerously short of troops in May, had planned an imposed conscription of Irishmen to send to the Western Front, she became enraged. She was relieved that her brothers were too young for drafting. The article read that anti-conscription pledges had been nailed to the front doors of churches while Irish politicians and labor unions refused to comply should the bill become law. Britain had even tried to sway French bishops to encourage the Irish to enlist in the French army, if not the British army, 'in order to defend fellow Catholics in France and Belgium suffering from the German invasion'. Their plan failed. However, the article added that Irish recruitment was becoming less important with America having entered the war.

"I can only imagine how my parents would have fought this had they lived," she mumbled to herself, proud of them but still angry with them, at the same time.

Since 1916, the Huiman Company Recruiters were paid by the British government to recruit thousands of Chinese laborers to supplement the shortage of Allied forces fighting the war. Even with the Americans having joined the war in 1917, the British military needed help urgently. The mandatory Irish Conscription law failed to pass Parliament and Russian forces pulled out of the war when the Marxist revolution resulted in a treaty with Germany in March, 1918. Chinese recruitment was the military's answer to finding labor manpower.

Hong Kong had malaria outbreaks that prevented recruitment there, but the other provinces, such as Shandong, provided thousands of able-bodied young men, who joined not only for the money offered, but to escape the cruel regional war lords and for the opportunity of an adventure away from the peasant agrarian existence in their provinces. What was not anticipated was how disposable their numbers were to the British.

They were not being enlisted as soldiers, but as laborers. Thousands died at the front where they were relegated to digging trenches, transporting munitions and supplies and repairing tanks. Mass graves were dug in Basra, Iraque, for the hundreds of Chinese who died delivering water to British troops fighting the Ottoman Empire.

In February 1917, when the Germans first learned that the British were beginning to transport Chinese workers to Europe, a German submarine sunk the French passenger ship, the Athos, where it was recorded that over 600 Chinese men were lost at sea.

The British then devised a secret plan that had the Chinese laborers sent to British Vancouver and from there transported by train, first to Montreal and then to the Canadian Atlantic coast and finally shipped to Le Havre, France. Packed into locked train cars like cattle and closely guarded, the volunteer workers from China were treated more like slaves than as volunteers in the war effort.

Da Yan decided to join. He knew this was an opportunity away from his futureless life in the Shandong Province. His grandmother, the village Wu (shaman), had told stories before she died of three of her sons, his uncles, who went to America to build railroads. Then with the money they earned, it was learned that they had opened a small restaurant and an apothecary in a place called Boston's Chinatown. Da convinced one of his brothers, the youngest named Chang, to sign up with him. Both lied about their ages not realizing that the British didn't care anyway.

"We will find these uncles in Boston," he promised Chang. "We will have a good life in America. We have no life here in China, only poverty and misery."

"But I am afraid, Da. Before us is a great unknown."

"Little Brother, is the bad life that we know now better than an unknown future life?"

With that reality, the brothers decided to leave their homeland together.

"How will we find our uncles in America when the British plan is to send us to Europe? Help me understand, Da?" Chang had seen a map and found himself confused by Da's plan.

"Is your plan to travel from Europe to America once the war ends and if we are still alive and have enough passage money?"

"We will be able to find our uncles because the British are sending all Chinese recruits through Canada first. That will be our opportunity, Chang. I give you my word that we will find a way to escape the army before boarding a ship to Europe. From Canada, we travel into America. Remember it is the Year of the Horse. We will use the horse's elements of energy, strength and independence to make our journey. We will make new lives for ourselves just as our uncles did."

Although both young men were thin and barely a few inches over five feet tall, as farmers, they were strong. Da, the older, was the practical one and he would do whatever it would take to reach a goal. Chang, still in his mid-teens, relied on his brother's abilities but would not ever compromise his own values of fairness and honestly. Sometimes, that frustrated Da but he admired Chang's character.

Keeping a small amount for themselves, the two men divided their recruitment bonus money equally among their four remaining farmer brothers. Farewells were difficult. Before they left, as per custom, Shandong liquor and red dates were placed on their grandparents' and parents' graves as their farewell, anticipating that they would never see China again.

"Must we swear our allegiance to the British King George, Da?" Change questioned.

"No, Brother, we owe allegiance only to the Shen, the spirit gods. And to ourselves," he quickly added. "Remember, we carry our shaman Grandmother Wupo's blood in us."

They endured the misery of the long sea journey where there was a lack of food and fresh air for the Chinese recruits, with many sea sick which made the living conditions abominable. Both brothers suffered for days with nausea and vomiting, to the point where they seriously doubted their decision to volunteer for the British. But as the illness subsided, and the ship finally arrived in Vancouver, their thoughts returned once more to the next steps in their journey.

"Da, there are thousands of miles between Vancouver and Boston. If we escape now, how will we be able to cross a continent with no money and speaking only Chinese? I am very worried your plan will fail. The more I think about it, I see us either ending up in the European war or dying somewhere in America far from Boston."

"You are right, Chang, and that is why we will change our plan. Since we have now learned that the British will be transporting all of us by train to the Canadian coast, there is no reason to rush our escape now. We will remain with our countrymen until the convoy reaches the east coast. Does that make you feel better?"

"Then we would have to travel from there to Boston, still a long and arduous journey. But, Da, you show only courage while I am fearful. I hope I will not shame you or myself."

"Chang, you are no coward and will never be one. Our family may be poor but all are honorable. So, this is my promise to you. When the soldiers herd the workers onto the inconspicuous steamships headed to France thinking they are fooling the German submarines, we will not be aboard. We will be finding our way to our esteemed uncles. That is our new plan."

"Do not worry, Da, I will follow your lead at all times."

"Tonight, our train journey begins. But we must be extremely careful. If we are caught we can be shot as deserters," he warned.

141

August 1918
Canada

During the week long cross-country train ride through the Canadian mountains, the brothers observed the shift changes when the guards were distracted and eager to get off duty. They saw the gaps that would allow possible escape while the guards were sorting and distributing food into the box cars or when the Chinese emptied their defecation pots.

Always trying to pick up English words, Chang asked "Why do the guards call us 'chinks'? What is the meaning of the word?"

"I think it is an insult word, like when they call us 'yellow' when we are not yellow."

"So, I will call them, 'sei gwailou', a bad white devil every time they call us a name. I will say it with a smile and they will never know what I called them." That made Da laugh and he wondered if he could keep a straight face should Chang follow through with this.

Because there were certain complacent guards at mealtime who would leave the doors on each side of the box car open in order to get some fresh air into the foul-smelling cars, the brothers had the awaited escape opportunity. The guards who did this did so more for their own comfort while serving the meals than for the comfort of the inhabitants in the car. Although the guards were armed with rifles and side-arms, the guards leaned their guns against the outside of the boxcar, as they distributed the meals twice daily. The guards took it for granted that orders from superiors were followed without question, ingrained into the Chinese mindsets after centuries of war lords.

The complacency displayed by the Chinese made the guards believe that the idea of an escape seemed highly unlikely. They were more right than wrong as there had never been any escape on record.

While the food was being distributed with the usual shouting from the guards, the laborers pushed themselves into positions on the food line.

Da said to Chang, "It is now or never. I heard someone say that the next stop is the final one where everyone will be transferred to the ships. This may be our last chance." Chang nodded his head in agreement. Like his brother, he began to ease himself to the end of the food line and towards the opened back door.

The brothers being small in stature and agile, silently eased themselves to the ground from the rear box car door left open for air. One man from their province noticed their descent but quickly turned his head away as a sign he would keep their escape attempt to himself, probably out of fear of retaliation from the guards and assuming the brothers would be caught and shot anyway.

Da whispered, "Remember what I instructed you to do, Chang. Do exactly what I do."

They then positioned themselves head to toe lying in the middle of the train tracts under their box car with arms and legs tightly held close to their bodies. They waited and prayed to their ancestors. Hidden from view while the train was stopped, their concern was how visible they would be once the train pulled forward and all the cars had passed over them. The hope was that guards never looked under the cars and never looked back once the train was on its way. They had already learned that the soldiers never took head counts after the meals so two missing laborers would never be identified until, perhaps, at the end of the journey.

They listened as the guards slammed the box car doors shut. The signal was given to start the train to its final stop. The brothers could not help but wonder the fates of the laborers after they were loaded on a ship headed to France and delivered to the front lines of a war that had no meaning for them, other than survival. The train whistle rang out and slowly, at first, the wheels moved down the track. Speed began to pick up and the sound of the engine grew louder.

It took nerve to remain motionless as the train began to move only inches above their bodies. One false move would result in the loss of a limb, then death from bleeding out. Da silently prayed while Chang's prayers were audible, even with the deafening noise of the train taking on speed above them. As soon as the train fully passed over them, the brothers slid over the side of the tract into bushes and out of site.

Weeks later, the brothers found their way to Boston's Chinatown but it was only made possible by the kindness of people they met during their journey. As they began to learn some English, they would offer to work for food. In most cases, clergymen were kind, especially the Negro ministers.

One kind Black minister in Maine, who gave them shelter, told them, "You boys remind me of my parents' story. They searched for freedom without papers and in fear of the authorities. Only you are traveling in a southern direction when their travels took them north from the south." Although the brothers did not understand what the minister had said, they recognized kindness. Without being asked, they repaired his broken fence as payment.

Along the way, they would be directed to a city's Chinatown, where they always received help from countrymen. The Chinese business men maintained a strong network that protected their own and provided protection from the police because of the known prejudice. It was such business men who formed associations that established Chinese cemeteries because the Chinese were not permitted to be buried in cemeteries for whites. Schools for the few Chinese children in the population were also created by the Chinese Business Men Associations.

From such a network, Da was able to learn the location of the Boston Chinatown. Through such networks, arrangements were made for them to ride in the back of Chinese delivery trucks heading south. After the uncountable miles on foot, these rides were a luxury to the brothers who had never before ridden in a motorized truck.

Fiona knew she was living in the most vibrant city in the world but, still a teenager and alone, she feared venturing out. As inviting as Central Park appeared, her memories of her night alone in the Dublin park still haunted her so she dared not walk through it alone, even in daylight.

Sam decided to end her self-imposed isolation and get her out into society "Fiona, there are so many things to do in New York besides sitting in your room reading the newspaper. Friday night I am taking you to the movies."

He kept his word taking her to her very first silent motion picture. It was the 'Little American'. In it, Mary Pickford played an American nurse in France who falls in love with two soldiers, a Frenchman and a German and Fiona was still teary eyed when they left the theatre.

"Oh, Sam, that was so beautiful it made me cry. So romantic and sad at the same time. Thank you so much for taking me to see it."

"Well, enough with the crying, next time, we go for laughs, Kiddo."

The following week, he escorted Fiona to the Columbia Theatre on 7th Avenue where there were 'clean' burlesque shows similar to vaudeville. Stars like Will Rogers and Joe E. Brown made her laugh like she hadn't laughed since her early childhood.

Politically, Sam was against the war. "I'm a pacifist," he called himself. She wondered if that kept him from the draft or that he was too old to serve.

Excited to take her to the latest Charlie Chaplin movie, he felt the need to explain Chaplin's message in the movie. "It is very important that you understand what Charlie Chaplin is trying to get across to the audience in 'A Shoulder to Arms'. In his satirical way, Chaplin is ridiculing war and everyone in it. That it is not just a simple comedy as many believe and are too stupid to comprehend."

Fiona understood that Sam's passionate agreement with Chaplin's message was because he shared Chaplin's belief. But in her rebellious heart, she believed that war was often necessary in order for people to win freedom from oppressors. *Isn't that what America did in the Revolutionary War and Ireland is doing now?* However, she decided there was no reason to debate Sam on the subject.

She discovered that Sam was a very intelligent man in a very dirty business. It made her wonder why, with his intellect, he hadn't taken a better path with his life than the one he had taken. *But then, look at me,* she thought, *sometimes events beyond our control happen to us.*

He took her to a minstrel show where she was amazed by Black Bill Robinson's 'Stair Dance'. "My God, Sam, how does he do that? And so easily? I would break my neck if I tried to dance going up and down a flight of stairs!" Thinking of Brian, she added, "Although on our ship I did meet a boy who could walk down stairs backwards while he spoke with folks behind him." That bothered Sam but he acted as if he didn't hear it.

"Speaking of dancing, do you know how to dance, Fiona?"

"I never learned, Sam. Unless you count a bit of a pub's Irish Jig as a child, why?"

"You'll see next time we go out," he replied with a mischievous smile. Fiona liked it when Sam was happy when he saw her having fun. The last thing she wanted to do was to discourage Sam's enthusiasm at introducing her to new enjoyable entertainment.

Fiona was relieved that he never required any more from her than her sincerest thanks for these dates. She knew she would never get involved with him beyond their working together and hoped that it was enough for his ego to be seen in public with a young girl on his arm.

At the knock at the door, Mrs. Jacobs told Mina, "It's just the delivery boy. That's how I get the newspaper and groceries now that I cannot go out shopping everyday as I did in the past."

"I can do that for you now, Mrs. Jacobs, and save you some expense."

"We'll see, Mina, but right now the boy counts on the little tip so I don't want to deprive him of that. His family lives on the fourth floor and every year there seems to be another baby added to the family."

Reading a newspaper was a new experience for Mina, although most of the reading was done out loud by Mrs. Jacobs. Mina learned the value of the newspaper as it served in teaching her to read English. Reading articles to her and then having her practice re-reading, Mina was learning the language and, very importantly, together they shared the news of the day. They would read articles and discuss current events and human-interest stories. Even the smallest article would sometimes elicit a passionate response from her teacher.

"This is so sad. The very last Carolina parakeet, the only member of the parrot family native to the United States, has just died in the Cincinnati zoo."

Then she read something that made up for the parakeet article when she read that the Bird Migratory Treaty was undergoing passage that would outlaw killing and selling bird feathers used in women's hats.

"Now that is a wonderful news, don't you agree, Mina? Shame on any female who is so vain as to have birds die for feathers for her hat."

They read about the twenty-two-foot-high memorial erected in California memorializing the Donner Party of pioneer families trapped in the same amount of twenty-two feet of snowfall in the winter of 1845 where thirty-nine people out of eighty-seven died of starvation even after eating their horses and dogs.

With the war news, most of the articles were depressing so it became their daily habit to search for at least a few good news articles to end each day's session.

"Here's one, Mina. The National Park Service just hired the first woman park ranger. Albeit due to staffing shortages caused by the war, but still a giant step for women desiring federal work."

"Not sure how many women would want that type of employment, Mrs. Jacobs."

"It's still a start for women, Mina. Someday, women your age will have far more choices than you have today. You will see it happen in the years to come. But mark my word, there are men who will not allow it to happen easily and without a fight. Women will have to demand rights, like the Suffragists are doing today."

"Who are suffragists?" Mina questioned and to which received a lengthy explanation supportive of the movement from her teacher.

"Very courageous women," replied her teacher who then explained the movement and its goals.

September, 1918

Boston

"Did they teach you in training about our history as being the first police department in America?" asked Officer Muller of the young cadet assigned to him.

"It was called 'The Watch' then, started in Boston in 1631," replied the cadet, proud that he knew the answer.

"Right, and we in Boston should be proud of that history."

Officer William Muller was first generation German, tall with fair hair and blue eyes. Even his stylish handlebar mustache was light blonde. He had been born in Boston and completed school before entering the police academy. His politics were liberal when compared with his police colleagues. He was disappointed by many of his Irish coworkers who, although new arrivals or first generation themselves, treated immigrants harshly, especially the Sicilians. Not to say that Officer Muller couldn't easily smash in a deserving culprit's head with his 14-inch club if needed, but he preferred a peaceful solution to a problem when possible.

"Officer Muller, how long have you been on the force?" asked the young cadet officer assigned to Muller that day. Expecting a routinely dull day, conversation helped pass the time.

"Almost six years, Simmons. I'm sure you know that is an important milestone because then our salaries go up to $1,400 annually. All I know is that things are better now than ever with modern patrol cars and wagons and police call boxes."

"But I'm sure you hear the strike talk among the men, right? Do you agree that the police should be recognized as a trade union?"

"Well, I do know that eighty to ninety hours of work every week needs to be looked at by the commissioner. Policemen need family time and those hours make that difficult for the married men."

"I guess it's good that we are both single, then," the cadet answered.

"Well, I hope not too long for myself as I have my eye on a pretty nurse, although she doesn't know it yet."

Muller had been assigned District A-1 where he walked the same beat covering the North End and the Downtown waterfront. He was proud of the work he did keeping people safe. His navy-blue uniform was kept spotless and the badge that he wore on the left side of his coat was polished brightly as were his uniform's copper buttons.

While they walked the beat, they noticed a conductor frantically waving to them from a parked trolley car.

"Stay behind me and watch," Muller ordered Simmons.

"Good, some excitement, I hope."

"Never think that excitement is a good thing in this job, Cadet. But you will learn that lesson quick enough." Muller walked quickly to the trolley, twirling his club in his right hand. The cadet following him a few steps behind.

"There's a drunk causing trouble, Officer." The conductor was relieved to have help as he failed in trying to handle the situation himself. "He's been upsetting a young woman passenger and he hit a young Chinese man who tried to intervene."

Officer Muller could see that although the trolley had stopped at the curb, the inebriated man continued to harass a young woman. He had pulled off her hat saying, "let me see your pretty red hair" and was pushing a Chinese man who was still trying to come to the woman's aid. The conductor said the man had even shoved him when he demanded the Italian get off the trolley.

"Ok, Mister, I think you had better come along with me peacefully," advised Muller as he pushed his baton into the drunk man's ribs. When the man turned to hit the policeman, Muller hit him hard in the neck with his club and tossed him out of the trolley and into the street.

For the briefest of seconds while Muller had his back turned to speak with the woman, the man came at him with a knife, ready to stab him in the back.

Seeing this, the Chinaman jumped onto the man's back causing him to lose his balance and drop the knife.

Instantly, the cadet kicked away the knife and grabbing the man's wrists, applied the handcuffs.

"I hate you coppers and I hate the Chinks but, most of all, I really hate uppity bitches who think they are too good to accept a working man's compliments," the prisoner sneered directing his last statement at the young woman. He continued shouting obscenities as Simmons held him while Muller called for a police wagon.

"You may have just saved my life," Muller told the young Chinese while reaching to shake his hand. "Thank you for your brave act," Muller said with sincerity. "What is your name?"

"I am called Chang Yan," he answered the policeman, bowing politely.

In broken English he nervously explained, "I work in my uncle Ming's restaurant. He sent me out to buy supplies from Lee, our distributor uptown." Muller could see the two full bags still at his seat on the trolley, being watched-over by the grateful young woman he had assisted.

"This young Chinese fellow is a courageous person, Officer. That man is twice his size," she stressed as she pointed at her assaulter. She had retrieved her hat and was pinning it back on with a long hat pin. She pondered a moment and then said," I should have stuck him with this pin."

"I will need names and details in order to process the arrest and then you can be on you away again," Muller told the conductor and the young woman.

"My name is Jane Rider and I would like to reward this gentleman." Muller could hear the distinct sound of an upper-class education in her voice and he wondered why she rode the trolley when her class of people usually rode cabs. Then he noticed she wore a Suffragist badge.

As she reached into her purse gratefully smiling at the Chinese youth, he politely refused her offer. In halted English, Chang insisted that it was his honor to be of assistance.

"Then I will respect your decision and again thank you for your gallant behavior, Mr. Chang." She did not realize that his last name was really Yan but Chang did not correct her.

When the boy reentered the vehicle, the other riders clapped their hands applauding him. He shyly looked down, with eyes on the floor, looking a bit worried that he may have shared too much information with the policeman.

Muller understood the distrust that immigrants had for the police, knowing that many had immigration tales best never told. Everyone has something for which they are not proud or which may not have been entirely lawful.

How one got to America is not as important as how one conducts himself once here. This new young Chinese immigrant is an honorable person and someday his descendants will be good American citizens just like the rest of us with immigrant parents and grandparents, Muller thought and truly believed. *All they need is to be given the same opportunities given to our immigrant families. But because they look different it will most likely take longer,* he sadly realized.

After Chang Yan re-boarded, the trolley went on its way with the conductor seen patting the young man on the back as he went to his seat in the rear of the vehicle. Muller wanted to wave to him but as he watched the trolley pull away on the tracks, the young Chinese man never turned around.

The prisoner, as he was being hauled into the police wagon threatened, "You'll be sorry, Copper. I'll get even with you, your dumb bastard. I got friends who know how to hurt people and cops don't scare them!" but his threats bounced off Muller. He knew the Sicilian mob avoided the police and kept to itself in their various districts, more of a problem for their own people than for average Americans.

While the angry man kept shouting out insults and how he would get revenge, Muller asked the cadet, "Did you get this bum's name for our report?"

"It wasn't easy but I did. Mario Russo. His excuse is that gets drunk after working his terrible job every night."

Muller walked over to the police wagon and faced the handcuffed man through the bars on the window. Face to face, the man quieted down, probably curious as to what the policeman had to say.

"I'm curious about what you said about getting drunk because of the work you do. So, what is your job?" Muller asked him directly.

"I empty the tenements shitty outhouses every single night. I'm a "night soil" remover," he answered belligerently. "What do you think of that?"

"Then I think you are right. You do have a shitty job," Muller agreed as the wagon drove off.

Cadet Simmons asked, "Are you worried about a guy like that turning up on you some dark night as he threatened?"

"I have better things to think about," he answered, sorry that this day's assignment took him away from his chance of walking with Nurse Mary Moran.

Pianos were the rage and being sold to anyone who could afford one. Tin Pan Alley on West 28th street between 5th and 6th Avenues became one of the busiest areas in the city where all the major sheet music was being sold by music publishers. Song writers like Ira and George Gershwin and Irving Berlin were writing songs with melodies that everyone was singing and humming. Favorites included 'Over There' and 'Oh, How I hate to Get Up in the Morning' as part of the war effort. Igor Stravinsky wrote a Ragtime concertina that spread from America to Europe. Fiona loved learning and the American music thrilled her.

Sam told her, "I am going to show you the city, Fiona. Enough of you hiding out in your boarding house every night."

He started with Manhattan's Tin Pan Alley, because he saw how enamored she had become with American music. They would walk or take trolleys to the other neighborhoods so that she could learn the geography of Manhattan island. They visited Gramercy Park, the East and West Sides, Chelsea, Murray Hill, Lower Manhattan. She loved the merchant stalls in the garment area where she purchased clothing articles for less money than department stores charged. Sam taught her how to haggle and barter and she became adept at it. Sam allowed her to learn each neighborhood's unique character and flavor from Chinatown to Little Italy to Harlem.

"But we only walk around in the safe ones," he quickly added, "because there are some that are still dangerous with criminal gangs, such as Five

Corners being one with a long history of your people being some of the worst criminals." Smiling a crooked smile, he waited for her reaction after the insult to the Irish.

She surprised him when she calmly responded, "Aren't we criminals, ourselves, Sam? After all, couldn't we be arrested for what we do?"

Sam did not answer which she understood to be a 'yes'.

Thanks to Sam's encouragement, Fiona had begun to walk the city by herself on Sundays during the daytime to view the sights for which New York is famous. She kept a journal and added the Empire State building, the Chrysler Building, the Woolworth Building and Grand Central Station to her list. Especially, she loved to sit on a bench whether on the Hudson River or the East River side and watch the boats sail by. Sometimes she could see a Steamship coming into harbor bringing a shipload of new immigrants to the city's shore for processing at Ellis Island. It brought back her memories of her friendship with Mina and the Turners and Brian Kelly and wondered how their lives were evolving.

I wonder if they ever think about me? How different my life would have been had there really been a Brooklyn family awaiting me, she thought with sadness. But with her innate resilience, Fiona brushed away the thought that was beginning to depress her and pondered her future instead.

"There is a better future for you, my girl, only you need a bit more time," she told herself out loud, reinforcing her will to make a life-altering change by audibly hearing her own words.

Not long after, she visited St. Patrick's Cathedral on Fifth Avenue. She had learned that in order to raise funds to build it, the Irish donated hard earned money and did most of the construction. Many donated family heirlooms to pay for the construction and women donated their gold wedding rings to be melted down for the church's chalices.

The splendor of the Cathedral's interior was inspiring, even for non-believers who were awed by the peace and beauty of the stained glass and religious art work. Parishioners sat in pews praying while visiting tourists meandered from altar to altar interested in the magnificent statuary equal to any in Rome. Fiona found a quiet side altar near the rear of the church. She lit a candle and knelt. She whispered her prayers because hearing her actual words made the prayer more real.

"Lord, it's been awhile and, so far as the church's roof has not caved in on me yet, please accept my 'hello again' and my 'please and thank you' prayers.

I pray you have my parents with you in heaven and I pray for my brothers' well-being. The less said about my aunt, the better. I thank you for my escaping Madame and for getting me to America. I pray that you forgive me for the way I have had to earn a living. I know it is shameful and a sin so I certainly would not be opposed to your guiding me as soon as possible into another profession and away from Sam. I even pray for Sam, who is a good man in many ways except for his choice of occupation. For that he will have to come to you himself to ask your forgiveness. But I don't want to overdo my requests today, so I will end now, Lord."

As she left she took a few coins from her purse and inserted them into the collection box for the poor. She crossed herself with the holy water from the font in the vestibule and descended the Cathedral's front steps to Fifth Avenue, which bustled with the noise from people, cars and horse drawn wagons. Fiona took in a deep breath and felt better than she had in years. She had a smile on her face and found herself humming a tune as she bought some roasted chestnuts from a vendor on the corner. An odd and unexpected thought came to her mind, *I wonder if Mina's Boston is as alive as New York is?*

She headed to Sam's place, which was a studio apartment on the west side. Separating the area with a curtain, he had allocated the half of the apartment with the window for the light needed for his photography studio and the other half as his living quarters. *Why he lives like this with all the money he makes is still a mystery to me,* was Fiona's ongoing thought about Sam's lifestyle. *Someday, instead of a rented room in a boarding house, I will have my own apartment,* she promised herself.

He had promised to take her dancing which was to be a new experience for Fiona. She was looking forward to this special treat. She headed to his place because she refused to allow him to pick her up at her boarding house. She insisted on maintaining respectability in public if she couldn't in her work. Besides, she had no intention of giving her landlady any gossip. As a single woman she never wanted any unseemly talk about her from any of the women living in the rooming house. She knew, without a doubt, that her Irish landlady would pick up on Sam's age and ethnicity and give Fiona a hard time about that. *If they only knew what I do every day,* she thought embarrassed, *then walking out with a gentleman Jew would be mild in comparison.*

Although wondering if she would be making a fool of herself if she tried dancing, she was still excited about learning something new. As angry as she could get with Sam with his constant posing demands, she was grateful that he was broadening her knowledge and experiences socially. He single-handedly was transforming her into a genuine American. To her, even her Irish brogue seemed to be disappearing, although every time she spoke a listener would still comment on it and would ask from where in Ireland she came.

At the Harlem nightclub where Sam had made reservations, they were escorted to their table which was up front by the band.

"Sam, this place must be expensive."

"What are you worrying about, Fiona. Can't I treat my model out to hear a great jazz band. How much more American can we get than to listen and dance to genuine American music?"

Ragtime's inviting sound filled the room and the young trumpet player received numerous bouts of applause because he was an exceptional musician.

"Do you know who he is?" Fiona asked.

"Sure, that's Louis Armstrong. He's just a teen ager but ain't he great already? He's going places, I bet."

Sam explained that Ragtime was part Negro Blues and part Jazz, making it a pure American sound.

"And Europe is eating it up," Sam said proudly, as if he had something to do with its success.

As Fiona watched the couples dancing together, Sam pulled her to her feet even though she protested that she wasn't ready to dance.

Sam told her, "Ragtime is a one- step dance. It's like walking around the room together. Just follow me," he insisted.

At first, their timing together wasn't in synch, but within a few minutes Fiona took to it as if she had danced Ragtime for years. Even when Sam tired, she wouldn't let him stop dancing. They started putting their own moves to their dance as they copied the more experienced dancers around them. Fiona circled under Sam's extended arm and Sam dipped Fiona at the end of a dance.

Sam protested, "You're killing me, Fiona, I'm not as young as you are and I need to rest." As Sam was saying this, a tall handsome young man tapped him on the shoulder, the sign for permission to cut in and change dance partners. Before Sam could find an excuse to not hand Fiona over to the new partner, they were already dancing away from him. He reluctantly returned to their table and ordered a drink, all the while jealous of how happy Fiona looked with her new young partner.

"My name is John Tarrington. What's yours?" he inquired.

"Fiona Burke." She couldn't hold back a smile as she was enjoying the attention of the young man with an upper- class accent.

"If I may boldly ask, is that gentleman your father?"

"Oh, no, Sam is my employer," immediately knowing that she would have to carefully measure her words. "I assist in a photography shop downtown. Having recently arrived from Ireland, he generously offered to show me the sights of the city."

But before they could continue conversing, Sam tapped the young man's shoulder so that he could cut in and resume dancing with Fiona.

"Sam, John is teaching me the newest dance, called the Fox Trot, so I need a little more time to learn it. That's alright with you, isn't it?"

"It is the latest dance fashion with two-steps and is going to make the old 'One Step' and everyone who dances it obsolete," John said. He delivered that information with such a cavalier attitude that Sam disliked him immediately. However, since Fiona requested more time in order to learn the new fad, Sam returned to the table, ordered another drink and watched the couple continue dancing and laughing together.

When Fiona returned to their table, John asked if he might join them. Rudely, Sam said that would not be possible because they had to leave.

"But it's still early, Sam," Fiona complained, confused by Sam's reaction.

"Since the young lady would like to stay longer, I will gladly see her safely home," said John, although looking directly at Fiona and not Sam for an answer.

She wanted with all her heart to stay having fun like a normal girl, but she knew Sam well enough to see that he was serious about leaving and not without her. To avoid a confrontation, especially since Sam had more than a few drinks, she thanked John for his offer and for teaching her the Fox Trot.

"Fiona, I really think you are the 'bees knees' and would like very much to see you again."

"Maybe next time…and thank you for the dance lesson," she replied as she picked up her gloves and purse from the table and begrudgingly left the club with Sam.

"You're mad at me, right?" Sam's words came out slurred from all the alcohol he had drunk while watching her dance. "Besides, he's a Limey, couldn't you tell? You Irish are not supposed to like the English."

Using a tone, she had never used before with Sam, she answered coldly that he needed to mind his own business. They did not speak during the cab ride home and Sam never invited Fiona out again.

Mina realized how unhappy she was in her marriage. The first three months, Carlo would leave one or two evenings a week to socialize at his men's club, as he called it, but was always home early enough for them to go to bed together. Then her husband started going out every evening and returning late, after she was already in bed, often asleep. She would try to stay awake for his arrival but most often could not. She found herself angry at his insensitivity and also fearful that he may think their marriage is a mistake. Even though she was questioning the marriage herself, thinking that he might be questioning it shamed and worried her.

She made a firm promise to herself that she would allow more time before she complained since it could be a passing phase. After all, he had an easy and free bachelorhood until his parents intervened with the marriage arrangement. She wanted her husband to think of her as supportive and accepting. *So, I will be silent and be an uncomplaining wife and hope this behavior ends soon.*

Instead, as was Mina's taciturn nature, she immediately rebuked him as soon as he returned one night. She knew she would incur his anger with her demands but did not care. The rent was unpaid and she had to face the landlord.

He barely got through the front door before she ranted, "You must stop this gambling, Carlo, before you completely ruin us!"

"Just because I'm married, there is no reason for me to give up the life I enjoyed before you came into it Mina."

"Carlo, do you realize that we have no rent money again. You make gambling more important than our life together. I don't know what to do anymore. How will we pay our overdue debts?"

"Being at the club each night is necessary or I will never be invited into the mob. I need to join, we need me to join to make our lives better. Don't you want to move to a swanky neighborhood some day and out of this rat-infested tenement? Don't you want nice clothes? I do. I look at the 'made men' and the family's soldiers in their fine suits and Italian leather shoes and I want the same. My job at the plant is only a placeholder until I can be made Cosa Nostra. You must accept my reason once and for all. My winning streak will return and we will pay the bills so stop nagging me. Just give me time."

"My father approved our marriage only because he was convinced by your father that you were never going to have any ties to Cosa Nostra. Did the Don lie? I don't want that life and if you do then we have no future together."

"But you have no say in this, Mina, and I don't believe that about my father. Why would he? Why don't you understand that what I want is what you get as my wife?"

I am too hurt to speak and will hold my tongue now, she promised herself knowing that it would only worsen the argument but changing her mind she went on. "I cannot go on like this. Someday you may come home and I will be gone," she threatened.

"And where will you go? To your brother? I will find you and drag you back because you will never be allowed to shame me," said in a voice she had never heard him use before. He was a stranger speaking to her, not her husband.

Mina finally awakened to the realization that she had no options that would allow her to leave her marriage. If she had the money for passage back home to her parents, she would return to Sciacca. But she was kept penniless. She was trapped.

Despairingly she realized, *Controlling the family's finances is always in the hands of the husband. Wives have no financial power. Police ignore wife beatings. Women have no more rights in America than anywhere else.*

She hid her shame as best as possible from Basilio and Carmela, since they had their own financial burdens. And the last thing she wanted was for her parents to hear how unhappy she was. She knew now that she could not change Carlo. Each day became harder to bear as he took his frustrations out on her and she became colder towards him. *As long as I can remember, everyone called me a 'mind changer'. If I am truly one, then why didn't I change my mind about this marriage before it was too late?* she berated herself.

October, 1918

New York City

After months in New York Fiona decided that, with a bit more cash saved, she could disappear from Sam just as she had done from Madame. She had two reasons for her plan to leave. Sam's photographs were becoming increasingly vulgar and Manhattan's Spanish influenza epidemic was reaching alarming rates.

The city was reporting numerous influenza cases which were a serious concern because it surely would get worse before better. She could see the illness in the fevered faces of pedestrians and trolley riders as workers trudged on to work to make a living even though ill and, without realizing it, spreading the illness. Even Boy Scouts were citing 'Spitters' by handing out written reminders not to spread the flu with spitting on the ground or in the subway.

She thanked God every day that she left prostitution when she took the modeling job for Sam. But Sam's photography was growing more aggressive in stretching the limits of lewdness. What had started as coquettishly erotic pictures, with an exposed breast or a glimpse of derriere while still having strips of silk and feathers strategically in place, changed to unacceptable boundaries for Fiona.

Sam had learned that there was a great deal of demand for anatomical close-up photographs to replace that which up to then were provided only in drawings. As risky as the business was becoming, he was considering to relocate to Boston where he was going to partner with a group of financial backers specializing in erotic photography that included adult models with animals and young children which horrified Fiona. She knew she would have no part in

Sam's new business plan and she surmised that only hardened criminals would partner in such a venture with him.

As Sam removed his head from under the camera's cloth cover, he said, "I don't see why you are complaining about letting me take the close-ups, Fiona. What difference does it make to you? When did you develop sensitivity about your body parts after all the nasty things you have already done in your short life."

He continued carefully choosing his words. "Seriously, Fiona, we have come to a crossroad in our business relationship so I have a proposition for you. A group of fellows in Chicago and Boston are interested in going into business with me. With their financial backing, I can pay you more if you are willing to continue working with me on new projects. It means relocation to Boston right away and later to Chicago. Moving around will be necessary to keep our operation safe. Otherwise, we end it here and I find someone else more willing."

Fiona was no fool. She suspected that his partners were gangsters and she knew that she would be required to perform more than modeling once she agreed to be part of this ugly arrangement.

Since her plan was to leave Sam anyway, why not have him pay her fare to Boston? She knew she would lose him once she reached Boston. The thought of looking up Mina excited her so she lied to Sam that she agreed to his latest offer.

Her easy agreement flummoxed Sam but he believed his bluff worked. He was relieved because he dreaded having to break in a new girl into his illegal but lucrative business. So, he took Fiona at her word that she would meet him in Boston. After all, she had kept her word and shown up in New York from Dublin.

October, 1918

Boston

He paced, swinging his baton easily while he whistled a tune, waiting for the trolley to arrive. The young Boston cop tried to appear as if their meetings were accidental and not deliberately planned. He looked forward to the walk together to the tenement building to which the young nurse was assigned.

The Public Health Nurse, Mary Moran, descended the trolley steps, holding her medical bag in one hand while lifting her skirt with the other. The policeman envied the gentleman who had taken her elbow to help her safely reach the sidewalk. Everyone in the neighborhood respected the nurses, except some men who complained about the birth control education being offered to their wives.

"Good morning, Nurse Moran," said Officer Muller with a wide smile. "We meet again."

"It does seem our schedules coincide, doesn't it?" She answered his smile with a knowing one of her own.

"Although it may be that my hours will be prolonged very soon as the influenza is worsening every day. With thousands of physicians and nurses deployed overseas to military bases to serve in the war effort, it has left a great shortage of us left to care for civilians. Then if that's not bad enough, many nurses are choosing to work in the civilian hospitals leaving even fewer of us to work in the outpatient setting. I'm not sure what to think but, unfortunately, the physicians are predicting that we should expect conditions to worsen before getting better."

"At the precinct it was reported that on September 12th the Port of New York was placed under quarantine which could happen here at Boston's port, too. If it will slow down the infections, then I'm all for it," he added.

"But I apologize, you don't need to listen to my complaining. I truly love my profession but I cannot help being frustrated. I can try to teach infection control, good hygiene and other therapies which I learned in nursing school but none of those will *cure* anyone. They may help prevent the spread but there are no cures other than each patient's ability to survive. So, I make sure the patients are clean and the bedding is clean, give aspirin, ice packs for fevers, apply mustard plasters and Vapo Rub to the chest and even make hot soup. Sadly, I return the next day to learn my patient died so I close the patient's eyes and comfort the bereaved as best as I can and make arrangements for the body to be taken away. One of the most difficult changes I confront is to get the Sicilian families to stop hugging and kissing their ill and their dead which contributes to the spread. That cultural change is one of my greatest challenges."

She continued after taking a deep breath. "But it is the children who break my heart the most. Some days I wonder if I can bear to go to work when I witness the terrible poverty of children going hungry, malnourished and underweight. Two days ago, I found two toddlers in their apartment alone with the corpses of their parents. They were filthy and starving and confused as they sat next to the bodies crying for attention. That is the worst part of my job, never knowing what misery I'll find in the next apartment."

She hesitated a moment before adding, "But please forgive me. Enough of my complaining although I do appreciate how you patiently listen to me. I choose carefully what to share with my family for they worry about me too much. In fact, my father wanted me to go into teaching, not nursing. It was a hard-fought battle, to say the least."

His heart went out to her. Everyone knew that if a patient had any chance at survival it was due to the visiting nursing care they received. However, one nurse could never visit every apartment in the tenement every day. Considering that the nurse cleaned the patients, their linens, gave medications, applied poultices, educated the families and frequently had to fire the stove and cook for the bedridden, the policeman appreciated his job in comparison with hers.

"Well, here we are," Mary said when they reached the building's entrance.

"Yesterday, I started with fifteen patients and by evening I had treated fifty. Wouldn't I love to have you as my nurse assistant," she joked with the officer.

"Oh, I don't think I would be much help to you as I'm a bit queasy when it comes to blood and vomit and such. Of course, I hate to admit that I may have just ruined your image of me as a strong hero of the law," he smiled.

"To tell the truth, Officer Muller, seeing you in uniform inside this tenement would most probably alarm my patients greatly. They are very suspicious of the police as you must know only too well."

"The Boston Police need to fix that, I agree. Anyway, for now, I wish you a good day, Nurse Moran, and stay well yourself. There are reports of many nurses becoming infected. Please don't let that happen to you," he said sincerely with true concern which she could not help but notice.

"And you take care of yourself, as well, Officer Muller."

Mary watched the young officer call to the small homeless dog that lingered around the building, day and night. For the last few days, he had been feeding the little dog and had finally gained its trust. The terrier-mixed mongrel went to him immediately with none of the fear it would show when others would call to it and it had progressed to eating from Muller's hand. *That poor stray dog distrusts everyone but it trusts Officer Muller. Animals can recognize a good person and he is one, of that I'm sure,* she thought to herself.

When Muller saw Mary watching him, he told her, "I'm going to take this little guy home later, if he'll let me. I think he deserves a chance, don't you?"

"I do. You have a good heart, Officer Muller," and Mary meant it.

As Mary Moran watched him walk away with the dog following him, she looked up and could see many inhabitants watching for her arrival. Some were hanging out their windows calling out to her to visit them first while others were coming out to meet her with the same requests. So many were eager to get to her before the others that she hoped confrontations would not result. *It's going to be a busy day, a very busy day,* but Mary welcomed the thought as she felt truly fulfilled helping others.

At the end of each day, surrounded by her family at the dinner table, she would recount only tidbits of her day's work, but still her parents worried for her health and safety in the tenements among the immigrants. They were very pleased and relieved when she lately began to speak of a young handsome police officer who escorts her most mornings when their morning arrivals coincide.

"When will we meet this nice gentleman, dear," Mrs. Moran asked.

"Mum, I swear if he doesn't get passed his shyness soon, I will literally drag him home myself to meet you," swore Mary with such determination that no one at the table doubted her for a minute.

One to poke fun at his older sister whenever given the chance, Mary's brother, Danny, elbowed their father laughing, "now, Dad, wouldn't that be a scene with Mary dragging a policeman home like a cavewoman capturing her man?"

"Mind your own business, Danny," Mary warned her younger sibling. But even Mary had to join in laughing with her family at such a thought. "Let's just hope it doesn't have to come to that," she said.

October, 1918
Dublin

Madame swore that it had to be the soldiers who came to her brothel and transmitted the Black flu to her girls. Furiously, she closed her door to all soldiers but it was too late and difficult to enforce. Three of her six whores were dead within a week. Sugar was one of them leaving Spice devastated. The musician refused to come anymore and even the police on her payroll were absentees. Her once thriving business was dying along with her workers.

Dublin had always been an unhealthy city with its poverty and overcrowdedness. With the arrival of this deadly strain of influenza, young healthy adults were succumbing quickly to this disease that no longer only took the old and very young. There was no immunity for anyone.

Many victims had their skin color actually turn blackish which explained why it was called the Black Flu. In most places it was known as the Spanish Flu. The papers reported over 250 deaths per week just in Dublin and thousands throughout Ireland. The newspapers reported worldwide infection with hundreds of thousands infected and dying everywhere. The disease was being compared to the Black Plague that swept through Europe in the middle ages.

"Go upstairs and carry the bodies out to the sidewalk," Madame ordered the Negro women, all still uninfected. Madame would not venture into any of the rooms of the deceased and kept a handkerchief around her nose all the time. She had even greatly reduced the time she spent in the parlor with her girls.

The older Negro worker refused to carry out the order. She was the cook and had always been more out-spoken that the others. She balked that she was fearful of contracting the disease and brazenly reminded Madame that there were men for hire to do this work.

"How dare you after all the years I have carried you!" Madame was indignant. "Where is your loyalty to me?"

"I never say no to you but this time I do say no! I'll help wrap the girls, that's all. I liked some of these girls. But carrying the dead bodies out to the street like they are garbage is asking too much." Beth adamantly stood her ground while the others watched her insubordination.

"What about the rest of you? Will no one bring the bodies out of the house?"

With no answer, only silence, Madame had her answer. Surprisingly, there was no punishment as she was fearful of losing her few remaining staff. Instead, Madame went outside and waved two men off the street who she hired to remove the corpses of the deceased to the curbside.

At first, the men haggled wages. Madame wanted the bodies out of the brothel as quickly as possible to avoid the smell of decaying bodies so she paid more than she expected. *They are ruffians but who else would be for hire for such work*, she reasoned as she doled out money to them.

"Just get the job done and leave," she ordered. She could hear the crude men loudly assess each girl's physical attributes as they glanced at each nude body under the cloth wrapping.

"Lord, this one must have put a smile on many a customer's face," said one of the men as he leered at the dead girl Honey's large breasts under the cloth wrapper. All the bodies were naked since Madame had ordered the Negro women to remove the clothing as soon as each died.

"No reason to waste good clothing in graves when they can be used again," was her order to them. "Put them away for the new girls I will have to find."

When the men finished, the house became eerily quiet. The bodies were at the curbside in two neatly balanced piles in front of the house awaiting to be removed to the mass graves awaiting them. The remaining inhabitants of the brothel watched from the windows unbelieving that their young co-workers were gone and left outside awaiting the wagon that would add their bodies to those already unceremoniously collected. The homes of the rich and the poor had no alternative other than to place their dead on the sidewalks for pickup.

The corpses were piled up and taken away by horse drawn wagons and buried. The cart men wore masks over their faces for protection, but they still ran the high risk of contracting the disease themselves. Contagion was everywhere.

The physicians were at a loss as to a cure. Whiskey became a favorite recommendation and, in no time, whiskey could no longer be purchased anywhere as everyone quickly bought up the available supply. Others advocated sucking on formaldehyde and lactose lozenges. Another recommendation involved wrapping oneself up in linens soaked in vinegar. None proved to be successful. Once the high fever hit with congestion in the lungs and dysentery, many victims died within 24 hours. As if the war in Europe wasn't enough of a hardship, Ireland's war for independence from Britain was being waged simultaneously with the epidemic.

Madame retreated to her room with a bottle of whiskey and gave serious thought to her current circumstances. She finally accepted that the wars and the plague had ruined her Dublin business. *The only ones making any profits on this disease are the whiskey and vapo-rub manufacturers,* she thought with envy as she devised her new business plan. *I can be as successful somewhere else as I have been here,* she arrogantly assured herself.

She pulled out her substantial savings from her safe and packed her expensive jewelry. There was ample money saved through the years for her to afford to travel abroad first or second class. And there were enough funds to start a new brothel in America. She decided on Boston because she heard so many Irish chose that city. She would then be among her own and feel less like an immigrant she hoped. *And I'm quite sure that the Boston police who are Irish will be like the Dublin police, very willing to work with me for the right sum,* she anticipated.

Although the Flu was pandemic, she trusted that the medical conditions were far better in America than in Dublin. America was the place to go. Madame left at dawn the next morning without a word to the remaining women leaving them stranded in the brothel.

"Our ancestors made this new life possible for us, Brother," said Chang as he and his brother cleaned up the dirty dishes from the Chinese restaurant tables. "We must set up a shrine to them soon."

"Yes, but Uncle Ming has played an even greater part, Chang," said Da and he meant it even if it offended the spirits.

The brothers had located one of their father's brothers after much searching among the Boston Chinese community. He owned a small restaurant that served mainly Chinese customers and a small percentage of sailors who had grown accustomed to Chinese cuisine. When the two raggedy young men introduced themselves to their elderly uncle, he was suspicious at first. But he became convinced of their blood relationship to him after questioning them closely and at length on relatives' names and histories that would only be known to family.

They were told that their other two uncles died just recently from the influenza disease that had struck Boston starting in August. "Nephews, my heart broke with their deaths. As brothers, we had struggled and suffered hard labor and injustices together for many years in this country. We sacrificed everything to start our business, frequently in the beginning going without food ourselves so that we would have enough food to feed our customers. It took this disease to separate us and this scourge will take many more lives before it ends, mark my word."

He shook his head and added, "Of course, you will hear that some whites are blaming the Chinese for bringing in this disease. Just more to add to all the other prejudices used against us. Nephews, prepare yourselves as you will experience much discrimination if you have not already through your travels."

"We understand, Uncle, because we met many people who disliked us merely for being Chinese. But it seems like a miracle that we are in America now, in Chinatown and, most importantly, we found you, Honorable Uncle," beamed the teen aged Chang.

"Nephews, the gods have graced both you and me. By finding me at this time, you two will benefit as there are no sons to inherit our business but you."

"Uncle, respectfully, may I ask why there is not even one son between the three of our uncles?" asked an incredulous Da.

"You have much to learn about America. Chinese have been instrumental in building the railroads, highways and blasting tunnels through the mountains. Our men were needed and were put to the work unwanted by whites and paid lower than whites who did. Then laws were passed that excluded Chinese families from entering America, so you will notice the extreme shortage of Chinese females everywhere. Laborers who had families in China will never see them again. Most men choose to remain in America and send earnings to their families. Very few return to China, just as my brothers and I had decided to remain. It is a very unfortunate situation. Sadly, our birth rate continues to decline in this country which is not the case with other immigrant groups. The only Chinese women here are those who entered the country before the Chinese Exclusion laws were passed. Sadly, you will see that currently we exist in mostly a male society."

"Uncle, are you telling us that we may never be able to marry or have sons ourselves?"

"As difficult as that may be to accept, it may be your reality as it has been for me and my brothers. Only time will tell."

Both young men did not respond. It was a condition unknown to them when they decided to emigrant. As their uncle's words sunk in, so did their feelings of loss and disbelief.

Uncle Ming made an important decision. "I will teach you all I know and you will study diligently to learn English. Speaking only our language will hold you back in this society. I will enroll you both in the Quong Kow School while you also learn our restaurant business. Very importantly, I will teach you the herbal medical regimens handed down from my mother, your grandmother. Our customers come to us for helpful medicines, so you will become herbalists like I am."

"Uncle, we are here to learn from you and to serve in any capacity in which you need us," was Da's response, as Chang nodded in agreement.

"As you know, your grandmother, my mother, was a midwife and a Wu. She taught her children many elements of our traditional Chinese medicine. She taught midwifery to her daughters and medicines to her sons so that each of us would have a skill in addition to the necessary skill of farming. Even though your uncles and I worked as laborers on the railroad construction, the money we earned to purchase this restaurant came from our prescribing and providing herbal medicines to our fellow countrymen. We were the healers in our Chinese railroad camps. White doctors were not available to us and our people trusted us more anyway."

"How did you get the ingredients for the medicines you needed?" Da asked knowing how complicated that must have been in the remote camps.

"Some were easier than others. Some powders we had brought with us from Shandong. For the rest, we made remedies with what we could find. We caught caterpillars to make fungus for energy. Squirrel feces was abundant and we used that in our medicines to relieve pain and invigorate the blood. Deer antlers were found in the garbage piles after the white railroad workers ate their venison. Catching snakes was trickier. But once we became adept at it and learned how to recognize the poisonous ones from the nonpoisonous, we had snake blood available, which became our best-selling pain relief product. Since it relieved muscle stiffness, even some white workers became our customers. Of course, we charged them higher prices, just as they did to Chinese in their commissary." Uncle Ming smiled at the memory.

Ming's nephews laughed at that. But their uncle then became serious, so they did, as well.

"But we sold poisons then and I still do today. It is part of my business that you must understand and accept. Even today, when a customer requests a poison, I comply. I do not, nor will you, ever question the purpose, especially when one particular customer makes such a request."

"Who is this customer, Uncle?"

"His name is Feng-Fu and he is the leader of the Jin-Bo, the Gold Waves Gang from Ping -On- Alley, near the old Chinatown gate. He knows he can receive free service from me anytime and that exempts me from making any protection payments to the gang as other merchants must do monthly."

"Uncle, do you think that he kills people with the poison?" Chang asked naively when Da was sure of the answer without his uncle's acknowledgment.

"As I told you, it is not our place to ask the purpose. Our only responsibility is to explain the type, mode of administration, duration, and expected effects of a chosen poison. Do you clearly understand this?"

In unison, the brothers answered positively, as they instinctively knew that was the answer their uncle needed to hear from them. However, this information was unsettling as their Grandmother was known to use her medicines to cure not to kill, or so they thought. Chang looked especially troubled with this directive.

Months into the marriage, Carlo continued to be a selfish lover where only his needs and his timing mattered. He never lifted a finger to help Mina with lifting the heavy loads up or down the flights of stairs as other men could be seen doing. She had to look at the wedding ring on her finger to remind herself that she is a wife and not an indentured servant. Her marriage continued to disappoint and trouble her. She constantly found herself looking back to see where she missed clues to his true nature.

After their wedding she had nervously asked her husband's permission to continue working for Mrs. Jacobs. She had explained to him that there was a small salary, free English lessons and, importantly, charitably helping a sweet old lady who needed assistance.

Carlo, surprisingly, gave her no argument. He told her she was allowed to continue but that she was to hand over her salary from 'the Jew' to him each week. He always referred to Mrs. Jacobs as "the Jew" and never by her name, no matter how many times Mina would correct him.

At first, Mina took his easy approval as a sign of progressive thinking on his part, which contradicted Carmela's impression. However, once she became aware of his gambling losses, she understood. Unabashed, he would take her cash away from her each week with no hesitation or delay.

Fiona was right when she said that love is needed first, then marriage. She found herself frequently thinking of her shipboard friend. *I really miss Fiona.* Mina did have Carmela, but she was more like a substitute mother than a girlfriend.

181

"Shut the door quickly, Mina, you are letting out all the heat," was Carmela's greeting to Mina's visit as she entered the apartment.

"And good morning to you, too," Mina answered sarcastically as she responded by quickly closing the door. She had decided that it was time to speak with Carmela about her marriage problems. Before she could begin the difficult conversation, she was handed a letter.

Mina's mood immediately improved as soon as she realized the letter was from Fiona. Amazingly, it was as if thinking of Fiona actually brought her wish to come true when she read of Fiona's planned trip to Boston. Carmela could see her excitement but waited for Mina to explain the letter.

"It is from my dear friend, Fiona, a wonderful Irish girl who travelled with me on the trip over. I cannot wait until she visits. You will love her, too, Carm. She is beautiful, smart and very wise for someone my age. She is an amazing problem solver, too."

Carmela, although pleased for Mina, also felt a pang of jealousy which she immediately dismissed. "I will make a wonderful meal when you have her visit here. We know the Irish have no cooking talent so we will introduce her to good Sicilian food."

She missed Fiona and never understood how they had lost each other on Ellis Island or why Fiona never wrote to her after all these months. Because Fiona told her that she did not know the Brooklyn address of her family, Mina never had a way to write her. She only knew that her friend proved to be a force of nature, so strong and independent and she admired her for that. That's why she changed her mind about asking Carmela for advice. Instead, she would wait until she sees Fiona.

Early one autumn evening, Basilio knocked on Mina's tenement door. He wanted to speak with Carlo about problems at the distillery plant.

"Carlo, are you feeling alright? You look flushed?" Mina asked holding her hand to her brother's brow as he entered the doorway.

"I'm fine, Mina," as he gently pushed her hand away. "But everyone at work is coughing or is at home ill. This influenza is one for the records they say. Anyway, I'm here to speak with Carlo about work issues," he stated as he crossed the threshold into the apartment.

Mina's husband impolitely did not get up from his chair to welcome Basilio but did gesture for Basilio to sit down at the table with him.

"Mina, bring Basilio something to eat."

"Nothing, thank you. I can only stay a short time so I can get home to Carmela."

"Then tell me what you want, Basilio, and quickly because I can see that Mina's right, you don't look so good. If you have this flu then back off from me right now."

Ignoring the comment, Basilio informed Carlo that the men have safety concerns at the distillery plant and are looking for an approach to take with the plant managers. "I thought maybe you can tell me what you think we should do as we would respect your advice, Carlo. You have been at the plant longer than most of us."

"Alright, so what exactly is wrong with the safety?" Carlo liked hearing that he was respected by the workers. It helped his wounded ego knowing he had little of it from his supervisors at work or at the social club where he played dice and cards.

"I'm sure you are noticing that with the increase in the production quotas there's a decrease in quality everywhere. More serious is the noticeable stress on the cylinders which is making conditions really unsafe. In our area, management even has us using brown paint to cover the cracks in the equipment, as if hiding the problem would make it go away."

"Did anyone formally complain to the managers?"

"You know how the men are. Everyone is afraid to speak up. We are hesitant to complain, afraid of losing our jobs."

"Look, all management is concerned with is increasing production as fast as possible. There is talk of new laws being passed about prohibition on alcohol and the bosses know the law is coming soon. That's why they are cutting corners and overfilling the molasses tanks. Tell the men that we just have to live with that reality," voiced Carlo in a dismissive tone as he finished his glass of red table wine and pushed back his empty dinner plate.

"But, Carlo, we are speaking of over two million gallons of molasses at risk of explosion!"

"Like I just said, live with it. Look, you can be the hero but leave me out. If you want to be the workers representative, feel free, but you may lose your job. Bosses don't like even a whiff of union talk but go ahead and start a union, I don't care. But remember, the managers don't care about any of us and would find other new immigrants to replace us in a minute. And you have a wife that you should be thinking about. My advice is keep your mouth shut. If anyone has to, then let one of the abrasive Irishmen take the lead, not you."

"But you have seen the steam leaks and felt the serious vibrations, haven't you? Lives could be at stake. Our lives. Then what do all our families do if that happens?"

"All the more reason to be extra careful on the job. You are still young, Basilio, so just keep your eyes open and mouth shut. You need your job. Ask yourself what would you do if you lost it? Would you take a job taking away the merde from the shit houses every night like my friend Mario?" As he said that, he thought about Mario lingering in a jail. *The stupido. He never could hold his liquor or his tongue*, thought Carlo, knowing he still missed his low-life company each night.

Mina felt ashamed and disappointed in her husband once again. Although he mentioned Carmela with some concern if Basilio lost his job, he was typically unconcerned about anyone other than himself. Mostly, she was sickened with how condescending he was behaving with Basilio who came to him respectfully for older brotherly advice.

After hearing Carlo out and realizing it was a mistake to seek his help, Basilio politely ended the discussion out of respect for his sister. As he was about to leave, he remembered he had a letter addressed to Mina that had been delivered to his apartment. He reached into his pocket and handed it to his sister. With a goodbye kiss to her and a nod to Carlo, he left. Shaking his head as he descended the tenement stairs, he thought, *my poor sister is married to a bastardo and a strunz.*

Back in the apartment, Carlo immediately took the letter from Mina and opened it. She saw him quickly pocketing an enclosure from the letter. "Read it out loud to me, Mina," he ordered since they both knew he could not read English well.

"Oh, it's from Jack Turner! His family and I became close during the voyage." It was easy to guess that the enclosure had been repayment money he had promised when on shipboard. It was verified as she read his written gratitude for the food-sharing during those last hungry days on the ship.

Jack wrote that he had good news and terrible news but decided to begin with the former.

"The good news, Mina, is that everyone is doing very well here in New Jersey. My brother and I, along with Sean Kelly, have started our own construction business which is growing every day with new work. Brian passed the fireman's exam and couldn't be happier although he frequently asks after Fiona and you (but, mostly, Fiona and I know you know what I mean!).

I miss Jack's sense of humor so much. Carlo never laughs and he never makes me laugh, either, she realized sadly.

The girls are becoming very American, already losing their brogues and taking on a Jersey accent and we wonder what your Boston accent sounds like now. I, with my little education, am so proud of how well the girls are doing in their schoolwork. They are teaching me rather than the other way around. I thank God every day that we have been spared so far from the dreaded influenza that is still spreading. I have to

applaud the good decision made by the New Jersey officials to close the schools temporarily to reduce the chance of infection. I believe the exposure to all the filth in steerage probably gave us an amazing immunity, wouldn't you agree?

Often, we reminisce about the voyage and how much we all hope to see you and Fiona again one day. Surviving that difficult time in steerage together bonded us in a special way and our crossing paths into each other's lives has been a blessing. Please write me if there is a possibility of a visit someday. We would welcome you with open arms. *How wonderful a visit would be*, thought Mina?

There are many job opportunities here in New Jersey if you and your husband ever considered relocating. I would gladly help you as you had helped our family. If you are in touch with Fiona, please share my regards and my offer to her, as well. For some reason I never obtained her Brooklyn address. *Inexplicably, none of us did*, Mina remembered.

With that, Jack included his address and, as he had promised, he included money in his letter which he said was his repayment to Mina for her kindness in sharing food on the ship when his family was hungry. Carlo had already confiscated the money and would not tell Mina the amount when she inquired.

The bad news came at the end of Jack's letter. **Mina, I thought to leave my terrible news until the end of my letter. You may have noticed I have made no mention so far of Winifred in my letter. That's because of my heartbreaking news. My Winnie drowned attempting to swim to New Jersey from the infirmary on Ellis Island. Her body had washed up at a place called Staten Island.**

Jack's letter went on but Mina could read no more as her eyes filled with tears. Her memories of Winnifred were those of a wonderful mother, a devoted wife and a dear friend. How cruel life can be.

"Is there anything important in the rest of the letter?" inquired Carlo as he prepared to leave for the evening.

"I think his wife's death is important enough." She said no more because she knew it would easily result in an argument.

"Do you have any other friends from the ship who owe you money that I did not know about?" Carlo could not hide his pleasure at the unexpected money he had pocketed.

"No."

"Too bad. And I want you to know that I do not give you permission to write this widower. He is a single man now who has a dead wife and you are a married woman, so I forbid it. I don't like how he seemed to like you very much from the sound of his letter. Besides, who would want to live in New Jersey?"

Mina sadly folded the letter disregarding Carlo's diatribe. She continued to think about Winifred and her family and, for the first time, to imagine living in New Jersey among friends.

Mina's thoughts were interrupted as her husband donned his coat preparing to leave the apartment. "Carlo, please stay home with me tonight." She feared what would happen if his gambling losses continued and one night he would not come home. Mafia reprisals were common knowledge on the North End when their loans went unpaid. "We need to pay the rent. Where will the money come from if you keep losing your pay to those criminals you gamble with? Now give me the money you took from the letter, it's my money and I can use it to pay our bills."

"Silencio, your money is my money," he sneered while taking a step towards her as if to strike her. "Those criminals, as you call them, are my friends and my future business associates. This is my way into the local family. Once I am accepted, then our money troubles will end. But until then I have to spend time with these fellows so they get to know that I can be trusted. I do not understand why my family back home is not helping. So, I need to do this on my own."

His look softened as he glanced at Mina. Pulling her closer to him, he added, "Mina, I feel my luck is about to change. I have made friends at the club. But, don't worry, I am no fool. I know the mob uses 'panem et circenses'," making reference to ancient Rome's use of bread and circuses to distract the people from reality. "I see the loose puttanas with *figa* available for the taking and free drinks that can make a gambler spend more and lose more. But, these do not distract me, I am faithful to you, Mina, all I do is gamble."

"But Carlo, you are not good at gambling. You are always losing. You think I believed you when you said I must have lost my gold necklace? I know you must have pawned it. Next you will be taking my wedding ring!"

This infuriated him. "You don't know anything." He pushed her away from him. But she didn't stop admonishing him. "You must stop now before it is too late. Is losing all your money the only way to be friends with these people? How many times must I remind you that I want no part of our being involved with Cosa Nostra? Do you really want to become a criminal, a killer?"

"There are other jobs, the 'bread and butter' jobs, like bookmaking, loan-sharking, collecting protection money from merchants. The best job is the 'no show' job that can be arranged with the unions so a guy gets paid for not working, can you believe that? That's what I want," shouting back at her at this point.

"I don't care about any of that. I just want us to have the normal life I was promised before we married. You are a smart man and a hard worker when you try. Can you promise me to try to stop the gambling and give up this wrong road you are on? Are you willing to do that for us, for our marriage?"

Losing patience, he grabbed his wife and pushed her hard against the wall. "This is cazzata! You are the one who needs to change, not me. You are the one who has to work harder to be the Sicilian wife I thought I was promised. You must be quiet and obey me. You must be proud of me," adding with a sneer, "and stop being so cold in bed if you ever expect to do your job and get pregnant."

He quickly admonished," And don't you dare run to your brother complaining about me because I will know if you do and you will be very sorry," he threatened.

That said, he slammed the door as he left. The impact caused the picture of Pope Benedict XV hanging on the wall to fall with the frame broken and the glass shattered. *If Carmela were here she would warn me that the Pope's picture on the floor is a bad omen and maybe she would be right,* was Mina's fleeting thought.

Mina should have known not to follow him into the hallway but she did anyway. "Di la verita?" Mina demanded the truth from him loud enough that neighbors were opening their doors. "So, I should expect that this will never be different? Your behavior will never change? I need to know, Carlo. Tell me the truth so that I will finally know that there is no hope for our marriage to continue."

At first, she thought he did not hear her or that he was pretending not to hear her until he turned back towards her in a rage and forcefully pushed her back into the apartment. He removed his coat and began to beat her. After washing his hands from her bloodied nose, he again donned his jacket.

"You forced me to do that. You will never leave this marriage, never. I cannot allow you to shame me in the eyes of my father or your family or even this tenement." He left without another word.

Salvatore Buterra, the Don of the North End, worked out of the office in the back of the social club on Prince Street which, for appearances, was a club to help immigrant Italian and Sicilian men find jobs and assimilate into American society. In actuality, it could be said that it did just that but in the wrong way with gambling and racketeering. Men who met the criteria could be accepted into this branch of the Patriarca Family. Once a member, assignments would include loan sharking, extortion and even injuring rivals or anyone owning a business who refused to pay for 'protection' insurance.

Although not in the prostitution business himself, Buterra allowed a number of whores to frequent his club to draw in the men, as long as they didn't interfere with the gambling. What they did at the end of the night was their business. They were to keep the men gambling and drinking the cheap liquor supplied by the club, which contributed to the men losing money at the games.

"Boss, Vitale's credit is at his limit again. What do you want to do with him?" asked Gus, a senior member known as the 'Collector'.

"Extend his credit limit some more and see what happens. Maybe he will start winning for a change." At that they both looked at each other and laughed.

"Don Vitale is a don in Sicily and married into the Palermo family so we must show respect. His father paid up the last debt called in, but his spoiled kid just doesn't know when to stop. My problem will be when his father stops covering for him. He has already made it clear that I should ignore the kid's requests to join our family which is no problem for me. I wouldn't take that hot-headed kid in anyway. So, we just wait and see," said Don Buterra. "It may become a serious problem eventually but, for now, I am not going to think about this fool. I am going home."

Gus wondered how the boss felt about his own son, Antonio, joining the family business in a few years, but he dared not ask such a personal question. The kid was attending the local parochial school.

The Don was devoted to his two familias although he kept both separated. Work was work, home was home. His wife was a Sicilian girl from Taormina who made him proud as the devoted wife and mother to their one son and three daughters. She never questioned anything about her husband's business and enjoyed the benefits received from it, such as a small home with a yard where she grew vegetables and in which their children played safely. She contributed generously to the church each Sunday when the basket was passed and never refused if there was a special collection for charity. Most evenings, her husband came home for dinner so she was pleased that he made the effort for family time. It was her understanding that her husband had given his men the order to never bother him at home unless it was for an emergency. And since he ran an effective and efficient organization, she could not think of even one such instance.

Although Buterra loved his wife, power provided him with entitlements for which she would never know. He was still a virile young man in his early forties, as he saw himself, and there were ladies available to him at will. He was always discrete. He had a roving eye but a discerning one. He preferred young whores just starting out in order to eliminate any possibility of venereal diseases. His preference was for Polish, German or Irish girls with fair hair and eyes so different from his saintly brunette wife. The new penniless immigrants provided a plentiful supply of desperate young women more willing to work free-lance in his club than in established brothels. Sometimes the couch in his office saw as much action as the gambling tables.

November, 1918

Boston

Each day, after Carlo left for work, Mina walked the few blocks to Basilio's tenement where she worked for Mrs. Jacobs. Her routine would be to look for the homeless mongrel so she could feed scraps she saved from home but it had not been seen for quite some time. She sincerely hoped it had not died from the cold nights with the recent snow or from human cruelty. Because it was a male she had been calling him 'Luigi', a name meaning 'fighter' and that was what he had to be to survive in the tenements.

Once she climbed the stairs, she would stop for a quick visit with her sister-in-law before going down the hall to Mrs. Jacob's apartment. "Carmela, have you seen the small dog recently?"

"Never mind the dog," as Carmela grabbed both Mina's hands. "I have an announcement, Mina!"

"Si, Carmela, but may I remove my coat first?"

"I can finally tell you! I am pregnant!"

"Oh Dio! that's wonderful, Carmela. I am so happy for you and Basilio. And for me to be an aunt!" Mina hugged Carmela as they both jumped up and down together like the joyful girls they still were.

"And our child's godmother, si?" asked Carmela, already knowing what Mina's answer would be.

"Si, who could love your child more than I?"

"Our prayers have been answered, Mina! Basilio and I are overwhelmed with happiness after these past years of trying to have a baby. Thank you,

Saint Felicity! Now if only the child is a boy to carry on the Amato name, it will be perfect."

But then she quickly added with her eyes raised to heaven "but we'll take a healthy daughter, too, St. Felicity," apparently still speaking to the saint and superstitiously not wishing to jeopardize the pregnancy by only requesting a son.

"I have been dying to share our news for two months. But your brother, the worrier, wanted us to make sure everything was going well before letting out the news. Nurse Mary told us that my pregnancy appears normal and there was no reason not to share the good news now."

Mina was excited for her brother and Carmela. She told Carmela that she knew what wonderful parents they would be. She found herself thrilled about the prospect of becoming an aunt. She knew her parents in Sicily would be excited, yet regretful, wondering if they would ever get to see their American grandchild.

"Have you written parents, yet?"

"Of course, but it will take some time before they receive the news. We know how happy they will be but it breaks my heart that neither of our mothers can be here with me for the delivery."

"Well, I will be with you, count on that, Carmela."

"Now it is your turn to become pregnant, Mina. Our babies can be close in age. Wouldn't that be wonderful?" Carmela's words struck a nerve in Mina. Becoming pregnant actually frightened her. She recognized that her imperfect marriage and frightening financial situation were contributing to her lack of passion in Carlo's bed. The last thing she wanted right now was to become pregnant. Secretly, she had been following Nurse Mary's instructions as to how to avoid pregnancy.

"We'll see, Carmela," as she let her voice trail off. "Just be so very cautious until this influenza epidemic ends, for both you and the baby. People are sick and dying on all the floors of both our buildings. You should stay indoors and away from people. I'll help you with the shopping and the housework."

"Isn't Carlo concerned about your exposure with you coming and going each day in both our buildings?" Carmela questioned Mina.

"Honestly, I think he just enjoys the pay I bring home each week," she replied sarcastically.

"Oh, and about the dog. I don't know if it is true but someone said that they had seen Muller, the policeman, take the dog home with him."

Mina hoped it was true since the officer did have a good reputation and gossip was that he and the nurse liked each other. "How nice for little Luigi. He will finally have a good home with someone like that."

"Nice for the terrier mutt but even nicer for the rats with the dog gone," sighed Carmela who did everything she could to keep the rats out of her flat. "Even the cats around here are afraid of our tenement rats."

Carmela became very serious. "I know I worry too much for Basilio but this disease is a scourge. The Riccillo family lost their youngest child yesterday. I didn't leave my apartment but I heard through the door that the mother refused to let the health workers take her little one's body. She struggled with them and neighbors had to intervene. Finally, Nurse Mary convinced her to let go of his corpse. So sad, Mina."

"Mrs. Jacobs read in the paper that it started in Kansas at a military base and then to Boston with sailors on a receiving ship. Then ships left Boston harbor for Philadelphia and New Orleans where it spread quickly there. Thousands of soldiers are infected and dying and now it is spreading everywhere. In last month's edition of the Boston Globe, it was reported that 202 people died in one day on October 1st. As hard as the doctors are trying, no one can explain the cause or the cure, so you must stay away from crowds as much as possible, Carmela."

Mina deliberately withheld the news that she read with Mrs. Jacobs about the Home for Italian Orphans already operating at full capacity to accommodate all the newly orphaned children in the North End due to the deaths of their young parents.

Carmela had been noticing Mina's healing bruises but had kept her silence. She accepted Mina's excuses at first but no longer believed Mina had so many accidental injuries. Carmela noticed that she would not visit when Basilio was home whenever there were bruises that could not be hidden by her clothing.

Finally, Carmela spoke out. "What is Carlo doing to you and why? I know you hide your injuries from your brother which is sensible, knowing how angry he would be."

"Carmela, you have been good so far in not making an issue of this. Please, you must continue to not say anything or there will trouble. Somehow I will find a solution."

"I see so many women with blackened eyes and broken bones in this building because poverty brings out the worst in husbands. But I never thought it would happen to you, Mina. You must be careful but if it gets worse, I will be forced to tell your brother."

"It won't get worse, I promise."

"Tenement life is difficult, Mina. So much poverty. When a working man is seriously injured, he loses his job. Do you know what happens then? Or he dies and his wife is widowed with seven children. What does she do? It is terrible just to think of it."

She continued, "There is a depraved world out there and the poor suffer the most. All I can do is close my eyes to it and not dare go out after dark. City poverty is harder than it was back home in the countryside." Advising her younger sister-in-law, Carmela added that poverty frustrates men even more than women. "Through centuries of deprivation and war, women have had to learn patience and fortitude for the survival of their children and themselves. Most men have not nor ever will learn that type of resilience. My advice to you is to find out what sets off your husband's anger and learn to control it. You can avoid being hit by him if you stop doing what makes him angry. You must be smarter than he is."

Sitting quietly, Mina sipped her tea while contemplating telling Carmela the truth about Carlo's gambling. But then changed her mind. *Carmela can be very insightful but she has no idea how serious my problem is and for which there is no easy remedy. She would be shocked to learn of Carlo's desire to join the mobsters or his gambling habit causing the continual loss of our income.* Mina was too ashamed to tell her the whole story. Some things must remain between a husband and a wife.

After Mina left to see Mrs. Jacobs, Carmela was surprised when Basilio came home early from work. Carmela knew something was terribly wrong since her husband was more likely to work overtime than to leave work early.

"The boss sent me home because he saw I was sick. I tried my best to hide it, Carmela, but I couldn't. Now I'll be docked wages for the hours missed which is not good for us."

Carmela recognized how he worried more about the loss of income for his family than his own illness. "Basilio, never mind money! People are dying everywhere from this influenza curse. Let's get you in bed and I'll find the visiting nurse who is somewhere in the building." She helped him undress and applied a cold compress to his fevered forehead, before she went in to the hallways searching for the public health nurse.

Although many victims of the influenza succumbed quickly, Basilio had fought it. He had been harboring the symptoms for two days when it finally worsened. Lying in bed alone while Carmela searched for help, he began to consider the seriousness of his condition for the first time. Like most young adults in good health, neither Carmela nor he ever thought they would be victims of the disease. They believed that, like most diseases, only the old and young were the most vulnerable. Then the newspapers began to report that this disease was killing young adults in greater numbers than any other age group. Up until then, Basilio concentrated on making a living. The more hours he worked, the better take-home pay. With so limited non-working time spent at home, he was unaware of the realities of what was happening around him even in his own tenement building.

That changed when he began to notice a serious change in his own health. First, he developed a fever, but he had kept it secret from Carmela and kept going to work. Then the body aches came, but still he went to work. He tolerated the accompanying cough but then had trouble taking a deep breath. Once his supervisor observed his output had slowed and then saw how ill Basilio appeared, he followed the company rules and sent Basilio home immediately. Basilio was reprimanded for risking contagion to his fellow workers. Then, as he left the building and as if the illness wasn't enough of a concern, he worried if there would be a reprimand on his flawless employment record.

To save money, Basilio's daily routine included walking to and from work, but on this day Basilio knew he felt too weak to make the long trek home so he waited for a trolley. Even ill, he felt guilty for spending money on the trolley that he knew Carmela could put to better use, especially with the baby coming.

Carmela had managed to assist him to undress and get into their bed with difficulty due to his weakness and her advancing pregnancy. Alone while she searched for the nurse, he couldn't catch his breath so he struggled to get himself into a sitting position. Even the slight elevation enabled him to take a deep breath instead the shallow ones that had forced him to mouth-breath.

His lungs burned with the accumulation of fluid. His whole body seemed to be turning against him and shutting down. He inadvertently glanced at his fingernails in disbelief as they began to turn a blueish color. *This cannot be happening to me? Could I be dying? Is it really possible that I will be leaving Carmela alone with our unborn infant? Worse, could I have already infected Carmela?* These were his last thoughts as Basilio's condition rapidly declined and while Carmela frantically roamed the building searching for the nurse, who could have been on any of the tenement's five stories.

November, 1918

Boston

The Boston Public Health Service assigned nurses to provide health education and care to the immigrants in as many tenements as possible, but there weren't enough nurses. The influenza epidemic was so out of control in Boston that the Agency telegraphed the National Red Cross Headquarters requesting nurses to be sent to Boston to assist in alleviating the crisis. Twenty-eight dollars a week was the incentive offered to nurses willing to take on assignments.

"I am very pleased to see you have taken to wearing a gauze mask, Officer Muller. Good for you as we must take every precaution available to us, right?" She was well aware that the morning contact with the young officer had become a daily routine and definitely not accidental. She admitted to herself that his attention pleased her although, after these many weeks, she wondered why he never suggested meeting after work for a movie or dinner. He had shared that he was not married so she decided that she would have to take the initiative shortly because of his shyness.

Removing his mask so he could converse easier, he said, "It's worth a try wearing the mask, I suppose, and the precinct ordered it. It wasn't my idea but maybe it will help considering the characters I come into contact with every day."

"Well, quite honestly, we both should continue to wear the masks even though there is no evidence that they really work. Hundreds of medical folks died last month who wore them so that is disconcerting. In fact, now I have to carry two bags, one for clean masks and another for soiled. Then they have to be boiled and dried daily. All I know is that tying these four strings to my face and hair is very troublesome so sometimes I don't wear the mask. But that doesn't mean you shouldn't!" she quickly added.

The tall, handsome police officer liked to listen to her because she was smart, passionate and opinionated and he admired her independent nature

"And how is your adopted dog, Officer Muller? Is he adjusting to a princely life after being such a little tramp?"

"The smart little mutt has adjusted very quickly to two square meals a day, a soft bed and kindness, I'm happy to report. My parents took a liking to him right away so he gets even more spoiled by them when I'm not home. I named him Max."

"A good German name, Max Muller," she remarked trying to sound German.

Muller tried his best each day to time his rounds with the pretty nurse's arrival time and became very disappointed when it was missed, to the point of ruining his day. Too frequently of late, their arrival times have not been coinciding.

To keep their conversation going, Muller told Mary that he was first generation American and asked how long her people had been in this country. "We're all immigrants here, just some of us arrived earlier than others."

"I'm proud to say that my maternal grandfather, Thomas Barry, arrived in Boston back in 1863 like so many other Irish forced to leave Ireland. As he tells his story, he was no sooner off the ship arriving penniless and emaciated when he was recruited right on the Boston dock into

the Union Army. And once my mother gives him a little whiskey, he will sit in his favorite chair and tell his story to anyone willing to listen."

"Tell me some of it. I love history," said Muller meaning it since he found anything about Mary to be interesting.

"Well, as he tells it, right on the dock, the army recruiter immediately handed him a navy blue wool coat, new boots and a voucher for hot food, so it seemed to him to be a good start in the new country for a 17-year-old who arrived with nothing and no one. So, he signed his name to a paper and found himself on a train headed to the South along with thousands of other young Irishmen. He fought in the Civil War until it ended and is deeply grateful to God that he had made it back home 'in one piece', as he puts it, when so many others had returned missing limbs or not returning at all. He said that the Irish recruits and the Negro soldiers were used as cannon fodder by the Nativist commanders. They were considered expendable so they had no hesitation in sending the recruits up and over hills repeatedly while being mowed down by the Confederates. But the Union had the numbers so, as the piles of blue-uniformed bodies mounted, more men would be sent forward to follow after those who had fallen. They had to climb over the hill of their dead comrades to reach the enemy. After massive losses, the confederates finally retreated but only because they were outnumbered. "Heck of a way to win a war," he would always conclude each time he retold his Civil War stories, and always lost in his painful memories of the needless loss of good young men on both sides. Even sounds a bit like the war going on right now in Europe, doesn't it?"

She continued when she saw that Muller did seem to be listening intently. "If anyone is still listening to him, then Grandpa tells of the war in 1846 where the Irish played a role, too, that made him proud. It was called the Saint Patrick's Battalion and led by John Riley. It was also made up of newly immigrant Irish. They deserted their American artillery and infantry battalions for a number of reasons. Some say it was because Mexico promised higher wages and citizenship. But most believe, from letters written to relatives, that it was because they were following their consciences. The Irish saw America as the same type of foreign ground invader into Mexico as England had been in Ireland. As Catholic soldiers, they were treated with deplorable discrimination. They were forced to attend Protestant services and their prejudiced Nativist senior officers issued the harshest punishments to them for trivial offenses. In one letter back home, a soldier wrote that when the American soldiers disrespectfully rode their horses into a Mexican Catholic church and joyfully desecrated it with shouts and hoots, even having their horses defecate by the altar, he made the decision that he had been fighting on the wrong side of the war. Anyway, they helped win a number of important battles until Mexico ran out of ammunition and money. The Americans won the war and the Saint Patrick's men were arrested for treason and hanged. Grandpa says that the green Flag with the Irish Harp under which they fought still flies on St. Patrick's Day in Mexico and in Connemara, Ireland, where John Riley was born. As you can guess, my grandfather, like most Irish, is a grand story teller," Mary ended wondering if she had gone on too long.

"And I would say that you have inherited his talent, Miss Moran."

"Well, you will be spared from any more of my banter now that we are here at my building. Please have a safe day and I hope to see you tomorrow," Mary said looking into his eyes as tenants from the building began to call to her.

As she walked away, he wondered, *she must have a beau, probably one of those wealthy brainy doctors. I just need to get my nerve up and ask her if she is seeing anyone. Even if it means that I will hate what her answer may be, I still have to do it.*

The next day, he noticed that wisps of her auburn hair escaped from her nurse's cap as she walked briskly in the cold autumn wind. If asked, the policeman would describe her green eyes as 'so beautiful as to take your breath away.' Officer Muller found himself in love with this woman but was too shy to know how to tell her without scaring her. He didn't know how to ask if she had a beau already. When he had mentioned being single, she had not said anything about herself. *Maybe I'm right and there is someone already courting her,* he thought unhappily.

"Officer Muller, I am especially grateful for your company today. I have never seen the streets so eerily empty in broad daylight. Such a strangely uncomfortable feeling to see barely anyone in the streets."

"Not so surprising considering all the closures. Schools, parks, theaters, businesses and even the railroad is limiting service now. Less crowds, less spread is the prevailing thought. Although, no one wants to say it, with so many ill, the closures are because there are fewer workers to carry on business."

"And those not infected are terrified of catching the illness," she added. "The hospital reported ambulance workers not reporting for work because of their fear of exposure."

"One good thing for our department is that crime is down," he added on a positive note. "But, at the last count, so are we with twenty percent of the force out ill so far."

He smiled at Mary. He had no idea with all this talk of disease how he could segue into letting her know his intentions were honorable and that he wished to ask her permission to see her on their personal time, as little as it was with both their long work shifts.

"Things are truly bad now that even Masses have stopped on Sundays. I never thought we would live to see the day that would happen, did you?" Mary knew he was Catholic from previous conversations they had shared, although she secretly looked for him at their church but never saw him at Mass.

"I'm sure Masses will resume soon," but he changed the line of conversation since he was a lapsed Catholic.

"Miss Moran, when people are scared, they make up all kinds of reasons to explain the cause of their fears, mostly with little evidence. At the precinct

I heard my co-workers blaming Germany for starting the epidemic as part of a secret war weapon that backfired and spread everywhere."

"I never heard that rumor. I've heard that it started in Spain."

"That's what I read, too, and that's why it is being called the Spanish Flu. Anyway, with Muller being a German name, I can't sound like I'm defending Germany, so I keep my opinions to myself at the precinct. Times are hard and people are scared and are always looking for a scapegoat."

"I agree." Mary took on an irritated tone when she added, "It's the politics and prejudices that upset me the most, too. We would have far more additional nurses if the Red Cross didn't ban Negro nurses from serving in the Army and Navy Nurse Corps or in our white hospitals. Some wealthy families are hiring them as private duty nurses but that is the limitation placed on them with the exception of working only in colored hospitals. It's a disgrace, an absolute disgrace."

She took a deep breath. "Well, that said with me proselytizing my politics on you, I must be off. Thank you again for your company," smiled the nurse, as she waited for him to ask her out. When there was no response from him, she frustratingly turned to enter the tenement. "Please keep that mask on anyway, never mind what I said. Best to be safe than sorry, Officer Muller."

He was disappointed with himself as he continued on his beat thinking, *next time I am going to ask that we begin to use our first names. I am taking too long in letting her know my feelings for her.*

As she looked over her shoulder at him walking away, she also made a decision. *Next time I will take the lead or we will never get this relationship off the ground!"*

November, 1918

Boston

Instead of visiting Carmela that morning, Mina went straight to Mrs. Jacobs' apartment. After the housework chores were completed and the English lesson completed, they shared lunch together. Mina loved the lunches Mrs. Jacobs had prepared from the groceries Mina bought at the Jewish merchant. She believed that she was most likely the only Sicilian who even knew what a cheese blintze was.

"Do you dream at night, Mina? As I am very old now, my dreams are always about my past and seem so real. Last night I dreamed my father was calling to me. He kept saying, 'Shayna maidel, my pretty girl, come to me.' I was never pretty but he would always tell me I was beautiful in Yiddish when he would hug me and say 'bei mir bist du sheyn'. Actually, I find comfort in such a dream because I believe death is a reunion with those we love. What do you think, Mina?"

"Frankly, Mrs. Jacobs, I think I am so tired I just sleep and don't dream much," Mina lied because she really spends sleepless nights worrying about how to end her marriage.

With the weather a bit milder, Mina opened the kitchen window just a few inches for fresh air and welcomed the breeze that came billowing through the sheer curtains that had been hung there for many years. Permanently yellowed from the unavoidable ash from the coal burned indoors for heat and cooking, Mina unsuccessfully tried to bleach them to their original whiteness. Often, Mrs. Jacobs would tell Mina to disregard the house work for which she was hired and instead spend extra time learning English by reading the newspapers with her.

"Come, Mina, let's begin our lesson," she would request as she sat at the table with paper and pencils and a recent newspaper.

"But I must finish cleaning and then I need to get more coal for later, Mrs. Jacobs."

"Never mind that. Your lesson is more important."

Mrs. Jacobs always reinforced to her student the importance of speaking English in America, otherwise she told her that she would remain a foreigner in the eyes of the citizens. She believed that was part of the reason for prejudice against many immigrant adults who never made an effort to assimilate by learning English and instead left it to their children to learn.

"Mina, it takes 'chutzpah', which means a type of nerve for an immigrant to truly assimilate into American society. You have it and your future children will be grateful to you for having it. It sometimes takes a generation or two for it to happen in many immigrant families because they are fearful or they just lack motivation, as you can witness right here in this building."

Mina could not help but think of Carmela as an example but she remained silent.

"Did you know that a long time ago an Irish woman, Ann Glover, was hanged here as a witch because she could only speak her native Gaelic and not English?"

"If they hanged people today for not speaking English, then they would be hanging everyone in this building and most of the North End," laughed Mina, but she knew Mrs. Jacobs was right.

A large part of each day's lesson involved reading the latest news articles in the paper. Mina would read aloud about the 'Great War' as the war was being named. Thousands of soldiers were dying every day in the trenches and those returning home were critically damaged by the inhalation of the mustard gas used by the Germans against them.

"From what has been said, this war may be wiping out a generation of young men in many countries, not just ours," the older woman commented. "A horrible waste of life is taking place." Mrs. Jacobs saw the war as a gruesome example of young men needlessly dying because of old men's arrogance and ineptitude.

"Some intellectuals have voiced how upper class British men have been given leadership roles in the army for which they have no warfare experience or knowledge. The thought is that these officers may be responsible for numerous blunders resulting in the needless deaths of uncountable numbers of soldiers who follow their rash commands. Such an unforgiveable waste, if true!"

She moved on to another article. This time she read it to Mina as it held a particular interest for her. It was written about the Russian Czar, Nicholas, and his family's execution by the Bolsheviks ending three centuries of the Romanov dynasty.

"Murdering the Czar, his wife and children must have been brutal, but Jews were long persecuted under the Romanovs. Maybe God has his own way of meting out justice," was Mrs. Jacobs' comment. This surprised Mina. After her deep expression of sympathy for the soldiers in the trenches, the coldness in her teacher's voice for the Czar and his children was just the opposite.

"Who are the Bolsheviks?" Mina inquired.

"Apparently, an organized group that has taken control of the army and, therefore, the country. Dictators cause such revolutions and have only themselves to blame when the people finally revolt. Only time will tell if the Russian people prosper under the new regime or will it become just another kind of monocracy headed by thugs rather than by patriots."

With the older woman's ability to change a subject quickly, she said, "Speaking of God and religions," which they had not been, "did you know that Muslims have ninety-nine names for God in their prayers while we have so few? Someday I hope that people will realize that we all pray to the same God. We just give him different names."

With this said, her teacher then began to discuss the different religions of the world, many new to Mina, especially those in India and the Middle East. Mina listened intently, appreciating that she was learning far more than English every day. She admired Mrs. Jacobs for her sincere tolerance of other religions and nationalities considering how intolerant everyone was against her for just being Jewish.

"I am unable to practice my religion as I had before. I stopped going to temple when Irving passed but I have wonderful memories of our kind Rabbi. I miss the Ha Motzi prayer over the braided challah bread, Passover feast and many other beautiful ancient ceremonies, just as you have in your religion. But one can be spiritual even without attending organized houses of worship. Prayer and kind acts are the answer to gain heaven, that is what I comfort myself with, as I try to do both as much as I can. I wonder if we will ever learn to love each other as all our religions teach?"

Her mood brightened up as it always did when she spoke of her deceased husband. "I was just a poor peasant girl until my husband educated me. He would tell me 'Bei mir bist du sheyn' which means 'to me you are beautiful' even though I was never pretty, in fact, I was quite plain. But Irving loved my thirst for knowledge and that's what made me beautiful to him, I think. I see that thirst in you, too, Mina, so never lose it. As Irving taught me, I want to teach you what I can. Keep in mind that knowledge is power and women need to understand that. I believe you are a very capable young woman and I am so grateful that you allow me to share what little I know with you."

"Little, you say, but you are a wealth of information, Mrs. Jacobs." Mina admired how Mrs. Jacobs could jump from one subject to the next and patiently answer any questions raised. But Mina did begin to notice that she would sometimes forget which language she would be speaking and revert back to the Yiddish of her childhood.

"Mina, you and my nurse, Mary, are my favorite people in the world. I don't know what I would do without you two," expressed the elderly woman as Mina was leaving for the day. Mina realized that she and Mary were her only visitors except for the delivery boy.

"Is *'Bubbe'* the correct Yiddish word for grandmother? If it is then that's how I think of you."

"And you are my special granddaughter, Mina."

Their visits together ended too soon to suit Mina, but she had her own obligations at home and the old woman accepted that. Joyfully, following each visit, Mina felt as if she had attended a class at a private school.

One day, Mary Moran examined Mrs. Jacobs while Mina was attending to the household chores. Then she took Mina aside while the old woman napped in her chair.

"She told me she had 'a shittem mogan' last night. For once, I did not need her to translate that into English for me as you can guess from the sound that it means diarrhea. So please keep an eye on her. She has no other symptoms so I wouldn't think it is anything serious for now."

"I will, Mary. You know I will."

"Actually, I've been meaning to tell you, Mina, that you are responsible for the noted improvement in her. Even her attitude is so much better. Since you have come into her life, she's no longer depressed. She looks better than she has in months and I am positive it is due to your care and companionship."

Mary went on, "You have no idea how pitiful it was for me to see how lonely she had become. I tried to spend time with her but you understand I have work here every day that goes well beyond my normal work hours. Sometimes I can only visit a person weekly as it is impossible to visit everyone in this building. Since you alone have lifted her spirits and given her a purpose in teaching you English, how about you pretend to take longer learning the language? She lives for your lessons," Mary requested half-jokingly.

"Mary, I really do enjoy my time with her and she generously pays me for the small amount of housework. Truthfully, I would come here even if she was unable to pay because I learn so much from her."

"I've seen your progress, Mina. Your English is now good enough for you to travel anywhere, to go to school and even to find a meaningful job if you so desire. Don't you know how freeing that confidence is for you as a woman?"

"It would be easier if my husband would speak English with me but he will only speak our Sicilian dialect at home," replied Mina trying not to sound too disloyal to Carlo.

Mary continued with her encouragement, "Unfortunately, that is only too common among so many immigrant families but I recognize how very different you are from most of the young girls I meet in this tenement. They seem to be content with so little and think marriage and babies are all there is to life. Mrs. Jacobs sees that difference in you, too."

Mina wanted to agree with Mary since her sister-in-law Carmela was certainly one of those girls referenced by Mary. All Carmela wanted, besides having children, was to remain in her Sicilian comfort zone, never really assimilating into the larger outside society.

The problem that holds me back and holds him back, as well, is that Carlo is a Philistine, Mina thought to herself, remembering Mrs. Jacobs describing the type during one of their lessons. *Carlo is a fool not to allow us to practice English. It would benefit him in his job with his non-Italian co-workers and supervisors. After living in Boston for three years, he is still very limited in speaking English, and barely can read it and that is his own fault. He expects us to live here just as if we were still in Sicily.*

After Mary's visit and her encouragement, Mina finally opened up to her teacher. She had slowly entrusted Mrs. Jacobs with her unhappy marriage situation bit by bit during the last weeks. Mina knew her teacher had seen the bruises but was too polite to ask about them. She knew she could trust her with Carlo's gambling behavior and that she would keep it secret from Carmela, understanding the importance of Basilio never knowing the truth.

Almost as a mother can read a daughter, the old woman provided advice while fully understanding that divorce was out of the question for Catholics. However, she did stand firm on recommending separation from Carlo should conditions deteriorate further. She even offered Mina to come stay with her if needed and Mina knew she was sincere in her offer. But it was an offer that could never be taken for fear of how Carlo would react, possibly violently.

"But Mrs. Jacobs, I want you to know that there is a sweet side to Carlo, too. It is the gambling disease that keeps that part of him in the shadows. It is the side I thought I loved but have seen for a long time. I can hope it returns but I don't believe it ever will. I am just grateful to have you to hear me out."

"Mina, take it from this old woman, life is not meant to be spent unhappy. Too often, we innocently take a wrong road. I have only myself to blame for not moving from this building years ago when all my Jewish neighbors were doing so. In your case, your life's path was crossed with Carlo through an arranged marriage. Don't allow this to change your life against your better judgement. You deserve all the happiness life offers so don't allow an unsuccessful marriage to ruin your future. You are being tested whether you realize it not. Will you continue in despair to live an unfulfilled life or will you use all your God-given blessings to change it? That is your challenge, Mina."

The next visit found Mrs. Jacobs not feeling well. She was running a slight fever and she had soiled herself. Mina couldn't disguise her concern with all the news of the Spanish flu that was spreading intensely throughout the North End and within the tenements. Every day, coughing was heard through the thin walls. Inhabitants quickly passed each other in the hallways afraid of contagion. Socialization among neighbors had become a thing of the past.

Beyond belief, the newspapers began to report that deaths throughout the world were adding up into the millions. Mary Moran could be seen exhaustedly visiting apartment after apartment with people calling out to her for help. And there was no hiding it anymore as bodies of the deceased were being carried out of the building by public health workers amid the wailing of relatives.

Mass graves were necessary for the vast majority of deaths because the immigrants had little money for formal burials. With the deaths of carpenters, coffin makers and grave diggers, the city had run out of coffins and graves.

"I will go and find Mary. She always knows what to do. Just rest and I'll be back quickly," Mina said, hoping to make them both feel better with Mary's presence.

"Don't overreact, Mina. Mary has no secret cure. If she did, she would be the first to end this plague. Besides, she just saw me two days ago."

"But you weren't ill two days ago."

"I will just nap. Stop worrying. I should have known better than to have gone downstairs to sit in the cold air watching the few children allowed out to play. It was unwise and now I am paying for it. Mina, put your mind to rest. I am going nowhere until I have you speaking English as if you born in Boston.

On second thought, though, let's not aim for that annoying nativist New England accent," at which they both laughed.

Mina left to return home after making Mrs. Jacobs as comfortable as she could. She could not find the nurse and Mary did not visit Mrs. Jacobs that day. The disease was rampant in the building and Mary could not keep up with everyone needing her help.

November, 1918

New York City

At Grand Central Station, Fiona bought a ticket on the Federal Express train to Boston with the money Sam had given her for the train and a hotel room. The plan was for her to meet him at an address in Cambridge the next day. He told her that his new partners wanted to meet his model before finalizing any deal with him.

"Fiona, when we meet the group of new partners, my plan is to have you pose as Mata Hari wearing just jewelry, nothing on your bottom or top. That should get their attention, right?"

"And look where it got Mata Hari, Sam. She was just killed by a French firing squad for espionage, in case you didn't read about that in the newspaper."

"Fiona, don't make light of this because it is important for both of us."

Fiona said nothing. Her plan differed greatly from Sam's. Up until then, Fiona had only posed with Sam and Madame in the room, no one else. She was shocked that Sam would have made an arrangement where there would be an audience of men enjoying her shameful posing for them. But she consoled herself with knowing that his plan would never take place. She humored Sam and counted on his trust in her. Her one hope was that he would not be hurt by these 'partners' with the cancellation of their private Mata Hari show.

Before she boarded the train, Fiona tore up the paper with the meeting address and watched the cold winter wind scatter the shreds onto the already littered train tracks. She watched as the tiny pieces floated and blew in all directions. In that moment, Fiona was reminded how similar her life has been to the unguided fragmented bits of floating paper. But, disregarding the thought, she began to formulize her plan to change her life.

I will have to outsmart them all. First, I will find a different hotel from the one Sam proposed and it will need to be as far as possible from his meeting address. She knew that it would not take long before Sam realized she would not be showing up at the arranged meeting. She wondered what Sam's reaction would be after all the months working together. *I really don't owe him anything,* she rationalized, *and I probably made him richer than he admits.*

But part of her would always be grateful because, without his help, she never would have been able to leave Madame or Ireland, which held only unhappy memories for her. And he never forced himself on her for which she would always remember gratefully. *He will find another desperate girl just as he found me. There is no shortage in any city. I just hope his business partners will not penalize him in any way but that's now his problem, not mine.*

On the train, she thought she would have the time to carefully calculate her next moves. She planned she would visit Mina in Boston using the address given to her on the ship. She said it was her brother's address but he would give Fiona her new address now that she was married. *Mina is a good influence on me and will help me make myself into a person like her, if that can even be possible. But even before locating Mina, I will find a real job,* she swore to herself.

Increasingly, women were needed and joining the workforce, especially with men away at war and, sadly, with many men not returning from the war. She had heard from talk in her boarding house that the Prince Macaroni factory in the North End was hiring women workers and was growing its operation, so her plan was to start there. *They may be hiring only Italian women and not Irish for a spaghetti factory but it will be worth a try,* she considered.

And she read an advertisement in the paper by a rope factory that was hiring in Boston because of the growing demand for rope for the warships, giving her another possible lead for a job. Regardless, she knew she had enough money saved to see her through her plan. Her landlady explained how bank deposits and withdrawals worked so she was determined to place her savings in the Bank of Boston upon her arrival. *Finally, with banking there will never again be a need for me to find hiding places in my room or sewn into my clothes!*

When she thought of Mina, she hoped that marriage hadn't changed her from the caring and innocent girl she was during the weeks of voyage. She missed the sweet girl who could never make up her mind but, who in the end, would always make the right choice.

November, 1918

Boston

After spending over a year serving in France and a month in the hospital re-cuperating from his injury, Henry Jackson was honorably discharged from the army and ready for his new civilian life in Boston. He was a proud Colored American soldier who served in the 93rd Division of the 369th Infantry Regi-ment from New York respectfully called the 'Harlem Hell Fighters.'

Their division were the first to arrive at the Rhine River, pushing back the Germans after spending 191 days in trenches. The French government awarded each member of their regiment the Croix de Guerre medal for their valor in combat.

"It was our good luck that the American army didn't know what to do with us colored soldiers so they placed the regiment under the command of the French army," he told his friend Andy who was helping him find a job in Boston.

"How so, Henry? What does it matter if you die for the USA or you die for the Frenchies?"

"It matters when you are treated with respect as the French do. America hasn't learned to do that for us coloreds, yet. The French called us heroes and treated us as equals. I can never forget that."

"Well, I am just glad you got yourself back. And better work is waiting you here, my friend, with no Germans shooting at you or working our dirt farms in Alabama."

Both men came from share cropper families, raised in dire poverty and perpetual debt and subjected to harsh segregated Jim Crow laws down south.

Once the boll weevil infestation ruined the cotton crop in 1917, a mass migration of southern blacks took place, migrating to the north where work could be found in the major industrial cities that were hiring coloreds and women because of industrial expansion and a need to fill all the vacancies caused by the war.

Henry ended up in New York while Andy had connections in Boston. Unlike Andy, who found employment in the rail road as a conductor, Henry joined the army.

"Man, the army changed my thinking about life. Sure, I saw combat first hand but the difference was that we fought side-by-side with the French and with colored soldiers from Northern and Western Africa. I witnessed how the French practiced democracy and equality and I gained pride from our African brothers. I sure hope I can adjust to America again, Andy, because I know it won't be as good as I had it over there. Can you believe that our boys were even allowed to date the French white women and nothing was said against it? I had too much of Alabama still in me so I was too scared to start any of that but I could have and knowing that was freeing. I did okay with the French for a poor southern black boy, that's for sure."

"Well, should I call you Henry or 'Henri 'since you are so French now?" his friend teased him.

"I guess I'll be fine once I get adjusted again as to how things are done here, but it may take some doing is all I can say. I'm still having nightmares. Hard to forget the bombing, the filthy trenches and the faces of friends killed around you and the faces of the enemy soldiers that I killed."

Both had nothing to say after that. Eventually, Henry thanked Andy for sharing his place and for the job interview with the railroad that he had arranged for him.

"I owe you, Pal."

"Never mind that. The good news for us Negroes is that the rail road likes us for conductor jobs and believes in hiring veterans. So, you have two good things going for you which made it easy for me to get your name on the interview list."

"Are you sure I can make a good conductor? I have my doubts about it to be honest, Andy."

"Look, like you already know, it may not be as bad here in Boston as it is in Alabama, but there is still plenty of troubles for us coloreds, so be prepared,"

216

Andy warned. It was important to make sure his friend understand that the north could be as prejudiced as the south, just different in how it was presented.

"The South is wide-open with their prejudices. The Northerners, they are sneakier with theirs," he added. "But you just make sure the passengers are comfortable and safe and you will be fine. Most people are real nice."

Andy's rooms, which he offered to share with Henry, were located on the north slope of Beacon Hill in Boston's West End, where there were hundreds of well-established working black families. Although the less desirable side of the hill, it was home to working coloreds and some whites and where many worshipped in the Baptist Church together, although the coloreds had separate seating. New arrivals from Louisiana, the West Indies and the Caribbean islands were adding to the American Negro population in the area. Many of them were Catholic, not Protestant. However, when the Baptist church sponsored a Thanksgiving Church Supper and Dance, all were welcomed and that was where Henry met Chloe Richard from Louisiana.

The dance was held in the church's hall which had many purposes, such as wedding receptions, christening parties and any other church related events. The pastor and his committee members decided that the community needed a joyful holiday event and the church ladies insisted on a Thanksgiving dance.

As the pastor's wife, Rebecca, put it, "time to let the young have a fling what with the soldiers beginning to return and the young girls lookin' for husbands."

Reverend Parker, being far more reserved than his wife, presented it as an outlet to celebrate life after all the deaths in the news. He proudly informed his congregation of the latest government reports that had the influenza infection rates lowest among Negroes.

"Science cannot explain it but it certainly contradicts white America's notion of Negro inferiority," he pronounced proudly.

And so, to celebrate Thanksgiving, the committee decorated the hall with lights and placed paper flowers on the tables, since real flowers were too expensive in November. A local jazz group agreed to play at the party for free thanks to the church-going wife of the saxophone player. And everyone agreed to provide various ethnic dishes, making the cuisine interesting, although turkey was still the main course. Some attendees brought Southern fried dishes and buttery desserts. The newcomer West Indians brought their Island rice and coconut dishes and the Creoles added their spicy ones to the buffet table. Unlike some strict factions of Baptists in the south, this New England congregation allowed dancing and beer.

"After all, did not Jesus imbibe wine in the parable of the wedding?" Reverend Parker preached from the pulpit. "And I'm sure that wedding had music and dancing, too."

Chloe had been standing in a corner with her sister and a few other Creole friends, occasionally looking around as the music played and people began to dance. Henry could not take his eyes off her, later telling folks that 'it was love at first sight.' Andy had spotted a young lady he had already been acquainted with through the church so he moved to ask her to dance, leaving Henry feeling uncomfortably alone.

I fought Germans so asking for a dance shouldn't scare me, he thought, but it did. However, he manned-up and asked Chloe if she would like to dance. When she jokingly answered what sounded like 'oui', he became even more infatuated. They introduced themselves and began to dance to a soft song that allowed them to hear each other speak while dancing.

"Do you really speak French or are you like me and only know a little bit, 'un peu de francais'?" he teased.

"Considering I am a French Creole from St. Martin's Parish in Louisiana, I do speak it but it is quite a bit different from Parisian French. So where did you learn your 'un peu' of the language?"

"In the army when my battalion was fighting in France." That was all he had to say. Chloe knew at that moment she wanted to learn more about this interesting veteran.

After the first dance, as they sat at a table together with Andy and his lady friend, Miriam, the couples became at ease with each other and talked of everything from local news on the epidemic to politics and religion. Chloe called her younger sister, Rene, over to join them,

which added to the energy at the table as the younger sister did not hold back any of her political views on the war or society.

"Every family has its renegade and Rene is ours," joked Chloe as she put her arms around the teenager.

"I am not a renegade unless being a renegade means trying to fix up this world that all you adults screwed up," she responded defiantly.

"Ok, no sister-fighting," interjected Miriam. "And for your information, young lady, I know that *I* did nothing to screw up this world. It was screwed up from the time I was born into it," which left everyone at the table saying 'Amen, Sister.'

Proudly, Chloe clarified that Rene was currently interning in their father's medical office and will be going on to school to eventually become a physician like their dad. "Right now, Rene is instructing women on birth control which is no easy subject and not always well-received. She is very brave. It often takes her into white neighborhoods where our people are not welcomed as she works with the Public Health nurses in some of the tenements."

"Frankly, I have not found the company of whites has much to recommend about it. The way we are treated frequently makes me dislike them as much as they dislike us." Rene spoke her mind even knowing she was causing embarrassment to the church-going people at the table.

To try to remedy the silence that had struck, Rene went on to quickly add, "but the other day there was an Italian woman who proved me wrong. She defended me when a vegetable vendor refused to sell me tomatoes. She berated the vendor and, from the little of the language that I could pick up, reminded him of all our Negro men bravely fighting overseas. Then she went on to say something about Negroes having been Americans a lot longer than Sicilian immigrants have. All I know is that she went out of her way on my account, which rarely happens."

"We all experience discrimination, Rene, I don't think any of us will disagree with you about that. But like you just pointed out, there are good and bad people who come in all colors that's what you have to remember, Girl. We need to do our best to not antagonize situations," said Andy.

Andy was right but Henry remembered back home in Alabama where Andy had frequently been referred to as an 'Uncle Tom' by some folks for his soft accepting nature.

Chloe returned to discussing Rene's work. "As Catholics, Rene and my father believe in the importance of birth control although our church is not in agreement. But our family believes that we each must follow his or her conscience. Rene plans to go into obstetrics which makes our family very proud of her," Chloe added knowing the recognition would please her sister.

"Anyway, we are happy to be here as we weren't sure we could attend, not being Baptists. But Rene, being persistent and inquisitive, made the effort to find out, so here we are and so *were* our Creole shrimp dishes!" which made everyone laugh since she used the past tense denoting how quickly their contribution was eaten. Miriam, Andy's friend, was the only one at the table who had eaten some of their dish and raved about how delicious it was. "That's why whenever there is a buffet line, I get on it fast before all the best food is gone. Let that be a lesson to the rest of you who missed out on the girls' shrimp dish!"

Shyly looking at Henry, Chloe added "I'm so glad Rene and I did come here."

"So am I, I mean, we all are glad you came," Henry stuttered but his attraction to Chloe was apparent to everyone at the table.

"Mesi, which means thanks in Creole" she responded looking around at everyone.

Mrs. Parker, the Reverend's wife, upon hearing the words 'Creole shrimp' mentioned, made her way to their table. "Who here brought that shrimp dish?"

The sisters hesitantly raised their hands, asking "was it too spicy, did someone not like it?"

"Young Ladies, your dish was eaten in a flash and people are still talking about how delicious it was. I just wish I could have got some but apparently one had to be very fast on the buffet line to get any!"

The girls beamed and promised that they would make a dish for her and the Reverend as a thank you for allowing them, as non-Baptists, to the dance.

"We are all God's children, remember that always," replied Mrs. Parker.

Hearing this, Chloe felt compelled to share a recent occurrence. "I know Rene told her story of kindness but I have one to share, as well, because something happened to me that proves how some people are more God's children than others. I was sort of not paying attention to my surroundings, daydreaming about what I would wear to today's party, when out of nowhere a young man pushed me to the ground with him on top of me. Of course, I immediately began to pummel him with my fists until I realized he actually saved me. A horse had gone wild and was pulling an empty milk wagon at full speed around the corner right where I was about to step. I truly believe he saved my life." She turned to her sister and deliberately added, "and he was white."

"When I thanked him with all my heart for his brave deed, he smiled and told me, 'Actually, I never take a trolley but I decided to wait for one today because I'm not feeling well enough for the long walk home. I guess that our paths crossed at the right time.' Then the trolley arrived and the young Italian man was gone."

Everyone at the table agreed that some things cannot be explained. A serious question was raised by the pastor's wife. "Do people like that come into our lives accidentally or are there no coincidences in life, just mysteries that sometimes have explanations and other times not. Food for thought," she said with a knowing smile.

Henry added what he was told by his mother. "We are tested every day, some of us pass and some of us fail and the guy in Chloe's story sure did pass."

"Your mother sounds like a very wise woman," Mrs. Parker said, meaning it.

"And now that I have had a chance to listen to your lovely accent, Chloe and Rene, would you be kind enough to explain the difference between Creole and Cajun? I have wondered about that for a while," she inquired of the Louisiana girls.

"Of course, Mrs. Parker," was Chloe's response. "In a nutshell, here is the easiest way to explain the two cultures. Creoles, like Rene and me, are an ethnic group descended down from colonial French landowners who sired children with their African slaves or their African wives since some did marry their mistresses. Although they clung to the French language, in time

changes happened. For example, the language formed was more a 'pidgin' French, easier for the landowners and the African slaves to communicate with each other. For example,' I love you' in French is 'Je t'aime' but in Creole it is 'Mo laime' twa'. Instead of 'oui' in French, it became 'wi' in Creole. And some African traditions also got mixed in with Catholic practices as the Africans did not let go of all their religious beliefs from the homeland."

"The Cajuns, on the other hand, are white descendants from the French Arcadians dispelled from Canada in the 1700's by the British as punishment because they refused to pledge their allegiance to Britain after the English won the war in Canada. Families were forcibly separated having to return to France while the majority of the Arcadians were exiled to the Louisiana territory, thousands of miles away. They are country folk who learned to navigate the swamps and bayous and managed to maintain their French and Catholic heritages, although with their own unique cultural changes added to both, as well."

Rene interrupted what she saw was becoming a boring educational conversation. "My sister is a teacher, as you can see by how she delights in lecturing. The important thing to know about both ethnicities is that our food is absolutely spicy and delicious!"

With that, everyone laughed agreeing, including Chloe, although she knew she could have gone on much longer on the subject. Her thought was pleasantly interrupted when Henry asked her to dance. They danced just about every dance that night.

As the weeks went by, they spent every spare moment they could find to be together. It wasn't easy with his new conductor job and her teaching position. So, Sundays became their day together whenever Henry's schedule allowed it.

One Sunday afternoon at a family picnic, her parents agreed that they could sit separately from the family as it was a known fact that Henry was now formally courting Chloe.

"Just like your students, I am always learning from you, Chloe," and Henry meant every word. He was very proud that he had found such a refined and educated woman who could answer all his questions whether it was science or history.

"I've heard it said, 'Educate a woman and you educate a family,' and I know now how right that sounds after meeting you," he said while talking her hand in his and kissing it the same way he had seen the French men do.

Henry was still adjusting to his conductor job which, at times, was difficult for him after living in France. It was a requirement for conductors to cater to the passengers, right or wrong, which made Henry feel like a colored servant at times. But the pay was fair and he never had to get dirty, so he forced himself to accept conditions as they were and to be grateful.

Chloe had graduated from Howard University, the same college that her physician father had attended and the one Rene would be entering in the fall. Her father decided to move the family to Boston when he was offered a prestigious position in the Boston Hospital for Coloreds.

Cloe was thrilled when she was offered a teacher position at the Mother Mary School for Girls. She loved teaching her second grade girls, all of whom were colored or foreign-speaking immigrant children for whom some of the other teachers had no patience. One dark olive-skinned child shared with Chloe how happy she was to have her as her new teacher because the previous white teacher would wash their mouths out with soap whenever any one of the students would accidentally speak in her native language. Because of the shortage of nuns in the poor parish, the few who were available were assigned to teach the white American girls. Regardless of the innate discrimination, Chloe found the school and faculty an otherwise welcoming place to work.

She frequently had to remind Henry that her job was contingent on her remaining single as no married teachers were allowed employment at her school. She held only a temporary certification and her deportment was under continuous scrutiny so there could never be a hint of untoward behavior or she would be at risk of losing the job she loved.

"I want to marry you, Chloe. Are you telling me we have to wait until you are ready to stop teaching? How long will that be?"

"Please be patient, Henry, 'piti piti', a little bit longer" she smiled using Creole that he loved to hear.

"I want to marry you, too. But look at it as a chance for us to save some money which will help us later after we marry and I am no longer allowed to teach."

Henry was not happy about the delay but appreciated how the woman he loved felt. It was beyond his understanding why a female teacher had to be single to teach when a male teacher could be married.

Henry thought to himself, *I bet France has no such stupid requirement. The 'Frogs', as the English soldiers called the French during the war, were far ahead of the 'Limeys and the 'Yanks' when it came to common sense and fairness.*

Fiona stepped into the train car, smiled her nicest smile at the Negro conductor and settled into a window seat. She watched him assisting a group of nuns with their horse-hair trunks and she watched the bustling Grand Central station crowds all heading to various destinations. As Fiona tucked her loose blonde tendrils into her bonnet, she made herself comfortable for the trip to Boston. Once the train was in motion, the rythmatic sound of the wheels and the rolling motion of the train car caused her to drift into a much-welcomed twilight sleep before a loud commotion gained her attention.

Three women who were sitting together were being hassled by a rude man towering over them while spewing derogatory terms at them. They were trying to ignore him which only seemed to increase his hostility towards them. Ungentlemanly, not one man in the car came to their rescue and the conductor had already left their car to collect tickets in the next.

"You rich bitches, with nothing better to do than cause trouble, are the reason my marriage ended. I blame you all for causing such unrest in my home that I was forced to throw my wife out and deny her seeing our children. This is due to your brain washing her. She is devoted to your stupid political fiasco. You are dangerous people and must be stopped at all costs," he spewed with no ending of his diatribe in sight.

"She went on marches with your kind, leaving me with undone laundry and cold dinners, to be ridiculed by the men on my job. I was called a man who cannot control his wife or head his household properly because of your ill-conceived ideas of women's equality with men. I tell you, it will never happen. You will never vote. You are wasting your time, you are all lesbians with no men in your lives. If you had men and children then you would have no time for such lost causes," his voice filled with rancor.

The Negro conductor came into the car when he heard the raised voice. Once he evaluated the situation, he calmly and politely asked the man to move to the next car.

"Sir, I'm sure you understand that this is upsetting the other passengers, which I am sure is not your intention. I have a very nice window seat ready for you in the next car, with your agreement, please."

At first, the conductor's offer was refused. "Even though you are not a white man, surely you can't be siding with these women who are endangering our way of life as men?" Henry

Jackson had to hold back his temper. He had to call back on everything the railroad taught him about customer service if he wanted to keep his new job. Without responding to anything directed at him, Henry continued to patiently invite the volatile passenger to accompany him to the next car, which finally happened once the man realized he had said everything he had intended to say to the three women who had not uttered one word.

A short time later, as everyone watched, the conductor returned to speak with the women. He introduced himself, made apologies to the women for the verbal abuse that they had experienced and ensured them that there would be no additional harassment during the trip.

"But, Ladies, a warning. I strongly advise avoiding that gentleman when we reach the station."

Fiona had watched the entire episode from her seat, even holding herself back as she instinctively wanted to aid the three women, but she waited thinking that the gentlemen in the car would do so. Seeing how wrong she was when not one man came to their defense, she finally realized who the women were and what they represented. The three were Suffragettes.

Even with her scant knowledge of the movement, Fiona was greatly impressed with their courage and determination. Suffering abuse, such as was just displayed on the train, these women are dedicated to attaining equal voting rights for women. She realized that she shared the same beliefs for liberty for which her parents gave their lives and that explained her affinity with these rebellious women. Because there was a long ride ahead and because there were many empty seats around the women in the otherwise crowded car, Fiona stood up and moved in their direction.

"May I sit with you?"

"Of course, young lady. But, as you have seen, it is at your own risk, as some on this train disagree vehemently with our politics," was the reply delivered with a wide smile by the older woman in the group. She was the one who had tried unsuccessfully at first to calm the man down. *Apparently, it would take more than this recent episode to disarm this lady,* Fiona thought, *although the two younger women still appeared visibly shaken.*

Fiona introduced herself. "My name is Fiona Burke and, being Irish, I know all about troubled politics firsthand. I can assure you I lived them not so long ago."

"Then it is our turn to introduce ourselves, Miss Burke. I am Lucy Burns and with me are Carrie Smith and Jane Rider."

"I see you are Suffragettes by your sashes." The women were wearing the purple, gold and white sashes across their dresses.

"Actually, we are *Suffragists*. Our name does get confused with our European sisters who are called Suffragettes," Lucy clarified for Fiona. They explained they were headed to Boston's Back Bay where the MWSA headquarters was located.

"Please excuse my ignorance but what is the MWSA?"

"Sorry, we should have realized that. It is the Massachusetts Women's Suffragist Association."

"What is the difference between a Suffragist and a Suffragette?" asked Fiona who was genuinely interested in learning more.

Carrie answered this time. "Suffragist is the American title. We Suffragists believe in obtaining equal rights for women through peaceful actions, such as marches, picketing and speaking on corners or anywhere else that we can. We print and distribute brochures in English, Italian and Yiddish to get the word out to people in different neighborhoods. Margaret Foley, one of our Boston Suffragists, speaks at factories during lunch hours."

Then Jane joined in. "In contrast to our peaceful movement, our sisters in England often resort to radical actions in order to gain attention to the cause for women's rights. Our goals are the same, we just use different strategies."

As the time passed in conversation, Fiona became captivated by their ideals and stories of bravado. Although the male passengers feigned disinterest in their conversation, Fiona could see that some of the women passengers were listening intently.

"Please tell me more," Fiona asked with sincerity.

"Are you sure you are open to hearing our story from last November? It isn't a pretty one but certainly a true one," inquired the leader, Lucy. "It may scare you, too, Fiona, if you are weak at heart."

"Miss Burns, I am anything but weak at heart, so please continue."

"The horrid experience took place this time last year and will remain forever in our memories."

Lucy went on explaining how all three went to the capital together where Lucy and another leader, Alice Paul from New Jersey, led a group of around 30 women activists. They were called the Silent Sentinels. On November 23rd, as they peacefully and silently picketed the White House with their placards advocating for women's rights, they were suddenly attacked by armed guards. The women were beaten with clubs, manhandled, groped and thrown into police wagons where they were taken to the Lorton Reformatory, called the Occoquan Workhouse.

"For weeks, we were denied our rights, the beatings continued and some of our ladies were stripped naked and put in chains. It was a nightmare for all of us. I doubt that even a hardened criminal would receive the same cruel treatment we had."

Carrie picked up at that point. "We had all agreed to go on a hunger strike, but to retaliate, the guards forced- fed rancid food to us through tubes, filthy tubes, I might add."

The youngest member, Jane, finished the narration with "Thank the Lord, their brutal treatment eventually leaked to the public, and within a month we had a trial and we were released since there were no grounds justifying our arrest. And as expected, there were no charges pressed against the police force or prison guards."

"But the happy ending is that we are very close now to achieving our goal. Britain has just given women older than 30 the right to vote and to run for seats in the House of Commons. Our 19th amendment is on its way to ratification by the states as we speak," Lucy announced proudly and in a voice a bit louder so those in the train car could take note.

"It was worth the price," voiced Carrie as she rubbed her wrist where there was a noticeable permanent scar. They all agreed in unison. However, based on what Fiona heard, she was sure that these women must still suffer nightmares from their experience as she still did from her mother's murder, her father's torture and her own brutal rape.

"As close as we are to gaining passage of the amendment that will finally give women the right to vote, it could still take a year before final passage with the states' ratification, so we cannot lose our momentum. That's why we are traveling to add support to our Boston suffragist sisters. We need Massachusetts to ratify."

"We are always excited with new members if you think you would like to join us and we haven't frightened you away. I do believe the worst days of our struggle are over although we cannot let up until the law is finally passed," Lucy stated firmly, looking at her friends for affirmation.

Fiona felt close to these American heroines. They were fighting for the rights for all women although not all women were willing to make the sacrifices for the cause as these women were. *Just like the few Irish patriots who make sacrifices for independence while others sit on the sidelines awaiting the outcome*, she thought bitterly.

Fiona reached for her Celtic amulet from inside her dress where it was hanging and squeezed it. Her thoughts traveled to the memory of her mother and the other two hundred courageous women of Cumann na mBan who followed James Connolly as part of the Irish Citizen Army in the rebellion in April, 1916 in Dublin. Although the Manifesto to the Citizens of Dublin called for every person's support of the uprising for freedom from Britain, only the patriots heeded the call while so many others hid in their homes. Even with the limited numbers volunteering to fight for the cause, it still took the British army six days long to quash the civilian rebellion.

Fiona accepted membership with the Suffragists on the spot and spent the remainder of the train trip learning how and where she was to start as a new recruit.

Meanwhile, a few cars down, Henry was looking forward to the upcoming end of the line where he was to meet his friend, Andy, at the station. *Glad this day is almost done*, was his thought, relieved that the angry white man calmed down for the rest of the trip. Otherwise, he knew it could have escalated into a really bad situation for everyone, not the least for him. He had to hold himself back from punching the cowardly woman-harasser. *Only two more stops to go before I'm done for the day. Then Andy and*

I will head to Mamie's restaurant and get some of her southern fried chicken that we Alabama boys love so much.

But it did not go that way. The angry man had been waiting on the train platform after he disembarked to continue his tirade against the suffragists. When the women, including Fiona in their group, saw that there would be a continuation of the harassment, they looked for police protection but none was in the immediate area. The man came at them and shoved the bag out of Jane's hand where it fell open with her personal belongings falling onto the concrete platform and the train tracks. He cursed them while his face turned an unhealthy red and spittle sprang from his mouth with every angry word. When Lucy blocked the younger women with her body, the uncontrolled man went to slap her which could have pushed her down onto the tracks. But someone from behind him had caught his arm before it met her face.

The man yelled, "Get your hands off me, your black bastard." He unsuccessfully fought to pull away from Henry but couldn't since Henry was younger, stronger and army-trained.

"Look, Mister, where I come from, we don't hit ladies, so you need to stop right now," were the words that calmly came out of Henry Jackson's mouth before he even had time to think of repercussions.

The man turned to punch Henry but Henry blocked the punch with his one arm while using his other one to push the man away from him and the women. Losing his balance, the man fell onto the concrete station platform. Then he began to scream at the top of his lungs, "robbery, robbery, help me!"

By then, a crowd of people that included Andy Jones had made their way over to the area, as did two policeman who immediately began to wrestle and handcuff Henry.

"That's right, Officers. Arrest this thief. He was trying to rob me. You can't even trust conductors today, especially the Sambo ones," voiced the man jubilantly having turned the tables on Henry.

Henry tried to explain as the police began to roughly restrain him. Had it not been for the immediate and insistent testimony of the women explaining that Henry had come to their rescue from the mentally unbalanced man, he surely would have been unfairly arrested. Even a few people on the platform supported that the conductor was not at fault and that there certainly was no robbery attempt.

The officers ordered everyone to leave the area and they then sent the unruly man on his way without so much as even a warning. Disgusted that the police were not going to arrest the conductor, he called Henry 'an ape in a uniform,' as he left the station.

Henry called back at the man. He wasn't positive but he was pretty sure what he said in response meant 'go to hell' in Creole. Chloe, at his insistence, was even teaching him some 'naughty' words, he thought gratefully. No one understood what Henry said to the man and that was for the better.

Lucy Burns rebuked the police for not arresting the man for attacking them but they ignored her. Demonstrating his personal prejudice for suffragists, the older policeman told her, "You women bring trouble like this upon yourselves," as he walked away followed by the other patrolman.

As Carrie and Jane collected the garments strewn on the platform, both Lucy and Fiona thanked the Negro conductor profusely for being a gentleman and their hero.

"If not for you, we really could have been hurt today. I cannot thank you enough," said Lucy.

"No need to thank me, Ladies. I believe what my momma taught me. She said that we are tested all day long to either choose to do the right thing or the wrong thing. I know that helping you today was a right thing."

Fiona was still inquisitive. "What was that you said to him as he left?" she wanted to know.

"Oh, I don't think you want to hear its translation, Miss."

She gathered it was something rude and inwardly was delighted. "Just too bad that he didn't understand what you said."

Following their final offering of gratitude, the women headed out on their separate ways. Henry walked over to join Andy who was tipping his hat as the women passed him on their way out of the station.

Shaking his head with a concerned look on his face, Andy cautioned, "Brother, you are a good Samaritan but you have to be more careful 'cause you ain't in France no more."

Madame entered America via the Boston Harbor, not Ellis Island, and not from steerage. With advice from other passengers, she found a comfortable hotel within walking distance of the harbor. After resting for a day, she obtained a map of the area and began her daily walks up and down the front and back streets.

As she looked around the harbor, she noticed men everywhere. There were noisy saloons and huge active warehouses throughout the area. Using her keen business acumen, she immediately went into a planning mode. *Sailors, dock workers, marine supply factory workers and civil servants all in one small harbor area and the only females seen to service them are the lowly street walkers. Instead of dirty alleys, I will offer them a first-class brothel.*

Once her mind was made up, Madame searched for the right location. With talk of the war ending soon, she was convinced that the timing seemed perfect. And, as she suspected, with the war and the flu epidemic having taken a toll on the area, many large homes were vacant and going for reasonable prices.

After a few days of orienting herself to the area, she located just the building she wanted. It had been a former boarding house whose proprietors had died in the epidemic. The bank accepted her low offer to remove it from their long list of foreclosures. Ideally, there was a rowdy saloon on the corner which would easily bring in business once she opened her brothel doors.

She knew her next step was to introduce herself around. Importantly, she knew she had to seek out the local gangsters and police in the area in order to make alliances, as she had done so successfully in Ireland. It would cost her many American dollars but she knew it to be an expected cost for doing business when you were in her line of work.

Within one week, Madame moved into her house and personally began supervising the building's renovations. There was no shortage of immigrant Italian mason and construction workers. Madame took advantage of their need for work so she negotiated wages far less for their skills than she would have had to pay Americans performing the same work.

Her demanding ways did not ingratiate her to the workers. Taking orders from a woman was hard enough for the men but taking orders from a woman of low character was worse. They all knew the type of business she was setting up. But the immigrant workers accepted the wages she paid and were grateful to have weeks of guaranteed work.

"Gentlemen, when all is completed, I want you to know that you will each receive a discounted rate on your first visit here as part of my thank you for your good work."

She made this offer to hard working family men who were not the typical types to ever become future customers of her establishment. The men joked about her offer as they headed to their homes, giving them a much- welcomed laugh after a hard day at work and for many days after. Some even jokingly shared Madame's offer with their wives who did not think it funny.

Thanks to the purchase price of the house being lower than Madame had expected, she had ample funds to cover all the amenities she could now afford and upon which she insisted. Four rooms on the second floor and three more on the third floor were planned for her working girls. A room off the kitchen was being finished which would be shared by the cook and maids. But for herself, she had a large bedroom and an office designed in the rear of the home's first floor overlooking the yard's garden.

She ordered a special water closet equipped with all of the newest products the Standard Manufacturing Company had available, including a full-length cast iron tub and a wash stand with a marble top. But her 'piece de resistance', as she called it with her improper French pronunciation, was the new indoor porcelain toilet complete with a metal pull chain that emptied the elevated cistern in order to flush the contents of the toilet bowl. *No more outhouse for me ever again in my life*, she promised herself. *I deserve to live first class from now on.*

The house already had two outhouses and she had them cleaned and repaired with new seats and fresh painting. Those were designated mostly for use by the workers and clients. She made sure her girls had chamber pots and wash basins in each room to be used in- between customers without losing precious time with trips going downstairs to the outhouses. However, the indoor bathroom belonged solely to her.

Madame knew she needed to hire a strong man with few moral principles to provide security for the house when a customer failed to comply with the rules. *I hate the extra expense,* she thought, *but it was different in Ireland, with most of the clientele being upper class. There was little need for any strong-arming there. But here with the mixture of customers off the docks, a bouncer-type was a necessity.*

After visiting a number of taverns, she began advertising her new brothel's opening. She was pleased with the interest she received. At one tavern, Madame noticed a large burly and tattooed sailor sitting alone with a half empty bottle of vodka in front of him. When he spoke to the tavern server, she could tell he was Russian from his accent. He was a giant with an ugly face, which explained why he was alone. He was older than she would have liked, maybe late fifties, but with his scars and tattooed arms, he could meet the strong-arm qualifications she needed for her brothel. Just looking at him would scare a normal person.

"May I join you," she asked but sat without waiting for his answer. She gestured to the barkeep to bring another bottle and a second glass, as the sailor eyed her suspiciously. "I see you have hurt your hand by the look of the dried blood. An accident?"

"Not that it's any of your business but I hit a snotty Chinese kid who got in my way today at the market. They are letting too many Chinese into Boston."

"Well, I'll get to the point then." But, instead, she stopped to fill the glass that had been placed in front of her and then slowly took a sip of the vodka from the new bottle.

"What do you want from me, Lady?" the impatient sailor asked. He moved the new bottle away from Madame and closer to him.

"I'm hoping to hire the right man to fill the position of a body-guard and bouncer for my new brothel on Water Street," she explained as the cheap liquor burned in her throat. "You may have seen the construction taking place on my building these past weeks."

"As a matter of fact, I got turned down by your construction foreman when I asked for work there. He better watch his back is all I will say cause' I like to get even with those who do me wrong."

"Well, the work was finished yesterday. I am ready to open my brothel once I find my right-hand man."

"What does a right-hand man do?"

"A little of this and a little of that, depending on what I need done."

"Maybe I am that man. I can do a little of everything. In fact, there is nothing that I will not do," he boasted. "My name is Vlad and I tell you that I'm sick of working on the barges and fed up with low pay and years at sea. So, if you pay me well, I will give you much loyalty as we

Russians are known to do. But you must also be loyal to me. I am willing to do whatever you ask as long as you keep paying *very* well, Lady."

Vlad emphasized the word *very* in his heavily accented English. He had already finished half of the new bottle as he spoke. "So, Lady, maybe I am the man for the job, yes?"

"Call me *Madame*, not Lady," as Madame's tone changed to a controlling one. "If you are being truthful with me, then I think you just might be perfect for the job and can start right away on a trial basis." She spoke to him trying to sound French. She could not help herself as she pushed her bosom forward and blinked her eyelashes as she spoke. But it had no effect on the sailor. *He must be very drunk not to notice my attributes*, she rationalized to herself.

During his many trips around the world, he had picked up enough languages, so he thought he would impress Madame by speaking French to her. Even intoxicated, it did not take long for him to realize that she did not understand a word he said. He knew then she was a phony but it did not matter to him. As long as he no longer had to go to sea and was being paid well to work on land after all these years, her secret was safe with him. She could pretend to be as French as she wanted.

"Your first assignment is to find whores for me. I cannot open without the working girls. But not the diseased ones. Only those young and healthy enough that they can work for a few years. Can you recruit them and bring them to me? Can you do that? More importantly, can you convince them to work for me even if they are reluctant or refuse? I cannot start a brothel without enough whores."

"I can be very persuasive, Lady, how much do I get for each girl I bring to you?"

236

Madame reminded him, "Call me Madame, please." She needed this big Russian brute, as brazen as he was.

It took some negotiation but they arrived at a mutually agreed upon price for each girl he brought to the house.

He was eager to start his job, especially the procurement part and added "And part of my job is to 'test' each girl, agreed, Lady?"

"Again, please call me Madame." She wondered if his memory was damaged by his alcohol intake but she was in no position to disagree since the second Vodka bottle was now empty and his slurred words took on a bullying tone which frightened her.

"Agreed," she answered with no hesitation. She had enough experience with men to wonder just how much sexual performance he had left in him considering his advancing age and the gallons of liquor in his system.

November, 1918

Boston

As Mina knocked at Carmela's door, she sensed something was wrong because of the delay in answering her knock. When Carmela finally opened the door, Mina could see that Basilio was in bed when he should have been at work.

"What's wrong?" Mia blurted out as she made her way into the small tenement bedroom area. Holding her pregnant belly, Carmela followed her in hysterics.

Mina went to his bedside but could see that Basilio was covered in sweat and his breathing was shallow. Even with his color turning cyanotic, he did not want to worry the two women in his life.

Switching between English and Italian, he told saying, "Mi sento molto male, I feel very ill" and quickly added to not worry them, "but I am strong and will get better soon. I just need rest."

Carmela was beside herself regardless of his words and had been anxiously awaiting Mina's visit. She told Mina that a few days ago, Basilio had said that many of the men at work were ill and it was thought that the influenza had hit the plant. Then he had been sent home early from his job because he was sick and everyone feared contagion.

"The nurse came and did everything possible to make him comfortable. She prepared a chest poultice, gave him medicines and even some whiskey that she carried in her medical bag."

"Did Nurse Mary say what else we should do for him?" questioned his sister quite aware of the seriousness of the illness.

"No, but she did tell me not to sleep in the bed with him until he gets well. She told me that my priority is to keep myself and the baby safe. So eventually when Basilio seemed to be sleeping, I rested on the mattress you had used when you lived with us and I stayed in the living room."

"I must have fallen asleep because I suddenly awoke in the middle of the night when I heard him speaking. I thought he was calling for me. But when I went to his bedside, he was delirious. He did not recognize me, Mina, and kept pointing to my hair telling me that I had a black cat on my head!"

For all her saints, Carmela was still very superstitious. To her the black cat was a terrible omen of death.

"When a person has a high fever, they say crazy things that do not mean anything. Our job is to get him better." Although younger than Carmela, Mina recognized she would have to take charge of the situation. Mina tried her best to calm her sister-in-law, all the while trying to hide what an emotional wreck she was herself. She kept reminding Carmela of her pregnancy and that she should try to rest while Mina took over tending Basilio.

"What good will it do for anybody if you come down with this yourself? You cannot risk losing the baby, Carm," Mina warned Carmela, insisting she leave the room. "Better I catch this than you."

"I cannot lose Basilio, Mina. *We* cannot lose him," she shouted at Mina.

Mina knew how devastating their loss would be but pushed it from her mind and concentrated on believing that her brother would fight this illness successfully. But reading the news reports with Mrs. Jacobs only confirmed the high mortality rate of this disease, especially among young adults.

Mina sat at his bedside applying cool cloths to his fevered forehead. She realized that he could not swallow after she attempted to get water into him. She watched him burning up with fever. She watched each breath he took become more difficult for him. She pulled him up into as much of a sitting position as she could in an attempt to ease his breathing struggle.

From outside the bedroom door, Mina could hear Carmela calling on God and Saints Cosmas and Damien, the healing saints, pleading for her husband's recovery. She listened and began to add her own prayers. No matter what happens, Mina promised herself that she would not leave her brother's bedside, no matter what. She would stay holding his hand. If Basilio were going to die, then she would be with him at the moment his soul left his body.

"I will never leave you, Basilio, I will be right here with you." Then she changed her mind and told Carmela that she was going out to find Nurse Mary. "Surely there must be more that can be done for him."

The tenement building was permeated with the smell of sickness. It was to be expected since the disease had been spreading throughout the North End since it started in late August. *The odor is unbearable, as it reminded her of the seasickness stench in steerage, but it is worse here,* thought Mina, as she knocked on doors searching for the visiting nurse. The dingy, poorly lit halls never smelled fresh even before the epidemic, with ethnic cooking smells and full chamber pots and unwashed inhabitants who barely had weekly baths. But with the influenza breakout the air was polluted with the odors of vomit, defecation and death.

It was common knowledge that some grieving families delayed reporting their family members' bodies for removal, especially with the deaths of the children. Being poor meant their loved ones were designated for unmarked mass graves with not even the dignity of a coffin or a grave stone marking their time in this world. The Sicilians, as per custom, would lie the deceased out in the living area for all to pay farewell respects with hugs and kisses to the corpse, unaware and unaccepting that the custom spread the disease to the living.

As doors grudgingly opened to Mina's knocks, she would be met by bleary eyed tenants, some sick themselves while caring for loved ones.

"Please help me, is Nurse Mary with you?"

"No, I saw her go upstairs" or "No, but if you find her tell her we need her here, too," were the responses received.

Mina went floor to floor shouting out for Mary until she realized that she was among many looking for the nurse. At the top of the 5th floor, the nurse came out of an apartment and stood at the railing looking down at the families calling to her. Even one floor below, as Mina looked up, she could see that the nurse was exhausted. Her uniform appeared soiled and her nursing cap askew. She had a toddler in her arms that she had just found in the hall alone crying. *Ignorantly, someone placed this child in a dark hallway alone probably to prevent catching the flu but not realizing how many other horrible things could happen to this poor innocent,* she thought.

"My brother on the 3rd floor is dying, please come to the Amato apartment right now, please, I beg you, Mary," Mina shouted so she could be heard over all the other requests being shouted now that the nurse had appeared.

"I have been waiting longer than you," a distraught man screamed at Mina. "My three children are suffering and need the nurse before your brother," he added with a threat in his voice as he climbed the stairs closer to Mina and headed towards the nurse, seemingly intent on pulling the nurse to his apartment.

"Stop this, all of you! Children come first, always," yelled Mary as she descended the stairs instructing the man to lead the way to his apartment. As she passed Mina on the stairway all she could offer was, "I'm very sorry, Mina." She then transferred the naked toddler in her arms to Mina.

"Take this child and find his family somewhere on the fifth floor."

Mina, being a stranger to the child, set off screams from him. Fortunately, some family member must have recognized his screams and descended the stairs to Mina and took him from her arms. The days of neighbor helping neighbor seemed to change with the influenza onset. Everyone in the tenement went into a survivor mode of 'every man for himself.'

Disheartened, Mina returned to the apartment. She did not want to tell Carmela that children were the priority for the nurse instead of adults so she planned to say that she couldn't find the nurse. But before she could finish, she became acutely aware of Carmela's unusual silence. She could see her kneeling quietly at her husband's bedside.

"Carmela?" she called as she closed the front door behind her.

She must be praying to her long list of saints for Basilio's recovery, was Mina's immediate thought as she looked at her sister-in-law kneeling next to Basilio's bed where a candle burned softly giving off shadows along the wall.

Carmela turned her head to look at Mina but remained kneeling when she said, "Mina, Basilio is gone. I have lost the love of my life."

"Dear God, no! Tell me you are mistaken, Carmela. Are you sure he isn't breathing?" as Mina ran to the bed asking numerous questions when knowing in her heart the answers would not be the ones she wanted to hear.

"Mina, my unborn child has lost his father and you have lost your brother." Although distraught, Carmela exhibited a calm that took Mina by surprise. It was as if the last twenty-four hours had provided her with an anticipatory grief that prepared her for the inevitable finality of her husband's death. Her hysterics were apparently finished and a stronger than expected Carmela emerged.

Unlike Carmela, it was Mina who fell apart and had to be consoled. "I should have been with him. I told him that I would stay with him but I changed my mind and went to find the nurse instead. Why didn't I keep my promise to stay with him? I am so ashamed of my indecisiveness, Carmela. Thank God, you were with him at the end. Will he forgive me for leaving him?"

"Your brother loved you with all his heart and would never blame you for trying to find help for him. We will grieve and make plans together. He would want us to be strong for each other and his baby. We will help each other get through this."

"Mina sat on the floor next to Basilio's body, disoriented not only by her brother's death but also by the appearance of a tragically heroic new Carmela.

Together, the two women suffered their loss, crying as they prepared his body for burial in his best Sunday clothes.

"Why does he have these fresh scraps on his knees and elbows?" Mina questioned while they were preparing his body for burial. "They look recent and still bloodied."

"I asked him the same question when I was helping him undress to get into bed. He told me that while he was waiting for the trolley, he fell on the ground while getting a girl out of the way of a runaway horse and milk wagon. Can you believe that as ill as your brother was, he still saved someone from serious injury yesterday?" That set Carmela off into another crying episode as she thought of her husband's kindness and courage.

"Yes, I can believe that," Mina's voice was hoarse from crying.

It was decided that Mina would telegram her parents. She knew the difficulty she would have trying to find the right wording within the limitation of a telegram. She would follow it up with a long letter to them right away. *How can I write to my parents that they have lost their last son?* Mina agonized.

As Mina sat with Basilio's body, she cleaned the bedroom area with vinegar hoping it was not too late in protecting Carmela from infection. Meanwhile, Carmela went to the parish priest and arranged an immediate cemetery burial for the next day. There would be no mass grave for her husband, no matter the cost she insisted. Understandably, Carmela was traumatized by her husband's loss but knew she had to give him the same respectful burial that he would have given her, if the circumstances had been reversed, even though it would mean using their savings.

Like Mina, she had never been without the love and support of men in her life, first her father and then her husband. She could not imagine her future without Basilio but she had another life growing in her body that demanded her care and full focus. She knew she had no choice but to be as strong as she could be.

"Carm, when you are ready, I want you to come live with me and Carlo. You took care of me when I first arrived in America and we will care for you and the baby. We are family and will get through this together. You are not alone." *Carlo could never say no to my offer, could he?* she worried.

"Thank you, truly, for your kind and generous offer. But as soon as I can arrange it, I will return home to my family in Sciacca. I will raise our child in Sicily surrounded by both our families there. You should write your parents that they will have Basilio's child in their arms soon. That may help them in their grief, God willing."

All Mina could do then was to hold her sister-in-law. It was not the time to question how Carmela thought she could afford to return to Sicily. Mina was heartsick knowing that she and Carlo were in no financial state to offer help with Carmela's passage expense so she remained silent. She hoped Carmela would not sink into a depression when she realized there was no funding for a return trip home.

With Basilio's death and the arrangements with the church that had to be made quickly to prevent his body being taken away by public health, Mina was unable to visit Mrs. Jacobs that day and never got word to her.

The following morning, still in the midst of Basilio's final burial arrangements, Mina went to check on Mrs. Jacobs and tell her the sad news about Basilio. She opened the door to Mrs. Jacobs' apartment with the key given to her but was immediately overcome by a stench far worse that the toilets in the alley. The elderly woman must have expired during the night as her body appeared to be in rigor mortis. The results of her dysentery were everywhere. Already well into her years, the fever and diarrhea must have dehydrated her during the night. *How sad that my dear friend had to die alone.*

Mina was devastated at the loss of her brother and now Mr. Jacobs, the two people she loved so much. The thought of never seeing them again overwhelmed her as she tried to think what next she had to do. She had to be strong and take responsibility for the burial of her friend and teacher since there was no one else.

Covering her mouth and nose with her scarf, Mina struggled to place the old woman's body on her bed. It was then that she noticed a letter addressed to her on the dining table where they had shared many memorable lunches and lessons together.

To Mina Amato:

Mina, I write this letter to you tonight before I am unable to do so, because I now know I caught more than a cold. I think it is influenza. If this letter is on the table, then I have either died or am totally incapacitated. Since you did not come yesterday, I pray you are not ill. Maybe, I will be here tomorrow and maybe you will be here to see me tomorrow, too, I can only hope for that. With all the death around us, God only knows. But I write this as a last will and testament so that legally you will have a right to all my earthly possessions should anyone question you so keep this letter safe.

Very importantly, make sure you look in the bottom drawer of my dresser. Irving had a carpenter make a secret compartment in the back as a precaution against all the theft in the tenement. It proved successful after my apartment had been broken into and the money never discovered by the intruders. Make sure you find it!

Sell the furniture but not until after you find the dresser drawer where the cash is hidden. Please ask Nurse Mary if she would like the book collection and the three oil paintings that she had always admired.

But all the money is yours, Mina. It will give you freedom if you use it wisely. I encourage you to consider enrolling in the Boston School for Secretaries. There are Katherine Gibbs secretarial schools found in other states, too, so please keep that in mind since you do have friends in New Jersey. You would excel in that profession. Please do that for yourself and to make me proud that the money made your life better for you then it is now. I don't want you to remember me as a yenteh, a busybody, meddling in your life. I have always wanted only the best for you, my beautiful girl.

You have been a darling friend, a helper, a student and a granddaughter to me. I truly hope that my savings can help you change your life.

Sincerely with love, Mrs. Irving Jacobs

Mina could not stop crying for the sad loss of her mentor and friend. But she found herself crying with joy, too, when she discovered the money left to her. She could sell the furniture and use the money to pay the back rent and still have quite an amount left.

"Thank you so much, Mrs. Jacobs," she cried, and added a prayer "I pray you are at peace with your husband Irving. I will always remember you."

She cleaned the body and dressed Mrs. Jacobs in her best dress and shoes. She cleaned the apartment as best as she could. Carmela was waiting for her return. She knew she needed to prevent her mentor's body going into a pauper's grave which would happen if the public health agents were notified. So, she quietly left the apartment, locked the door, told Carmela she would return soon and walked directly to the synagogue in the Jewish section.

As she exited the building she asked passing neighbors to let Nurse Moran know that she wanted to speak with her tomorrow in Mrs. Jacobs apartment. She kept Mrs. Jacobs death secret because of the past robberies. She was convinced that looting would take place. She wanted Mary to know about the books and paintings that were bequeathed to her.

A young woman with two children at her side greeted Mina. Mina repeated her request about Nurse Moran to her as she had been doing with everyone coming and going from the building. "Nurse Mary visited us yesterday to check on the kids and me' cause I'm pregnant again. But she didn't look so good herself, I'm afraid."

After asking directions, Mina located the Shul. A workman, who was painting the front door to cover the derogatory graffiti that had been written on it, pointed her to where she would find the rabbi.

Rabbi Milstein welcomed Mina and was saddened to hear the news of Mrs. Jacobs' passing. He told Mina that much of his congregation were flu victims and that he prayed every day for an end to the dreadful disease. He remembered that the Jacobs had faithfully attended the shul for many years until the husband passed away.

"Do you know what a mitzvah is, Mrs. Vitale?" the Rabbi asked.

Shaking her head that she did not, he then explained. "Most people interpret it as a special kindness. And that is exactly what you are doing for our friend, Esther Jacobs. Actually, in our religion it is more a commandment to be followed as we are expected to perform kind acts, much like your religion."

"Rabbi, I could do nothing less. I loved her dearly."

"I make you this promise. I will have everything handled immediately. Members of our temple will pick up her body today, prepare it and have her buried next to her husband, Irving. I will give you directions to our cemetery so you can visit."

"Yes, I would appreciate that, Rabbi."

"We have a tradition of placing a small stone on the grave for each visit. It is done using the left hand and it is our symbol that the deceased has not left our memories."

"Then I will gladly do that."

As she began to leave, the Rabbi continued to thank her saying that many other non-Jews would not have made the effort she did to ensure that her Jewish friend received a religious burial.

"No, Rabbi, please let me thank you. You have made it possible and I am very grateful."

From the money left by Mrs. Jacobs, Mia left him a donation to cover expenses and felt relieved that she was able to prevent her dear friend from ending in an unmarked pauper's grave.

Carlo will be so relieved when I tell him about this inheritance from Mrs. Jacobs, she thought excitedly to herself. She was determined to tell him. She committed herself to telling him. *He is my husband and has a right to know.*

Then she changed her mind. She decided that Carlo would not be allowed to know about this money. He would not be allowed to take this away from her as he had taken Jack Turner's. *This money will not go to gangsters to pay gambling debts or, worse, be used for more gambling. This money will stay my secret money and be hidden from Carlo.*

The news was spreading in the tenement building as fast as the influenza. The nurse had not shown up for two days. Fear set in as the inhabitants knew how unrealistic it was to believe that there would be a replacement nurse for them.

After missing Mary for three days, Officer Muller's concern mounted. Along with his cadet, he went into the tenement and questioned inhabitants about Mary. Upon seeing two policemen, most of the people were silent when questioned, some he guessed could not speak English or pretended not to speak English. Fortunately, a group of young mothers provided information, mostly in broken English, once they realized that the policeman was genuinely troubled by the nurse's absence and that his questions had nothing to do with police business.

"She looked very sick the other day. I felt so sorry for her," one relayed to him as another added, "I even told her to go home and take care of herself."

Another added, "We know you like Mary. We all see how you look at each other. When you see her, please tell her we miss our angel."

With this information, Muller decided to find Mary right away. He would go to her home or to any hospital if that is where he could find her. It was important that she know how much she meant to him. He was angry with himself for taking so long to tell her how he felt.

Using the tools available to him back at the precinct, it did not take long to learn her home address. He was determined to go to the Moran's home right away.

"Cover for me, Simmons. I'll be back later," he told the cadet.

"I hope your lady friend is alright, Sir. She's the one you talked about, right?" The cadet remembered hearing from Muller on their first day out together that he had found the woman he hoped to marry.

Muller just shook his head and left the precinct trusting that the cadet would think of a plausible excuse if anyone asked for him.

Quickly picking up a bouquet of flowers at a pushcart vendor, Muller made his way to the Moran home. He visualized surprising Mary while she was recuperating and having the opportunity to meet her family. He knew she would forgive him for the unexpected visit and would see it an overdue sign of his affection for her.

He found a black wreath on the front door. When the door was opened upon his knock, he was bewildered that the door was answered by an older woman with reddened eyes, as if she had been crying. Because he was still in his uniform, he immediately introduced himself to her saying, "I am Mary's friend and am inquiring as to her health as I only learned today that she may be ill."

Without a word, the woman stared at him but then allowed him to enter the vestibule. He could see a number of people gathered in the parlor, a few women weeping quietly with rosary beads in their hands led in prayer by a priest. A group of men at the other end of the room were passing around a bottle of whiskey as they spoke with lowered voices.

They all looked at him questioning the reason for a policeman's presence until the woman who had led him into the living room said, "He's here to see Mary."

Excusing herself from the group praying the rosary, a woman came forward who looked like an older version of Mary. He knew she had to be Mrs. Moran.

"Would I be wrong if I guessed that you are William Muller?" she asked as she placed her hand on his arm.

"Yes, Ma'am, I am."

"William, our darling Mary passed yesterday. We have just returned from her burial," she could barely get the words out as her lips trembled and the tears welled in her green eyes, the same eyes as Mary's.

The shock set in so quickly that Muller began to feel faint for the first time in his life. Catching himself, he leaned against the wall to keep from falling.

Mrs. Moran called to one of her sons. "Danny, get the good officer a chair and a stiff drink right away."

Instead of her son, it was her husband who came to give assistance. Mr. Moran gave his wife a questioning look as he set a chair under Muller.

"Yes, he is the one that our daughter was always going on about," she said with no compunction about Muller hearing it. Even heartbroken, she possessed a strength that he recognized had been inherited by her daughter.

Danny, Mary's brother, brought over a drink saying, "this should help, Officer."

"I thank you but I don't want a drink. I just want Mary back," said with tears clouding his eyes.

"Don't we all, don't we all," replied Mrs. Moran with her hand squeezing his shoulder.

"I can't believe she's gone." He couldn't hide his despondency and shock at her death. Not knowing what to do with the bouquet that had fallen to the floor, he picked it up and meekly handed the flowers to Danny.

"She thought highly of you, Boyo, and spoke of you often," Mary's father informed him as he took the drink from Danny's hand and drank it himself.

Hearing those words, Muller crumbled under the finality of it. As the Moran family members consoled him, he shamelessly cried as he had never done before, nor ever would again in his lifetime. Muller was filled with regret for the loss of the woman he loved and blamed himself for never having told her.

That month the newspapers reported that hundreds of courageously dedicated nurses in the military and the civilian sectors continued to die as causalities of the epidemic. Mary had been one of them.

William Muller never married after that. He devoted his life to the police force, quickly rising high within the ranks. Every year on the anniversary of Mary Moran's death, he would visit the cemetery with his dog and leave a bouquet of flowers on her grave.

Fiona got settled in a respectable boarding house that had been recommended by her Suffragist friend, Jane Rider. Jane had arranged an interview for her at the Hedley Soap Company's factory on City Road where candles and soap were made and packaged. The company was expanding and was hiring female workers.

"My family has lived in Boston *forever*, so we know everyone…or I should say my father does. Anyway, the interview for you has been arranged and I'll go with you to keep you company."

"Jane, you have been such a good friend. If I get this job, it will be due to your kindness."

"You will get this job entirely on your own, I have no doubt of it." Jane sounded far surer than Fiona felt.

Jane did not work as she came from a wealthy New England family. But to her parents' credit, she was educated to the importance of social justice and the responsibility of the rich to assist the less fortunate so she involved herself in charitable and political causes.

"I'm a bit nervous, Jane, I must admit." Fiona sat with Jane as they waited for her name to be called by the interviewer. Jane was busy smelling soap samples on display and playfully placing them under Fiona's nose.

"Fiona, stop worrying. Just tell the hiring person about your last job in the Brooklyn department store and that you are perfectly willing to learn everything there is about soap production. Even let the interviewer know that you know that sheep are the main source of the tallow used in the products so that you sound educated on the subject. You had sheep in Ireland, did you not?"

"We were too poor to own sheep, Jane, but the wealthy landowners had herds in the fields if that counts as my knowing about sheep?" she answered a bit sarcastically as she was amazed at Jane's naivety at times.

Not nonplussed in the slightest, Jane continued, "then forget mentioning sheep and just be your charming self and that should be enough for you to be hired."

I had to lie to Jane about the department store, Fiona thought. *Just imagine what she would think of me if the truth were known about how I have earned my living in New York and, worse, in Dublin.*

Fiona and Jane smiled at each other as Fiona's name was called. Nervously, Fiona left the waiting area accompanied by the hiring person leading the way to a private office. Wearing a new dress and hat purchased in the garment area of town, Fiona put on the radiant smile with which she was blessed. Fiona's interview went smoothly. She was relieved that there were very few questions regarding her past experience. She was hired on the spot and told to report for work the very next day. With the factory being closed on Sundays, she knew she would be able to participate in many suffragist marches held on Sundays.

Fiona was happier than she had been in years. She thanked Jane profusely as they left the factory together. When asked, Jane denied using her family's influence, but Fiona knew better.

"I don't believe you, Jane, but I am so grateful. You seem to be guiding me from the first time we met, happily for me."

Jane brushed it off. "Noblesse oblige" she said which required Fiona's asking for a translation.

"It just means that those of us blessed with more should feel obligated to help those not as blessed."

Jane would take no credit for her help and probably had only a slight understanding of how immensely important the job was to Fiona. Fiona believed that meeting Jane was an unexpected blessing and was grateful that their paths had crossed.

Fiona could not help but notice that many of the Suffragists were like Jane. They came from well-to-do families where money never seemed to be an issue. Yet, interestingly, the first question Jane asked Fiona was the amount of the salary offered to her by the hiring agent.

"Jane, I didn't even ask because I was so eager to be given the job," Fiona answered, somewhat embarrassed. "Was I supposed to ask?"

"Fiona, I don't want to sound critical. I'm relieved that you have the job but I'm sure that the men performing the same work as you will be paid higher. That is just another wrong to which women are subjected but will certainly not be solved soon. However, since we cannot right all the wrongs in the world, let's celebrate your new employment with my treating us to a lovely lunch. That will give us time to discuss your very first march coming up soon."

"I would be quite pleased with fish and chips, Jane. I do not need anything too fancy." In reality, Fiona was uneasy with the thought of an elegant restaurant's dining room.

"Today is a special day so I think our celebration requires lunch at Del Monico's. You will love it, Fi." Of late, Jane had begun calling Fiona 'Fi'. Apparently, rich people liked nicknames.

Just as Fiona feared, she was awed by the surroundings with crystal chandeliers and real flowers in vases even in the midst of winter, not to mention the elegant customers eating lunch as if they had all the time in the world. Soft music floated through the air so as not to interfere with the conversations that were taking place, some about business but most customers appeared to be ladies of leisure spending an afternoon at lunch.

Once seated, she became alarmed that she was out of her element. Fiona feared that she would not only embarrass herself but also Jane. Fiona softly confessed, "Jane, I hate to admit this but I am only 'shanty Irish' and have no idea how to act in this place. I sincerely do not want to call attention to us should I make an etiquette mistake."

Shocked at what sounded like an insulting term, she asked Fiona to explain the term 'Shanty Irish'.

"Shanty Irish are the poor Irish. We never learned proper etiquette and such. The 'lace curtain' Irish are those who are a level higher due to money or education who struggle to not be seen as shanty."

"Fiona, embarrassing you is the last thing I would ever do, so here is our plan that should make you more comfortable," she whispered so no one seated near them could hear.

"You will watch me closely. You will calmly pick up whatever utensil I pick up and you will copy my actions. You will see very quickly that you have nothing to stress over." Jane proved to be one of the kindest people Fiona ever met.

Fiona imitated how Jane sat straight in her chair, never allowing her back to touch the back of the seat. She allowed Jane to order for her and learned how she made the selections for the various courses. She watched which fork Jane picked up first. Fiona was determined to play the part of a lady, for Jane's sake, even though she was not, nor ever would be, on Jane's level. In her heart, she was grateful to Jane for allowing her a glimpse of the well-to-do life although it was one to which she would never belong nor ever be comfortable in.

The young women shared stories. Jane spoke about her family dating back to the Mayflower, her boarding school days and her family pushing her to consider marriage proposals being offered, none of which interested her, she stated emphatically. "So far, they all have been terrible bores, but I'll know when the right one comes along…I hope," she added. "You already know our harrowing experience in Washington when we were jailed, so enough said about that," referring to Lucy's telling the tale to Fiona on the train. "So, tell me more about you, Fiona?"

Fiona, holding back most of the truth, related her early childhood in Dublin. She lied about having been raised by an aunt after her parents died from an illness. She spent most of her time speaking about the tortuous Atlantic crossing. "But, Jane, honestly, as awful as the voyage was, the wonderful people I befriended made it far easier. We took care of each other and that made all the difference."

"Fiona, how right you are about how some people can make a positive difference in one's life. In fact, something did happen to me recently that I will not soon forget. I was on a trolley when I started to be harassed by an Italian man, but this time not for my Suffragist politics. I know he was not thinking correctly because he was very drunk, but the impression I got was that he was asking me to date him or something? Can you imagine the absolute audacity?"

"You are very pretty, Jane, so I am not surprised, but go on with your story."

"Well, after the drunk pushed the conductor who tried to remove him from the trolley, a Chinese man came to my rescue. I think he was young but, with Asians, who can tell their ages with their long braids down their backs and their strange oriental clothing? Anyway, he not only bravely came to my assistance, he actually prevented a policeman from being stabbed in the back by the same man. He was our hero that day. I'm sure I will never see him again but his actions certainly made a difference to me and an even greater one for the policeman."

"It goes to prove that there are strangers who, for good or bad, come into our lives. I suppose that is what makes life so interesting." Fiona tried to erase thoughts of the many people who had hurt her. Instead she thought of Mina, Margaret, the Turners and now, Jane. She even visualized Brian Kelly with his puppy-dog eyes.

"Well, aren't you being profound, Fiona! Let's toast to that." They raised their crystal glasses of minted ice water.

As Fiona sat in the exclusive restaurant dining among the city's elite, listening to the soft violin music, she believed it was a turning point in her life.

The following Sunday, Fiona found Basilio's building after studying a North End map and finally asking directions from the trolley car conductor. She found herself happily excited to be seeing her friend again. Instead, she was concerned when she found Mina, Carmela and a priest consoling each other.

Mina was thrilled by Fiona's surprise appearance. She wanted to squeal with joy like any teen ager at seeing her long-lost friend but instead knew better since Basilio was just buried.

Although neighbors were sending their condolences, people were avoiding the apartment since no one really understood how the influenza contamination spread.

The burial had taken place that morning in Cop's Hill Burial ground after a small prayer service at St. Leonard's. Both Mina and Carmela were dressed in black. Like most Sicilian widows, Carmela would most likely wear black for the rest of her life if she never remarried.

Fiona offered her sincerest condolences to Carmela. She told her some of the wonderful things Mina had shared about her brother on their journey together. Although she never tired of hearing good stories about her husband, Carmela insisted that Fiona sit and take some refreshments. Fiona was hungry so she was very grateful for the tea and pound cake. The priest got up to leave and blessed them with the sign of the cross in Latin. Even Fiona knelt for the blessing which surprised and pleased Mina. At that point, Mina insisted that Carmela rest in bed for the baby's sake. She led her to the bed, removed her shoes and covered her with a heavy blanket, as the apartment was cold even with the coal stove burning. Mina reminded herself to refill the coal pail for Carmela before she left for the day. Basilio always did that but Mina knew that she would do it going forward. Climbing the stairs with a heavy pail of coal equaled carrying wet laundry up the stairs, both miserable tenement tasks.

With Carmela out of the room, they were then able to be emotional and speak freely. After hugging and eagerly speaking over each other, they quickly discovered that their girlish friendship was as strong now as it had been on-board the steamship, even after these many months of separation.

Mina insisted that Fiona go first, starting with how they missed each other after clearing the admission process on Ellis Island. Fiona lied about the Brooklyn family being in a rush to catch the ferry as the excuse. She went on about how she had done some part time work in a Brooklyn department store but that the job had ended. She said that she decided it was the perfect time to find Mina.

"Brooklyn is noisy and dirty. I'm hoping Boston is nicer. Just knowing you live here makes it nicer, Mina."

"True, Boston has beautiful sections and marvelous history. But as you can see, our tenement row houses don't fit in that category. Half the tenement is made up of people from Sciacca with everyone related to each other which doesn't make it too foreign for me. But I confess that I do get homesick for the open country side and I truly miss my parents. Do you get homesick, too?"

Mina would never ask such a question if she knew how sad my memories of home really are? "Not so much anymore, Mina, as I try to look forward to my new life here…although my new life always seems to be *in development* and not *developed,*" she laughed emphasizing the words. "So here I am on your doorstep. But I am so sorry about the loss of your brother. My

timing could not be worse, could it? I know how much he was loved by you. Does Carmela know what she is going to do now?"

"First, your timing is a gift. I've just lost my brother and a good friend this week, both to influenza. Now I will be losing Carmela, too, but in a good way, I suppose. She told me that she is returning to Sicily to live with her parents and have the baby there. Her plan, now that Basilio is gone, is to raise the baby in Sciacca surrounded by both our families. I think her plan is a wise one but I will miss her dearly."

"Can she afford passage back home?" Fiona asked politely although doubt-ful seeing the condition of the run-down tenement building and Carmela's walk-up apartment.

"Another testament to my brother. Amazingly, even with his low salary, Basile had purchased a life insurance policy with Phoenix Mutual for a few cents every paycheck and he made sure Carmela kept it safely filed away.

Carmela could not stop crying as she told me about the policy. She is so grateful that he had been so wise in doing such a thing. She said she had even argued with him that it was a waste of money since they were both so young and healthy. But he refused to cancel the policy, thankfully, as we see now what a true gift it is for Carmela to be able to use it in returning home."

Mina thought back to when she first learned of Basilio's life insurance and had asked Carlo if he had such a policy. She could never forget his selfish answer, 'No, why should I leave money for your next husband to enjoy?'

"Fiona, I will miss my sister-in-law terribly but now I hope to have you here. Please promise me you are planning to stay in Boston permanently?"

"I plan to, Mina. Actually, I already have a job in a soap factory here which I attribute to the kindness of one of the suffragists I met on the train coming to Boston who helped me through the process. And I am joining their ranks with my first march this afternoon down Commercial Street. I understand you are grieving and need to stay with Carmela. But in case you change your mind, as we all know you so often do, then come and cheer us on. I'm sure you want to be able to vote someday, right?"

"You always amaze me! A Suffragist, good for you! But instead of talking politics, first we must catchup."

Fiona went first, describing her made-up Brooklyn family and about working in the fashionable Loehman's department store on Fulton Street.

"So that's why your clothes are so pretty, Fiona," sighed Mina.

"Never mind that, I want to renew our friendship, just as if we never separated months ago. She happily described how exciting New York City is with the numerous theaters, movie houses and concerts and went into detail about the ones she had attended. Mina could not help herself as she quietly laughed when she watched Fiona show her how to dance the Two-Step.

"Oh, Fiona, I feel guilty laughing at such a sad time but you are always so much fun."

"Now your turn, Mina. Tell me all about your life and tell me in this lovely English that you have acquired since our voyage together. I actually understand your every word for the first time. No more pantomiming necessary!"

They both laughed while imitating all the pointing gestures and facial expressions they used on the ship to communicate with each other and which were still fresh in their memories. As the visit went on and Carmela slept, Mia began to open up to Fiona. She told her about her wonderful Jewish teacher responsible for her improved English and about the busy marketplace where she loved to shop but the conversation then led to her disappointment in her marriage. She even shared that she had thought of divorce but knew that it was impossible unless she could find a way to support herself.

"I need your friendship now more than ever, Fiona, and your advice." She even explained the inheritance and why she had to hide it from her husband.

"Carlo would squander it quickly with his gambling and I see it as my means to leave him if I ever finally make that decision to end my marriage. I believe the inheritance could last long enough for me to enroll in secretarial school, which is something I have been giving thought to. Anyway, it just gives me a small sense of security for now."

Fiona thought hard at what Mina had just shared with her. "Listen to me. First thing you do, Mina, after your husband goes to work tomorrow, is to put your money in an account at the Boston Bank. I did that when I arrived here and now I have such peace of mind. And there are ways to get your money when you need it without even going directly to the bank. Most

importantly, no one can touch the money but you, giving you independence from your husband. I can teach this to you when you are ready to learn about banking."

The very next day, as advised, Mina opened an account at the bank and kept her bankbook hidden in her corset. She thanked God for her best friend, her personal 'angel', Fiona.

December, 1918
Boston

He finally acknowledged to himself that his losses were beyond repayment. He was stunned when his father sent word that he was finished bailing him out after years of warnings about his gambling. The final blow arrived with his father's acknowledgement that he would do everything in his power to prevent Carlo's acceptance into the Boston Cosa Nostra family because of his consistent immaturity, poor judgement and because the Don had given his word to Mina's father.

He seriously began to consider his situation. With the old Jewish woman's death, Mina no longer would be bringing in a weekly salary and he had lost the last of the money sent to Mina from a passenger named Turner who had owed her a debt. For the first time, Carlo began to fear that the mob could hurt him if he had no way to repay all the high interest loans they had provided him and which were due for repayment.

That night, when he folded his cards after losing again, another player, who he had never seen before, asked if they could talk. Carlo could see that this man appeared comfortable with the mob members so he hoped this would prove beneficial in some way. He didn't look Sicilian but, nevertheless, he seemed to have a connection with them in some way. *At this point, I have nothing to lose by listening to this guy*, Carlo nervously thought to himself.

"Look, I am in the photography business and I'll get right to the point. Buddy, I can see you are in big trouble with those gentlemen. I repeat, big trouble. But I tell you nothing that you don't already know, right?" as he pointed to the four mob members at another table who were glaring at Carlo. "I may have a way out for you. Let's go get a drink and I'll lay it all out."

After a few drinks paid for by the photographer, he explained that his usual model did not show up for an important business meeting. He blamed himself for foolishly trusting a Dublin whore to keep her word. "My own fault. I trusted her but that's what I get for doing a good deed."

He went on, "My new partners back there," as he pointed toward the gambling club, are concerned that I will not deliver the pictures I promised them for immediate distribution. You see, these pictures make a lot of money for everyone involved because, frankly, these are what you call 'dirty pictures' and they sell like hot cakes. From sailors to bankers, there is a lucrative black market for them."

"Here's where you come in. I can see you are desperate. So am I. See, I made a promise to those guys and I'm late delivering, just like you. I just arrived in town from New York and now need a model for the pictures fast. You need the money to pay off the mob and I need to take some pictures for them. Surely, to save your life you can find a young pretty girl who can pose for me for a few pictures that will get us both off the hook? But we need to get this done fast."

"Why don't you use one of the whores at the club?"

"Because what makes my photographs special is that I capture a kind of innocence in the nudity. The gals at the club don't meet my standard. Wish one or two did because it would solve my problem, but I don't see what I'm looking for in them."

After his questions were answered, Carlo saw that he had no choice but to accept the photographer's offer. The type of pictures that would be taken sickened Carlo but he knew he had no option but to agree to have Mina pose.

He rationalized, *surely, as my wife she would want to keep me safe, no matter the sacrifice because she loves me. All I have to do is make her understand how serious the trouble is that I am in.*

It was very late when he got home that night after drinking with the photographer. Carlo eased himself into their bed awakening Mia from her sleep. He stroked her hair, pulled up her nightgown and climbed on her even though she was only half awake. This had become his routine after a night of drinking and betting. She never refused her husband. Her only wish was for him to finish quickly so that she could go back to sleep.

But this night was different. When Carlo finished, he told her to stay awake because he had something very important to tell her. Mina sat up in bed while he paced around the small room.

"Carlo, its late. What is so important it cannot wait until morning?" Mina asked stifling a yawn.

"Because my life is at stake, that's why." With that said, the agreement that he was forced to make was explained to her. Posing for a few 'provocative photographs' would save his life, he stressed. When he explained in more detail, Mina was stunned that he had offered her up to do this unholy thing. All she could think of was that, although she was married to the man standing in the room with her, she was really all alone. Her brother and Mrs. Jacobs were dead and Carmela on her way to Sicily. All of this came to her as a terrible weight, too heavy to carry any longer. She prayed that she would see Fiona soon.

"As my wife, you must do as I tell you, no matter how distasteful it is to both of us. Must I remind you that when we married you promised in the vow to love and obey your husband. It will only be one session and I will be there with you and the photographer the whole time, I promise," he said, as if that would reduce her anxiety and shame.

Mina began shaking her head vehemently nodding 'no' and began crying, "I cannot do such a thing."

Carlo repeated, "I will be killed if you do not fully cooperate, don't you understand this?"

"Your weakness has dishonored you. Now you will be dishonoring me, your own wife. Surely, you can think of another solution," she pleaded disbelieving such a demand was being placed on her by her own husband.

"This is the only solution or I am a dead man." There was not a doubt in Carlo's mind about that. "If the Jew had left you money when she died, then maybe I could have paid the loans, but no, she went and left it to other Jews at her temple. Guess she didn't think much of you after all," he repeated, not for the first time since Mrs. Jacobs' passing. *Thank God he believed me when I told him nothing was left to me.*

"I should have left you months ago," she yelled back at him. That was when he hit her causing her nose to bleed. She fell back in the bed and wept, hurt more by her husband's disrespect for her than the pain inflicted.

"I was told that your full face will not be shown in the pictures, so I can hit you again if necessary. Don't make it necessary."

Realization that this horrendously shameful act was going to be forced on her and that she was helpless to prevent it made her physically sick. She barely made it to the chamber pot under the bed before she vomited up bile.

How did my life change so terribly in just a few months? What could I have done better? Like abused women are known to do, she began to blame herself instead of her husband.

The photographer arrived at the apartment with his new Number 1 autographic Kodak camera equipment which cost him twenty-one dollars. He immediately set up for the session. The tenement was dingy, but he was prepared. He had brought two background screens with him. One screen had a boudoir background and the other a Christmas scene. He had brought additional accoutrements, such as feathers and costume jewelry. As instructed, Carlo had prepared Mina that she would have to be naked for all the photographs.

Sam could not hide his relief at seeing Mina. "I usually don't work with models I have not seen, and I took a big chance with you, Carlo. But I am relieved to find that our model is very pretty. It is important that a model be slim but still have curves and not be flat chested. So far, so good!"

"What is your name, Miss?" Sam asked.

Carlo answered, "She is Signora Vitale."

Sam was surprised that the model selected by Carlo was his *wife*. Sam never expected that. *But then desperate people do desperate things,* he realized. *What I need most right now, is for the two of them to follow my instructions uncomplainingly so we can get this done and I can get the pictures to Buterra.*

"Did you tell her about the special anatomical close ups?" He worried she would refuse once she realized the nature of those specific intimate poses.

"No, I did not tell her because I don't know what that means."

"Never mind, just make her do exactly as I tell her to do, with no balking from either of you, and we can finish as quickly as possible, for both our sakes."

Mina had to be prodded frequently about the poses as she would freeze out of innate modesty. Sitting, standing, reclining, with and without props but always naked, she complied as if in a hypnotic trance. Her humiliation reached its peak when the special close ups of her private parts were forced on her. The session finally ended after a few hours, leaving her disgraced and sickened by what she had been forced to participate in.

Before leaving, Sam took Carlo aside and quietly made another offer to him. "I understand that this is an unusual situation with her being your wife, but it went quite well considering she never modeled before. Maybe you would consider another session in the future?"

Without hesitation, Carlo said he would consider if the price was right.

After the photographer left, Carlo pondered the offer. He disregarded Mina's sobs as he sat down at the table with a pencil and paper and calculated numbers. The money he just earned would pay off his gambling debt. *But think about what a few more sessions will bring in?*

December, 1918

Boston

After Fiona's visit with Mina on the day of Basilio's burial, she proudly partic-
ipated in her first Suffragist march down Commercial Street to many cheers
with the 19th amendment on its way to passage. There were still vulgar dis-
senters on the sidelines who yelled obscenities but not like previous years when
the women marchers were endangered with physically injuries. Still someone
in the crowd threw dog feces which hit the hat of one of the women marchers,
but she carried on as if nothing happened. Such was the strength of the dedicated suffragists.

Fiona was proud to be one of them. She held her head high, carried her
placard and felt clean for the first time since she was fifteen and lived with her
family in Dublin before the raid that had drastically changed all their lives. But
her life had turned around and she liked the new life she was making for herself.

Thanks to Jane, Fiona was happily working as a packer at the soap manufacturing company. While she listened to her coworkers complaining about
the long hours and low wages, Fiona silently smiled to herself feeling grateful
to be living a normal life among normal people.

She loved the aroma of the finished soaps as she boxed them and could
smell the dust from the soap on her clothes long after leaving work.

Since she wanted to prove herself, she volunteered to march in the dangerous position of being at the end of the line of marchers. That position was
one where a marcher was always most vulnerable to a physical attack because
it was the position closest to where the crowds gathered on the sidewalk and

behind the marchers in the street. She followed Jane's recommendation to cover her ribs with cardboard for protection in case of shoving or punching were to happen. In the privacy of her room, she also practiced the ju-jitsu moves she learned in Dublin from Sugar and Spice. She remembered having to use one on shipboard one night but pushed that memory away like so many other memories best forgotten.

From where she marched, Fiona could see a child running with a hoop about to be under a building where men were running away because a piano was breaking from a hauling rope two stories above. Without any hesitation, Fiona dropped her placard, ran to the child screaming to stop. As the child glanced at her, she grabbed him and threw them both just a few feet from where the piano fell to the ground breaking into pieces, making a cacophony of different notes as it did.

Marchers and bystanders began applauding Fiona while the child was mostly concerned where his hoop had ended up. A group of men in suits, for whom the crowd made ample room, ran to Fiona, helping her up to a standing position. Both her elbows were scraped under the torn sleeves of her white dress but she still maintained what dignity she could with her ripped clothes and concealing her pain. One well-dressed man, with grateful tears in his eyes, approached her while holding the hand of the boy. The previously noisy crowd became silent as they watched the man with his son approach Fiona.

"Antonio, give this brave lady your thanks for saving your life."

"Thank you for saving my life, Lady."

"Miss, he is not eloquent but he is sincere." He gestured to one of the men in his entourage to put his son in the sedan parked in the street. "Let me introduce myself. I am Salvatore Buterra. You have done a great service protecting my only son, Antonio, for which I am now in your debt."

"Thank you, Mr. Butera, but your son's safety is reward enough."

"I have four daughters and only this one son. It is important to Sicilians to have our names carried on by our sons so I am in your debt. Please, Miss, I must have your name."

Fiona then identified herself and could not help noticing that he seemed taken aback that she did not appear to recognize him. Being Irish and new to the North End, she was still learning who were politicians and who were Mafioso. She believed she would be guessing correctly that he was the latter.

"How can I repay you? Some deed that I can make besides buying you a new dress to replace this torn one?" he asked, taking her hand into both of his and looking closely into her eyes.

"Dio, what extraordinary eyes! The double colored eyes of an Indian goddess who brings good fortune." He made that up because he was known to be a charmer and well-read even without a formal education.

She smiled her special smile and extricated her hand gently from his.

"Maybe someday, if I need your help, then I will ask a favor, so thank you for your kind offer," she lied since she never thought for a moment she would ever request anything from this gangster.

"Your Irish lilt explains why you do not know who I am but that is alright. Just know that I am a man of my word and we will meet again, Miss Burke."

His men picked up her bonnet and placard, but it was the boss who insisted on handing them to her. His hand remained on hers for a longer time than normally expected and Fiona did not want to impolitely pull her hand away. So, she left her small hand in his large one for the extra seconds it took before he withdrew his hand. She recognized the look he gave her because she was only too familiar with lustful looks.

As he made his way to his automobile, the crowd opened to make room for him. The door to the car was being held open for him by one of his men, all were dressed similarly in dark suits that did not totally conceal the holstered guns they carried. She overheard his order to have flowers and a new dress sent to her.

Mr. Buterra turned and waved to Fiona before entering the car. Fiona was not so naïve as to not realize she had just met a powerful gangster boss.

Fellow Suffragists then began hugging her and complimenting her on her courageous act. Then two sister suffragists stood her between them, hooked their arms through hers and the march resumed.

The commotion caused an onslaught of additional onlookers from windows and from workplaces wanting to see what happened and, now that it was over, the onlookers slowly disappeared. Unknown to Fiona, one of the most interested onlookers was Madame accompanied by Vlad.

Madame could not believe her luck in finding Fiona again and pointed her out to her bodyguard. Although from her viewpoint she could not hear what was said, she did recognize Buterra thanking Fiona for her courage. *Fiona is always full of surprises*, she thought and not for the first time. *And I may have a surprise for her, too, real soon.*

"That girl used to work for me and I want her back in my house, no matter what you have to do. Do you understand?" she told Vlad who was leaning against a lamppost smoking a cigar wearing the new suit Madame bought him the previous day.

Madame kept as much of a physical distance as possible between them. Not just because of his unpredictable nature but because of his poor hygiene. He never bathed and food particles could be seen in his straggly beard and between his broken teeth.

Yesterday, she secretly empathized with the distressed tailor who tried holding his breath as he measured Vlad who never seemed aware of his own body odor. Madame knew that, as soon as they left, the tailor would take Vlad's old clothes and burn them in the trash can in the back of his shop.

"A whore Suffragist, I never would have guessed that connection being they are all lady-lovers," he laughed very amused at the idea. "Sure, sure, when do you want her?" was Vlad's response to Madame.

"Not yet. First, you will follow her at a distance so as not to be detected and learn where she lives and where she goes. When the time is right, I will tell you to take her." *And I will not lose her this time*, she swore to herself.

And I will have my first Suffragist, teasing himself with his perverted thoughts.

Madame was disappointed with her new business. There was more competition than she thought in the harbor area and her income was lower than she expected. She attributed it to having a poorer working-class clientele and unattractive whores in her brothel.

"I don't like the quality of tramps you are bringing in," she informed Vlad.

"You find better, you think?" Vlad had no fear of Madame. He knew he could easily bully her anytime he wanted. He could detect fear in her eyes sometimes when they spoke.

She put up with his insubordination because she had no other choice and because, frankly, he did scare her. She walked away from him which only made him deliberately laugh loud enough for her to hear.

With Fiona back in my stable, things will turn around quickly, she consoled herself. *I'll advertise her and win a higher clientele once again. Maybe I'll post some of her photos that Sam had shared with me that he took in Dublin. That would get the attention my house needs.*

A week later on the following Sunday, Fiona decided to pay another unexpected visit to Mina hoping to find her at her apartment. Since she had the day off, she took a trolley and enjoyed the glances she received wearing her Suffragist sash over her dress. *How times are changing for Suffragists*, she thought. Even a gentleman offered her his seat in the crowded trolley car.

The windows of the trolley were partially opened, so the combination of the trolley's speed travelling up and down hills and the winter wind, male and female passengers held on to their hats. Fiona enjoyed the clanging of the trolley bell and she enjoyed watching the busy markets and people hustling back and forth. She was excited to see Mina and share with her all the amazing events of the previous week, including the successful march, the child's rescue and meeting a real gangster boss. She was basking in her new-found freedom.

She hoped to catch Mina alone and she did. But found herself concerned with her friend's appearance. Since her last visit, Mina was noticeably thinner and had dark rings around her eyes. Even under the terrible conditions on the voyage together in steerage, Mina always took pride in her appearance to the point of vanity.

"Have you been ill?" Fiona asked with sincere concern.

"I am ill, but it is another type of sickness, so please bear with me as I try to explain what shamefully happened to me."

Mina loved Fiona for her consistent confidence and personal strength which she had shown time and time again during their voyage. Just being in

269

her presence gave her comfort. So, with more control than she thought she had, Mina began to explain what she was shamefully forced to do in order for Carlo's debt to be cancelled with the loan sharks.

"My own husband made me feel so dirty. The positions that the photographer forced me to take are unspeakable, even to you. If you can imagine the most indecent poses for a woman then you will know how I was photographed. You are the only person in the world to whom I can tell this. God rest his soul, but I could never have told Basilio. Even my gentle brother would have killed Carlo." The thought of never seeing Basilio again brought on a new barrage of tears.

"Mina, stop crying now! This is dreadful and I will help you put a stop to it."

Mina looked closely at her friend. "You seem different, Fiona. Even stronger than I remember. What has changed?"

Taking her distraught friend's hands in her own, Fiona sighed, deep and long. "My guess is that the events in our lives have changed us both. In many ways, we will never again be the girls we were. But that is life. You and I will make the saying 'what doesn't kill you, makes you stronger' true for us…starting today."

"Without you, I would be alone, Fiona."

"Does anyone else know about the pictures?"

"No, of course not!"

"So, you have been suffering alone. For that I am so sorry but we will change that."

"Fiona, what can be done? I am so ashamed and so fearful it could happen again because Carlo has not stopped gambling."

"First calm yourself. Everything can be fixed with enough thought and enough time, I promise you." Fiona pulled out a handkerchief from her purse and handed it to her. It smelled of soap from Fiona's job.

As Mia finished describing her fear, which seemed quite possible to Fiona if Carlo was still gambling, she had to hide how shaken Mina's story had made her. She struggled silently thinking, *it is too much to hope that this is a coincidence but how could it be? Could it be Sam taking these pictures? Could I have caused this dreadful episode in Mina's life by leaving Sam with no model for his gangster partners? How can all our lives be so unknowingly connected?*

Taking Mina's face in her hands, Fiona asked, "Mina, you will have to answer this question before I can offer any help. Are you going to stay with Carlo or are you willing to leave him? There will be no changing your mind this time, no matter what." Fiona demanded a decision knowing her friend's proclivity to vacillate. "This is far too serious and you are only fooling yourself if you think it will get better. In fact, unless something is done, you are right to fear that it could happen again."

"What do you suggest?"

"You do nothing for now and do not allow despondency to set in. Trust me, I will have a plan soon." The words tumbled from her lips while her brain was focusing on a favor that was owed her.

Mina remembered Jack Turner's letter. She quickly retrieved it and handed it to Fiona. "Please read Jack's letter now before you leave." The letter was placed in Fiona's hand as Mina tried to collect herself after their emotional visit. Mina could see the tears that filled Fiona's eyes as her heart broke reading about Winifred's end. But all she said when she finished reading was, "you and I will accept Jack's invitation to New Jersey very soon."

Mina truly believed that somehow her friend would help her out of the hell in which she was living and for the first time she began to have real hope.

"You show up unexpected and at a time when I am desperate, like an angel…like one sent to rescue me because I cannot rescue myself. Fiona, do not laugh at me because it is true."

Fiona could not help but laugh at the idea of her being anything even remotely angelic but she would never discourage Mina's beliefs. "I'll only agree with Jack being an *angel* because our moving to New Jersey would be a 'Godsend'," she said jokingly. Then seriously added, "it would be heavenly to live where we would be surrounded and supported by friends who care about us and where we could start our lives over the way we both want to."

Ming's business was prospering. Having the assistance of his nephews made up for not having sons. He could not love them or trust them more than if they were his own children. He marveled at how respectful and grateful they were to him and how they uncomplainingly balanced schooling and long work hours. With their help, he expanded the number of tables in the restaurant and extended seating outside on a patio during the summer months. This enabled him to put away additional savings and to continue to send money home to family in China.

Although it was common knowledge that discrimination was a daily fact of life in Boston, his nephews learned to avoid problems by keeping their heads down and by conducting business honorably and honestly. There was never any trouble other than with one particular patron who Ming assigned to wait on himself rather than to subject his nephews to any abuse from the bully.

Unfortunately, the Russian sailor, now a brothel manager as he called himself, had acquired a taste for Chinese cuisine during his years overseas. To Ming's despair, he had made Ming's restaurant his local choice for food, as well as for medicines, particularly, aphrodisiacs.

One afternoon, after Chang returned from an errand picking up fresh vegetables from the Chinese open market, Ming noticed him trying to hide his bruised face.

"Chang, come here. Let me look at you."

"Uncle, it is nothing worth noting."

"Let me decide that," Ming stated while turning the young boy's face toward him.

"Tell me what happened to you to cause these injuries."

"Uncle, I am ashamed. I tried to defend myself but Vlad is far too strong, as you know."

"So, it was the Russian who did this to you?"

"He smelled drunk and was telling everyone that he felt like getting some exercise, as he put it. I should not have looked up at him, that was my mistake. He recognized me and called me yellow eyes and pushed me down spilling the bags of vegetables into the street. As I tried to collect the spilled food, he pulled me up and hit me a few times before he walked away, laughing that he hated 'chinks' but loved our food. Some of our people helped me up and helped gather our purchases but no one dared to confront this giant bully and who could blame them?"

The older brother, Da, suggested contacting the gang leader, Feng Fu. "Feng will right this wrong, Uncle, if you ask him?"

"When the time is right, I alone will handle this situation, you will see," was Ming's calm reply. Internally, Ming was furious. *The time for revenge is now. I have tolerated this Russian beast's rudeness and disrespect for too long but deliberately injuring my nephew is intolerable and will stop. I will see to it.*

Fiona wrestled with the decision. She decided to find Mr. Buterra and see if he would keep his promise. She truly never thought she would ever collect on his offer. However, she believed that he would be the solution in preventing Mina from ever being forced again to pose for obscene pictures. Or so she hoped.

Fiona kept trying to sort out all the connecting pieces as best as she could. She literally abandoned Sam with no notice of her plan to stop working for him. In fact, she tricked him into thinking she would meet him in Boston, leaving him to face the mob partners without a model. Carlo owed the same mob gambling money and he somehow met Sam. Then the two of them used Mina to solve both their obligations. And Mina is frantic because she believes that they plan another session soon. *And I am sure she is right.*

She decided that she had no other option but to ask Don Buterra for help. *I'll will ask him to keep his word. I will ask that he stop Carlo's mistreatment of his innocent Sicilian wife because of his gambling debts. I'll explain that she is my dearest friend and that I am counting on him to make it stop. Then the debt will be repaid in full with my gratitude. The question that remains is will he be willing to stop Sam and Carlo when he may be involved in the dirty business?*

It was not difficult to find the gambling club. What was more difficult was entering the premises. To gain entrance she had to walk a gauntlet of mobsters hanging around, smoking and joking with each other. They blocked her entrance, and, at the sight of a pretty woman, some began to make unseemly remarks.

"Shut up, you idiots. She's the gal who rescued the boss' son, the Irish gal, the Suffragette."

"Is Mr. Buterra in? I would very much like to speak with him." She addressed her request to the older man in the group who recognized her. She ignored the others as if they didn't exist.

"Oh, the Don will be available to you, pretty lady, as long as you are available to him," remarked one wise guy while the others snickered.

"Please excuse these bums," the older man apologized as he escorted her into the club. She was told to wait as the same man went into an office. The smell of alcohol and cigarettes permeated the premises which made her nauseous, *or is it due to fear*, she wondered.

In just moments, she was ushered into Don Buterra's private area. As he sat behind a desk, his eyes narrowed as she approached. "Miss Burke, this is an unexpected but nice surprise. Please sit down. Can I offer you espresso, a strong Italian coffee?"

"Tea would be lovely. I'm Irish in case you forgot," she told him with a smile.

Never taking his eyes away from her, the boss called to Gus and told him to bring tea.

"Did ya' say tea, Boss?" Apparently, tea had never before been a request so he had to be sure he had heard correctly.

"Yes, tea, you ass," Buterra responded before he realized his rudeness. "Please pardon my language, Miss Burke. Sometimes my temper takes over but Gus understands."

"So, does your visit mean that you wish to take me up on my offer?" As he said this, he could not keep his eyes from moving over her body before lifting them up to meet Fiona's eyes. Most women would be insulted by his behavior but not Fiona. She found this as proof that she was in control, even if he did not know it yet.

"Yes, Mr. Buterra, indeed I do," she answered while crossing one leg over the other very slowly and looking directly into his eyes.

Once the tea was delivered, their polite conversation centered around Fiona's inquiry as to how Antonio was doing and Buterra complimenting her lovely and unusual eyes until they finally arrived at the point of the meeting.

"Now tell me what you want. A promise made is a promise kept."

Fiona left out no details of the spousal abuse received by her dearest friend, a sweet Sicilian and practicing Catholic girl. She provided Carlo's name and address and described the shameful photography session for which he had forcibly subjected his young wife in order to continue his gambling habit.

"My request is that you make sure he never hurts his wife again, either by physically abusing her or by forcing her to do immoral things against her will."

Carlo Vitale, I should have known. Such a strunz to use his own wife. Well, even his father cannot save him this time, Buterra thought.

"This is my request and I know you will handle delivering the message as you see fit. I put my full trust in you." She slowly uncrossed her legs enjoying that she could see him watching her every move. She deliberately raised her arm, which automatically raised her breast higher, to fidget with a tendril of hair that had slipped from under her hat.

The mob boss was clearly smitten with the Irish girl. Being married never stopped his adulterous behavior. But he realized that this situation required him to be a promise keeper first, not a lothario, not yet anyway. *But soon,* he promised himself.

January, 1919

Boston

It was the first time that Carlo had not come home from his evening out. Mina was exhausted with worry all night because she was at a loss as to what to do. *Maybe he went directly to work? But what if he was arrested or taken to the hospital? Should I go to the gambling hall and ask about him?*

But before she could decide her next step, Carlo was delivered home by two men who banged on the door before dumping him in the hall outside their apartment. His eyes were blackened, his nose broken and he had multiple cuts and bruises. Mina helped pull him to his feet and, with his arms around her shoulders, got him to the bed where he collapsed groaning. She kept questioning him as to what happened.

"Who were those men? Were you robbed, or hit by a vehicle?"

Shaking his head, he replied that it was none of her concern.

"None of my concern? You are my husband, so this is a serious concern," as she began to inventory the visible wounds. He forcibly pushed her away. No matter how she implored him for an explanation, none was offered. Only groans and words of self-pity were expressed. He ordered her to leave him alone.

"But I want to help you, Carlo."

"Merda, just leave me alone."

She relented knowing when it was useless to argue with him. But before she closed the bedroom door she reminded him that Fiona would be coming to dinner. It had been planned that they would dine together after he left for his usual night out. She told him that she would cancel if she could but that there was no way to do that.

"I could not care less about you and your friend. You can both choke on your dinners, just leave me alone."

She had pity for him in his current condition but felt there had to be a gambling connection. What was most disturbing for her was that the terrible pictures were supposed to have repaid his gambling debt in full. Did he incur more debt so soon that he couldn't repay? And if he misses work due to his injuries, will he lose his job? However, Mina knew that none of these were important to her any longer because of her plan with Fiona.

Ignoring her husband as he requested, she closed the door to the bedroom and went about her daily routine. In the afternoon, she went to the market to purchase the bread, meat, chorizo, cheeses, tomatoes, olives and peppers needed to prepare a special meal for Fiona. She made the purchases using a small amount of Mrs. Jacobs' money. In his current condition, it was not likely that Carlo would be questioning her on how she paid for the food. For that she was grateful. Although his being home complicated Fiona's visit, they could still converse with lowered voices. Her spirits were high just knowing Fiona would be arriving shortly.

The afternoon had drifted into evening quickly. Fiona had not arrived. Mina knew that there had to be a logical reason. As she glanced out her window, she noticed that snow had begun to fall, already covering the trash bins and cracked sidewalks of the tenement buildings. Few pedestrians were out and the ones who were held their heads bowed from the biting wind. The temperature had dropped very quickly once the winter sun went down and the apartment was becoming uncomfortably cold so she added more coal to the stove. She rarely used coal during the day in order to save it so that Carlo would come home to a warm apartment each evening after work. But unknown to him, she had been treating herself to heat during the daytime, again thanks to her inheritance from Mrs. Jacobs.

She peeked her head into the bedroom to check on her husband. He turned painfully onto his back, moaning but telling her to leave him alone again. "Should I get a doctor?" she asked.

"No, go away." She did just that but not without some guilt. *Maybe later, he will explain what happened and let me help him.*

Mina kept vigil at the window looking for her friend. Concern was starting to build, but mostly disappointment. She worried now that it was dark and the streets empty. *These streets are unsafe at night for a woman alone even in good weather.* As disappointed as she felt, she trusted that Fiona was using good judgement in cancelling her visit. She never doubted that Fiona would not have a good reason. Her only hope was that it was the weather that caused Fiona's absence and not something more serious.

Fiona knew that she was running late to Mina's. She had a few unavoidable delays. Work ran over and the trolley was late and slower than usual because of the inclement weather. A light snow began to fall, blurring the street lights giving a dizzying effect at first, but then turned heavier, almost diminishing visibility altogether. Fiona never liked the inky dark, so she hurried her steps. She hoped she would be permitted to stay the night at Mina's if the storm continued and the trollies stopped running. She could see Mina's tenement in the distance where it stood looking as dreary as ever amid the previous piles of snow now dirty from traffic and animal defecation.

Although concerned about the weather, Fiona enjoyed a satisfied relief thinking about Mr. Butera's promise that Carlo would never abuse Mina again. She never wanted to know how.

Mr. Butera would accomplish his promise and never wanted Mina to know anything about her part in it. She just wanted the result to be successful.

She looked forward to finalizing the arrangements for their escape plan once Carlo went out for the evening as was his usual routine. *The snow shouldn't stop Carlo since his nightly destination is within walking distance,* she remembered having been there herself to see the mob boss.

She reviewed the plan in her head as she walked hurriedly. She and Mina had agreed to meet on January 15th at the entrance of the Boston Public Library at 12 noon. This would provide time for Mina to pack a bag once Carlo left for work and for Fiona to have ample time to respectfully resign her job at the soap factory. Together, they would take the train to New Jersey where Jack Turner would be waiting for them at the train station as already arranged. Fiona had already corresponded directly with Jack and received his confirmation. The money Fiona and she were pooling together would provide lodging and hold them until jobs could be found. Jack assured them that there was room in his home for them and that there were many job openings in his area. Jersey was growing industrially and employers were seeking new female hires to fill vacant positions left because of the influenza epidemic and the male casualties of the war.

The usually busy street was empty of pedestrians and vehicles which gave her an uneasy feeling. The storm had created a ghost town. She wished the cold wind would be at her back instead of her face, but the excitement of the escape plan made her forget her discomfort. *I'm almost there*, she told herself as she pushed on.

Suddenly from behind her, Fiona felt a large hand placed roughly over her mouth and the other around her tiny waist. A sedan had pulled up to the curb so quickly that wet snow splashed over Fiona and her captor who then let out a string of profanities at the driver.

As she was carried into the back seat, the large man held her down and took liberties with his hands as she tried to stop him. He had an Eastern European sound to his voice as he barked orders to the silent driver. Fiona was deliberately being held face down in the captor's crotch, to stifle any screams and to, no doubt, provide the criminal with some degree of perverted pleasure. It was not a long ride to their destination and once she smelled the harbor, she could guess that they were still somewhere in the North End.

Her greatest shock was to see Madame when she was carried into the house and tied to a chair in a back room on the first floor of what looked like a bordello. *My god, how can this be?* Shocked to the bone at seeing Madame in Boston, she was even more dumbfounded with her predicament.

Menacingly, Madame addressed Fiona through clenched teeth trying to gain control of her anger while, at the same time, maintain her false French accent. "Fiona, it is my delight to see you looking as lovely as ever. It was my good fortune to see you at the suffragette march the other day. What a surprise it was for me. Mon Dieu, you even played the heroine and saved a child, an important child, *bien sur*. But, as you can guess, repayment is due. You owe me much and I expect to recoup. You will work for me again. I suspect you may need convincing of this, so that is going to be arranged by Vlad."

"Madame, please don't do this to me. Surely, you can understand why I left. If you had ever had the chance to leave prostitution when you were younger, wouldn't you have taken that opportunity yourself? You are punishing me for something you would have done, too."

Pleading, she continued, "I didn't leave you. I left selling myself. There's a difference, Madame." Fiona lied because she had always wanted to leave this woman who she detested.

Unmoved, Madame walked out of the room and left the Russian to begin 'convincing' Fiona.

All Fiona could think about was how Madame just destroyed her future. She was devastated imagining Mina waiting for her at the Library alone and confused. She searched deep within herself for strength that would be needed to get her through this ordeal but only felt the deepest despair. For the first time in many years, Fiona began to cry and told her Irish ghosts to go quiet.

Mina 's worry grew when there was no word from Fiona. She visited her boarding house, but no one knew anything helpful, only that no one had seen her. Then when Mina visited the soap factory where she was sure she would find her, she was informed that Fiona had not shown up. As her last resort, Mina went to the Police Department. An officer at the front desk listened to her and filled out a missing person report, but left Mina feeling that there was not going to be much effort put into it.

"Why don't you sit down and wait for Officer Muller, who has your location on his beat. He should be arriving here shortly if you're willing to wait, Miss."

While Mina waited, she watched the dynamics of the busy department. Mounted police, detectives and officers, criminal and lawyers, all coming and going. The desk sergeant called her back to the desk where a tall officer stood.

"Muller, this lady, Mrs. Vitale…. that's your name, right?" as he looked at Mina to verify. When she shook her head 'yes', he continued speaking, "Ok, her friend is missing. Here's the report so see what you can find out."

William Muller walked her back to the bench where she had been sitting and asked her a number of questions and for a description. Mina provided a complete description of Fiona, including her unique eyes. Muller wrote it all down, ending their conversation with a promise to investigate.

"But Mrs. Vitale, sometimes people don't want to be found, especially new immigrants who tend to move around where work can be found. Could that be the case with your friend?"

"No, something is wrong. I think something has happened to her," said like the loyal friend she was.

"I'll be in touch but don't get your hopes up too high," as he walked her to the door, ending the conversation as politely as he could. He knew too well the difficulty in finding a missing new immigrant in the crime ridden tenement neighborhood where no one trusted the police and no one would share any information with him.

As she walked home, she knew that something was very wrong. Mina felt torn apart by this devastating change in their well-laid out plan. *Should I cancel it or carry on without Fiona?*

She made a decision. She would be at the designated meeting place with the hope that Fiona would still arrive as promised even though there had been no word from her. She would not deviate from the plan. She would leave while Carlo was at work and take the train to New Jersey where Jack Turner would be waiting. *There will be no turning back, no changing my mind this time, no matter what*, she promised herself.

Madame held one of the new American Tobacco Company cigarettes that were beginning to be smoked by women. Since the war, a culture shift was taking place where women craved more independence, particularly after working in factories earning wages while the men waged war. Cigarettes were branded as being stylish and 'deliciously toasted' so there was an increase in women smokers among those who could afford them.

Ever trying for a glamorous stance, Madame held her cigarette with one hand while cupping her elbow with the other. Eventually, she poured her visitor two fingers of Jameson's Irish whiskey.

The mob sent a collection man monthly to all the North End brothels. The payment provided guaranteed protection from the authorities, trouble makers and sometimes other brothel competitors.

She learned long ago, in her experience with men, that liquor loosened tongues. Especially, when the wine-drinking dagos were given real whiskey. The more liquor, the more information. And information was power.

"So, what's new in your world, Gus?" She was glad she only had this one dago to deal with. Sometimes they sent two collectors.

After his third drink, he laughingly told her of a recent debt paid by the boss to some Irish girl. "The boss told this broad that she could have any favor she wanted. So, what does she ask for? Not a car or jewelry or money, but to have some poor jerk beat up, can you believe that? So, we beat the shit out of him and another guy."

"That does sound odd, doesn't it? What does this woman look like, Gus, since you say she is Irish then maybe I know her?"

"She's no tramp so I don't think you would know her. Unless you know any suffragettes," he smirked.

"What does she look like?" Madame continued even though offended that Gus would think she only knew tramps, which was truer than she would have liked to admit. Madame was fearful that she already knew the answer Gus was about to give.

"Blond hair, very pretty but what the boss can't stop talking about is her two different colored eyes. She's a head-turner and she sure did turn the boss' head."

"Do you know what the debt was for?" Madame cunningly asked as she poured him another whiskey, knowing the favor had to be repayment for rescuing the boss' kid, which she witnessed the day of the march. She began to seriously second guess her decision to have kidnapped Fiona.

"Yeah, she pulled the boss' son from getting crushed in an accident. It was a close call, too. Not many dames I know would have done what she did."

"But do you know why she asked Mr. Buterra for a favor to beat men up?"

"Naw, not really 'cause noone said nothin' about it. But when we gave those guys the beatin' of their lives, there was talk about dirty picture taking which had something to do with it. Mr. Buterra believes good girls should be left alone, especially good Sicilian Catholic girls."

Gus continued with his story and with his drinking. "You shoulda' seen it. When we was almost done beatin' these guys, the boss hisself bends down and tells them that they are dead men if he ever hears of this problem again in his North End. Then he tells the gumba that he must be a 'frocio', a faggot to do such a thing as take dirty pictures of his own innocent wife. 'I will let you live for now, out of respect for your father, but you are never to show your face in my club again, never,' that's what he said, word for word."

Madame asked, "what about the other man?"

"Oh, the Heb? He was the older guy who took the pictures. To that guy, the boss tells him that their business together was over and, if he wanted to live, he better go back to New York on the next train and never show his Yid face in the North End again."

Could that have been Sam Goldman taking pictures? Who else could it have been? she reasoned. *He must have left Boston and returned to New York right after that warning. Too bad they didn't kill the cheating shyster! But I still don't see Fiona's connection unless Fiona is sleeping with Buterra! That is the only thing that makes sense for him to grant her wish to have the men beaten to save some friend of hers. And I have his mistress locked up in a room as punishment for leaving me in Dublin. Maybe these damn Wops are looking for her right now? If I release her, she will go straight to her mob boyfriend and make me the subject of the next beating. If I don't release her and the mob boss discovers that I am forcing her to work in my house, there will be hell to pay.*

Madame was frantic realizing she had a life-threatening problem that re-quired fixing immediately. Based on what Gus told her, Fiona has a connection to the mob boss, no doubt a very intimate one, even if this story about picture taking of someone's wife is still a puzzle.

The only solution is to make Fiona disappear for good. I can't leave any trace of her that would track her back to me. Vlad. I can't imagine Vlad to be above killing if the price is right.

Madame excused herself, telling Gus she had to greet her first customer of the evening. Just after she left, Vlad opened the door without thinking and for just a moment he saw Gus sitting with a drink in his hand. And it was suf-ficient time for Gus to recognize Fiona gagged and tied to a chair with bruises on her face. She seemed to be staring into space with a look as if she didn't know where she was. Vlad closed the door quickly but not fast enough to pre-vent Gus from seeing what was happening.

No wonder that bitch had so many questions about the Irish girl? Is Madame into kidnapping good girls now and forcing them to be puttanas here? Gus was con-fused by what he witnessed but was sure that he had better let the boss know right away about what he saw.

Pretending he saw nothing of any importance, Gus started humming as he casually finished his drink. He knew Vlad was listening from the other side of the door waiting for a reaction from Gus. Tangling with the giant was the last thing Gus intended to do.

"I'll give you a good-bye, Madame, I gotta' be going," he called-out loud enough for her to hear, and for Vlad to hear, as he made his way to the back door to leave, but not before pocketing the protection money that had been left on Madame's desk. "Thanks for the drinks. See you next month for the next collection."

Thinking, *holy shit, I gotta' tell the boss what I seen,* Gus made his way to the boss' office as quickly as he could with the information he was sure the boss would want to hear. But the boss was not at the club. Instead he was told that the boss went home to be with his family for the evening.

Gus was unsure what his next move should be. He certainly did not want the boss' wife to hear any of this and yet if he waited until morning would the girl's condition be worse? *With a bruised face, she must be refusing to become part of the brothel. What the hell is Madame thinking? Kidnapping a Suffragette? Madame must be crazy.*

Once she saw Gus leave, Madame called Vlad into her office. She explained *their* predicament and emphasized the pronoun *their* since both would be considered equally guilty by the mob boss if he ever learned of the kidnapping. Vlad said nothing about how he had opened the door that had given Gus a view of their prisoner.

"So, we can't let them know that we have Fiona. Can you make her disappear, Vlad? I see no other way around this mess that we have gotten ourselves into, can you?"

"Is there extra money for me?"

"Fifty dollars," she answered without hesitation.

"Make it one hundred dollars and I will solve the problem. And I have one other requirement."

"What is it?" asked Madame impatiently.

"I require a few hours entertainment tonight with her. You owe me that much since you wouldn't let me touch her other than to hit her some," he stated in a tone that meant there would be no negotiation. "Now it's my turn for some satisfaction before she dies."

"Just make it fast. This is serious for both of us. We could be the ones dying if we don't take care of this problem. All they know is that she's missing but have no idea where she is. No one would think to look for her here, so that is in our favor. Once you make her disappear, our secret will be safe," she said knowing that eventually she would have to do something to rid herself of Vlad, too.

She walked out of the room, leaving him wondering how fast he could get to the Yellow Eyed Chinks to get some of that special aphrodisiac herb they sold. *I need to be able to perform well for my time with Fiona tonight*, he thought perversely, knowing that he had been having some trouble getting an erection lately. The last time he blamed the girl and fiercely took it out on her for his physical failure.

January 14, 1918

10pm

Vlad frequented Ming's restaurant and frequently bought medicines from the Chinese businessman. His patronage was unwelcomed because he was surly and unwashed and disrespectful. Chinese customers were uncomfortable when he would sit at a table and loudly demand service ahead of others. Even overcharging him did not dissuade his returning to Ming's, although more often than not, Vlad left without paying his bill with the excuse that something was wrong with the food. Ming never wanted to cause a scene so he tolerated Vlad, fervently wishing each time would be the last time he would come to the restaurant.

The proverbial 'last straw' was reached when Ming learned that Vlad had humiliated and bullied Chang in public. Ming wanted revenge. Too many times during these past months he and his nephews took the abuse out of fear of retaliation from this criminal who boasted that he managed a brothel.

The Russian told them, "Sorry to say, no Chinks are allowed to visit our establishment so don't think because I eat in your restaurant that I will allow you the privilege to enjoy our girls. But I hear you have your own Chink brothel in Feng Fu's part of town. I am going to go there to try it out one night myself. I want to see if those little gals can accommodate a guy my size, if you get my meaning." His laugh was as twisted as he was.

Ming seethed silently but knew he would get justice when the time was right. His opportunity arrived when Vlad appeared that night as the restaurant was closing and the last diners were preparing to leave. Because his nephews worked the restaurant and attended school during the day, Ming managed the dinner business alone many nights.

"Ming, stop whatever you are doing right now and get me some of your special sex medicine. Give me a large dose that will keep me performing long and strong tonight." This request, which was more an order, was issued loudly enough for everyone to hear as the giant Russian bully stood in the center of the restaurant.

Ming continued to politely bid farewell to the departing customers, who looked relieved to be taking their leave. The Russian had established a reputation in Chinatown as a bigoted trouble maker. Ming lost business whenever Vlad appeared there.

"Please sit, Mr. Vlad, as I need a few minutes to prepare the powder for you. You will be pleased with the results, I promise. It is very special with strong effect."

"It better work or you will be sorry, Ming, I promise you that. Tonight is very important for me. I need to be at top performance for many hours."

Ming went to the private area in the rear of the restaurant where he kept a locked apothecary closet. He deliberately bypassed all the aphrodisiacs. Instead, he went deep into a locked drawer in the cabinet. The cabinet contained many toxic powders used through the centuries by assassins to eliminate enemies. Ming opened the drawer with the key that he always wore around his neck. He pulled the drawer open and carefully touched the bag that held the toxic 'heartbreak grass'. He poured a lethal dose of the fast- acting poison into a small paper bag. Estimating the Russian's height and weight, Ming added an extra spoonful of the powder to ensure success.

"Hurry, Ming, the lady awaits my full attention."

"Mr. Vlad, this should serve your needs very well. Just mix all the powder in water and drink immediately once you are home. Remember that you must drink all of it to get the results for which it is intended," Ming instructed trying to disguise the rancor in his voice. "Remember, drink all of it at once. And because you are a loyal customer, this is my gift to you, no charge."

"Free or not, it just better work fast. You don't want me coming back dissatisfied, if you know what's good for you." With that, Vlad snatched the bag out of Ming's hand and left as quickly as he had arrived.

Oh, it will work, thought Ming, as he watched the hated man leave. Within minutes of ingestion Ming knew that there would be intense cramping, abdominal pain and vomiting followed by internal bleeding of the organs and, finally, a painful death by morning. *I have done a great service for the woman unfortunate enough to have the Russian coming to her. And I have done a great service for all the rest of us, as well.* Ming suffered no guilt and knew he would sleep well knowing he had achieved his revenge. As Ming closed his business for the night, he hummed a folk song from his childhood which he did whenever he solved a serious problem.

"Muller, see that girl sitting over there? She's a waterfront tramp who says there's a big Russian going around kidnapping the whores off the streets and forcing them into his new brothel. She says he tried to rape her in an alley the other day when she refused to go with him, but he couldn't get his "man-thing" up…her words, Muller, not mine. She says he got away when some sailors came in answer to her screams. She says this guy has all the street walkers afraid and something has to be done," the desk Sargent said insensitively with a smirk. "Anyway, go down there and visit this new joint to see if there's any truth to what this dame is reporting. Here's the address."

With Mary's death, Muller found himself accepting as many assignments as possible with the hope that work would take his mind off his loss. He believed that diving into police work would be the remedy for his misery, and so he did exactly that.

He went to the address and because it was early in the morning, he found the brothel quiet, as he expected, with all the inhabitants asleep after working all night. He rang the bell a number of times and then began loudly banging on the door until a worker finally answered. He pushed his way passed her and into the parlor and bluntly ordered, "Where is the Russian who works here?"

The frightened maid pointed to a back room, so Muller went in with his baton ready. He found a young blonde girl tied to a chair looking at him with pleading eyes and a giant man tossing in pain on a dirty mattress with liquor bottles strewn around the floor.

As Muller was untying the girl, he immediately noticed her eyes when she looked directly at him, grateful for her rescue from the brute on the floor. The two different colored eyes matched the missing girl's description given to him yesterday by the young Italian girl. But the Russian started to thrash about taking Muller's attention away from the captive. Before he could stop her, the young girl took off once her wrists and legs were set free. She ran faster than Muller ever expected, considering how she appeared to have been abused.

He then concentrated on the giant still on the floor who was groaning in pain while holding his abdomen. There was some vomit in the bedding and there appeared to be blood in the excrement in a pail nearby.

He's really in bad shape so maybe arresting him will be easier than I expected. He doesn't look like he has a lot of fight in him right now. Muller quickly handcuffed the weakened man's hands and used cord to tie his legs, the same cord that had just been untied from the girl's legs.

"I'm Officer Muller. Do you hear me? You're under arrest for kidnapping and rape." He had to use a loud voice in order to be heard over the man's groaning, wondering if the man was too sick to even understand him.

He was proved wrong when the prisoner muttered, "Muller, a Kraut son-of-a-bitch name, you go to hell."

"Mister, you have the influenza. You might need the hospital before going to jail."

"I have no influenza. The Chink did this to me. He did this to get even with me for pushing his kid around. He made me sick all night. He ruined everything so am going to kill him, I swear!"

Then the prisoner started vomiting again. Muller quickly backed away to protect his uniform boots. He pulled out his mask from his pocket to prevent contagion spreading to him, even though its value had been questioned by Mary. *Mary!* Everything seemed to remind him of her.

He returned his attention to the man on the floor. "Mister, your talk of a Chinaman sounds like delirium to me. Spanish flu does that. Lie there quietly until the police wagon gets here."

"No, I tell you, it's the Chinaman who did this to me," but at that point Vlad was bent over in acute misery with a bloody drool coming from the corner of his mouth.

"I'm no doctor but it would be better for you to save your strength. Help will be here as soon as I make the call."

Influenza was Muller's diagnosis and the one he was going to pass on when the back-up officers arrived so that they could take precautions.

Muller left him alone on the floor and went to call the precinct for the police wagon. He used the phone in Madame's office. Within minutes he was joined by a woman in nightclothes and heavy make-up for so early in the morning.

"Are you in charge here?" he asked her.

"Yes, this is my house. What is the problem, Officer?"

"I'm Officer Muller. I am following up on charges made against the Russian who is tied up in the next room. I just called for the paddy wagon but he may need a hospital. Looks like he has the influenza. Is anyone else sick here?"

"No one. I run a healthy house, in every way," she stated.

Not long after, the back-up arrived. "Fellows, be careful. Wear your masks if you have them 'cause this guy is really sick," Muller warned. They saw him wearing his mask so they pulled out theirs and placed them on before touching the prisoner.

"Jackass coppers, listen to me. You have it all wrong. It was the shit medicine the Chink gave me. I know it was him. That yellow bastard poisoned me," Vlad insisted as his speech slurred and he writhed in pain.

"Disregard what he says. He's delirious and keeps repeating nonsense about some Chinese," Muller explained to his fellow policemen.

When Vlad noticed Madame, he pleaded, "I think I'm dying, help me." But Madame turned her back to him and moved as far away as she could. By the time he was carried out and locked in the paddy wagon, he lost consciousness. They placed him on the cold floor of the vehicle. His last thought was about burning Ming's restaurant to the ground. Vlad was dead before he reached the jail. His cause of death was listed as influenza.

Madam, who had been awakened by the servant, still could not believe what had happened. As she questioned Muller on the charges and if there was evidence supporting the charges, she reached into the pocket of her robe and began to remove money so that the officer could see the bribe that was being offered.

"Put your money away. I need you to tell me why there was a young woman tied up in your back room? Then I need to look around and question your other employees about the Russian. So, what I need you to do is to sit down, be quiet and let me do my job."

"But I have a right to know."

"For starters, kidnapping, felony assault and rape. We have a victim down at the precinct ready to press charges against him even though the one in your back room ran away. After I question your employees, there may very well be additional charges against him, and maybe against you, too."

"If the brute had a woman in the back room against her will, I had no idea that he did that." Although she would never admit to Fiona's kidnapping, she knew she would be arrested once Fiona found her way to the police. Or worse, once she reached the mob boss. She didn't know which was worse.

After Muller interviewed all the women in the house, he advised them to not fear coming forward with any accusations of kidnapping and rape which would be added to the list that would be presented to the judge. Muller warned the girls that if they did not show up as witnesses, they would run the risk of Vlad being freed and he would resume his harsh treatment of them again. He guessed that the Russian's condition looked moribund as he was being placed in the wagon, but no one knew that he had already died.

When asked her part in these crimes, Madame blamed the Russian. She swore she was unaware of any of these accusations. Muller looked to the girls for their reactions. But they remained silent and did not implicate Madame, probably because she paid well in comparison with the other brothels on the waterfront. And there was a possibility of blackmailing Madame which crossed a few of their minds.

Once Muller left, Madame collapsed into an upholstered parlor chair. She knew she had to do some damage control with the girls since she knew that they knew she was as guilty as the Russian. *Vlad, the stupid ass! If he had gotten rid of Fiona last night when I asked, the policeman would not have been an eye witness to her confinement and assault. But no, he wanted it his way and I foolishly agreed,* she lamented. *But why didn't my mob protection money prevent this fiasco? Isn't that what I've been paying for?* she thought angrily while she counted out money she planned to pay her whores for their continued silence.

11 am
Buterra received Gus' news and was furious.

"Why didn't I know about this yesterday," he demanded grabbing Gus by the front of his jacket with both of his meaty hands.

"Boss, you were home with your family and you don't want us disturbing you at home so I didn't," said Gus, hoping Buterra would understand that he was only carrying out his standing orders.

"Are you sure, 'cause it makes no sense to me," as Buterra calmed down and straightened Gus's wrinkled coat lapels.

"Boss, I know what I saw. It was the dame that saved Antonio. She's hard to miss."

Taking Gus' word, Butera and three of his men climbed into the sedan, guns loaded and headed to the whore house where Gus swore he saw Fiona Burke kidnapped and tied to a chair in a back room the evening before.

When the gangsters barged into the house, it was alive with activity. One whore was leaving with her suitcase cursing like a sailor at Madame, who sat there in a fugue state. The other women looked dazed as they sat around the parlor smoking cigarettes and drinking coffee to stay awake. Some were counting the money Madame had given them as bribes.

Gus pointed out Madame since all the women were similarly clad in night clothes sitting around the parlor.

"Now who has the nerve to be entering my house when we are closed and without my permission?" she demanded as she rose stiffly from the armchair. She was prepared to throw the intruders out herself but then she recognized the mob boss. Brazenly and taking the offensive rather than a defensive stance, she barked at him, "Why didn't my protection money protect me from the police raid this morning? Isn't that what I pay you for?"

Without any hesitation, Don Butera grabbed the woman by the throat and demanded, "if I don't find Ms. Fiona Burke in the next minute, you will be dead and your whorehouse set on fire, do you understand me?"

12 noon

Before Madame could think of an explanation, there was a thunderous sound of an explosion. Screams could be heard coming from outside on the streets. Everyone in the house turned in the direction of the noise that sounded like an oncoming freight train coming from the rear of the building. They had no time to react as the wooden building's walls and roof caved in on them and swept them away in a towering wave of a sweet-smelling muddy substance.

As the huge wave of muck rapidly pushed everything in its path down the street carrying debris and screaming victims, Madame desperately reached for

Buterra who had grabbed onto a floating beam enabling him to keep his face above the mire. Victims were being submerged into the thick substance with some unable to raise themselves because of the viscous weight. Shock set in with the realization that an explosion had released tons of thick molasses from the distillery's holding tanks causing a rushing river of molasses destroying everything in its wake.

Madame desperately grabbed a hold onto Buterra's coat sleeve. Looking directly into her unbelieving eyes, Buterra peeled Madame's grasping hand away from his arm and watched her being helplessly tossed along the bubbling muck and debris flowing to the harbor. As he clung to the beam for his survival, he looked for his men but they were gone.

12 noon

Mina stood at the top of the library's steps with her carpet bag as she awaited Fiona at the designated time and place as planned. She wore her best dress and her dark hair was knotted in braids coiled around her head. All she needed was Fiona to complete the escape plan to New Jersey.

Although she had received no word from Fiona, she prayed she would still show up. Because she knew that Carlo would be at work, she took the huge risk of leaving a note for Fiona taped to her apartment door, confirming that she would be at the library as planned and had purchased the train tickets.

It was a beautiful day, unusually warm for January, and surprisingly so soon after the recent frigid weather. Mina scanned the street hoping to see Fiona. Instead, she was shocked to see Carlo a half block away angrily approaching her. His fists were clenched, and his face distorted in anger. *He must have found the note I had left for Fiona*, she thought horrified not knowing what to do next.

At the same moment, but on the opposite side of the street, she saw Fiona. She carried no valise and was running as fast as she could towards the library. Apparently, Fiona had seen Carlo, too, as they eyed each other and increased their running speed.

Fiona was frantic at seeing Carlo and knew there would be an unavoidable altercation. But after the terrible experience from which she just escaped, she believed nothing was going to stop her now. If he became hostile, which was very likely, they would go inside the library and have the police called. She and Mina were going to make the trip to New Jersey where the Turners and the Kelly family were waiting for them. She pictured Brian and wondered if he might be part of her new life there but realized that this was not the time to think about that.

As she ran towards the library, Fiona was aware that her face was bruised and her hair disheveled but little did that matter now that she was free. She was eternally grateful that the Russian brute returned last night mysteriously so sick that he was unable to follow through on his threat to hurt her. Still tied up in the chair, she had to listen to his moaning through the night, as he drank vodka thinking that would alleviate his stomach pain. At one point, he had asked her opinion if a doctor should be called. As if she cared. Her only thought was that she had hoped he would die.

We will not allow Carlo to ruin our plan. Fiona concentrated on that thought as the distance to reach Mina narrowed.

Where is Fiona's suitcase and why does she look so unkempt, was Mina's first thought, as she watched helplessly as both her husband and her best friend raced towards the library. She dreaded the confrontation about to take place once the three came together. *What kind of scene will Carlo make in public? Will he dare strike me?* She prepared herself to scream which would bring people to their aid, she hoped.

Suddenly, came the thundering sound of a huge explosion from the direction of the Purity Distilling factory. Fiona and Carlo stopped in their tracks at the sound and looked back behind them. Screams and chaos immediately followed as a tsunami of thick dark molasses roared around the corner.

A huge brown wave, three stories high, roared through the streets, toppling the wooden structures, automobiles, trollies and people. There was no time for anyone to escape as everything and everyone became trapped in the deep thick bubbling molasses. School children at lunch time, laborers, housewives, merchants, and horses were swallowed up and could be seen thrashing about trying not to drown in the thick paralyzing substance. Victims caught in the flood were completely covered with molasses and struggled to grasp for air through mouths and nostrils filled with the thick substance as they were being swept away in the flood.

Mina thought back to Basilio's visit the previous month when he told Carlo his concern about the safety of the plant's tanks. *My God, my brother was right, look what is happening now!*

Patricia Sabella

When the stone library building shook, Mina fought to maintain her balance. The wave finally leveled midway up the concrete library steps where Mina had been standing at the top.

She watched in horror as both her husband and her friend were caught in the wave's thick muddy substance enmeshed with debris from the collapsed buildings. They struggled amid the detritus of lumber and stone from the surrounding demolished structures, their bodies covered with the muck.

Carlo appeared to have been struck by a large piece of floating lumber from a wagon wheel which managed to push him closer to the library steps. Both he and Fiona could be seen gasping for air as the viscous substance covered them entirely and already had started to harden. Neither could stand and repeatedly kept falling face down into the thick swampy mire. The weight of Fiona 's long skirt was dragging her down each time she fought to rise.

"Oh, Dio, oh my God!" Mina kept repeating to herself as she rushed down the steps.

She held her skirt up high trying to prevent losing her balance as she entered the pooling molasses which still had a strong current even as it was leveling. Since the flood had pushed Carlo nearer the library than it had pushed Fiona, Mina headed in his direction first.

As she pushed herself chest deep through the muck, she worked her way toward her husband. Then with just the slightest hesitation, as she watched him struggle to breathe, Mina changed her mind and quickly turned to save Fiona instead.

Epilogue
The Great Boston Molasses Flood

In Cambridge, a forty-foot high wave of molasses swept through the city at thirty-five miles an hour, killing twenty-one and injuring one hundred fifty people at 12 noon on January 15,1919. It took days to complete a search for victims in the mud and under the debris. Gunshots were heard throughout the city's north end as horses and dogs trapped in the muck were euthanized. Homes, businesses, schools, the railroad and the city's waterfront were destroyed as the flood made its way to the harbor. Like every disaster, there were economic and social effects that tragically changed people's lives.

There were a number of suspected contributory causes of the catastrophe at the Purity Distilling Company, including questionable construction that led to the cylinder stress failure that collapsed the fifty-foot tall, ninety-foot-wide steel tank that held 2,300,000 gallons of thick molasses weighing an estimated 26 million pounds.

But many believe the company deliberately ignored proper safety checks and disregarded worker complaints in order to be ahead of the imminent Prohibition laws which did result in the 18th Amendment being ratified in 1919. The change in the weather may have played a part, as well. The cold weather increased the thickness of the molasses which made it extremely lethal.

When Jack Turner and Brian Kelly drove the girls to New Jersey in Brian's new Ford, the girls still smelled of molasses and Fiona's blonde hair had become a shade of henna.

CPSIA information can be obtained
at www.ICGtesting.com
Printed in the USA
FSHW021944291118
54134FS